SOHO IN THE DARK

CW00683956

Das Petrou

Dassos Petrou

SOHO IN THE DARK

FICTION4ALL

CONTENTS

INTRODUCTION

Soho was once a seething hotbed of creativity. Between the seedy sex shops and massage parlours, ad agencies rubbed shoulders with production companies, recording studios, illustration studios, editing suites, and publishing houses. And after working hours, the bars and bistros were full to gunwales with creative types and celebrities from the world of showbiz. It was clearly the place to be seen.

Sadly, London's exciting, dynamic, sizzling quarter that the media world generated in abundance in a once hard-edged Soho (and Fitzrovia) has gone forever. The advertising industry has shrunk, shrivelled and dispersed. The film companies, production studios and facilities houses have gone the same way. All that's left are the ghosts of a once-thriving, unique and tightly-wound community of creatives on a mission. These stories are inspired by that loss.

THE CONNOISSEUR

Some things that should be obvious are so terrifying; you don't want to let yourself know them.

Jason Watts was an artist's artist. A genius. He owed nothing to the modern system of education, which he considered to be corrupt, pretentious and totally lacking in substance. In an era where modernist subversion and token sensationalism were the norm, Jason could draw beautifully rendered, anatomically perfect, classically inspired figures with stunningly, free-flowing finesse. It was easy to conclude he was born at least a century too late.

A highly-respected figurative artist who taught him in his first year at college declared, "At the age of nineteen he can draw the human figure from his head better than I can from life!"

Even in his early teens he was driven by an obsessive nature, and from that time he spent years in an intense study of such dusty old tomes as *Constructive Anatomy by* George Bridgeman, *Anatomy for Artists* by Eugene Wolf, and *The Practice of Painting and Drawing* by Solomon J Solomon. These artist-authors were the last in their line. They understood what (for them) was the dreadful truth - Modernism was an unstoppable force that would soon suffocate traditional art, wiping out all the well-established Classical values and replacing them by a kind of anarchy. By writing

11

down the long-established methods of their craft they hoped to preserve them, in the same way that the monks of the Pachomian monastery in Upper Egypt buried the sacred scrolls of the Nag Hammadi library after the draconian proclamation by Bishop Athanasius in 367 A.D. banning all non-canonical books.

Those (now-apocryphal) texts on the craft of drawing and painting were not written in vain because they succeeded in passing the baton. Through their teaching Jason Watts mastered the methods of long-dead Academicians, acquiring a detailed knowledge of human anatomy and perspective, and an encyclopaedic knowledge of traditional painting techniques, including scumbling, glazing and the application of mid-tones, half-tones, washes and highlights. Every specialism he needed to create the kind of art he had always loved – beautiful, figurative, romantic painting – was part of his armoury, and he put these weapons to good use. His pictures were astonishing for their sophisticated technique and flourishes of bold embellishment. On seeing his work people were nearly always shocked to discover that, not only was the artist very much *alive*, he was only in his twenties.

Despite the accolades of the discerning few, Jason achieved very little success in the London galleries. He quickly discovered it was impossible to make an impression as a traditional, figurative, romantic painter in an art world hostile to those qualities. Subverting the long-entrenched principles of the Modern art world was like trying to bring down Everest with a chisel. Things had moved too far along the path of a politicized culture driven by aesthetic theory, and supported by a kind of post-rationalism – leading to a preference for 'The Shock of the New'.

He kept up the good fight for a while, but in the end, he had to eat, so he wound up entering the commercial art and graphics field, where everybody he worked with understood and embraced his genius totally. Over the next few years he created slickly rendered visuals and beautiful storyboards for ads, building up a phenomenal reputation in the process. Through that he came to the attention of the animation film industry. From there it wasn't long before he landed a three-year contract as a concept artist in Hollywood.

Leaving England to work abroad was not something he had ever geared himself up for – but the offer was too good to turn down. Life in Southern California was wonderful. But he and Rebecca had a habit of spending money like it was covered in lice. For a while, things were going incredibly well. He helped design two major features and created designs for several other productions. But when the time came for his lucrative contract to be renewed, it wasn't. So that was that. He didn't see that coming at all. It might not have been such a surprise if he'd stopped to remember how he always failed to sensor his personal views in conversation with colleagues, and even his superiors. Although he liked them all, he generally had a very low opinion of their talents.

Jason never meant to upset. He was just honest. He always felt that he had full license to express himself as he pleased, for the simple reason that his astonishing talent was irreplaceable. But he was wrong, and like his great hero Michelangelo, who suffered from a similar talent for rubbing people up the wrong way, he missed out on the proper financial rewards his abilities deserved.

As if losing his job wasn't bad enough, his former employers took things to another level. They let it be known to just about every other studio that Jason Watts was more trouble than even his considerable abilities were worth. That became obvious when he started making enquiries around the different film companies to say he was available. Nearly all those approaches were cut short as soon as he mentioned his name. The two job interviews he did somehow manage to arrange were distinctly uncomfortable, because in both cases he found himself on the receiving end of cold, unsympathetic stares.

Soon it became clear, even to his limited sensitivities about such matters, that he had been blackballed. He felt shocked, humiliated and badly let down. It was so unfair. Who else could have done such original and masterful designs on those two films he'd worked on? Felix Beerbohm and Terry Swift, his art directors, were just jealous, that's all. Average talents joining together to defeat him, like ants swarming a cockroach. But there was no time to dwell on that now, not with his bank account being so dangerously low. There was no choice. He and Rebecca would have to give up their beautiful, spacious, home (with swimming pool, huge garden, and A-list neighbours) and acquire something more affordable. Rebecca was distraught, and was often seen about the house, in one corner or another, in tears. Nevertheless, Jason had to steel himself to do what was necessary, and within a couple of months, they had moved into a medium size, shabby, semi-detached house in La Crescenta, on the outer edge of Glendale. That bought them a little more time, but even then, it wasn't too long before they were struggling with bills again. Soon the only money they had left was barely enough for the price of their airline tickets home. They were now seriously considering throwing in the towel.

It was about that time when Stan Freeman rang Jason up. Stan was probably the most talented of all the artists still working at the studio. He was a big, burly, bearded Texan, who had been awe-struck by Jason's work from day one. He said he had a possible nugget to throw Jason's way, but he needed to explain a couple of things first. Jason immediately felt there was a catch, but they met up that night anyway at a smart bar in Melrose.

"So still no luck with the studios then?" asked Stan.

Jason pursed his lips and shook his head.

Stan nodded sympathetically. "Ok… well, you might find this interesting. Back before I got into the movies I used to have an illustration agent. Nice guy, but a bit of an asshole, if you get my drift. So, this guy, Greg, he rings me up yesterday with a job.

15

Well, you know… it would've been great if I wasn't so snowed under. But, I got to thinking, it could be so perfect for my good friend Jason Watts."

Jason picked up his glass, took a sip, put it down, and wiped off the foam moustache with his sleeve. "Sounds interesting."

Stan wiped his lips and ignored the comment. "It don't pay the kind of money you're used to. But it's not too bad."

"Pff. I can't be too fussy at the moment. Work is work"

"Damn straight, Jas. And it's not just an itty-bitty illustration. It's a goddam mural. I mean, we're talking large, fuck-off panels, they want painted in the classical-style. And wait till you hear the subject matter: stories from ancient Egypt, Rome, Greece – all that shit. Maybe nine or ten paintings – I can't remember exactly. This is a job you were born for."

Jason couldn't help feeling there was a catch. "Is it outdoor?"

"No. It's up in Gladstone Pines. Place called the Wynand Centre - sort of gallery and arts education centre for the local community. Not even a half hour from here."

"Could be good."

"I reckon."

Jason did his best, but he couldn't help looking glum. It was hard not to be like that after all the disappointment he'd been through since leaving the studio. Stan leaned forward and gave Jason a pat on the shoulder. Not knowing his own strength, it gave Jason a jolt.

"Hey man," he said. Relax. "There ain't nothing to worry about. Way I see it, you go and talk to the guy over at The Wynand and you'll be sitting pretty - guaranteed. You just need to hear what the fellow has to say. Remember, the devil is always in the detail."

The next morning, after a sleepless night, Jason plucked up the courage to call the number Stan had written down for him on the stained napkin. The phone rang for quite a while before it was answered by a secretary, who seemed friendly enough. She seemed jovial and worldly wise, and was probably a grandmother. She checked through her diary and fixed up a meeting for Jason with Greg. That Friday Jason was sitting on a sofa in Greg's ninth-floor offices in Studio City. To cut to the quick, Greg joined him on an adjacent armchair and was knocked out by Jason's work samples, which he went through on the glass coffee table. He said that the work was perfect for the job spec at Wynand. But he did say that Howard, the guy who was in charge of the commission, was a tough, no-nonsense fellow – although his bark was worse than his bite.

Howard Donnellon, the administrator of the Wynand Centre, had made his way up the pyramid through hard work, a no-nonsense attitude to life, a tough hide, and a strong, natural business sense. His father was a tailor in the garment industry. As a schoolboy, he made extra money working at a grocery store. Leaving school without qualifications he began selling radio aerials for cars and other electrical goods out of a truck he purchased from a neighbour. He eventually founded a general import/export wholesale company. In just a few years he had set up his first venture, manufacturing cheap sound systems using clever techniques to achieve lower production costs to undercut the competition. Manufacturing capacity was soon expanded and he became a millionaire by his mid-twenties. Despite his lack of formal education, by his mid-thirties he had developed a very personal taste in figurative art that began to occupy him more and more. Through it he built up an impressive, if eclectic, art collection over the years, which included pieces by the French Impressionists as well as a few lesser-known works by John Singer Sargent, Édouard Manet, Joseph Sickert, Bernard Fuchs, Dean Cornwell and others. Eventually he indulged himself further in this diversion by founding the Wynand Centre.

The place didn't particularly stand out as an architectural masterpiece, being a pretty standard piece of stunted, block-like, 1980s California architecture, with a very plain white frontage. Jason drove just past it, parked up round the back and then walked around to the front entrance. Inside the small lobby a girl receptionist, who was far too young to wear glasses attached to a neck cord strap, dropped her pen as soon as he announced himself. Recovering, she stood up beaming and leaned over her desk holding out her hand. "Vanessa Hutchinson, Mr Donnellon's personal assistant.'

"Jason Watts."

Pleasure to meet you Jason. Would you follow me please?"

They passed through two sets of glass swing doors into a modestly sized exhibition hall, with a smooth wooden floor, pristine white walls, oak panelled up to about shoulder height. A narrow, arched skylight ran the full length of the ceiling. Jason immediately knew that his would be a really great space to create a mural.

At the far end, she led him through a wooden door into a small stuffy office.

"Please take a seat," she said. "Mr Donnellon will be along shortly."

She left the room with a friendly smile, closing the door behind her.

The room was poorly lit and slightly airless. He settled onto a 1970s, fabric-backed office chair. Between him and an oak swivel chair opposite was a large mahogany desk, with an ancient computer, four neat piles of paper, and an ink blotter next to an antique King James Bible. The window to his right had the blinds slightly open, creating striped shadows on a snarling fox's head, which was mounted to a small wooden plaque on the wall to his left. Behind the empty chair was an oak bookshelf crammed with antique hardbacks. He could make out a few of the titles from the spines, such as *Darkness Visible, Lucifer and Ahriman, The Ontological Proof of the Devil,* and *Paradise Lost.*

A gruesome but impressively executed engraving hung on the wall to his left, clearly a scene from Dante's Inferno, and probably by Gustave Doré. But he was unfamiliar with this image. He got up to get a better look at it. Some small type below the image revealed the title: *Dante and Virgil Encountering Lucifer*, from Canto XXXIV of Dante's Inferno. It also explained that was engraved by Cornelis Galle the Elder, after a drawing by Lodovico Cardi (both unfamiliar to him). Jason looked closer at the gigantic, leering, wide-eyed Devil, with three hideous faces, encased in ice, right up to his chest and gigantic bat-like wings spread out behind him. Staring madly, he ravenously devours three naked human beings, as if they were chocolate bars, and on the ice in front of him are the tiny, tiny figures of Virgil and Dante.

Jason considered how odd it was that people of extraordinary business acumen, with all their logic and hard-nosed pragmatism, were often suckers for this kind of fire and brimstone, religious/supernatural mumbo jumbo.

His cousin, Rita was a typical example. She was an incredibly smart and very successful lawyer, ruthless in her business dealings. But she would spend thousands on things like palmistry, mediums and astrologers.

Just then a deep, gravelly voice broke his concentration.

"Ah! Jason Watts?"

Jason turned to see a fifty-ish man with military moustache, and slicked back, slightly greying hair. He walked over from the door to take Jason's hand with an extraordinarily firm grip.

"Howard Donnellon. Pleased to have you on board."

Howard gestured for Jason to take the chair he had been sitting in before, and walked around to the large chair on the other side of the desk.

"Excuse my timing,' he said. "Meeting at my corporate HQ, over-ran. Had to drive back like a maniac from Orange County. Mind you, my wife says I always drive that way."

He sat down and then nudged his chair forward in a series of bumps. Satisfied with his perfect positioning, he moved a few papers around on the desk, and then rested his arms on it, and looked at Jason for what seemed an unbearably long time. Jason did his best not to look pensive. Finally, he spoke.

"Well Jason, soon as I saw those pictures of your work your agent sent over, I gotta tell you..." he held out his hands with raised palms, like a statue of a saint, "They blew my mind. Couldn't help thinking of all those Renaissance greats – you know who I mean: Titian, Michelangelo, Raphael and so on."

Jason coughed in embarrassment. "Well, uh... thank you. It's a great honour to be associated with..."

"No really."

There followed another long silence, as HD tugged at his moustache, still looking challengingly at Jason

Jason tried to retain his humility as best he could, much as he loved compliments. His thin moustache curved down in a thin dark line to a small beard that grew below his jaw, and just hugged the upward curve of his chin. It added poise, refinement and a sense of the dandy. Vincent Price would spring to mind, but he had cultivated it in honour of Velázquez. His small nose and calm intensity in his stare added to the look. His mouth was closed, thin and relaxed.

Howard gave up trying to analyse the expression. He decided to pick up where he left off.

"It's good to know that there are still people around that have the ability to create beautiful art. I can't tell you what a relief that is. Too much junk being held up as art. When we look around we can see it clear as day - civilisation is becoming debased, culture distorted, roles inverted, standards eliminated, materialism and greed celebrated, and the moral tone is close to debauchery."

Jason was truly shell-shocked by this barrage, having arrived there expecting to be quizzed about his suitability, education, qualifications and so on. He was not ready for this at all, although he did his level best to hide his discomfort. What he didn't know was that Howard was not known for his sensitivity and ability to empathise, so there was no danger of Howard picking up on that. Anyway, he had built up too much momentum in his soliloquy to focus on that sort of thing.

"In the final analysis, when a people can no longer distinguish truth and beauty from falsehood and ugliness, they are ripe for all manner of deception, oppression and enslavement.'

He took a large cigar out of a drawer and lit up from a desk lighter, taking in a deep puff before continuing. Savouring that for a moment, he finally closed his eyes, exhaled, smiled with satisfaction and continued.

"Tastes today are dictated by cultural vandals. And it's no accident. Not at all. It is my belief that this decay of our civilised values has been meticulously planned."

Jason coughed nervously. "By who?"

Howard answered his question in a roundabout way.

"That picture you were looking at over there," HD pointed towards it with his chin. "Fantastic piece of work, don't you think?"

"Uh, well yeah. Beautiful. I thought it was by Dore, but it's not."

Howard continued, oblivious to Jason's last remark. "What it shows is the devil, let's not beat around the bush. Is that an accurate representation of him – or is it just a visual metaphor for what he represents? That stupid idea they ram down our throats of a red guy with the little horns, tail, pitchfork, you know; fire and brimstone - that we all grew up as the standard version of the devil... paaah! Who knows what he really looks like?"

Jason wasn't sure if he was supposed to say anything, but Howard freed him from that necessity.

"One thing's for sure, he wouldn't stand out in a crowd, otherwise he wouldn't be able to do what he's been doing. We'd know it was him. Think about that for a moment."

Jason was starting to feel nervous. Was he actually implying that the devil exists? It certainly seemed that way. Was he an obsessive, or just a crank?

"He's elevating and exalting public lewdness and vulgar anti-social behaviour to a place of respect," Howard continued, "while vulgarising and lowering every higher moral value for the sake of convenience and personal gain."

Jason didn't have the courage to express an honest opinion. "I see."

"The way he's worked it, the sacred becomes a punch line. The sordid becomes a sacrament. The minister is a monster, but the sex worker has a heart of gold. He – I'm talking Satan, Lucifer, the devil, he's the one who profits from this celebration of self-contamination."

Jason was starting to wish he could wriggle out of this job, but he needed the money.

"Most people don't believe in his existence. That's fine. You may do, you may not. Me, I observe his influence everywhere."

Jason did his best to look convinced.

"He's screwing around with our understanding of the world. Everything we see and feel has become warped and twisted: our loves, our freedom, everything. Especially our appreciation of all that is good, including the appreciation of beauty that we're all born with. Do you like what passes as art today? Huh? Huh?"

"Uh… not particularly."

Jason felt a bit cornered, but he wasn't being dishonest in his answer. He hated most modern art in galleries and museums. But he couldn't see why you had to attribute that to the devil, or any other supernatural entity. It was random. Maybe it was down to failures in the education system, or even the impact of mass production and consumerism, and the faster pace of life. People don't have the time to think clearly and weigh things up in their heads.

"Come on, Jason. Be a bit more committed," said Howard. "These are important issues. Soon we'll all be living in a delusional fantasy world, where the devil and the dark elite who are nurturing his schemes, those 'intellectuals' who are supposedly smarter and more objective than the rest of us, rule from on high, with scientific precision and wisdom – dictating what reason is, what morality is, what beauty is. We have to call time on all that. And you're going to help us."

That really did put Jason on the spot. He couldn't help crossing his legs, interlocking his fingers around his knee, swinging his raised foot, and tensing up. Was he going to have to be a part of some kind of religious ritual, or exorcism, or something?

Howard's cigar had gone out. He lit up again and carried on where he left off, using his cigar as a gesticulating tool.

"It's my belief, Jason, that every time something truly *beautiful* is created in this world, the devil suffers a little defeat."

Jason relaxed.

"We want you to create something wonderful, an unquestionable masterpiece – a stunning mural that will glorify the magnificence of all that is great in the civilisation we inherited – and are in danger of losing."

Jason cleared his throat and said, "Well uh, it'll be an honour, sir. I'll certainly do my best."

"I'm sure you will, my boy. I'm sure you will."

Jason had an unconventional spin on the story of the rise of civilisation, and he put together a remarkable sequence of images. There were nine drawings in all, making a visual narrative from the first stirrings of conscious thought through to the rise of ancient civilisations, right up to the fall of Rome. The drawings were executed on large sheets of cartridge paper and done mostly in charcoal. The board of the Wynand Centre, were unanimous in their approval. Howard put his arm round Jason and said: "Jason - you just kicked Satan's ass."

Now he was ready to paint the real thing.

The daily journey to the Wynand Centre was no big deal, and when he worked after 6 pm, (which he did most days); the drive back wasn't too bad either. Gladstone Pines wasn't particularly interesting: more of a suburb than a city. But he did appreciate the cooler climate and spectacular views of the valley.

Jason was inspired by a whole range of figurative artists, particularly from the Orientalists and Romantics, including Jacques-Louis David, William Waterhouse, Solomon J. Solomon, and John Collier. The panels were all over five feet tall and eight feet wide, and the images worked mostly as diptychs.

Towards the end of the day in September Jason was up on his ladder adding a few finishing touches to the final scene. Anyone walking in at the time would have seen him in his black polo neck, brand new, tight-fitting Levis, and the sharpest pair of polished black winkle-picker shoes you have ever seen. Standing below the ladder the points of his shoes peered out over the metal step he stood on, like miniature missiles aimed at the wall. He was in deep concentration. His huge forehead made more prominent by the fact that he was balding, even at his tender age. But it was a very dignified and stylish way to do so, his short black hair combed back from a sharp point.

Sally, the receptionist had already gone home and Vince, the caretaker, had taken over at the desk. Maria had already done all the cleaning and gone home. Vince was now waiting beyond the double doors at the far end at the front desk, for Jason to finish up so he could get on with his other duties.

He was up on his ladder painting a milky glaze over the figure of Hermes, in the middle of the design, between the Gods and mortal man. At the top of the composition Zeus, Hermes, Poseidon, Aphrodite and some other Gods – all of them are looking down at the ordinary men and women below with awe and trepidation. The people below are no longer submitting to the divinity of the Gods. They're free, intelligent, sophisticated, self-confident individuals, calmly enjoying the hard-won fruits of civilisation.

The gallery area was pleasantly quiet. Jason liked that. And no one could sneak up on you in there because the polished wooden floor was impossible to walk on without making, at the very least, a loud squeak in shoes, and a puff-puff-puff in socks. Even in bare feet you'd hear a flopping sound. Which is why he almost fell off his perch when he heard a theatrically loud cough from close by. Twisting and looking down to his right he saw a medium size old man staring at him intently. The man looked to be (at least) in his seventies, clean-shaven, with a healthy mane of white hair drawn back from his forehead. He wore an extraordinarily wide lapelled, herringbone suit, silver and black tie and white shirt with a very thin grey stripe. Strangely there wasn't a hint of colour about him anywhere. He held onto an antique, bejewelled walking stick, and gazed at Jason with his upturned face, that was strong and owl-like, with a thin nose positioned high above the lips; and an aristocratic, domed forehead. His eyebrows were dark, well manicured, and far apart. The thin mouth was fixed with an expression of both disdain and self-satisfaction. The top half of his ears were covered by his hair, the chin was small and almond shaped, and the cheeks firm though thin. His flesh was so pale he was almost albino.

"It is a remarkable feat that you have achieved here, young man. Absolutely exquisite," he said in a pristine New England accent that sounded more English than any one in England could today.

"Very nice of you to say," said Jason.

"It is the philosophical and historical content behind the work which impresses the most; not just in this particular scene," He gestured towards the

28

painting Jason was now working of, showing the gods of Olympus looking down at mankind below, "but for the entire series. To me this visual narrative of yours is an open book. The images transcend even your, not inconsiderable, technical achievements, raising the aesthetic and intellectual sensibility of the whole work."

Jason wondered if this fellow was an out of work actor. Perhaps someone had hired him as a kind of prank. But who would do that?

"At the risk of sounding conceited, it verges on the tragic that there are so few individuals alive today with the requisite loftiness of mind to appreciate those sorts of qualities."

"Uh, thank you," said Jason, trying to work out how long this nut-job had been in there, studying him forensically while he had been peacefully unaware. The thought made him shudder. Jason hoped he'd go away, but that was looking less and less likely.

"It may interest you to know that I have met some of those people."

Jason stopped to look down. "What people?"

The fellow seemed to be indicating the Gods of Olympus with his chin. Was this some kind of joke?

"You mean them," said Jason, pointing to Zeus and Athena.

"Indeed."

Jason felt compelled to treat that affirmation with the incredulity it deserved.

"Oh, is that so?" he said, laughing out loud.

The old man thumped the end of his metal-tipped stick on the floor in a fury.

"Young man. When I tell you that I am on personal terms with these people I am making a statement of fact. Do not, I repeat, do NOT take up that tone with me again. You will come to regret it."

There was something conveyed at that moment to Jason that was in no way connected to the words the old man expressed. He was immediately aware of being in the presence of far more danger than he'd ever encountered in his life – and yet he couldn't say how he was so sure of that.

"B-b-but – they're *gods.*"

"I *know* that," said the old man.

Jason looked towards the window to see it was getting dark. He wasn't sure if he was shivering or not. There seemed to be a strange stillness over everything. Then the man's eyes gleamed as he broke the silence.

"You've definitely achieved a feeling of sublime grace with that image, particularly in the delineation of that exquisite group of naked dancers near the Acropolis."

Jason sensed that the ominous mood had dissipated. "Thank you."

"But I do have one particular concern. In the daytime scene, the dancers in front of the Parthenon, supposedly the Temple of Reason - are wild, and in a state of drunken debauchery. That seems to jar. And why are those giant figures of Aphrodite and Eros in the background of the night-time scene?

Jason shrugged. "No particular reason."

"Ha-ha-ha-ha. You are clearly playing down your knowledge of the mystery religions. You are either embarrassed or - more likely - discrete. But that is understandable. These learnings are not for the profane. Nevertheless, you have no secrets from me."

He stared at Jason with a leering smile then sent a chill through his spine.

"And those other figures", the old man continued, "the ones in the night scene, they are dancing in front of the Delphic Oracle with obvious dignity and poise. That is rather odd, isn't it? Especially when you consider that they are performing in front of the temple dedicated to Dionysius – the God of wine, the passions, or rather lust and debauchery, as some would say. Have their states of mind been cooled somewhat by the presence of Apollo, the father of intellect and reason? Or, am I right in my suspicions that you are knowingly depicting the balance that can be achieved between the Dionysian with the Apollonian."

Jason felt naked. These were concepts he would discuss only with his closest friends, such as Alan, Geoff and maybe sometimes Debbie, and the independent filmmaker and artist, Morgan Blake. Denial wouldn't work. But he tried to play it all down. "Well, I have looked into that notion a little, yes..."

"Of course, you have my boy. And not just a little. It is obvious that you are deeply aware of these principles. Are you then, an initiate of one the higher orders?"

"Sorry?"

"The Royal Arch, or the Rosie Cross, perhaps?"

Jason shook his head. "I don't know what you mean."

"Then perhaps you're connected to one of the older bloodlines?"

Jason laughed. "I don't think you could find a more working-class family than mine."

"So then, you are a classical scholar - perhaps you studied at Oxford or Cambridge, or one of the Ivy League universities?"

Jason laughed. "You couldn't be further from the truth?"

The stranger seemed mildly irritated. "So how did you know all this?"

"I read a lot. I buy books, mostly from second hand bookshops."

"What books?"

"Lots of them. Battered old Penguin Classics even. Like maybe in Euripides, who talks about some of this stuff in '*The Bacchae.*'"

"Stuff?"

"And in the nineteenth Century you have Nietzsche speaking about the Apollonian and the Dionysian a great deal, especially in '*The Birth of Tragedy*'. It's no big secret."

"Ah, I see. You're an autodidact."

"What's that?"

"A self-educated man."

"Is that an insult?"

"Mm. Not necessarily."

Jason was looking down at the fellow with incredulity. The man was impervious to Jason's glare. He took a business card from the inside pocket of his jacket and held it out expectantly.

"Roland Dockstader at your service," he said.

Jason thought it was a repulsive name. He was not in the least bit interested in taking the card, but he felt it would have been extremely rude not to come down the ladder to collect it. Reluctantly, he wiped his hands on a dirty rag and walked down the ladder to take the card. Without even giving it a glance he put it the back pocket of his jeans. At that precise moment, the man moved impulsively forward, and held out his open hand. Jason felt compelled to take it. It was like the hand of a dead man. His grasp felt cold, as if he'd come in from a snowstorm, yet outside it was sweltering. He fought back an urge to dash out to reception and get Vince to come into the gallery to evict this madman. Then Dockstader interrupted, with more of these sweet and sticky mind games.

"You have certain qualities Mr…"

"Watts."

"Thank you. Quite honestly, your knowledge of the arcane is something of an anomaly. For an autodidact, you have raised yourself to a level reserved for, may I say… higher individuals."

"What higher individuals?"

Roland Dockstader ignored the question. "The rituals you show in these paintings have been kept secret among the ruling elite for centuries. Take for instance the cult you depicted here," he pointed to a painting further along, "it was practiced in the Third Dynasty of Egypt. Let us give it its true name - Isis worship. Basically ancient, pagan, mother-worship, and its priesthood was exclusively restricted… and its followers carefully selected."

Jason felt he had to snuff out this weirdo's flame. "Socrates had something to say about supposedly 'superior' types," he interjected. "Plato quotes him in The Apology, where he says, 'the men most in repute were all but the most foolish; and that others less esteemed were really wiser and better'."

"How quaint," snarled the old man.

"The Cult of Isis", said Jason, "as far as I am aware, practiced social control, the subjugation of free will, and total exploitation of the people."

"Quite so," replied Dockstader, almost with a sense of pride. "That control model works very well. It was based on the pagan ceremonies of ancient Egypt and Rome, you know. The cult of Apollo comes from all that. You may have heard of the families of Rome who are called t*he black nobility.*"

Jason leered. "The ones that evolved over the centuries into the Venetian Black Nobility."

"Precisely. Today they're the power behind the western world."

Jason wished he'd never become involved in this discussion. He wondered if Vince would ever get up dodo his rounds, as he was supposed to have done over half an hour ago.

"I know," replied Jason. "That's what the cult of Apollo is today. That's why I've painted it."

"Very good! Yes, the Roman republic and empire of their ancestors was controlled from Rome by the cult of Apollo, which you have shown very well in your work. It was, of course, the chief method of fomenting debt in the Mediterranean, and it also acted as an intelligence service as well as being a cult – and was instrumental in creating other cults."

Jason nodded. He couldn't hide his understanding now. "From what I remember, in Egypt it fused with the cult of Isis and Osiris as a sort of direct imitation of the Phrygian cult of Dionysius."

"That's right," grinned Dockstader. "That was where they created the cult of Stoic irrationalism, which was based on Aristotelian Nicomachean Ethics. Your hero, Socrates was really just an idealist. But Aristotle, as we all know, was a true pragmatist."

Now Jason's emotions were triggered. "Ha-ha-ha. And what kind of pragmatist was that? Not a very impressive one. He turned the growing belief that the sun - not the Earth - was really the centre of the universe on its head. He looked backwards, to a time of ignorance. He actually proclaimed that the Earth was the centre of the universe. That makes him indirectly responsible for the death of Galileo in the 1600s."

Dockstader shrugged. "Not such a great loss."

Jason shook his head in disbelief. "You're joking, of course. In my opinion, what your 'elite' followers of Aristotle fear most is technological progress and an educated population. That would put an end to the possibility of total control of the masses by the elite."

Dockstader lowered his head slowly and lifted it to show another smile. "Which is why the methods that were used by the ancient priests of

Apollo in ancient times, including the promotion of Dionysiac cults – featuring drug cultures, sexually motivated counterculture, and extremist anti-establishment fringe groups – to foment a demented rabble against progress, enlightenment and rationalism, are important."

Jason was horrified and almost speechless. "Important?"

"Please allow me to continue. There are today individuals, special people who, it has to be said, regard most of mankind as less than human, which is (I hasten to add) understandable from their perspective. Indeed, one of my closest friends exhibits this quality admirably."

Jason frowned. "Oh? And what's so admirable about having disdain for mankind?"

"I didn't say my friend's attitude was admirable. If you listened carefully you would have understood the point. What I expressed was the fact that she is a perfect *example* of someone who has disdain for mankind. An admirable one."

"Oh."

"Yes. A most remarkable woman, and a very dear friend, despite her few odd predilections. But then, which of us is perfect?"

"She sounds dreadful."

"Oh, no no no. She's delightfully creative and original. Charismatic to the extreme – and she has an extraordinary mind. Extraordinary. She's a very good friend. Smart and cultured, with a quick sense of humour. She's a governor of one of our finest universities on the East Coast. But despite her unquestionable intellect and political nous she can be quite irksome, although I do try to forgive some of her eccentricities."

"People are entitled to be eccentric."

"Ha. Most endearing of you to say. But, I don't think you would be so defensive of her particular eccentricities. I myself despair of the peculiar urges she sometime entertains. But I do allow her some latitude because, after all is said and done, she is an inspiration."

"Well, I must get on...."

Roland talked over Jason, which irritated him, although he managed to keep his frustration in check. "Just recently, for example, she enticed two young children, a boy and a girl, to her brownstone home. How she achieved that is another story. I hesitate to describe how things developed from there."

Jason had a gut feeling whatever it was would breach the boundaries of good taste, and he wasn't wrong. Instinctively he braced himself.

"You see, my dear autodidact, soon after she procured these young people I went to visit her. I'd just been to see the marvellous Temple of Dendur, in The Sackler Wing, of the Met: built by the Roman Governor Petronius around 15 BC in Egypt, and dedicated to Isis and Osiris. My friend, well, she lives only a few blocks east of there. It had just stopped raining, and the sky was bright with a few long, black clouds drifting like battleships overhead. It was about six by the time I got to her brownstone dwelling. She buzzed me in, as she always does and I went right on up to her first-floor lounge, where she met me with a customary kiss on each cheek.

She was dressed head to toe in Agnes B. As she went to pour me a glass of claret I sat down at the chaise longue. That's when I noticed two children, a boy of about nine, and a girl of about seven, chained by their wrists and ankles to the wall opposite."

"Are you winding me up?"

"Not at all. Well, as you can imagine, I was rather taken aback. But I was also curious about their rather luminous pink colouring. It wasn't until I went over to take a closer look that I realised their skin had been completely peeled away. The boy was groaning and the girl was making kitten like meows of pain."

"Oh, please." Jason lifted up the corner of his lip in a mixture of disbelief and disgust.

"I'm stating a matter of *fact*."

"I-I-I don't… did you call the police, or what?"

"No. Of course not. She is my friend, remember?"

"Jesus." Jason's feeling of disgust was peppered with anger and frustration. The mix led to confusion. The only thought that made any sense was that he wished this person would go away. But no such luck. He was continuing the horror story.

"I did of course emphasise to Cordelia, (oops I shouldn't have named her, but I trust you are a cautious individual), I did emphasise to her that enough was enough and that her poor little victims should now be put out of their misery. However, even after a few days she had clearly not followed up on my suggestion. Quite the opposite. She went out of her way to perpetuate the situation by inserting various feeding tubes into them. She is, I'm sure you will agree, rather naughty."

"Naughty?"

Jason reacted as if he was chewing a lemon. Not only was this guy interrupting him in his work, he was also giving him the creeps. The repulsive turn the conversation had taken was more than Jason was willing to put up with.

"Look mate," he said, reverting back to his London vocab, "I really have to be getting on. So, if you'll excuse me..."

The smirk vanished. "Please don't misjudge me. Of course, I am absolutely repulsed and unsettled by the appalling behaviour I have described.

Those words of moral indignation were demolished by the subtle, self-satisfied smile that followed."

Jason took a moment to assess the insidiousness of this character before offering his succinct conclusion.

"You're nuts."

The smirk remained. "Not at all, my dear autodidact. Not at all."

Jason sneered; picked up the palette and brush he'd put down on his little side table and climbed back up the ladder.

But Mr Dockstader was not to be dismissed so easily. "Why be so angry? Rather you should try to see the bigger picture in everything. With your extraordinary talents, and knowledge you have the opportunity for a revaluation of all values. In the words of Robert Louis Stevenson, 'why man, do you know what life is? There are two squads of us - the lambs and the lions.' "

Jason looked down and spat out: "So what's that supposed to mean?"

"Accept what you are. The lions, my dear autodidact, are a different species from the rabble."

"Oh, I get it. You're talking about the difference between demi-gods and men."

"Indeed. And as your friend Plato declared in his Apologia, *'the demigods are the illegitimate sons of gods, whether by the nymphs or by any other mothers, of whom they are said to be the sons—what human being will ever believe that there are no gods if they are the sons of gods?'*"

"You and your associates may see yourselves as being above all men, but whatever you may believe, you're certainly not demi-gods. And I don't see ordinary people as rabble.

"Oh dear - such a shame. Such a shame."

He looked down again Dockstader wasn't there. There was no one in the gallery at all. But that shouldn't have been possible. Roland Dockstader couldn't have gone off without making himself heard. It's unavoidable. The room is echoey, the floor is wooden. You can hear a mouse crawl in there. Jason hadn't even heard the double doors click open, and swish back closed as they inevitable always do.

There was nothing else for it. Jason was baffled. He scurried back down the steps and went through those very swing doors to the tiny lobby. Vince was at the desk in his gleaming white shirt, with military epaulets and the ever-present red and blue biro lids peeking out of the top pocket of his shirt. He was watching the ball game. A veteran of the Korean War, he may have been in his seventies, but he was built like a tank. He made an extraordinarily big smile by sucking his lips in, which loosened his dentures so he had to stick out his tongue to push them back in place. Having completed that tricky task, he made a little sucking noise.

"How you doing Vince?"

"Hey, what's up Jason? You came through those doors kind of sudden. Everything OK?"

Jason sighed and said, "Yeah, uh sure. I just wanted to find out where that old guy went.

"Who?" Vince slurped up a couple of sips of coffee from his oversize mug.

"The old guy I've been talking to in there. Is he in the bathroom, or did he just head on out, or what?"

"What old guy?

"The one I've been talking to in there. You know... herringbone suit, full head of white hair."

"I'm kind of confused here, Jason. I've had the security camera here next to the TV the whole time, and I can tell you now, there sure as hell wasn't no one in there with you while I've been here."

Jason was open mouthed.

"Oh... er... What are you saying? I've been chatting to him for god knows how long – fifteen twenty minutes..."

"Fifteen... Jason. Listen to me. I'm watching the basketball, but I keep an eye on the monitor all the time, because my jobs on the line, anything goes wrong. Know what I mean?"

"Sure."

"Well there ain't no one been in the gallery but you, son."

"You sure."

"Sure as hell. Come over here."

Jason went around behind to look at the ten-inch by six-inch monitor on the cheap black swivel stand. Vince rewound the tape half an hour, and then played it on fast forward. A grainy black and white picture came up, with the inevitable wobbly white bands going across the middle of the screen because fast-forward was on. The view was from the camera at the top corner of the gallery, high above the office at the far end looking down at the whole area. The huge empty wooden floor of the gallery was showing and on the far left of the screen was Jason up on his ladder painting – all by himself. There is no one else there at the foot of the ladder – or anywhere else in the gallery. The numbers in the timer on the top left of the screen ran forward from 17.55 to 18.30. The only thing of interest was Jason coming down the ladder twice to get more paint, or to wipe his brush with a rag. At no stage was there any sign of there being an old man at the foot of the ladder talking to him.

Jason was confused. "No. That can't be right. The guy was right there all that time, until about a minute ago. So… you sure that's for today, that footage?'

Vince became a little angered. "What are you saying? Sure, it's today. Why would I have yesterday's screen playing right now. You think I'm senile or something?"

"N-n-not at all. But that's mad because he was there, just now. I've been talking to him for ages."

"Look Jason. I don't rightly know if this is some kind of scam you're playing on me, but if you don't mind I'd like to get back to the ball game."

A wave of uncertainty passed over Jason. It was the type of anticipation that comes before heavy rain, from the sense of oppressiveness and electricity in the air. Somewhere in his mind there was an idea that was totally elusive. It brushed through him, almost completely out of sight, oozing discomfort and dread, while remaining hidden in the shadows all the while. What was that? For a moment, he felt all at sea and could only stammer.

"Yeah... shit. Sorry Vince. I don't know what's up with me. I've obviously been over-working. Going a bit stir crazy too. I think I'll call it a day."

"You do that, son. Mighty fine job you're doing on that there mural. Looking beautiful."

"Thanks, Vince."

Jason went back into the gallery, cleaned his brushes and washed his hands. Back out in the car park he fumbled around for his car keys. When he pulled them out a little business card fell out onto the tarmac. He held it up close. It was black with shiny, gold-embossed type.

Roland Dockstader
ANTIQUARIAN
65 Prospect Street

Rhode Island 02906
Telephone: +1 401-454-5500

What did it all mean?

THE FORGETTING

There are sacraments of evil as well as good about us, and we live and move to my belief in an unknown world, a place where there are caves and shadows and dwellers in twilight.
Arthur Machen, The Red Hand.

There was this definite thought that there should really be nothing at all ever. That was obvious, straightforward and clear-cut. Nothing is all there is - and always will be.

Well, not anymore. Now there was something. It started with the blackness that shouldn't have been there. It was too much. Now it was everywhere in every direction. How did that happen? If that wasn't bad enough now there was now an awareness of the blackness too: thinking. It was so aberrant, it was perverse. He was scared. But how could thinking happen? Where was it coming from? Suddenly it was impossible to deny.

"I'm doing it. It's coming from me."

And the change didn't stop there. The blackness was strobing, rippling - becoming unstable, tearing itself into strands, becoming brittle and then crumbling... leaving gaps. He was afraid of the spaces in between at first. They were bright. Then he became seduced by them. They were fascinating spaces through which the world of things started to be revealed. He embraced the change. These were staggeringly beautiful things, overwhelmingly rich with colour and shape. How was it possible?

Then the blackness was completely gone to fully reveal the world of *things*. At first it was overwhelming.

The wallpaper above the fireplace was thickly painted in a rich, matt, purple grey. Landscape paintings were hung on the walls. Portrait photographs were propped up on the mantelpiece and to one side there were glass cabinets crammed with knick-knacks and old, hardbound books. Looking back to the shelf, there was a leaf green Art Nouveau vase filled with blood red tulips, and to the side of it a bust of a Roman Emperor. Diffused light came from a small, white polished glass sphere held up by the statue of a female nude. Above that hung a gilded, tarnished, Rococo mirror. The near burnt out ashy pile of coals in the grating were flecked with wriggly worm-like flecks of glowing red. In front of the fireplace a Persian rug was spread onto the polished wooden floorboards. Lying flat on it were two short metal crutches, the sort you have to put your wrists through when walking.

That made him worry again. Whoever they belonged too was obviously still in the house somewhere. At the far end of the room, to his left, was a large bay window with rich velvet curtains which were not quite closed together. Through the gap, on the other side of the glass, were bare branches clawing at the moon.

Was this Crouch End?

"I'm thinking too fast. Slow down," he concluded. He breathed in. There was a definite but faint smell of stale incense. He lifted his head and discovered he was lying on a battered old, leather sofa that looked as if it had an exotic skin disease. A bristly blanket was itching his chin. He had no idea who he was, and he didn't have any inclination to worry about it. Anyway, he didn't want to be here any longer than he had to. Sitting up, he scooped the covering away to find that he had been sleeping in his jeans and a sweater. This sudden desire to act was inexplicable. There were not even any flashes of visual memory. What happened last night? Was he at a party? Yes! That was it. But whose party was it? Why did he stay over? Did he come alone? He held onto that thought as he looked around. Were there people asleep in the shadows - behind the piano, or even under the table maybe? He thought not, though he had no clear reason to be so sure.

Upstairs maybe? Yes, definitely. He couldn't find justification for his conclusions, but that didn't stop him accepting them fully. Another thing he was sure of (without knowing why) was that he had to get out of that house immediately. In a panic, he heaved himself up and swung his feet onto the floorboards when everything in the room went out of phase. The ceiling appeared to become unstable, wobbling before spinning and then shuddering to a stop after several liquid pulses. But that wasn't all. Something was clawing away inside of him, scraping his insides. He arched his back and struggled to suppress a groan. A horrible burning sensation coursed through him in a wave, but the pain quickly subsided, and with its departure came fragments of memory. He recalled a girl, with short blond hair standing next to a guy in a cream coloured Harrington jacket and blue jeans. They were both looking down at him – probably in this very room only a few hours ago. Who were they? What did it mean? Did it really matter?

He put on his boots, stood up, yawned, stretched out his arms and walked over to the slightly open door, pulling it slowly towards him. Quickly he stepped out into the hallway awkwardly, like a bad swimmer daring himself to step off the top diving board. To the far left a light was still on partially illuminating the terracotta-tiles. It was coming from a room that was probably a kitchen. He needed to have a piss, but he didn't know which of the closed doors would be the toilet. It was too risky. From somewhere up the stairs came the sound of snoring, which chilled him with worry. Turning around he crept slowly towards the oak front door, grabbing hold of the heavy chain, while taking care it didn't fall away with a clunk against the woodwork. He was lucky. No one had bothered to lock the Chubb, so he clicked the latch down on the Yale, opened the front door, and closed it as if he were replacing the cover of an unexploded landmine, before stepping out into the night.

Soon after passing through the front gate he stopped to look at the night sky, and the cool air sharpened his thoughts. Then he looked around and studied the narrow side street, and he was struck by a moment of enlightenment that it was probably Ferme Park Road just ahead. A wave of pins and needles rushed through him as he walked briskly towards it. It was either a sense of relief or elation. Turning right on Ferme Park Road he walked through a brick railway arch, and arrived at a familiar parade of local shops. Once they had been the ground floor of dignified red-brick, three-story Victorian homes. There was an off-license, a newsagent, a butcher, an antique store, a launderette, and a greengrocer among them. The streets were empty.

Ahead of him the sloping roofs of tall Victorian houses concertinaed away towards the line of trees, high up on the hill around Alexandra Palace in the distance. But with every step, he found it more difficult to connect his thoughts. He still couldn't recall his name, but his deep sense of rootedness to north London more than made up for that, in the state of mind he was in. The important thing was to head towards Wood Green. No reason really. He simply felt he should. Once he got there he would know what to do. But unless he could remember where he lived he could find himself walking around the whole night long.

He had to focus. He was intending to walk the full length of Ferme Park Road, which ran like a spine through his life. Disconnected scenes played out: firework explosions in slow motion. Him as a teenager playing electric guitar as his friend's mother brings in a tray of tea and biscuits; him again as a teenager in bed with an older woman while her husband is away: sitting upstairs on a bus with schoolmates on the way to the skating rink.

At the end of the parade he stopped. The scene ahead had a hypnotic effect on him. Was the silence soothing or terrifying? He struggled to snap out of it. A road sign by a side street indicated a dead end. But when he looked hard it looked like there was a narrow alleyway at the side of a run down, red brick house in the corner.

He was tempted to take a closer look but he didn't want to be diverted from his original plan, so he turned away to carry on walking up Ferme Park Road, and as he looked back in that direction he couldn't believe what he was seeing. The road had shrunk slightly in length, and the line of trees at the top of the hill was nowhere to be seen. He looked behind in utter disbelief and things had changed there too. The road was now closed off by a row of houses that faced him, forming a cul-de-sac. Where was the railway arch he had passed through only a minute ago? How was this possible? It was as if the road was healing itself from a fresh wound. Feeling totally disorientated he turned ahead once more expecting to see the concertina of redbrick pointed roofs heading off into the distance again, only to discover that that wasn't there either. Instead of being absolutely straight the road now snaked a little and was blocked by a low flint wall just a few yards from where he stood. A thick, unkempt hedge rose from the back of it, and there was now a Romanesque church behind that. He was feeling even more trapped than he had been in that house.

What kind of civic planning allowed for this kind of street layout? It was madness. These changes were insidious. They had crept up on him. Ferme Park Road was never like this before.

It was becoming a strain to think clear thoughts, and there was so much strangeness going on around here he didn't know where to start. Nothing looked the same on the second glance. What if that instability was to spread out to other places, like a cancer? The idea made him shudder. His thoughts swum around the idea of impermanence that waited for him, behind every wall, every corner, and every manicured bush. He became breathless with worry, heart pounding like it wanted to burst from his chest. Suddenly he remembered it looked like there may have been a narrow pathway in the shadows at the side of the house in the side street at the end of the parade of shops. It was covered with overhanging foliage. At the time, it seemed like a pointless exercise to check it out, but right now it was his only possibility of escape. Otherwise there was nothing but dead ends in every direction.

He went back the short distance to that side same street and turned into it, walking as fast as he could towards the corner he was thinking of. The lamplight here was weak. There was a small gap on the left of the end house there with a wooden fence at one end. He grabbed a fist full of foliage, that was mostly ivy growing from the large oak tree in the front garden and pulled it aside like a curtain. It revealed a narrow, cobbled alleyway, deep in shadow. He manoeuvred himself into it, breathing a sigh of relief. When his eyes adjusted to the darkness he realised he was in a long, ridiculously narrow cobbled alleyway. In fact, it was a bit of a squeeze walking through, and he couldn't help brushing his shoulders on the wooden fence on the left and the brick wall on the right as he went. After pushing past a cluster of overhanging leaves a little further on, he made out a patch of light in the distance. He felt a rush of excitement. There was definitely a road cutting across the end of this alleyway, but beyond the tarmac and the far pavement there was only pitch black. Was it a badly lit industrial estate? If it was, he didn't fancy being around that kind of place at night. His imagination ran riot, and he wondered if the thick blackness might signify an abyss. Not in north London, surely? Near the other end of the alley he made out some scattered blotches of grey, nestling inside the velvety blackness. At the very end, they resolved themselves into leaves and branches. He was safe. The darkness was just a park of some sort.

Again, he had that feeling of being in a familiar place, but not quite. It certainly felt like this was East Heath Road, but there was something different about it. And somewhere within his entanglement of his swirling thoughts he wondered, how could an alleyway in Ferme Park Road link up to the other end of Hampstead Heath?

Across the road he saw that a stretch of grass that sloped out of the darkness up to the edge of the pavement. There were no railings to separate the road from the park. Inside the darkness the feeble street lamps cast insipid shadows that fanned away from the nearest trees. Above them rose the upper storeys of a parade of Neo-classical grand, Portland stone buildings of the early twentieth century, with two tiers of smaller rooftop windows inset into the long-tiled roof that extended along the whole length of the block, then a gap and to the right of that the huge, green copper dome of the Planetarium. They seemed so robust. So, imperious. He felt sure he'd

54

be safe there. Marylebone Road was too established. Too cosmopolitan. Too dignified. That was a proper main road. It was a symbol of lost times, a return to a better world. Surely things would make sense again, wouldn't they? He was desperate to get over there. Cutting through the park was obviously the quickest way. He could take that path (that he was pretty certain wasn't there before). It was partially lit by lamp light and probably went right through to the other side. The idea was beautifully tempting, like the sweet music of the Sirens was to Odysseus, even though he knew to head towards it was certain death. He gazed at the darkness that was beyond the visible section of the path and imagined how warped and demented things could become there. It was too risky. He would make his way around the edges of the park, until he reached the other side, even though it was a massive detour.

Across the road, to his right as he went, was a seemingly endless row of dignified and commanding turn-of-the-century houses, with raised front gardens and stone steps leading up to their main entrances. He felt awed by their architectural splendour, but couldn't help thinking they were really nothing more than a formidable barrier funnelling him along. They seemed to be arranged like an endless line of tombs, yet they were probably full of happy, well-off families, all of whom were currently sleeping peacefully and contentedly. The contrast between himself and those clearly imagined people left him feeling sad, inadequate and alone. Operating in such a low gear, he couldn't think clearly enough to even recognise that.

On and on he went and it seemed like the park to his left and the row of large houses across the street would never end. However, there came a moment when he could see a Victorian mansion block rising above the dark mass of trees ahead. Despite all the unease he had been experiencing, he felt a sense of achievement mixed with relief. He started to run, head-down. In the corner of his eye someone in a dark blue Harrington jacket, khaki chords, and black Dr Martens shoes walked past going the other way. That would have been shocking if he wasn't so focused on getting to that corner. It was the first sign of a human seen since he woke up.

He stopped running to catch his breath, his mood shifting from a vague sense of anxiety and suppressed hope to one of relief. Here there were railings separating the park from the street. Here the road followed the eastern edge of the park. There was no question. Running across at the end of this road were the glass and steel buildings near Great Portland Street on Euston Road. He had come a long way further east than he expected, but that was fine.

He crossed over to the Victorian mansion block, not least because he was fed up with hugging the edge of the park for so long, so. The gloomy light from the lampposts gave the large, red brick, apartment block the appearance of a stage set. Higher up the tall, bay windows loomed over balconies that stretched the whole length of the building, with ornate, cast iron rails on the two levels below. All of the front entrances were inside arched porches, ten steps above street level. This is when things started to take on a different flavour. Further along, at the top of one of these steps he spotted a girl sitting on the low wall near a door. Again, it was pleasing to see another human being. She attracted more than his curiosity.

He soon realized as he got close that she was a young and attractive girl. She was gripping her right elbow and holding a cigarette from two outstretched fingers. It was cold enough for him to need a scarf and coat, yet she wore only a lightweight, unbuttoned, grey, cashmere cardigan over a black Chanel dress. A cold gust made her shiver. She breathed out a long plume of smoke, then gripped herself tighter, inadvertently pushing up her breasts. When he was almost level with her he could hear muffled music coming out of the partially open front door beside her. He couldn't help staring. In an instant, she was gazing directly at him. She seemed startled. Her eyes widened and her eyebrows shot up and she immediately twisted round to crush her cigarette into the low brick wall. He quickly looked the other way and hurried along, hoping to avoid distressing her further. But it was no use. Behind him a girl's voice (it must have been hers) was shouting out, "Jason! Jason!"

He was worried she was calling out to a boyfriend to come out of the building and save her from him - this over inquisitive stranger - so he was almost running by now. But it was no use. There was a flurry of footsteps behind him, getting close. He spun around, in the hope that he could think of something to diffuse the situation before he got a fist in the face. But almost as soon as he did a pair of soft, warm perfumed arms wrapped themselves around him. That same girl was standing on tiptoe in black ballet shoes and kissing him on the cheek. Her breasts were pushing into him and it felt wonderful. He had no idea why this was happening. Confused and aroused he leaned back to get a better look at her face while she continued to cling to him. There was something familiar about her pale, ghostly skin, ruby red lips, shoulder length dark auburn hair. Even her large circular golden earrings.

"Well? Aren't you going to say hello, or anything?" she said.

Her, small green eyes and dark eyebrows, jangling bracelets and bangles were stirring up powerful, but fleeting images. This was the sweet and unfathomable Debbie Wright. The thing he recalled most about her was the feeling of perpetual disappointment. All she ever wanted from him was friendship. She had never invited any other kind of relationship. Among his group she was known as Little Deb, because there was another, taller girl called Debbie.

She said it again: "Jason?"

The smell of her last cigarette lingered. She was talking fast and breathlessly.

"Say something. What are you doing wandering around the streets this time of night?"

"I'm not really, uh…"

He pursed his lips and frowned, but she didn't wait for him to finish.

"So… do you have to be anywhere in a hurry? Please say no."

The best he could do was shrug and a smirk. It seemed to be enough. She grinned as if she'd just won big on a roulette table. This was really nice but he couldn't suppress a feeling that something was not right about all this. Then it hit him. It had been more than twenty years since he last saw her, and yet she hadn't changed – not in the least. Down to the puppy fat and dimpled cheeks. That was just crazy. But then an idea overwhelmed him that made no sense at all: this must be the real Debbie. Yes. That must be what it was. He tried to work out what that meant, but her voice broke the spell.

She'd been talking and he hadn't noticed.

"And so, it's nearly over and everything, and it's only a works party. But that's OK. So… you coming in, or what?"

She raised her voice, in mild frustration, "Huh?"?

He had to say something. "Uh… so uh, what kind of party did you say it was?"

She frowned, as if struggling for the right words.

"Kind of a wrap party, I guess. Our Spring/Summer collection went out yesterday. There's a bunch of people from client side (most of them are OK, actually), the whole design team, of course, and all the buyers, sadly. And that's…"

She let go of him and put her hands to her hips, in an angry, matronly posture.

"This is so crazy." She pouted in feigned hurt. "It's been like... decades since I've see you and you need to know what kind of party we're having before you come in and talk to me?"

Her voice reached him as if from a great distance – but it reached him. Things he saw and heard floated to his senses through a mist: he was like a drugged observer of events unfolding on the other side of a theatrical screen.

"I-I'm sorry. I'm just... I'm not feeling right at the moment," he said. "I was going to s..."

She put her finger on his lips.

"Sh. It's ok, hon. You can tell me later."

She put her arm in his and led him towards her front porch when, without warning, she let out a little scream. He had doubled up and fallen from her grasp down onto his knees, like a penitent monk. She couldn't have known that his mind and body were on fire, as memories burned their way to the surface, flashing up at random like wildfires in his consciousness. The pain went right through him, settling mostly in his stomach.

He remembered now. After Rebecca's death, selling the house and moving in with Alan and Jenny. They were so good. They took him in because he couldn't cope. He didn't want to be alone.

Debbie watched, worried and confused. His eyes had started to water.

"Can you hear me?" she said. "What's the matter love?"

She stepped around his back to haul him up by the armpits, struggling without success. Then she came around to face him, and tried again. She managed to help him up off his knees. He sighed, dusted his trousers down, straightened up, and looked at her in embarrassment. The pain had now faded with the memories. All of those images were gone now.

"S-s-sorry about that," he stammered. "I'll be alright. Don't know what came over me."

She shook her head, smiled, and took his hand, leading him up the steps. It's not so much that he decided to go along with it all. But what was the point of resisting? This was actually making him feel good. In fact, the pain had almost totally vanished. Curious.

They entered the wide, carpeted hallway and she slammed the door behind her with her heel, giving him a squeeze around the waist. Had she ever been so affectionate to him before? He thought not, but he couldn't be sure.

Joy Division's *She's Lost Control* came from the third door along on the ground floor. The hypnotic bass vibrated through him. He wondered if there was a Byzantine ceremonial going on – maybe even a child sacrifice. She led him in. It was a surprisingly large living room – white walls, minimalist décor. A few fashion-conscious people (mostly in their twenties and thirties) were mostly at the edges of the room mingling. Only two couples were dancing. Obviously, the party was thinning out, but one person stood out like a sore thumb; a huge, bald guy, with the physique of a wrestler. He was wearing a tight-fitting suit. and sitting at the side of the table where the food had been spread. He sat with his fat legs spread wide, in a Neanderthal pose, holding a plate piled up high, and eating a large sausage roll, and scoffing away. His mouth was covered with crumbs. Unsurprisingly, no one made any effort to speak to him. He was obviously some kind of hired muscle, though why anyone would need security at a party like this was hard to imagine. After taking another large bite the ape caught his stare and returned it with an aggressive frown. He quickly looked away.

There were a few older women among the guests, and they nearly all wore beige, loose-fitting trousers and silk blouses. Only two couples were still dancing. Debbie was saying something. The music was so loud he couldn't make out what. She put her lips close to his ear and he could feel her warmth. She led him to a sofa and then went over to say a few words to the guy at the turntable. The volume came down to a tolerable level and she came back with a couple of glasses of wine and handed one over to him with a smile.

"Red any good?"

He took it gratefully. "Fine."

"I didn't recognize you straight away. You look different. Hair's going grey, and I'm not sure about those sideburns but... have you lost some weight?"?

He had no idea. "Uh, maybe."?

She frowned, and then regained her flow.

"So, what have you been doing with yourself? It's been so long. I want you to tell me everything."?

She put down her glass on a coffee table and pushed both hands on his thigh and looked into his eyes with genuine enthusiasm. The feeling was electric. So lovely. He tried hard to remember specific moments about his life in recent years, so he could give her the type of answer she was expecting, but it was hopeless. Still, he had to think of something.

"Well... hard to say. What about you?"? It was the best he could do.

She laughed a little.

"Keeping your cards close to your chest, Jason Watts? Never mind. I'll get it all out of you later."?

So he was Jason Thompson. So what? The name summarises a person who had memories he can't access. He was someone else now. In this state of mind, he was attuned to things differently. In fact, better. It was like a blindfold had been pulled off. Now he could see that everything was in perpetual flux. It was like riding a wave. Jason Watts? So what? You can't make a name mean anything momentous and useful when you're trying to understand an imminent action in life. A label stops you thinking about what's been labelled. Forget the label. Think about the thing. That's what he now understood. The more thoughtful thinking is, the more attuned to reality it becomes. Things were so much clearer. Purer, directed thinking gives you the proper meaning about an action or thing - what was already meant, before it ever even happened.

"But you haven't changed at all," he said with confidence.

63

"Me? Why would I?" She looked offended.

He wasn't expecting that.

"So, like I was saying," she said. "After two years in London I went over to Milan (which was great) - just as a sort of a dogsbody. Low pay, but good for the CV. It helped me get the job at Salamander when I got back. Hey, you know, I have been so lucky. I've worked on some lovely collections, and got some amazing PR out of Vogue, Harpers, Marie Clare...

She stopped talking suddenly. A brown hand fell on her shoulder and stayed there firmly. It belonged to a small, middle-aged, pock-faced, man in a blue mohair suit. He was holding a large pink cocktail, with an umbrella a cherry, and a straw. He acted like he owned the place, which he probably did. A couple of underlings stood behind him; centurions with benign smiles.

"Oh hi, Shekhar," Debbie said, turning to see him. "This is my friend, Jason. We go way back. Jason, Shekhar, my boss."

Shekhar looked over at him, and pulled an infinitesimal smile, which he quickly followed up with a frown. Debbie noticed that and squeezed Jason's thigh to compensate.

Much to his annoyance, Shekhar sat intrusively on the armrest next to Debbie and broke straight into work-speak. He understood none of it, which was obviously the intention. It had something to do with a photo-shoot that went wrong. She listened, asked a few questions and apparently reassured him. Finally, Shekhar stood up and went away, taking his followers with him.

When he was gone she rubbed the hair in his head affectionately.

"Sorry about that. Shekhar gets very possessive of his staff. That's just how he is. He's been very good to me, apart from not giving me a pay rise in a couple of years. But that'll come."

He started to lose concentration again as deeply hidden thoughts started to stir again, but he managed to suppress them this time. Tears had been rolling down his cheeks. Debbie stopped to look at him in disbelief, took his face in both her hands.

"Oh Jason. What is it my love? My poor baby."

She leaned forward to push her lips into his, and they stayed that way for a while. When she pulled away she held her face close to his.

"It's OK," she said, before kissing him again and standing up.

He felt chastened and excited by her tiny, soft green eyes. Is this where he had gone wrong in the past with Debbie, he wondered? Had he never appealed to her sexually because he was just too much of a lad, too insensitive?

"Come to bed", she whispered. "I live upstairs."

He smiled and she took his hand. He didn't know if he had ever been this happy before. They left the party without a single backward glance.

It was pitch black on the first-floor landing and there was a faint smell of disinfectant. Debbie flicked a switch. Some weak lighting stuttered on revealing a surprisingly large, open space. An empty area in the middle was illuminated, but the edges were left largely in shadow. To create all this space, the walls of all the apartments must have been knocked down. But how was that possible with all the strict planning regulations for these types of buildings? He had expected to see a long, narrow corridor with doors running off either side of it, as in all nineteenth century apartment blocks of this sort.

From what he could see, this large, open plan space reminded him of his old school hall, not just because of the scale, but also the parquet flooring, sash windows and oak panelled walls. In some ways, it felt a bit like the upper floors in Liberty too. He spotted the upper part of a railing to a spiral staircase at one end, and dozens of clothes rails pushed alongside three of the walls. As his eyes adjusted better to the poor lighting he could see most of the rails were crammed with clothes, while others were a bit sparse. This was certainly not a living space. It was more like a warehouse than anything else. Or at best a hostel of some sort. Cardboard boxes and a few chairs were scattered all around too. But the weird thing was there were people busily at work in the shadows, moving clothes on hangers, putting away fabrics in a tall rack of wooden draws with glass fronts (the sort you get in men's clothing stores in St James. They looked like they had been doing that uninterrupted for some time. Yet how was that possible when just a few moments before the place was in pitch darkness.

The entire wall to the extreme left of the large space was a glass partition. It was completely clear of boxes, chairs and clothes rails. She led him over to it, and pushed at a part of it, which turned out to be a glass door. Initially it was dark in there, but she stepped on a foot switch and some more dim lights faded up as inset glass bowls in the ceiling. Again, there were clothes rails and boxes, this time in a haphazard arrangement, as well as a table with a reading light (turned off) a computer, and an old grey metal filing cabinet. This room, if you could call it that, felt like an office-cum-storage space which someone had dumped a double bed in.? Nothing about this floor made any sense.

"Is this your bedroom?" He asked.

She laughed. "No. It's my home."

He was quietly appalled, but he also too enthralled by his imminent prospects to allow that line of thinking to persist.

He stood by the bed and watched her walk around a stack of cardboard boxes to reach for something against the glass wall, and drew down the venetian blinds across the whole glass wall, including the door. She then came back to kiss him and then let go to hurriedly undressed down to her black bra and panties. Without saying a word, he took off his coat and awkwardly started pulling off his jumper and shirt. She seemed so confident and happy and her body was still young, her skin white, and her curves gentle as she climbed into bed and threw the duvet over herself. He followed her example of retaining a modicum of minimal modesty by keeping on his underpants.

"You coming in then?" she said as she flipped the duvet back for him.

After they made love she lay face down with her elbows bent, resting her head on the back of her hands. She seemed exhausted and content. He could not remember ever being this happy, and yet that wasn't saying much, because he could remember so little. He leaned up on his elbow and began to stroke her buttocks, and then he dropped back in stunned surprise. Standing behind the bed board looking down at him was the creepy, sweaty and pock-filled face of Shekhar, made even more creepy by a low light beside the bed, which lit up the roof of his eye sockets like a primordial cave. The security guy he saw earlier, chomping a pastry, was standing just behind him. Both of them were expressionless. Behind them were others, perhaps the hangers on he was with downstairs at the party. They were standing in shadow, so he couldn't be sure. He gasped in astonishment. How long had Shakhar and his underlings been there? Were they watching the whole time he and Debbie were making love? He felt humiliated and confused. But despite the embarrassment he jumped out of the bed naked, seething with anger and frustration. Rapidly hauling up his clothes and shoes from the floor, he scampered past the hateful voyeurs, stumbling over a stray chair leg as he went, yelling obscenities all the while.

Eventually he fumbled around and found a featureless white door at the back that opened into a tiny bathroom. It smelled of mould. There was a shower, a cracked sink, a nearly used-up bar of green soap, and a toilet. A dirty grey towel hung on a metal rail. He slammed the door shut, closed the lid on the toilet, sat down and got dressed. He didn't bother to wash.

When he finally came out Shekhar and his crew were foraging around the cardboard boxes and clothes rails to one side, completely oblivious to him. He was still shaking from an adrenaline rush, but he opted to just get out of there. He didn't want any trouble. Debbie's was still lying face down on the bed crying. He went over to take one last look at her and her flawless, milky skin. There was a large mole on the bottom of the left shoulder blade. Despite the scene that he had caused when he saw Shekhar and his cronies staring at them both, surely there was something terribly wrong. This was really not a normal reaction. She was so totally devastated, it was insane. There must be something happening here that he didn't understand. Each time she sobbed her whole body shook. She was so helplessly emotional that she hadn't pulled the duvet over herself. It was barely covering the back of her thighs. Was she having a nervous breakdown? Her soft, reddish brown hair completely obscured her face. He considered talking to her, to find out more – but his greater need was to get out of that place. He turned away, not even bothering to cover her naked body, storming out of the glass enclosure, tramping through the length of the shadowy warehouse and headed down the stairs.

When he had almost reached the last step someone a large figure came out of the shadows to block his way. It was the fat security guy. Up this close he stank of old sweat. The way he stood it was now obvious he was knock-kneed. Not even his expensive made-to-measure suit could hide that. His dark hair was slicked back and his eyebrows were thick. He looked down, as if to admire his own black patent leather shoes, and his double chin spilled over his tight collar. Then his dead eyes came up into a fixed, cold, dark stare as he spoke through gritted teeth. He had a deep, gravely cockney accent.

"Where you going buddy?"

His anger made him brave. "None of your fucking business."

The fat man grabbed him by the collar and dragged him down the last few steps to hold him up close. His face was now only a centimetre away. He was more or less growling now, so that he was spraying spittle.

"Mr. Skekhar doesn't like anyone upsetting his people. You've made Debbie feel very unhappy. Do you understand?"

He shook himself away from the fat man's grip. "Me? You have to be joking. It's you and your boss that did that. Staring at us in bed. What was that all about? Fucking pervs."

There was no warning for what was about to come. The fat man sniffed and looked to one side, as if distracted, raising his right hand to wipe his nose with the back of his wrist. Suddenly he swung back and landed a powerful punch into his face. He

70

didn't even have a chance to topple back onto the stairs as the fat man followed up with an uppercut into his stomach. He

doubled up. There was an unbearable burning and clawing inside him. The fat man opened the front door and kicked pushed him out, slamming the door closed behind him.

He stumbled down the steps, blood flowing down his chin from his nose and mouth, and collapsed head first into the pavement.

He was spread out face down, partly on the Persian carpet and partly on the wooden floor, when they found him, not far from the sofa. Alan and Jenny rushed down the stairs when they heard a thump from their bedroom. They guessed that something was up. Alan called for an ambulance as soon as they saw him, but they knew it was already too late. He'd obviously tried to leave the house, but he didn't even manage to make it to his crutches. He probably didn't even have remember that he even needed them.

Jenny sat on the sofa and burst into tears. Alan went over to comfort her. They discussed how the mixture of opiates the doctors prescribed for the pain didn't mix with the high doses of cannabis he was taking in the belief it would cure his cancer. All it did was totally screw his thinking.

They heard the ambulance pull up. Alan got up and went out of the lounge to pull off the chain and unlock the Chubb. There were two paramedics standing there, both big guys. They came straight in.

One of them kneeled down and held Jason's wrist, then looked up at his colleague and shook his head.

They carried him to the ambulance and invited Jenny and Alan
to go along.

In the ambulance Jenny had a phone call from an old friend, Rosie. She had called with sad news about an old college friend, Debbie Wright.

"What about her?" asked Jenny.

"She died in a car crash on the Archway Road on Tuesday."

"Christ. We're all dropping like flies."

She told Alan the news when she hung up.

"Shit. I remember her. Didn't she go out with Jason for a while?" he asked.

"No', she said emphatically. "But they were very close."

UNDYING TALENT

Through the huge bay window, the sun hung low over the turquoise sea, flooding the room with clean blue light. In the middle of the large, almost empty room, a slim, naked girl with long red hair stood very still, not even ten feet from where he sat. She had been like that for over an hour, making quick glances at the clock above the door every now and again, before turning her head back into position. One arm was raised above her head and the other rested on the back of a battered old wooden chair, where a piece of purple velvet was draped, spilling onto the wooden floor, where it gathered into complex folds.

He was one of five students sitting around her. Two of them were drawing on easels and the other three sat using drawing boards on their laps. The rest of the class had given up and gone back to the main building. These were the hard-core life drawers, but not all of them were any good.

When it hit six o'clock the girl dropped her arm to her side and shook her hands, so as to allow the blood to flow while she walked over to the wooden screen in the corner, where she would get dressed. Everybody seemed relieved it was over, but there was also a collective sense of achievement.

Imogen, who sat in front of the window and was almost silhouetted from Alan's point of view, theatrically leaned back over her chair, and stretched out her arms in a long, balletic yawn, like a cat seeking to be stroked. At that same moment

Dick and Phil, who had been sitting to the left of her, put down their boards and wandered over to check out Alan's drawing. He sat with his drawing board propped up on his knees, while pretending to evaluate his final drawing, knowing perfectly well that it was good. The line-work was bold and confidently executed, the figure correctly proportioned, and there was none of that clumsy foreshortening and incorrect anatomy you get in most students' work. Without question, this drawing was mature – and full of weight and grace. And that was why Dick and Phil had so much praise for it when they came over.

Rosie Tushingham, who noticed this outpouring, wanted to know what all the fuss was about, so she got up and strutted over, pushing through Dick and Phil as if they were nothing more than curtains, to get a good look at it.

"Oh... that's so gorgeous," she said.

Alan was surprised more by the softness and warmth of her breath than her voice.

"Cheers Rosie."

"My drawing was rubbish today," she said, as she straightened up. I don't know what's wrong with me."

Alan twisted round to face her. No. There was nothing wrong with Rosie. Like all the boys, He couldn't help being attracted by her all-black, Nico-like look, and her pixie-style blonde hair.

"Come on Rosie. We all get bad days," he said, even though he long ago concluded her drawing ability was limited. She pursed her lips to one side, and frowned, still looking at the drawing and

74

perhaps also weighing up weather Alan was being genuine or not. Even Imogen came over to get a good look, sidling up next to Rosie. By this time Phil and Dick had gone back to pack up their equipment.

"Oh. That is so perfect," she said with a pained expression, as if the drawing was discharging bolts of electricity. "You've captured her stance beautifully."

Alan's thick black rockabilly quiff wobbled as he turned around to look at her.

His eyes were deeply inset and in shadow, while his skin looked even paler than usual in the cool sunlight.

"Cheers Imogen."

Suddenly a deep, sonorous voice exploded Alan's aura of stardom,

"Ah! Is it already six?" it boomed. This was Raymond Jacques, the drawing tutor. He breezed into the room with his red silk scarf hung loosely around his neck, and his battered leather flying jacket left open. He sat on a tall stool, slightly behind Alan, taking a tin of tobacco from his jacket while also looking at Alan's drawing. Imogen and Rosie took this as a sign to pack away their equipment. Raymond commanded great respect. His knowledge of anatomy was staggering. He could draw the muscles and bones of the figure you may have been struggling with in your drawing, as well as explaining the mechanics of it all. None of the other tutors could do anything of the sort.

He would say things like: "The foot is attached to the tibia - like that… and it articulates at the base.

It's actually a lever. The fibula comes in on the outside and hinges to it here, like this." Then he'd draw another picture. "OK. Now, the gastrocnemius muscle attaches from behind the knee at the top and pulls the heel up at the back, while the muscles that attach to the base of the fibula at the front come down and splay out to attach to the front of the foot, like so. They are the ones that lift it up."

The students would bathe in the warm glow of his knowledge. He was the only graphics tutor who actually knew what he was talking about when it came to drawing the figure, and this gave him an air of sophistication and quiet calm. But just then that last quality was absent. If anything, he exuded despair - and even sadness.

"That's a nicely resolved figure, Alan," he said, while dangling a pinch of tobacco over the Rizla paper. Raymond was Belgian, but something about his deep voice and foreign accent hinted towards the Slavic. He rolled the tobacco in the paper; using both hands then lifted it up to lick the sticky edge, before mumbling something.

Alan wasn't sure he'd heard right.

"What's that, Raymond?"

"I said we may as well all give up," he said, as he lit his thin roll up using an ancient, battered brass Ronson.

That was what Alan thought he'd heard. What did it mean? Raymond took a seemingly endless drag and breathed out a plume of smoke. Everyone waited with bated breath for further clarification, as he brushed a fleck of tobacco from his lower lip.

But all he said was, "I've never seen anything like it."

Something about all this was really dispiriting. Raymond had left the conversation hanging. Alan almost didn't want to enquire further, but he felt obliged to.

"Never seen anything like what, Raymond?"

"That kid Jason Watts - he's made us all look like scribblers."

"I don't understand."

Scribblers; that was a word he hadn't heard since primary school. Was Raymond implying that the life drawing he still had pinned to his board was in that category too – a scribble? He was certainly looking at it when he said that word.

"I'm a bit confused. Who did you say?"

Raymond shook his head almost imperceptibly and took a deep puff of his cigarette.

"Jason Watts. First-year student. In front of me he drew me a male nude, with the arms outstretched and a slight twist, weight on one leg. It was like watching a Renaissance master at work."

Imogen, who had been stuffing her layout pad into her bag at the other end of the room, looked up and responded.

"Jason Watts? He's a bit weird, but his work is like, just so amazing. He can draw anything."

Alan looked from her, to Raymond and back again in utter confusion.

Raymond looked at Alan, raised his eyebrows and shrugged, in defeat more than affirmation.

"It's true," he added. "I've just come back from doing the course assessments for Year 1. Most of

77

that year is pretty average. But he's way ahead of everybody. I don't just mean the first years, I mean second years, third years and the tutors too"

Alan felt like the camera was on him in one of those Hitchcock shots where you zoom out while you move in, creating a kind of vertigo sensation. He couldn't speak. In blank amazement, he watched Raymond shaking his head and staring into infinity as he continued:

"He can draw any pose from his head - better than I can from life. And he's just nineteen. Nineteen."

Alan looked again at his own drawing, the one that everyone had been drooling over a few moments ago. Now it just looked sad and inadequate. "Jesus," he muttered.

Raymond shrugged and took out his Ronson again from his top pocket to re-ignite his half-smoked roll up, then lifted it delicately from his lips to let out another plume of smoke, before closing his mouth and turning down the corners of his lips in painful contemplation. It was difficult to know how to challenge Raymond's defeatism.

"Could it be some kind of trick?"

Raymond coughed, before he replied. "Ha. If it is, I'd like to learn it."

Alan winced and asked, "What's his name again?"

"Jason Watts."

"Hm."

Alan and Jenny lived in a first-floor flat, in the middle of a row of small Regency houses, between the grounds of an eighteenth-century church and the hospital. His live-in girlfriend, Jenny, was staying with a friend in London, which was a shame. He could've done with her being around, because he had left the life class feeling totally deflated. What a miserable situation to be in. To find yourself usurped by a first year. How was it possible? It didn't seem right. How could anyone be that good? Yes, some people are fortunate enough to be born with a huge reservoir of innate talent, but even then, they have to put in ridiculous hours of hard work and sacrifice to be anywhere near as good as the level of drawing ability Raymond was describing. People who are that obsessive tend to have under-developed personalities. It's like those boring maths geniuses, with their slave-driver parents. The effort involved in becoming so much better than everybody else leaves them devoid of personality. Probably this Jason Watts character is just like that. Boring, arrogant, quiet, and a bit shifty. Yeah. And another thing... these brilliant, ambitious types also like to keep their cards close to their chest, to cultivate a kind of fake, cold, reserve. They want to appear as if their phenomenal abilities come naturally to them, but really, they're just boring swats. An image of a slightly older, taller and skinnier version of the Milky Bar Kid, wearing gold, wireframe specs rose to the front of his mind. He was sure that he wasn't far from the truth. But right now, he needed to focus on tea.

Alan put the previous night's spaghetti Bolognese on the stove. Then he took a beer from the fridge and sat down by the coffee table, and picked up a book on the work of Augustus John that was lying around. He opened it out to a drawing of a nude girl that had been created with sweeping, sensitive outlines and rapid, pencil strokes for tone. She is face down, legs slightly bent, levering her upper body up with her elbow so that her left breast hangs down, sensually touching the blanket beneath her. It was a staggeringly beautiful and skilful piece of work, mixing knowledge, talent, subtly refined technique and experience with expression and sensitivity. How could anyone get to be that good? He was on a level very few artists had reached, when it came to figure drawing. Henry Tonks, his teacher at The Slade (and a great draughtsman in his own right) thought John had actually reached the same stratospheric standard as the Renaissance masters, Leonardo and Michelangelo. He wasn't exaggerating.

Augustus John was good enough to get into the Slade by the time he was just seventeen. Even before he graduated, he was recognised as one of the greatest draughtsmen of his generation. Probably the third-year students at the Slade, who were in their twenties, would have been looking at the drawings of the teenage John and wondering why they bothered - rather like Raymond reacted to Jason Watts, and most likely he would too.

Jenny called after a while. He listened to her talking about the great photographs she'd taken in the north London dress factory, of all these sad, poorly paid and over-worked women. He told her about how much time he'd spent on his thesis, and how it was developing slowly. But he didn't say anything about the genius in the first year whose ability had caused such anxiety and despair to Raymond Jacques.

That night Alan had trouble getting to sleep. Try as he might to find reasons to disregard what Raymond had said he couldn't ignore the fact that Raymond was never flippant about anything. His tendency was to find fault. He was even a little critical of a Rembrandt drawing once. So, when he said he was overcome by the brilliance of Jason Watts, he must have meant it. There was no point in avoiding that conclusion. That left him with the solace of despair, because there was no point analysing that issue any more. Now he was overcome by curiosity. He had to see those incredible drawings that had made that painful impression on Raymond for himself. A kind of fatalism overcame him, and he sensed it could be a life-changing experience, though he had no idea why that was so.

In the morning, after brewing up a strong coffee and munching on some toast, he left the flat in his favourite red and black plaid shirt, his US-made Levis 501s and a pair of black DMs. This was his cool rockabilly persona. It was like wearing a suit of armour. Ten minutes later he came down the hill to the side of the long, slightly bowed glass and steel, Bauhaus-inspired art school building, which was bathed in shadow. He entered the foyer and walked purposefully up the main stairs, taking two steps at a time, not even stopping on the mezzanine to buy a layout pad and pencils from the college shop. Reaching the first floor landing he turned left, moving away from the stairwell to push through the plain, grey double doors leading to First Year Graphics. On the left of the corridor was a row of small admin offices. Opposite them were two very large rooms. One was First-Year Design, but the nearest one was the illustration studio. The door was open. He plucked up the courage to go in and approach the nearest person, who happened to be a skinny boy sitting at the desk in his cubbyhole (all students had their own desk, which was walled in from the desks either side). This lad sported a thick mop of blond hair, which made him look like a young Andy Warhol, which was probably intentional. Being completely engrossed in a dog-eared paperback, he didn't notice Alan. Alan coughed loudly. This caught his attention.

"Hi. Any idea where I can find Jason Watts?"

He looked up at Alan over his transparent frame specs and blinked.

"Huh? Yeah... yeah! Sorry. He's on the other side, just before you get to the desks near the windows."

"Near the windows?"

He closed the book up decisively (a Penguin edition of Sartre's, The Age of Reason) and stood up, as if having been sparked to life.

"Here."

Alan followed him along a meandering route, among a narrow maze of desks. They came to a booth where a pretty girl with a neat brown bob sat on the desk swinging her legs. A tall, dark haired lad in a gleaming white shirt, black drainpipe trousers and carefully polished black Oxford shoes chatted to her while pinning up some drawings. Alan noticed they were obviously photocopies of Augustus John's work, although he wasn't actually familiar with any of them.

The kid went up to the white-shirted lad and tapped him on the shoulder.

"Jason. Someone to see you."

With that he zipped off. Jason stopped what he was doing and twisted around.

Alan held out his hand. "Hi."

Jason shook it firmly. "Hi."

Alan White. Good to meet you. I've heard a lot about you."

Jason laughed and said, "Doesn't sound good."

"Oh no. It was all very positive. It's not very often that Raymond Jacques praises anyone's work."

The girl exchanged a confused look with Jason.

"Better get my art history done," she said, totally ignoring Alan.

"Sure. See you lunchtime, Deb," he called as she left.

"So, uh… what can I do for you?"

Jason fixed Alan with his hazel green eyes, not so much in an unfriendly manner, so much as a deep curiosity. Alan had spent hours working out what he would say, and he tried to follow that script.

"I just really wanted to introduce myself and, if you don't mind that is, get a look at some of your work. That's if you have the time."

"Sure. Are you an illustrator?" he asked.

"Third year," said Alan.

"Oh, right."

Alan studied his face for any signs of concern or evasiveness, but the opposite was true. Jason seemed to be delighted by the request. He was nothing like Alan had expected. There was no reserve, no coolness. In fact, the opposite was true. He seemed to be a genuinely warm and friendly soul.

As Jason opened the draws in his plan chest, Alan pointed to the drawings on the wall.

"I see you're a fan of Augustus John."

Jason was looking down at the time. "What?"

"I was looking at a book of his work last night," said Alan. "I thought I knew all his work, but I've never seen those ones before."

Jason got up looking confused. "Which ones?"

"Those."

"Where?"

"There."

He laughed a little. "Oh no. They're not Augustus John's. They're mine."

Alan was sure he misheard.

"Sorry?"

"He is a big influence, for sure, Augustus John, I mean. But I did those."

"You?"

Alan was sure he hadn't heard properly. He was certain there was some confusion. "No. I mean those drawings on the wall there."

Jason nodded politely. "Yes. They're mine."

If was like a custard-pie-in-the-face moment in a Laurel and Hardy film. Had he ever felt this stupid? Words swirled around in his head, but they wouldn't slow down enough to be coalesced into sentences. He didn't know how long it took for him to say, "You uh... wow! That is incredible."

Jason Watts could have laughed out loud and humiliated him, but he simply waited for the truth to sink in so that he could show Alan some other work.

Alan felt as if he was in the presence of a deity. Over the next ten minutes Jason showed Alan a fantastic selection of drawings, including anatomical studies, pencil portraits (many showing people he had seen hanging around the college bar and several of the girl who was talking to Jason when he arrived). All of it looked as if it was by Augustus John. In the portraits, the eyes and lips were full of life and expression. Like John, he used fluid outlines, along with clean, parallel, diagonal pencil strokes for shadow. Alan was sure even Augustus John would have believed he did them. They talked for another twenty minutes or so, before Alan had to depart for his art-history review. They got on very well, and Jason was pleased to have someone who could half draw really appreciate his work for what it was worth. They agreed to meet up at the Wheatsheaf when Jason got back from Paris, which is where the first years were going for a few days.

When he got back home that evening Alan was buzzing. He was also confused. There was no denying the incredible quality of the work Jason Watts had shown him, as well as the extraordinary

85

facility he possessed. It was stratospheric. Frightening. Because of it, Alan's confidence in his own ability had been badly dented, probably beyond repair. There was no way on earth he could ever reach that level. Yes, he could improve a few notches, better than most mortals, but whatever he did, however hard he tried, he would always be looking up at Jason Watts. How could it have happened, that a nineteen-year-old kid could draw in the exact style of a great master? Alan's wounded ego prompted him to suspect there must be something criminal about it. He rummaged around every corner of his mind to cobble together an acceptable diagnosis, but it was a futile exercise. What exactly does it take to be that good? Was there a sinister secret behind Jason Watts' abilities? Could it really be some kind of trick, as he'd expressed to Raymond?

The first thing he noticed when he got home again was that a few more days of dieting had made a visible difference to Jenny's silhouette, which saddened him a little. He actually liked her puppy fat. She looked up when she heard him enter and squinted a smile that emphasised her tiny roman nose. She was pouring herself a glass of wine in the lounge. He walked around the table to kiss her on the lips. She showed him the bottle, and he nodded so she filled another glass and handed it to him. He raised it in gratitude and took a slurp. Her blonde, spiked-up, hair was now brown at the roots.

"Alan?" she pouted.

"Mm."

"I've just spent ages scraping that horrible, sticky charcoal sediment off the bottom of the saucepan."

He sucked in his lips and nodded. "Mm."

"Are you going to enlighten me?"

"Yeah, well, you know…that's not my fault."

"Excuse me?"

"When we were chatting on the phone last night you were just, you know… too interesting, so I forgot all about the saucepan."

"Oh, I see. So, it's my fault?"

"Looks that way."

She shook her head in mock despair. "I am going to kick you where it hurts."

She stood up. "I'm doing Bolognese again. Do you want to make some salad?"

Soon he was at the kitchen work surface chopping up lettuce, while Jenny stood by the stove, stirring the saucepan. She stopped to taste the sauce with the long wooden spoon, nodded, and then looked over at Alan.

"Fancy going over to the Feathers?"

"Why not?" He shrugged.

"Don't sound too enthusiastic. What's put you in this weird mood, have I done something wrong?"

"No! It's just, you know... shit, now I know how Raphael felt when he saw Michelangelo's Sistine Chapel for the first time."

"What? How did he feel?"

"He fainted."

"You're going bonkers. You haven't seen me for a couple of days and you're rabbiting on about Raphael and Michelangelo like I give a shit. I was

87

expecting a bit more of a warm welcome. Are you having a fling?

"No! No way. I just, you know. I'm a bit shell-shocked – and depressed."

"Bollocks."

"Do you know someone called Jason Watts?"

"Should I?"

Alan explained how Raymond came in at the end of the life class looking shell-shocked, talking about this first year that was so good that "we" (he was including himself in this statement) should all give up.

"You're saying there's a kid in first year who's better than Raymond?"

"I had to check it out for myself – so I did. I wouldn't believe it if I hadn't seen it with my own eyes. His work looks exactly, and I mean exactly, like Augustus John's."

She frowned. "What are you on?"

"I'm not kidding. You should've been there. I watched him drawing this incredible figure from his head. No word of a lie – the drawing he did looked more like an Augustus John than Augustus John could've done."

"So, let me get this straight, he does copies of Augustus John?"

"No. You're not listening to me. He draws like Augustus John. That's his style. It comes natural to him. It's what he does… they're proper, beautiful, original drawings."

Jenny seemed to be staring into space. He realised that her thoughts must have moved on a couple of stages. She nodded to herself then looked hard at Alan.

"When did Augustus John die?"

"Sorry?"

"Roughly, I mean. When did Augustus John die?"

A strange, almost devious look came over Jenny as she half-squinted with one eye and raised the eyebrow of the other. It made Alan feel nervous whenever she did that.

"Well, he was already an art student in the 1890s so..." he started counting his fingers, then he dropped his hands. "It's unlikely he died any later than the 1940s or 50s."

"You're not sure?"

He shrugged.

"A few months ago," she said, "I saw this documentary about a kid in Ireland (maybe he was four or five). The thing is, ever since he could talk, he was describing his past life as a grown man. He said he was a fisherman living on Mull, an island off the west coast of Scotland, hundreds of miles away from where the kid lived with his mum and dad, which was in county Cork. He would say that he died in a fishing accident. It sounds mad – but no one could explain how he was able to describe the island of Mull and its geography. He could name the family members from his past life too."

"Sounds a bit fanciful to me."

"Shut up a minute."

Alan leaned back in surprise. Jenny continued.

"His mother took him to psychologists and other experts and stuff to work out what this was all about. In the end, she saved up and they went to Mull by plane. When they arrived, he was able to show her around the place. They even found the house where he said he lived - and it was just like he described it – even the surroundings matched."

"Blimey. So, when was this programme on?"

"Maybe August."

"Right."

"If that kind of stuff is possible – and what they showed is very convincing - then this Jason Watts character might actually be a reincarnation of Augustus John."

Alan was left gawping in stunned silence.

But she wasn't done yet. "Didn't you say Raymond told you Jason Watts was nineteen?"

"Mm."

"So, if he's nineteen he was probably born in, let me see..." She splayed out her fingers and started counting, bending each finger in sequence. Satisfied, she lowered her hands and nodded.

"1961. Right. Now you've got a whole fucking shelf of books on Augustus John. Pick one out and look up when Augustus John died."

Alan winced. He had always been so disparaging about anything to do with the supernatural. Whenever she mentioned star signs, or the emotional energy left over by the dead being visible to sensitive people' (presumably like herself), he would wind her up, implying she was over-exercising her considerable imagination. Anyway, he was pretty sure that John could not have died any later than the mid-1950s.

"Alright, alright. Don't get your knickers in a twist." Reluctantly he went over to the bookshelf running his fingers along the spines before pulling out a pale-yellow hardback. It was a biography of Augustus John by Michael Holroyd. He was never really interested in Augustus John the man, just the work. Despite being a genius, as a human being John left a lot to be desired. Alan opened it up to the last chapter and within seconds he looked up, visibly shaken. "Jesus."

"Give it here."

Jenny snatched the book, ran her finger down the page, stopped at a particular sentence and laughed.

"Ha! 31st October 1961. What did I tell you?"

It would be hypocritical of him to admit it, but Jenny's reasoning could explain everything.

Half an hour later Alan and Jenny were sitting in an oak-panelled corner of the Prince of Wales Feathers, watching the regulars, drinking, chatting, cheering and groaning as the darts team (predictably) lost to a team from the other side of town. The cigarette smoke seemed particularly irritating, though it really wasn't any more intense than usual. Jenny was genuinely interested in the darts, so Alan was free to concentrate on his own despair. He considered again how he'd been so far ahead of everyone... and now there was Jason Watts, who had come along and changed everything. The extent of this kid's talent was obscene - unnatural. That's why he was now weighing up the supernatural explanation that Jason could be a reincarnation of Augustus John. It would explain things and even relieve some of Alan's misery, because it would mean that Jason Watts was effectively a passive cheat. That would partially relieve his wounded ego. But Alan's long held scepticism couldn't completely go away. It's surely the case that if you were reincarnated you would retain the personality and characteristics of your previous life - otherwise you're effectively someone else. But Jason Watts was nothing like Augustus John, despite their drawing styles being so alike. John was a thoroughly unpleasant human being: arrogant, selfish and bullish, while Jason was easygoing, and really just a very chilled out sort of guy.

When the darts were over Jenny was not in the least bit interested in any discussion of Jason Watts.

"Listen," she said. "I'm not going to say this again. If Jason was born after October 31st, 1961, then we might be onto something. But if he was born before that day, then there's no way he's a reincarnation of Augustus John. You can't be reincarnated into a person who's already born, can you?"

But Alan wouldn't let go, and she became bored, which was why she turned away to join in other people's conversations. He was left alone with his battered old penguin edition of 'Against Nature'.

About an hour later it was last orders, and Alan looked up to see that Jenny was getting floppy. Having mingled with people standing at the bar she came back and sat next to Alan again. He put the book back in his jacket pocket and told her he was looking forward to getting back, putting the kettle on and watching the late-night horror film on ITV. But things didn't quite turn out that way, because as soon as they closed the front door she lunged towards him, lifting up his sweater and pushing him up against the hallway wall and thrusting her tongue down his throat. She then pulled away and quickly opened the door leading to the stairs to their apartment and dragged him into the bedroom, where she pulled off his jeans, tugged off his jumper, and spread herself over him.

When it was over, she dropped beside him, and fell almost immediately into a deep, open-mouthed sleep. He lay there for a while, allowing the quiet glow of his orgasm to percolate, before carefully getting off the bed to wash. When he came out of the bathroom, he didn't feel like going to bed yet, so he went into the lounge to watch whatever was left of Frankenstein Must Be Destroyed. Peter Cushing in his mad scientist's laboratory was sawing the top off the cranium of a corpse, after which he took out the dead brain and replaced it with a living one. Then he put the cranium back, leaving a gooey red line at the join, and started up some machinery. Slowly the corpse was re-animated. Usually Alan would enjoy these far-fetched, electric moments in Hammer Horror films, with their over-the-top dramatic music, cheesy acting and low lighting. But he couldn't focus properly because he started thinking again about Jason Watts - whose genius was well beyond dispute. It may sound outrageous, but he was convinced that it wouldn't be outrageous to put him on the same level as the Renaissance masters, as Henry Tonks had said about Augustus John. Frustrated at his inability to enjoy the film he lunged at the remote, switched the TV off, and went over to the kitchen to make himself a hot chocolate. Finally, he went over and sunk into the sofa, put it on the coffee table, and waited for it to cool down.

It was early evening in the graveyard and it was getting dark fast. This bleak place was overgrown with nettles. Orange and brown, crusty leaves scattered around the patches of grass and mud. He was standing under the dark mute trees, gazing at the partly shattered, ivy-covered, grey headstone and the words: 'Augustus John, 1878-1961' that were engraved on its partly shattered surface. In the earth in front of the headstone, the soil seemed to soften and shift, as if a molehill were forming. Then a frantically clawing hand pushed out, enlarging the hole, allowing the reanimated corpse of Augustus John to emerge. He was wearing a shabby raincoat, like the tramp on the cover of the Jethro Tull album, Aqualung. At first his head was in deep shadow, but as he looked up his bloodshot eyes and ragged beard that was encrusted with mold and soil, became clear. When he gave a leery grin the rotting flesh cracked and peeled away from his face when, which made his lips crack up to the nose and down to the chin. Alan was terrified. He tried to run, but it was like moving through a pool of viscous fluid, as Augusts John's living corpse stumbled towards him, arms stretched out. Alan woke up with a startled groan, just as the festering fingers were about to grab him by the shoulders. Jenny was still fast asleep. His heart was beating fast, and he couldn't get back to sleep. So, he got up and went back into the lounge, and poured himself a brandy.

The next morning (Saturday) they were in the old town, where Jenny was trying out different outfits in the Oxfam shop. Meanwhile Alan was hanging around outside. It was clear this was not going to be a quick sale, if indeed she did buy anything. He walked along the road a bit and came to a shoe shop which had a nice pair of maroon DMs on display. Sadly, they were just out of his price range. Wondering slightly further afield he came to a weird shop that featured a human skull, black candles, a knife with strange carvings, a crystal ball on a plinth, and a ceramic statuette of a hand with life-lines drawn in across the palm and fingers. There was also a set of tarot cards and a large tome, which was opened out to a spread showing a range of strange alchemical symbols. It was called Bell and Candle, and he'd never had the inclination to give the place a second look before. He studied the artefacts with just a hint of revulsion and then it struck him. Surely, they'd have some books on reincarnation in there.

He felt a tap on the shoulder. It was Jenny. This could have been embarrassing, but luckily, she was too distracted to notice what kind of shop window he'd just been looking at.

"I've just seen Imogen in Oxfam. She's trying something on in there right now. I said we could go for a coffee. Wanna come?"

As Alan wasn't ready to be sociable this was a good opportunity for him to get away. "Uh, you know what?" he said. "I'm all coffeed out. I had, like, three cups before we left home. I'll just wander around the second-hand bookshops for a bit. You go ahead and I'll catch up with you both a bit later."

Jenny went off gleefully to join her friend and Alan sneaked into the Bell and Candle. Once his eyes adjusted to the lack of natural light, he looked around the small, higgledy-piggledy interior. It smelled of incense. At a cluttered bookshelf to the right stood a frail looking, white-haired old man in a black suit, which must have been at least two sizes too big for him. He was thumbing through a massive tome with some difficulty. There was another bookshelf, filled with more valuable looking antique texts, covering much of the back wall. A small, homely looking lady in her sixties and a younger woman were sitting at a desk just in front of that, intently looking over a ledger. The older woman had obviously dyed black hair and wore a heavy, beaded necklace over a colourful patterned dress. She reminded Alan of Mrs. Tiggywinkle, from the Tales of Beatrix Potter. The other, probably in her thirties, was in a white blouse and pale green cardigan.

Alan went over to them and coughed.

"Uh, sorry to interrupt you," he said. "I'm uh, I'm trying to find out about uh, reincarnation."

He waited for an interval while they bickered in a low whisper about some numbers. Then the older woman looked up, holding him in steady focus and eventually spoke, with more than a hint of irritation.

96

"Reincarnation?"

"Uh yes. That's right."

The younger woman stopped writing so she could look at Alan too.

He hadn't felt this uncomfortable since he was summoned to the deputy headmaster's office for failing to deliver his French homework for the second week running.

"What is it you want to know about reincarnation?" said the older woman.

"Uh… you know, general information, like how it comes about and what it all means - that sort of thing."

"That sort of thing?"

"Well, whatever you can tell me."

"Mm. Tell me now, would I be right in saying that you've never been interested in the subject before?"

"Uh… no."

"And is this sudden interest in reincarnation in relation to a certain individual, a well-known person perhaps?"

"Well… yes."

"I see. And just for the sake of avoiding us having to talk about abstracts, shall we say that this someone could be, for example, Augustus John?"

There was a pregnant pause before a shiver ran down his back and he thought the room was floating on rough seas. A thousand thoughts tumbled over each other in his head, becoming knotted up and wisp-like before fading altogether. How did she know? All he had asked for was some general information about reincarnation. He stared at the women in speechless amazement, then took a step back and stumbled, knocking a bronze candelabrum off the table.

"Do be careful!" shouted the older lady. "We wouldn't want to have to ask you to pay damages."

He was feeling totally overawed and confused by now.

"S-s-sorry," he stammered, kneeling down to pick up the candelabra to replace on the table it had rested.

"How did you know?" he said finally.

"Know what? You're not making much sense."

His mind raced. Had Jenny gone into this shop and spoken to these women already? No, impossible. He'd been with her the whole morning.

"About my interest in Augustus John, in relation to reincarnation."

Then the older woman said, "What a ridiculous question. It was obvious."

Alan was stunned into silence. This whole experience was making him feel very uncomfortable, and he wished he'd never come into this shop.

Both the women laughed uncontrollably.

Meanwhile, the other customer who had been looking at the heavy book, shook his head angrily, put the book he'd been studying back on the shelf, and walked out in a huff. With him gone Alan relaxed visibly.

"Could I please trouble you for a glass of water? I'm, feeling a bit dizzy."

"Bella." Said the older woman. And the younger woman immediately got up and went through a door at the back of the shop.

The older lady held out her hand. "I'm Cornelia, and you are…"

"Alan", he said, taking her hand.

The younger woman came back with a glass.

"And this is my daughter, Bella."

Alan took the drink. She had something of the librarian about her, with her dark hair tied back in a tight bun, and the wire frame glasses.

"Pleased to meet you," said Bella, also shaking his hand.

Alan smiled, and Bella sat back into her chair.

"Good. Now, where were we?" said Cornelia.

Alan coughed, and became alert again. "Augustus John… You know what? I don't understand how you could possibly have known that…"

Cornelia interrupted him, as her fat fingers began twisting the lid back onto her fountain pen.

"Goodness," she said, exasperated. "Do stick to the facts! You wanted to know about reincarnation or, as we call it, the doctrine of cyclic existence."

Alan shook his head and forced out the words. "I'm sorry if it irritates you for me to ask, and I don't mean to be rude, but it really is quite baffling, and I would very much like to stop you there before moving on. Now please - how did you know it was Augustus John who was integral to my inquiry?"

Cornelia sighed and folded her arms and looked up at the ceiling.

"The fact is," she said, "you just look as if you're interested in Augustus John. Doesn't he Bella?"

Alan could not have been more frustrated and perplexed. "What?"

"Yes. It's quite obvious," added her daughter.

These two witches were running rings around him, and he didn't have his wits about him to respond suitably. He shook his head, took a deep breath and shrugged in submission.

"Fine, whatever."

With that Cornelia gave him her full attention once more, as she took up where she'd left off.

"Now, back to the main point. We're not short of books on reincarnation. Bella, show what we have will you?"

Bella stood up and led Alan to the shelf where the man who was in earlier had been rummaging. From the lower shelves, she pulled out a large, dusty looking tome and handed it up to him. Alan took it and opened it out to the index. As he looked through that Bella took out a bright orange, glossy paperback and stood up to flick though until she found a particular passage.

"You can see here," she said. "It really is very succinct: 'The Monad, the Divine Spark, the Ego – whose individuality remains the same throughout the whole course of reincarnation – is truly a denizen of the three higher worlds, the spiritual, the intuitional, and the higher mental, but in order to further its growth and the widening of its experience and knowledge, it is necessary that it should descend into the worlds of denser matter, the lower mental, the actual and the physical, and take back with it to the higher worlds what it has learned in these. Since it is impossible to progress far during one manifestation, it must return again and again to the lower worlds,' and so on."

He had no idea what she was talking about, but he tried to look impressed. He took that book from Bella too, handing the other one back to her.

"Feel free to buy that, if you wish," said Cornelia. "How much is it darling?"

"Nine pounds," replied Bella.

"There you go. You'll probably find it very enlightening. However, I strongly suspect you are not being as open with us as you should be?"

Alan stopped reading and regarded her as her podgy fingers fiddled menacingly with her necklace.

"I'm sorry," he said.

She gave a knowing smile. "Clearly, Augustus John is the spirit in transition, that is of interest, but who is the suspected receptacle?"

A cold tremor ran through him. It was almost as if this woman was a burglar who had burrowed her way into his innermost thoughts.

He gave a shrug. "There's this kid," he said. "Well... he's nineteen and his drawings are inseparable from Augustus John's. The thing is... Augustus John died in 1961, and this kid was born that same year. You see where I'm going with this?"

"Yes. That could be an appropriate explanation, as long as he was born after the time of John's death – preferably at the exact time of his death."

Bella interrupted at that point. "Mama. The coincidence of dates may be interesting, but it's not the only possible explanation."

Cornelia's eyes widened and she turned to face her daughter with a look of utter disdain.

"What are you harping on about, Bella? If this young fellow was born soon after, or at precisely the same hour that Augustus John died, it would be exceedingly difficult to ignore the possibility of him being a reincarnation of the former."

Bella closed her eyes, and lowered her head slowly in submission.

"Now!" Cornelia said, filling the sudden silence with a smile of smug satisfaction, turning her attention back to Alan "I should like to hear the symptoms first, and any deductions will fall out of that."

"Symptoms?"

"The manifestations that make you think this is a case of reincarnation."

Alan shrugged again. "Well, that's pretty much it really."

"You're sure that he doesn't just procure these wonderful drawings elsewhere and bring them in, as homework, so to speak?" Have you actually witnessed him in the act of creating these things yourself?

"Yes! He did four or five of them, right in front of me."

"Interesting, but still… to my knowledge, reincarnation is not known to automatically confer the previous abilities and skills of the deceased into the new life."

Bella nodded in agreement, as Cornelia continued.

"I see."

Bella interrupted again.

"The question is whether this young man could be a passive recipient of Augustus John's soul, or if he has advance knowledge of magic and occult practices that enable him to channel Augustus John's soul?"

Alan was baffled, and Cornelia bashed the table with the palm of her hand in fury.

"Don't be so ridiculous!"

"I'm sorry. I don't understand…"

Bella wriggled her fat bottom into the chair so she could get more comfortable.

"Bella is suggesting that the young man in question may be a seriously powerful adept of the dark arts."

"Magic?"

"Precisely. That would be beyond anything you could imagine. He's only a young man, as you say. One would need decades of knowledge, built up through endless reading and practice – as well as secret initiations. No. It's a ridiculous notion?"

Alan nodded blankly.

Bella interrupted, obviously intending to clarify things. "There are different types of channelling: intentional, spontaneous, classic (of a particular entity), open (inspired speaking from an unknown source), sleep and dream, clairaudient and clairvoyant."

"Christ," said Alan, almost in a whisper, not least because most of this was just gobbledygook to him.

But then Cornelia confused him even further by raising her arms in despair, and scowled at her daughter.

"Bella, please. If I need your elucidation, I shall ask for it."

Bella submitted and Cornelia addressed Alan directly again.

"Now, where was I?"

Alan had no idea, and Bella was in no mood to be helpful, so Cornelia had to find the thread for herself. "Ah, yes. Channelling.

"Generally, a channeller will go into a trance, which manifests itself in different ways. Sometimes they go rigid, into a type of catalepsy."

"That's definitely not what happens with Jason. When he does these drawings, he's totally relaxed. No way is he ever catatonic."

"There are some channellers who are able to open their eyes during the process and walk around and behave quite normally – and so on."

"Do you mean for hours?"

"No, no, no, not at all. It would take an extraordinarily powerful mystic, someone with decades of experience, someone who has achieved the magisterial status of wizard, having built up a monumental store of knowledge of the occult arts to join with a consciousness from the other side to achieve that."

This was all beginning to sound rather fanciful to Alan, as it was completely off target. He was pretty sure that Jason had no interest in magic whatsoever.

"But first things first," said Cornelia. "You will need to find the date and the hour when this young man was born. Everything follows from that."

He didn't want to belittle Cornelia by saying he already knew that. But Alan couldn't help noticing that Bella, who was behind Cornelia, was shaking her head, in silent (and hidden) disagreement with her mother. Alan had no idea what that was about. Anyway, their ramblings were either unintelligible or sheer nonsense. They also managed to make him feel uncomfortable in their presence – so he thanked them for their time, made his excuses and left.

The daylight hurt his eyes. The street had definitely become considerably busier. Uncomfortably so. What should he do now? Jenny and Imogen could be anywhere: having coffee, checking out shoes and clothes, looking around the Saturday market, or perhaps going through the record boxes at Rooster. He didn't know where to start looking, so he gave up before he started and went to see a lunchtime screening of American Werewolf in London at the cinema in the town centre.

Jenny called out to him as soon as she heard him coming up the stairs. He found her stretched out in the bath using her big toe to block a dripping tap.

He went in and kissed her on the lips then leaned against the wall in preparation for whatever underwhelming news she was going to give him.

"Guess what?" she said, with a mischievous look on her face."

He folded his arms. "Tell me."

"Chloe called up Imogen this morning."

"Mm."

"She wanted to find out what she could bring her back from Paris. You know, being nice to her big sister. Imogen said she'd love a white shirt from Agnes B (as if you'd be interested)."

"Alan shrugged."

"And then…" she added, "She asked her when Jason Watts was born."

Alan perked up. "And?"

"Imogen remembered his birthday drinks at the King and Queen this year."

"When?"

"In July. It was his nineteenth."

"Shit. Augustus John died in October. That's a few months early."

"Yep. So, he was born when Augustus John was still alive."

She looked up to see his reaction, and he was desperate not to have one.

"Yeah, well… that reincarnation business was always a bit far-fetched."

Jenny, who had sunk lower and lower into the water, suddenly rose up a little.

"Look at you trying to sound like the cool sceptic! You totally believed me when I said about reincarnation!"

106

"I wouldn't go that far."

"Pf. Anyway that's not all. Chloe said something else – probably just as interesting."

"I bet."

Jason Watts is into magic."

He stared open mouthed as Jenny started splashing away at the bubbles in her usual carefree way, clearing bubble free zones on the surface of the water

"She said he's totally obsessed."

"H-how does she know that?"

"That's all I know. Chloe had to get off the phone after that, because the tutors were rounding everyone up for their visit to the Louvre."

He moved his shoulder away from the wall, blinking hard frantically as his thoughts ran wild. How could he have been so wrong in his initial assessment of Jason Watts? In the time, he was speaking to Jason, he didn't see any sign of the reserve and cunning that you'd expect from someone who dabbled in magic, like that guy who was the head of the Church of Satan, who was supposed to have had Marilyn Monroe under his spell. What was his name? Oh yes... Anton LaVey."

Jenny was getting bored at this point.

"Right," she said. "I need to wash my hair now. So, if you don't want to risk getting soaked..."

Alan went into the lounge and stood looking out of the window, facing the street below and the hospital beyond, seeing cars parking, people walking to and fro, perceiving nothing, trying to let it all sink in. He tried to remember the precise words Cornelia had used:

"It would take an extraordinarily powerful mystic, someone who has achieved the status of wizard – or Magus; someone with a monumental store of knowledge of magic - and beyond that - a considerable predisposition of soul - to join with a consciousness from the other side to achieve the results that you describe."

He pulled out a stick of tough liquorice he'd bought in town and started chewing.

What do experts in magic do exactly? Cast spells. He had read about Aleister Crowley who had a reputation for being a supreme master of magic. There were many rumours about what he got up to, perhaps unsubstantiated. But it was said he performed weird rituals, using rhythmic chanting and bizarre spells. He organised and took part in ceremonial orgies and animal sacrifices. Rumours are that he was driven out of Italy for sacrificing babies. How could Jason Watts, who grew up in an ordinary terraced house in north London, have done that sort of thing? Where would he do it? Did his dad have an unused garage, or something? He tried to imagine Jason in a black hooded gown in a candlelit room, with hieroglyphic charts on the walls, and skulls, skeletons, and antique globes and strange measuring instruments all around, while a large cauldron made of dark pewter bubbling away, creating a foul smell. Maybe there would be glass tubes and beakers brewing up colourful elixirs and strange potions. If Alan became too inquisitive, would he be able to cast a curse on Alan, giving him some kind of disease, or even sending him mad? Despite Imogen's information, it all seemed totally preposterous. Nevertheless, he wasn't looking forward to meeting Jason again.

The next afternoon the first years were back from Paris, and Alan was hoping Jason hadn't forgotten their arrangement for that night. All day Jenny was covering the floor with her photographs and drawings to prepare for a presentation on Tuesday. In fact, that's what she was still doing when Alan was about to leave.

"You going to get legless?" she asked after he kissed her goodbye.

"Not so as you'd notice," he said.

For days, he'd been agonising over what it was all about, Jason's supposed interest in magic. He still wasn't a hundred percent convinced it was true. It sounded crazy. How would anyone get into that sort of thing? But if there was something in it maybe it would explain the Augustus John business. Tonight, was his chance of finding out, but he had no idea how he would bring the subject up. If he was lucky it would fall out of the conversation naturally.

It was cold and the wind was coming straight off the sea and hitting him full-face. The pub faced the seafront, though the only entrance was on a side street. When he arrived under the portico he stopped to consider whether he should just forget the whole business and go home. In defiance of what he considered to be his cowardly predisposition, he grabbed the brass handle and pulled the heavy oak door open, to discover he was using more strength than was required. A wave of warm air washed over him, leaving him surprisingly invigorated as he walked in.

Despite the big crowd at the bar he managed to get served quite fast before heading into the main bar. The sun dropped just below the slate grey sea through the huge front window, leaving a dull yellow glow in its wake, and the large ceiling fan and wicker seats gave the place the feeling of a colonial clubhouse in India. Alan looked around and saw Jason sitting at a table in the corner with a bunch of people. Alan went over there and stood drinking on his own for a moment, but it wasn't long before Jason called him over to their table, standing up and reaching over to give Alan a good, firm handshake. Around the table were Debbie, Ryan, Sophie, Emily, Geoff and Ali. Debbie was the girl who had been sitting on Jason's desk the day he met Jason in the first studio. Jason introduced him to them all and then asked Geoff and Ali to shift over a bit so that Alan could squeeze in.

"Alan's a third year," said Jason to the ensemble. Ryan, a tall, lanky, good looking blonde Aryan type said, "Hey Alan. Maybe you can tell us what you think. Most of us here believe Jason is a killer and he should definitely be arrested."

Alan was stunned. "Killer?" He couldn't suppress a look of utter astonishment, which he quickly tried to disguise as irony. Unpleasant thoughts flashed into his brain and made him hesitate before taking the next step.

"Ha! Perfect. Who is he supposed to have killed?"

He waited in silence for what was to come.

"It was only a cat," said Debbie protectively.?

Alan feigned indifference, but he could feel his heart beating a little quicker and a sudden chilliness in his back. He imagined a wooden glade at night, where Jason is standing poised knife in hand, under a gibbous moon, wearing a ceremonial robe, by a stone alter on which the cat is to be sacrificed. Alan forced the image out of his mind to calm his racing thoughts.

"What colour was the cat?" he asked.

Jason and his friends looked at each other bemused.

"What's that got to do with anything?" said Ali.

Jason came to Alan's rescue. "That's OK, he said. "It was Tabby."

Alan was relieved. "Oh." This wasn't connected to a ritualistic murder then. That was a relief. "So, what happened?" said Alan.

"Murder", said Ryan. "That's what happened."

"Oh, shut up!" said Debbie.

Emily sniggered.

"Look. I didn't mean to kill the fucking cat," said Jason. "Where we lived in Finsbury Park, our house backed onto this wasteland behind the school playground that was at the end of the garden next door. Sometimes, when me and my cousins played in the garden, our ball would go over there, and we'd, you know, we'd have to climb over this low

111

wall to get it. Now we had two cats, Streaky and Tiger who were terrorised by this bruiser with one ear. I used to see him clawing at my cats and often chasing them in our own garden. Well, one afternoon I went into that wasteland with my little cousin Dean and while we were there we came across this scruffy beast. I had my granddad's pitchfork with me,

Ryan interrupted. "Oh right, so your intentions were non-violent."

Ryan, Sophie, Emily, Geoff and Ali all laughed. Debbie shook her head disapprovingly.

"It's not what you think," said Jason. "I only wanted to scare the bruiser by slamming the pitchfork into the ground near him, but he was unlucky he leapt right over to where I was thrusting it. The prongs went right through him and got stuck in the hard soil."

"Uh! This is getting worse. I'm calling the RSPCA said Ryan jokingly," as Geoff and Ali doubled up with laughter

"Oh, shut up," said Debbie.

"I didn't mean it. Honestly." Dean was distraught, poor kid.

How old was he?"

"I dunno. Maybe about eight?"

"Great influence you are."

"Like I said! It wasn't part of the plan."

More sniggering.

"Sure... so, what did you do after that?"

"I put my foot on the dead cat and pushed it off the pitchfork. I tried to wipe the blood off on some grass."

"Eee-yuk!"

Alan listened to all this in bewilderment. He was beginning to be ashamed of his suspicions and a change gradually began to take shape in the nature of his thoughts.

"We went back over the wall into our garden, and I put the pitchfork back in the shed. After that we went back into the kitchen and I drew batman and Superman for Dean until my aunt came to pick him up. We didn't tell my mum or grandparents anything."

Jason's pals continued to rib him about the incident, with the exception of Debbie, who seemed annoyed by them all. Eventually the subject ran out of steam, and was overtaken by hunger. Only Jason decided he wasn't going to go along to Samson's, a trendy burger restaurant not too far away. Even Debbie deigned to leave Jason's side to join them. Ryan and Ali even invited Alan to come, in the hope that Jason would join them, but Jason stood firm. He was going to the Market Diner later for sausage egg and chips, he said, and he had been looking forward to it the whole time they were in France. When they had the table to themselves Alan took the opportunity to get back to a more meaningful subject.

"I have to tell you after I came over to see you and your work, it's had a major impact on me. I can't get over the way you draw..."

Jason took a sip of his beer and his eyebrows lifted a fraction into his noticeably large forehead, which gave him a look not too dissimilar to a young Jack Nicholson.

113

Alan waited for a modest return, but there was no response. It was as if to say, "Yes. I know I'm good. You're quite right."

This left Alan a little lost for words, so he moved on, to fill the uncomfortable silence.

"What I was wondering was, how did you set out to draw the way you do. I mean, the knowledge and sophistication in your work must have come from somewhere."

"You sound like my mum. She used to look at my drawings and say, 'you didn't come from me. You came through me'."

"I can understand that."

Jason let out a loud burp. Then he stood up with his empty glass. "Fancy another?"

"Uh... Thanks."

Alan handed his glass to Jason, who went off to the bar. It was a few minutes before he came back with the beers and two packets of cheese and onion crisps, which he threw on the table. "Here you go."

"Cheers," said Alan, as Jason squeezed around to get back to his seat in the corner.

"To get back to your question, I was a pretty sickly kid. I missed a lot of school. Mum used to buy me comics when I was in bed, you know, the American sort: Batman, Superman, Tarzan and stuff like that. I used to sit up in bed and copy the figures, resting my pad on the tea tray. I filled in a lot of sketchbooks like that. But I didn't learn as much as I would have liked. One day I went into the library and started rummaging and found these books on anatomy for artists. They looked promising. I took them home and forced myself to draw from them. I bought an action man and started drawing him in various poses, trying to do the same pose a few times until I could draw it without the doll being there. Then I got a small plastic model skeleton and learned all the names for the bones, and after a year I started on the muscles. It helped a lot. But I still wasn't getting it. It was like that for a few years. And then I had the dream."

"What dream?"

Jason took a good long glug of beer and thumped the glass (not too hard) on the table for emphasis. "The dream that changed everything."

"Now I'm curious."

Jason took another sip of his beer and frowned, as if what he was about to relate somehow pained him. Alan couldn't help noticing he was getting through his pint fast. Neither of them spoke for what seemed an uncomfortable long time, and then Jason took another sip before breaking the silence.

"When my nan died," he said, while wiping the foam off his upper lip. "I had this dream."

"How old were you?"

"Thirteen. I'm not sure if it was the day after the funeral, or maybe a day or two after that. In the dream, I remember I'm back at the funeral, but it feels different. I'm not sure that the people there are my family, but they could be. We're all standing around the coffin... it feels like something is about to happen, and I'm kind of gearing myself up for it, but I don't know what it will be. Suddenly the lid opens up slowly on its own. No one has touched it. Everybody stands back, but I go forward and lean over to look inside. Nan's body isn't in there.

Instead all these beautiful geometric shapes start floating out. They're semi-transparent, and in amazing pastel colours: glowing triangles, squares, circles, as well as cubes, cylinders, cones and spheres. A fountain of shapes – so perfect. I am stunned by the beauty of it all. You could say I was almost mesmerised. When I woke up I felt this irresistible urge to grab my pad and start drawing. And what flowed out of my pen at that moment was absolutely the type of drawing that I had been struggling to create for years. It was a wonderful, wonderful feeling. The figures came out just right. All that stuff I was practicing and learning, it suddenly came together - like magic."

There was that word again, thought Alan. Time to take advantage of the moment. "Magic? Oh yeah. I hear you're very interested in magic."

"Love it," replied Jason without flinching.

An involuntary shiver ran through Alan, dissolving the delicacy and wonder of the story he had just heard. He resolved to meet Jason's eye as he spoke.

"So, uh, how did you get into magic? I mean - you don't seem like the sort of person who would be interested in that kind of thing."

Jason seemed utterly and genuinely perplexed. "Why not?"

"Well, I dunno. I mean... What's it all about?"

Jason chuckled, which made Alan even more nervous.

"I'll show you?"

Alan looked on as Jason rummaged around in his jacket pocket for a minute and pulled out a red

116

silk handkerchief which he dangled near Alan's face. "Now watch closely," said Jason as he closed his left hand into a fist and, pushed the red handkerchief deep into his now tightened red fist with the fingers of his right hand, until it was all in there. Alan took a big sip from his glass, feeling a bit bored. Meanwhile, Jason blew onto his clenched fist, and opened it out to reveal... the handkerchief was not there anymore. It had vanished.

Jason grinned and said mischievously, "See? Magic."

Alan burst into laughter, spraying beer in all directions. He struggled to stop himself laughing, leaned forward so his head hit the table. People started staring and Jason worried that Alan might be having a seizure. Finally, the cacophony subsided, and Alan sat up, wiping the tears from his eyes.

"You all right, mate?" said Jason.

"Sorry," he said, in a slight falsetto voice. Then he caught his breath. "I just can't tell you how funny that was.

At that moment neither of them knew it, but this moment was the start of a friendship that would last a lifetime.

Postscript

A week later Alan was walking home from the station, having gone up to meet a few old school friends. It was after six, so most of the shops in the Old Town were closed, but the lights were still on in the Bell and Candle. Curious, he crossed over to peek through the glass and saw Bella standing by the large shelves with a small pile of books under her arm. She was wearing another mohair jumper. This one was lemon yellow and much more tight fitting. Also, she looked completely different with her long, black hair loose, covering her shoulders and glistening from the lighted candles distributed all around the shop.

He pushed the door in, and stepped forward so the jingly jangly things tinkled like wind chimes. She twisted around to look at him and he was immediately surprised by her hourglass figure.

"Oh. It's you," she said.

The place smelled strongly of incense. He looked all around for Cornelia.

"I wasn't sure you'd be open," he said. "Is Cornelia around?"

"Mother has gone to Glasgow to hear a lecture at the Theosophical Society. Not my cup of tea."

"Have you come back to buy that book?" she enquired.

"Er, I'm still thinking about that. But... I wanted to say thank you. You were very helpful the other day, you and your mother, I mean."

She sucked in her lips and raised her eyebrows.

"Look," he said, as he tried to find some courage. "Can I ask you a couple more things about, you know, the guy we were talking about?"

He was pleased he managed to get that out, but he wasn't sure how to continue.

"You mean your outrageously talented friend?" she said.

"Mm hm."

"I thought we'd exhausted that subject."

Everything she said seemed to be a challenge.

"Well yes, but there's been a development, which kind of changes things and I would really be grateful if I could just get your take on it."

She seemed to go cross-eyed for a few seconds. Then she suddenly sparked into life and marched over to the table, took off her glasses and placed the books down so she could open a draw to pull out a set of keys, which she held up and jangled with an impish expression.

"I was just about to close up," she said.

"Oh, right. I'll get along then."

He was half way towards turning around to leave he heard her say," "Fancy a splif?"

He turned to face her again.

"Sorry?"

"What's the matter. Don't you smoke?"

"I do but..."

"Give me a minute."

She walked past him to lock the front door, pull the bolts, and then turn the closed sign around. Then she dragged down the blind over the glass door.

"Right. This way."

In a state of utter confusion, he followed her through a door at the back, which opened into a narrow room, which featured a sink and work top on the left, with a kettle, a cassette player, and a sofa.

"No need to stand," she said.

Taking his cue, he sat at one end of the sofa, wondering if he was making a big mistake. Bella, meanwhile, rifled through a shoebox full of tapes.

"What do you want to hear?" she said. "John Martyn? The Cure? Mozart?"

"You got Solid Air there?" He asked.

She rummaged a bit more. "Mm-hm." She slotted in the tape and pushed the button in hard, so that the soothing vocals and hypnotic baseline came up.

"Tea?" She said, still standing.

"No thanks," he replied.

"Fine."

She sat down at the other end of the sofa, and opened the lid of a battered old tin of Golden Virginia on her lap. Then she took out the cigarette papers, flattening one out.

"So, you're not into theosophy?" said Alan, as she took a large pinch of the dried, crumbled green leaves, forming the mass into a worm shape along the opened out, King Size Rizla.

"Not really," she replied. "Obviously mother and I share an interest in matters metaphysical and spiritual, hence the shop. But we tend to approach everything from a diametrically opposite standpoint. That irks her somewhat, as does any challenge to her way of thinking, which I'm sure you noticed."

He laughed. "What can I say? But, why do you let her talk to you like that?"

She gave him a sideways glance, and a corner of her mouth turned up.

He hadn't stopped to censor himself before speaking. It just seemed to come out. He began to wish he'd kept his trap shut. She put the joint to her lips, put a lighter flame to it, and took a long deep breath, till she was sucking in a centimetre of

120

glowing red at the tip. Then she took it away from her mouth to let out a plume of smoke and said, "Because I love her."

He found the floodgates to his courage open.

"Yeah. But still..."

"I was at university in London studying philosophy," she interrupted. "It was all going so well. I had a flat in Camden, and I really loved London. I found the course work fascinating at first, but when it started to get political things fell apart for me."

"Political?"

"Compulsory cultural Marxism?"

"Oh. So, you're right wing?"

She squinted in frustration. "No! Not at all. Just not into Marx, or semiotics, or linguistic theory. One of the tutors in particular - and some of the students - had it in for me. Like you, just then, they thought I was a Conservative, and the psychological bullying that followed was relentless. I was ostracised and had all sorts of vile, juvenile things done to me. I won't go into details, because it still pains me to remember. Anyway, the long and the short of it is... I buckled. I had a breakdown."

"What does that mean?"

"I was a gibbering wreck sitting in bed, staring into space, with hot tears streaming down my face. I didn't eat for days. I wasn't even answering the phone. Mum drove up, and asked the landlord to let her in. She came in and cleared my room out, pushed me into the car and took me home. She was so worried, and she was wonderful. Truly. She hired someone to look after the shop while she nursed me back to health. I've been with her ever since."

She handed him the roach and he took a puff, which caused him to immediately struggle to hold off a coughing fit as he said, "Christ. When did all that happen?"

"Let me think now... yes. It was eleven years ago."

Recovering somewhat, he said cautiously.

"Surely, it's time for you to go your own way now?"

She said nothing as he gave her back the roach, which she put it into an ashtray, then stood up to lift off her yellow mohair jumper, to reveal the pale, flawless skin of her stomach. She reached back to unclip her white bra. He was transfixed, feeling a mixture of astonishment and pleasure. Instantly he knew what to do. He was, at that moment, like an actor who had almost forgotten his lines when he stood up to wrap his arms around her. He kissed her cheek and then her lips, before bending down to kiss each breast softly. She breathed heavily and pulled him over to the sofa. Half an hour later they were lying down. She was playing with his hair as he lay back, contented and perplexed."

"Where did that come from?" he said.

"The moment," she replied, with a smirk. He admired her confidence and her impulsiveness. But he guessed these were qualities she couldn't switch on at will.

"Am I allowed to ask you about my friend now?"

"Feel free," she said, leaning over to take the roach out of the ashtray to light it again.

"He has no interest in the occult, alchemy, spirituality – whatever you want to call it," said Alan. "His only interest in magic is in illusion – tricks. Not the occult, or supernatural, or dark arts - or whatever you want to call it."

She laughed. "That is so funny."

"I know. And the other thing is - he was born two months before Augustus John died. So, no way is he a reincarnation of him."

"Don't be so stupid. That's like adding two and two and making five. Time is not as simple as you think? Thought is dynamic and it can actually accomplish material results. It can even act at a distance - not just in terms of proximity, but also of time. So, the thoughts of others can be accessed. Time is not linear."

"What do you mean?"

"It can split into different branches - like the Northern Line does after Camden Town."

"What are you talking about?"

Quantum theory describes it like this: systems interact with each other, outcomes split into alternative versions, and they're all real."

"Now you've lost me."

She smiled.

He told her then about how Jason told him about this wonderful dream where he is at a funeral and the coffin lid is opened before it is lowered into the ground and out of it float these beautiful, colourful, light shapes: triangles, squares, circles, rectangles, cubes, cylinders, spheres... he is awed and fascinated by them. He said he remembered that dream perfectly when he woke, and from that day he was able to draw the way he does now. He was thirteen.

She nodded seriously and stared at the ceiling. "He was chosen."

"By who?"

She got up and started to put on her bra while she said, "I think you'd better go now."

Soon after Alan was walking home and trying to put everything into order in his head. Having sex with a woman over thirty, accepting there was a glass ceiling to his creative potential, and coming to terms with the metaphysical nature of reality. It all seemed absurd, but in reality, that was just an illusion. There was a definite order to it all. He had felt it. It was just too difficult to understand, and even more difficult to accept. Much like Jason's genius.

THE RESURRECTION

The week before the day of the lecture had been a blur of rain and mist. The venue was a quietly dignified building on the southeast corner of Regents Park, with rows of Ionic columns and three stories of tall, narrow windows. Sadly, since its heyday, in the Regency period, it had fallen into some disrepair and was now a sort of temporary arts centre, which was scheduled for conversion into luxury apartments, but there was no sign of that happening any time soon. The lecture theatre was situated on the ground floor, and was an original part of the building. High ceilinged, light and spacious, it was laid out like a small, indoor, Greek Amphitheatre. Alan thought it was just the sort of place where medical students of the nineteenth century would have sat to watch autopsies being performed by leading surgeons of the day. However, on this particular afternoon the only thing being dissected was the subject of Divine Proportion. Alan's interest in the topic was connected to his love of classical and neo-classical architecture, but he also wanted to be able to apply its principles in the composition of his drawings and paintings. Having sat down at one of the upper benches facing the lectern, he rummaged around in his rucksack, so as he could take notes. Ultimately though, he decided against that. After all, it wasn't as if he was going to be tested or anything.

Finally, the speaker came in wearing a loose-fitting, grey flannel suit and carrying a battered brown leather briefcase. His unkempt mop of curly blond hair gave him an air of relaxed warmth and intelligence, which was pleasantly reassuring. Having removed a glasses case from his jacket pocket, he withdrew a pair of gold frame wire spectacles, and put them on very delicately, with the little fingers of each hand protruding prominently. Then he sighed and stepped up onto the lectern, gripping it with both hands, before looking around the room and coughing loudly. It had the desired effect, because the chattering from the benches came to an abrupt halt.

"Good evening, and a warm welcome to you all," he said, with a smile. "My name is Harold Cohen and I am a professor of Renaissance studies in the department of European History at London University."

His voice had the soothing qualities you'd expect to hear in a country sermon. It reminded Alan of the TV actor, Derek Nimmo.

"What we are going to talk about here today," he continued, "Is Divine Proportion, which will help us see how the objects of beauty can be appreciated in any form. We will be talking about the 'Golden Section' of the Greeks, and how it is not just a means of creating art and architecture, but that it also describes how nature takes shape, from the smallest sea shell to the furthest galaxy."

This was a good start, thought Alan. And for a few minutes at least, he was able to follow the flow. But when an element of mathematics entered into the mix, Alan's thinking became undisciplined, particularly when the speaker said,

"There are many points where you could cut a piece of string, and every one of them would give you a different ratio for the length of the small piece of string to the large piece."

Alan waited to see if he could latch back into the flow again, but instead found himself looking blankly around the room. It was no good. His consciousness was sinking into a sickly sweet, deep, marshmallow miasma and there was nothing he could do about it.

When Dr Cohen came to say, "This is where the ratio of both is 1.618 to 1, or, as we shall henceforth refer to it, Phi becomes significant," he tried once more to follow the flow, by focusing hard on the speaker, watching him speak, seeing his lips move. It was no good. He could no longer make out words, just low, hollow sounds, as if he was underwater.

The game was up. His attention was drifting further and further and he found himself looking absent-mindedly at the people sitting in the rows behind the speaker, as a dreadful sense of anticipation took slow possession of him, while he became somehow conscious of a sort of displacement, an uncomfortable awakening that was baring down on him by some unknown means, leaving him nervous and perplexed by its inevitability. Soon those people's faces began to lose their sharpness, and then bobbling perceptibly, like waves, before just one of them came inexplicably into sharp focus separating itself totally from the others. This particular face happened to be looking down. The forehead was large, and around the mouth was a suave musketeer-type moustache and goatee beard, and on the cheeks, were well-groomed, knife-sharp sideburns, reaching right down to a pronounced set of jowls. It seemed like minutes that he had been staring blankly at this person, when he then became hypnotised by his grass green corduroy jacket. He struggled to recall where he'd seen it before when he had a moment of enlightenment that struck him like a bucket of iced water had been swung his way, washing away his waking dream and leaving a dreadful realisation, followed by complete and utter confusion. There was no question. This person was Jason Watts. But Jason Watts was dead.

It was nearly two years ago that the cancer got him. In just two or three months this tall, dignified man of fifty-three was devoured inside out by the disease. In the end, he looked like a tiny, pathetic, shrivelled up octogenarian. In his last two years, Alan and Jenny had put him and Rowena, (his girlfriend after Rebecca died) in their spare room. This was during the period following Jason being forced into bankruptcy by his creditors, and they lost the flat. After a while it got to the point where Rowena couldn't look after him anymore, even with Jenny's help, so they had to arrange for Jason to go into a hospice after that. Alan recalled that strange moment in those last few days when he was sitting with Rowena by Jason's bed in the hospice, talking about the funeral arrangements. Jason had fallen into a deep coma and the doctors said he could expire at any moment. But something extraordinary happened. Jason suddenly sprang up, into a sitting position, and looked directly at Alan.

"Oh Alan. Hi!" he said, as if he'd just woken up to the alarm clock.

And then he immediately fell back into the deep sleep, from which he never emerged.

Alan gave the eulogy at the funeral, and then watched as Joy Division's, 'Walk in Silence' played while Jason's coffin slid slowly behind the curtains, on its journey to incineration.

So how could Jason be here now, alive, fit and well, taking notes at a lecture! This was definitely no ghost or vague spiritual entity that would dissolve way like autumn mist. It was the firm, solid, physical Jason – and he was just as much a part of the audience as everyone else.

Alan knew he would have been terrified if he was on his own, and he actually was scared for a second or two, until everything began to coalesce in his mind. Having all these other people around at the same time was powerful reassurance, a sort of paperless safety certificate. Still, the question remained, how was it possible for Jason to be here now, fit, healthy, solid, breathing? He had to know. A fiery urge welled up in Alan to talk to Jason, to ask him about absolutely everything – immediately. Fuck it! This was no time to be self-conscious. He shot up, oblivious of the consequences, and stomped down the steps and across the floor of the theatre, past the speaker (who smiled benignly at him) and shot up the aisle of the tiered rows of seats opposite, to squeeze past the people seated at the end of Jason's bench (who definitely weren't pleased). One of them, a bearded fellow in his forties (who looked like he was about to go hiking in the Welsh mountains after the talk), gave him a filthy look. Jason, meanwhile, was blissfully unaware of all this activity, focusing completely on whatever it was he was writing. Alan went right up next to where he sat and tapped him on the shoulder. Dreamily Jason turned around, looked up and smiled, before beaming into a wide-eyed look of recognition.

"Alan, how are you?" he said. It was so ridiculously casual. It was as if Jason had returned from a week's holiday in Margate, instead of having risen from the dead. Alan dispensed with formalities. "Jason... We need to talk. Can you come for a walk?"

Jason pouted, went wide-eyed, then shrugged and stood up to put his notebook and pen in his pocket to follow Alan out, squeezing past the thoroughly discomposed people at the end again. Alan didn't much care; although he did stop and turn around to face the speaker when they reached the door, to say, "Look... I'm really very sorry about all this, but we..." He searched around for a reasonable statement that would qualify such an interruption, but could only come up with, "we haven't seen each other for years."

The professor seemed to sympathise, nodding and smiling when he said, "Obviously your friendship must be of divine proportions."

That caused a ripple of restrained laughter, so that even Alan smiled.

They went out on the park side of the building, taking the few steps down to the pavement that was strewn all over with orange and yellow leaves, like tickets to a rained-out concert.

"Jason. You know you died, right?"

Jason simply nodded with a mild shrug. A million thoughts ran through Alan's brain, and none of them amounted to anything that would correspond to an appropriate response. His heart was beating fast, he was a little scared, but he knew he had to try to stay calm – even though it was superficially so.

"OK. Listen," said Alan. "When we get across that fucking road we can talk properly."

"Sure."

The sky was milk white, bestowing a soft and nearly shadow-less light on Euston Road. There wasn't the typical roar of traffic, because there simply weren't as many vehicles as usual, which was odd for a road which was virtually a motorway running across the northern edge of central London. It was almost empty of pedestrians too. Alan wondered if this was a public holiday that he wasn't aware of. But then he remembered there weren't any public holidays in October. As they crossed over to Great Portland Street Station he tried to make sense of it all, without success. When they came up to a car showroom not far from Warren Street Station they turned right more psychologically prepared to talk – and listen. "OK. Now tell me... Jesus, what the fuck is going on? You died. Ok, just give me a sec... I mean, after death, did you experience, heaven, angels or what? I mean, fuck... you being here now... you've been resurrected. There can't be many people who get resurrected."

"No, there aren't," replied Jason slowly, following it with that barely suppressed impish grin he would have pulled just before he was about to wind you up, or perform one of his many magic tricks. "And... did you talk to God?"

Alan was expecting at least a little reticence, but the response was immediate and confident.

"Yes. And we understood each other."

"You what?"

"That's all I can say about that."

Alan was stunned by such a show of monumental arrogance. But perhaps this response was not quite as egotistical as it seemed. And Jason did have a propensity for arrogance. But it could be that Jason understood (correctly or otherwise) that somehow his return made him one of a select group, like an angel or something. Alan felt that there might have been just a hint of anxiety in his blasé response. There was definitely a sort of rapid squint, which might mean he was somewhat embarrassed about his apparent divinity – as if it was an encumbrance. Of course, this was all pure speculation, but Alan suspected that Jason genuinely wanted to talk to him about how it was that this completely incomprehensible turn of events had come about - but he was definitely anxious doing so. Alan decided to give him a little nudge in that direction.

"So, where do I start? What's it all about? I mean... what the fuck?"

Jason pinched his nose, like one of those mediums you read about from the Victorian, who would appear to withdraw a stream of ectoplasm from their facial orifices. All around Fitzroy Square the leaves were falling like rain.

"Give me a second," said Jason. "I'm trying to work it out. To be honest, I only know bits, and it's tough getting my head round any of it."

Alan couldn't miss the pained look in Jason's eyes. Obviously, he had to temper his exuberance if he didn't want to aggravate whatever it was that was troubling Jason. The Telecom Tower loomed high to the right, like a monstrous hypodermic syringe. Before long they were walking past the offices of Solomon & Obadiah. The building was huge, stretching east to Whitfield Street and south to Tottenham Street. Although he was badly paid during his time as an art-director there, working mostly on British Airways and Fosters, Alan still had a soft spot for the place. He couldn't resist looking through the huge plate glass window, to see if there was anyone he knew in there. Sadly, it seemed strangely devoid of life. There was only the one receptionist, which was unusual. A cleaner was working around the waiting area, where there was no one seated. Where were all those expense account people returning from their obscenely long Friday lunches? The whole of Charlotte Street seemed empty of life and Alan's mood was now sufficiently impressionable to see the whole neighbourhood darkened by an ominous shadow. That may explain why he was struck by a tidal wave of fear when Jason gripped his arm. For an instant, he reacted as if he was being clawed by a zombie, however, he recovered quickly, and Jason didn't notice. He was working on building up some of his inner strength, and now he had a look of resolve in his eyes.

"I'll tell you what I can," he said. "But these memories, if you can call them that – they're a bit all over the place. I'm not sure how much sense I'll make."

"OK. Whatever you can say. Take your time."

Jason turned to Alan apprehensively, resting the knuckle of his forefinger on his chin, which is something he did when he was working on a difficult portrait.

"Everything was black. There wasn't anything else. That's the best way I can describe it. Then it kind of dissolved away and I found I was in your living room, sleeping on the sofa. It was the middle of the night, just after a party, I think."

"What? But you were in the hospice when, you know, when you died."

"I know, but I'm telling you what happened."

Despite being baffled, he thought it best not to interrupt any further.

"OK. Go on."

"At the time, I didn't know where I was. I just realise now, on reflection. My mind was like a blank slate. I didn't even know who I was. I was really desperate to get out of the house before anyone saw me, and I didn't even know why. And that's where it gets hazy again. I remember walking into the night, and somehow I end up in bed with Debbie."

"Whoa. You skipped a couple of stages there. You did what?"

"I was making love to Debbie."

134

"Making... wait. Which Debbie? Not Debbie Wright, the girl who was trying to get into your trousers the whole time we were at college?"

"What?"

"Never mind. Look, you do know that Debbie Wright was in a fatal car crash, around the same week you died, don't you?"

Jason frowned and raised his upper lip on one side, in a show of disgust, and said, "Alan. Why do you always do this? What the fuck has that got to do with anything? Why are you bringing up peripherals? This is really doing my head in trying to remember everything that happened. I'm not *meant* to remember. Everything that I draw out brings with it a major stabbing pain. I've got fucking a right migraine now – and I never used to get those."

Alan was stunned and humbled by this tirade. It would have been totally unconstructive to deliver a riposte, even if he had one. The main thing was he didn't want to cause Jason any more suffering than he was already going through. But he did want to know what the hell was going on. This wasn't simply a reincarnation of Jason, or some kind of ghostly apparition. This was a fucking solid, living, breathing, animated material resurrection with a totally brand, spanking new fully restored human body. Christ, even in those old Hammer Horror films, the mad scientist needed fresh bodies to re-animate, because when decomposition set in, it was too late. All that was left of Jason's body after he died was a pile of ash. Where would you start?

"Jas. I'm really sorry," he said. "I'll shut up and

let you explain everything in your own way."

Jason shook his head and sighed, like a schoolteacher despairing of a naughty child. Alan took that as a sign that the tension was now diffused.

The dull sky let a frugal light seep down to the almost deserted pavements and near-empty office buildings. It was easy to believe that the shadow of death was looming large over London. Then, out of nowhere, Jason said,

"But this was the real Debbie," puncturing Alan's melancholy reverie. "Huh?"

"She wasn't all sad and worn out by a breakdown and anorexia and all that, which we were all hearing about her over the years. I didn't think too much about it then, but she looked the same as she did at college."

"So... she couldn't have been real."

"No. I think she was. It just depends on your definition of 'real'."

Alan thought about that as they crossed Goodge Street, pulling a quizzical expression and saying nothing, preferring not to risk antagonising Jason again. However, by the time they were passing the Charlotte Street Hotel the silence between them was becoming painful. He had to say *something*, and just as he was about to, Jason beat him to it.

"She was crying," he said, "and it was because of me. I can't remember what I did though. All I know is I was absolutely desperate to get out of there, and I charged down those stairs to the front door."

"So, you have no idea what happened that led

to make you want to leave like that?"

"No. But I do remember walking along the pavement afterwards and then... everything went black."

"Again? Why?"

"Something happened. This time the blackness seemed to hang around for ages. I was in this massive tunnel and I couldn't see the end of it for ages, it was so dark. I just knew I had to keep walking. And then I saw a point of light ahead, and I don't know how far I had to go, but after a while the light got a little brighter, slowly becoming like a sun - almost unbearably intense - and I ended up walking right through it: it kind of swallowed me up and it felt invigorating and cool. Slowly it faded, and the dark tunnel wasn't there anymore. My eyes slowly recovered from the intense brightness, and I found I was high up on a hill, looking down at luscious woods, with vines, and plantations of olives stretched along a river. On one side was a range of massive snow-capped mountains, with their summits covered by clouds, which sometimes thinned out to reveal the powerful jagged peaks behind..."

At this point Jason stopped talking and became dreamy and distant. He then pinched the bridge of his nose and frowned intensely, as if in pain, before he was able to continue again. "

And then the mountain peaks would become lost again when the mists thickened for a while, before becoming wispy here and there, and allowing the blue sky to gleam through in some places. Sometimes the gaps in the mist revealed dark pine forests, that swept right down to the foothills."

"Sounds awesome."

"It was. There were these soft green pastures and woods below that sort of clung to the skirts of the mountains, and I could see flocks of birds and herds of sheep. To the other side, in the distance, huge plains were becoming lost in the mist. Behind me was a gorgeous, deep blue sea."

"Sounds like a typical near-death experience."

"Except this *was* death, remember?"

"Oh yeah. Sorry."

"One thing that confuses me now, but I didn't see anything odd about it then, those mountains were bloody miles away, but I could see the individual flowers growing on their slopes really clearly."

Alan perked up on hearing that. He'd read a couple of books on remote viewing that suggested something to him which he couldn't resist giving expression to. "Interesting," he said. "Could it be something to do with a kind of four-dimensional consciousness?"

Jason turned to Alan with heavy eyes. "No idea what you're talking about Al."

Alan scratched his head and tried to explain. "I read about these guys who were sort of psychic spies, in the USA, back in the seventies. They say they could set their minds free to see things that were many miles away, while their bodies were left behind in a darkened room. One explanation for that was that in the state of mind they're in to do that, which is similar to the dream state, they can see in four dimensions. It's called remote viewing. One of

138

them wrote a book about it. He said it was a divine gift, that kind of ability. Didn't you say you had a conversation with God?"

"What? Did I say that?"

"Fucking hell, Jason. That's not the type of statement I'm likely to forget, is it?"

Jason shook his head. He looked heavy-eyed and fatigued, as if he'd just woken up with a horrendous hangover. "Look, can we give it a rest for a minute?" he said. "Maybe talk about something else. I'm feeling a bit dizzy right now."

Alan did his best to hide his frustration. "OK. OK. I'm sorry. Just – you know, take it easy."

Alan was starting to think that if Jason had been suddenly resurrected, maybe he also had some place where he was living now. If that was true, it would show that there was some divine force pulling a lot of strings. He would try and a test that hypothesis, as subtly as he could. He put a fist close to his mouth and coughed, and trying to sound as matter of fact as he could he said, "So, uh... Jason. Where do you live now?"

"Camberwell," said Jason, rubbing his eyes.

"Fuck... Camberwell? But... you never lived in Camberwell."

"Well I do now."

As they walked past the post sorting office in Rathbone Place Alan reflected on the lecture and became struck by something he'd missed that had to be explained.

"Alan. Back in the lecture theatre I saw that guy Kevin Sharpe, you know, the sculptor guy who

139

had the studio next to yours."

"Oh yeah. He was there."

"But he didn't seem bothered about you being there."

"No. He was cool. I chatted to him on the way in."

"But... that's crazy. I mean - he was at your funeral. He *knew* you died."

"Well, he's obviously forgotten."

"How could he forget?"

"No idea. Why don't you ask him?"

"Maybe I will, if I see him again. Not that I'm too keen on the guy. His work is terrible. Absolutely talentless."

"Yeah. I don't like what he does either. But he's good company in the pub. Drinks like a fish."

"And what about Steve Ormsley, who used to play guitar with you. I saw him sitting right near you. He was at the funeral. I saw him crying like a baby. He should've been totally traumatised by you being there – alive and well."

"Well he was pretty relaxed when we had a jam in his studio last night."

"What the fuck? Didn't he even wonder how the hell you came back from the dead?"

"Never asked."

"This is insane. So, neither of them had any reaction to you being back in the land of the living?"

"Nope."

"Christ. Maybe I'm the only person who does remember."

"Could be."

Alan had to consider that idea for a moment. Was it possible that some all-powerful, divine entity had somehow constituted a completely new life for Jason, in order to make his resurrection fit in with everything again? That would involve some major tinkering. But wouldn't that sort of intervention require everyone who was part of Jason's life to have amnesia about him being dead? As they crossed Oxford Street it occurred to Alan, that induced amnesia wouldn't be enough. There would have to be changes to everyone whose life had been in any way connected to Jason. This was getting scary. Alan felt a sudden urge to call Jenny. Of course, he wouldn't tell her anything about Jason being here now – *alive* – over the phone. She'd have a fucking seizure. Or, most likely, think he was losing it."

That instant Jason stumbled sideways into Alan, almost knocking them both over. They were just entering Soho Square at that point, but Alan reacted fast enough to keep them both upright, by taking a firm hold of him and ushering him over to the nearest unoccupied bench.

"Whoa. Take it easy there, fella."

Jason looked pale and dazed as they both sat down. Jason wiped his brow with the back of his hand.

"Thanks Al. Just give me a second. Feeling a bit queasy."

"Sure. You just take it easy. I'm going to give Jenny a ring, see what she's up to. Won't be a minute."

Jason sighed and looked down between his

141

legs, as if he'd just run a marathon. Then he wiped his brow, which was covered in sweat despite the coolness of the day.

"Sure," Jason nodded. "You go ahead."

Just behind them on Carlisle St a small crowd of media types had built up outside the Guinness bar. Meanwhile, near their bench, in the square, a Goth girl dressed in black stopped and waited for her boyfriend to light a cigarette.

Alan got his phone out, punched in the number, and held the handset to his ear. All he could hear was a screeching, high-pitch, tone. What did that mean? He tried again, with the same result. Maybe her phone was damaged somehow. He would try the landline.

This time the phone actually rang as normal, but there was no reply, although he waited for quite a while. That was strange. She had a big deadline on an illustration job she was working on for the Radio Times, so she wouldn't normally go anywhere in that situation. She'd be ensconced in her studio upstairs listening to Radio 4. Perhaps she was struggling, and didn't have time to answer the phone. But she would always have trouble resisting any phone call, in any circumstances. He fought back an urge to go home right away, but when he saw Jason resting his elbows on his knees, with his head in his hands, in apparent pain, he didn't have the heart.

A forty-something man in dark glasses, black leather trousers, and a mop of bleached blonde hair was walking a white Airedale on a lead, heading towards the hut in the middle of the square.

"Uh, Jason?" said Alan.

"Jason sat up and looked at Alan with tired eyes.

"This bag is a bit of a pain. I'm going to drop it off at Capricorn Films. It's only down the road. You OK to move on?

Jason nodded.

They went out of the square towards Dean Street, passing through the throng outside the Guinness bar, and every step they took Alan could see that Jason was getting visibly more lethargic. They carried on, along the narrow alleyway where Private Eye Magazine was based, which was just around the corner from one of their favourite lunchtime venues, the faithful old Star Café. But this was no time to think of food. Turning into the road with the Old Hat Factory they headed towards Wardour Street. It was getting dark now, even though it wasn't that late. Confused, Alan looked up to see a massive cloud spreading itself across the sky, a black duvet moving in slow motion.

Soon they entered a small alleyway leading into a square courtyard, just off D'arblay Street. In Georgian times these four-story buildings would've been housing for many families, but now they were functioning as offices and studios for the media industry, although some of the lofts had been converted into apartments, for those occasions when the director would find he was working too late to go home, or for other occasions when a comfortable bed would come in handy. In the left-hand corner, the ground floor had a modern frontage, with the word 'CAPRICORN' emblazoned on the glass frontage, in foot tall, bold, sans serif type. Alan led Jason over there, pushed the buzzer by the door and waited. After a crackle a high, pitch male voice came through the intercom.

"Hi."

Alan leaned closer to it, "Oh hi. I'm a friend of Rosie's."

There was no reply. Simply the prolonged farting sound that indicated the door was now released. They entered into a reception with a bare brick-walled interior, with wooden floorboards, and a long, polish steel curved desk, with a thick, beech wood top, and a couple of plate glass shelves on raised plinths at each end, on one of these was propped a large computer screen. Behind the desk sat a pale, young lad with a mop of ginger hair, wearing glasses with thick black frames. As soon as he set eyes on Alan he nodded.

"Hi. Oh... I remember you," he said. "Alan West, isn't it? You've done a few voice-overs, here haven't you?"

Alan chuckled. "Just a few." That was a major understatement. He must've made two-dozen commercials here over the years, for various agencies.

"Is Rosie around?"

"Yeah. She's round the back getting drinks ready for an edit in Studio 4, but I'm sure she'll have time to chat. Do you mind just signing in first?"

"Sure."

The lad pushed a large open pad with a pen attached to it on a piece of red string. Alan took the pen to sign his name, the date and time in the appropriate columns.

"Great. Thanks," said the lad, turning the pad around so he could read it. "Go right on through. You know the way."

Jason followed as Alan walked over to the double doors on the right. They went through into the narrow hallway, where framed gold and silver discs were mounted along the whole length. Jason asked Alan if he knew where the toilets were.

"I'm bursting," he said.

Alan pointed to a small alcove to the right, and told him to meet him he'll be in the room at the end. Jason nodded and rushed off, in that direction.

Edit suites 1, 2 and 3 were bunched together on one side and 4 was on the right. It had a red light outside it, to indicate that a recording was in progress. Ahead the kitchen door was slightly ajar. When Alan got there, he pushed it in gently, and there was the unmistakable profile of Rosie Tushingham, with her blonde, pixie-style hair, tight three-quarter length jeans and black ballet slippers. She was trying to find a space for a pot of tea on a tray, which already had several cups and saucers on it, and a plate of chocolate biscuits. That done she lifted the tray. Having looked up she stood open mouthed and immediately put it down again.

"Alan!"

She rushed over to give him a big hug. He couldn't help noticing how she had filled out beautifully over the years.

"What are you doing here?" she was still holding his elbows as she spoke.

He held up his rucksack.

"Can I leave this with you and pick it up in the morning?" he asked.

She took it from him and shook her head.

"Is that it? That's a terrible excuse for coming over to see me."

He shrugged nonchalantly.

"Well, I had to think of something."

"You look a bit tired," she said. "Is everything alright?"

"I was..."

There was the sound of footsteps in the hallway. Instantly Rosie's eyes widened, along with her mouth. She looked as if she was going to say something but it turned into a little, high-pitched yelp as she collapsed with a thud onto the floor, where she lay twisted, between the kitchen and the hallway by the open door.

"Shit."

Alan immediately realised that the sight of Jason approaching must have given her the shock of her life. Why didn't he think? How stupid could he be? Rosie had known Jason even longer than he had. She was there at Jason's funeral with her husband, Derek. They gave Alan and Jenny a lift to the crematorium, and sat next to them at the service. Fuck. He should have considered all that before bringing Jason in there. Why didn't he do that? Maybe he was confused by the fact that some of those people at the lecture who would have known that Jason had died didn't react at all to him being there alive – sitting among them all. They had their studios on the same floor as him and they knew him very well, but they reacted as if everything was normal, Jason sitting in there among them, very much alive. This was all becoming totally incomprehensible. But the issue now was Rosie. He crouched down beside her. "Is Rosie OK?" said Jason.

Alan looked up to see him staring at Rosie with a look of pain and distress.

"What do you think?" said Alan.

Jason looked as if he didn't know what to do with himself, as Alan tried to shift Rosie into a slightly more comfortable position, inadvertently he lifted her T-shirt and felt the warm, soft flesh on her back. He rubbed it, in the hope that massaging would help her somehow.

A runner who heard the commotion came out and asked what was going on. Alan stood up. A big guy win a black polo-neck sweater rushed out of studio 4. He had no shoes on. "What the fuck happened here?" he asked.

More people came out from other rooms, including the red headed guy in glasses who was at the reception desk. This was all getting a bit too weird now.

"Did you see what happened?" the bearded guy said accusingly to Alan.

He was trying to work out how to explain that seeing Jason was probably the prime cause of Rosie collapsing, because she would have expected him to be dead, and that the sight of him, living and breathing must have been a total shock to her. God knows how they would react to that explanation. Best to obfuscate.

"It's crazy," he said. "She uh, she just came out of the room to say hello and I don't know what came over her. She just dropped. Could it be her blood pressure or something?"

No one said anything for a few seconds. The bearded guy just shrugged.

"Shall I call for a doctor?" said the redhead eventually. Everyone ignored him.

The guy in the black polo neck came over and checked her pulse. More people were rushing out of various rooms to see what was going on. It dawned on Alan that the best thing for him and Jason to do right now was to take full advantage of the chaos and make a swift exit. He tugged Jason's sleeve, and they walked back along the hallway discreetly, taking a turn into the alcove where the toilets were. Alan remembered there was another door there opening into the room where staff stored their bicycles. Alan tried it. Fortunately, it wasn't locked. They went in and navigated the obstacle course that was caused by the piles of bikes, reaching the fire door. Alan pushed the bar and Alan was relieved to be out in the courtyard again, although Jason was still anxious. "Was that all because of me?" said Jason. Alan simply looked sideways at him. Jason winced. Alan immediately felt sorry for Jason because of the confusion and guilt he must have been going through. It seemed unfair, because it wasn't his fault he found himself back in this world - alive again. Somehow it had happened, and there would of course be all sorts of repercussions from that. Reality seemed to be in a mess. If Alan wasn't careful, he would lose his grip. He had to keep his composure.

"OK. Look. Let's get away from here," he said, putting his arm around Jason's shoulder. "I just need to walk for a bit and get my head around what the fuck is going on here."

That wasn't going to be easy.

Was everything that had happened since he went to the lecture just a figment of his imagination? There were many reasons to justify being distressed, especially given that, for nearly an hour, he had been walking and talking with someone who had been dead for over two years. But Jason hadn't been plonked back into the world just like that. The way things were now it was as if his death never happened. Whatever tinkering had been done – it's not been done only in the present. The main change is to the past. There's no question that things have been shifted going back at least two years. That's how long Jason said he was living in Camberwell. Crazy as it sounds, what it means is that the previous segment of time which everyone had gone through has now been re-edited, so that they have lived it differently.

If that's what's happened, he reasoned, then it's like we're all nothing more than fucking chess pieces, and some God-like chess player has dropped the whole game he was playing on the floor and then he's tried to put everything back on the board like it was before, only some of the pieces are now in the wrong places. It's a mess. If it had been done properly then Alan wouldn't be able to remember how things were before – namely that he should be dead. Neither would Rosie. But as soon as she saw

Jason walking towards her, she was a scared shitless. That's why she fainted. So, she knows what he knows. But it gets more complicated, because some people that knew Jason was dead (or they should have known) didn't even flinch when he was sitting there right in front of them in the lecture theatre. There was that guy Kevin Sharpe, the sculptor (at least that's what he called himself) who had his studio next door to Jason. He didn't seem bothered. Neither did Steve Ormsley, who used to play guitar with Jason. The thing is, they were both in tears at the funeral. So, it's as if their whole memory of Jason's death has been wiped from their minds.

But what other chaos had been caused to his life, as a consequence of all these changes? The metaphysical tweaking done to accommodate Jason's re-insertion into reality must now affect everyone whose lives intersected with Jason. Were he and Jenny together even in this version of reality? The signs aren't positive. He'd tried to call her quite a few times on his mobile, and all he got was a drone that meant her mobile was now a dead line. There was no reply on the landline either. The only way to find out if their relationship was still alive was to go home, to Crouch End, NOW. He almost didn't even want to be with Jason now. In fact, if anything, he wanted to get as far away from him as possible. He wished he'd never gone to that sodding lecture. Jason's Resurrection has clearly cast a shadow over everything, and it's as if reality can't cope with it.

And then he suddenly wondered, why the fuck

150

was it so dark?

It was no later than four o'clock when they went into the film company. They couldn't have been in there more than ten, fifteen minutes, max. He looked at his watch and stumbled. "Fuck!"

"What?" said Jason.

"What time do you make it?"

"Jason looked at his watch too, then he turned to Alan totally baffled. "That can't be right. Eight twenty-five."

"This is mad." He fumbled around and got his phone out of his pocket.

"Yeah. Fuck knows how it's happened, but we've skipped four hours somehow. It's night time all of a sudden."

"But how? Is that my fault too?"

They were turning into Lexington Street now,

"Look, Jason. No offence, but I need to go home now. I'm worried about everything. It's hard to explain, but I just want to go and find Jenny... see that she's there... I'm going to get the underground to Finsbury Park from Piccadilly Circus."

"Sure. I understand. I'll walk that way and get the number 12 to Camberwell."

"Fine."

They turned out of Lexington Street into Brewer Street and that was when it happened again. This was opposite the Left-Handed Shop that a tall, slim, dark haired young man in a North Face jacket saw them both and stopped in his tracks, right in front of them, in the pavement. He said one word, in a low breath.

"No..." and then he immediately he collapsed,

exactly as Rosie did in the recording studio. But unlike Rosie he hit his head on the curb and cracked it so hard that there was blood. Jason rushed over to the prostate young man and said, "Robert. Wake up."

"Do you know this lad?" asked Alan.

"Of course, I fucking do, he's my son."

Alan stood open mouthed. "Your what? I didn't know you had a son."

"Alan says," of course I do, and you're his fucking godfather!"

"But you never had a son!"

"What the fuck are you talking about, Alan?"

Alan glared at Jason and the prostrate young man he was cradling, before shaking his head slowly.

"Right. That's my lot. Sorry Jason, I'm off."

Not stopping to look back, he hurried along Brewer Street, leaving Jason kneeling by his 'son' in confusion and disarray. He had a strange and brooding apprehension that there definitely had been a seismic shift in his life - a catastrophic, and all-embracing, emotionally devastating disaster. Jason had been his best friend and an inspiration in every way, and he loved him for everything he'd done for him and everyone else. But his return to life had been totally unsettling. Everything was alien to him now. It even felt as if autumn, his favourite season, had been hijacked. His mind was running on overdrive as he turned into Swallow Street and walked under the white arch/bridge to the station entrance at the end of Glasshouse Street.

Jenny was the priority now. He needed to know she was OK.

Looking around it felt as if debilitating dread was everywhere. The people rushing in and out of the station all seemed to have pale and worried faces, reflecting his own state of mind. It compounded his anxieties. His heart was pumping, and his head was spinning. He hurried through the barriers and in an attempt to calm down, he stood on one side of the escalator until he arrived at the bottom, trying to ignore the stressed out folk rushing down on his left.

The train carriage was crowded and he had to stand all the way to Kings Cross. But it didn't matter. He was too pre-occupied with how he would tell Jen about Jason, and what he would find when he got back, to dwell on the woman's rucksack that was digging into his back, and the sweaty stained armpits of the guy standing ahead of him.

At Finsbury Park, there was a W3 bus ready to leave just as he came out of the back entrance to the station. He managed to jump on just as the driver was closing the doors. In two minutes, it stopped at the start of the seemingly endless, canyon of large, redbrick Victorian houses that was Ferme Park Road.

Stepping out of the bus and back into the night, he walked towards the parade of small shops. He was nearly home now. Ahead the rooftops and leafless trees were silhouetted against the iridescent, moonlit sky, mottled here and there by dark, drifting clouds. He had almost taken it for granted as he went that the house would be abandoned. But he didn't want his imagination to run away with itself.

Outside Londis a girl in a white cycle helmet was fixing a metal mesh basket full of groceries to her bike. She turned towards him as he passed, and her face caught the strong yellow light from the shop window. There was definitely something about it that disturbed him. Maybe it was much older than he thought, or too expressionless to make him feel easy or comfortable. Picking up his pace, he crossed over, and walked a little further in the same direction, and then turned left just before the brick railway arches.

The first thing he noticed outside the house was that the hedge was ragged and overgrown and the hydrangeas were dry and sagging. In fact, the whole front garden looked shabby. That was desperately unsettling, because when he left home it was trim and neat, and yet seeing your best friend return from the dead is good preparation for any absurdity, but there was no time to dwell on that. At least the upstairs light was still on. A feeling of trepidation overwhelmed him. He stood poised, with keys in hand, at the front door. For some reason, he decided to knock first. While he waited he glanced nervously over at the neighbouring house. As he expected, the devious old lady was there watching, behind the slightly lifted curtain.

"What the hell does she do all day?" he wondered.

He knocked again but his rapping evoked no response. There was nothing else for it. He tried the key and the door opened. He stepped in and turned on the hall lights. His bicycle was leaning against the wall, though Jenny would never allow that. Bikes had to go in the shed. Looking ahead he saw that the stair carpet looked grubby, and the kitchen door was open. But the lounge was his first port of call. He went in. In the prevailing gloom, he couldn't make out the outline of the glass cabinets that Jenny's grandmother left her. Turning on the dimmer switch he discovered why that was: they weren't there. This was not a good sign. Maybe she'd moved them somewhere. The table, sofa and several wooden chairs, and of course the immense fireplace with the antique clock on the mantel were still there, but there was a stack of books piled awkwardly against the wall. Why was that all about? Jennies framed pictures and furniture were gone too and the bay windows were filthy. Jenny would never let them get that bad. Only his paintings and photos were on the walls. The room felt characterless. None of this was relieving his worries. He turned around and went up the stairs, two steps at a time, and went straight to their bedroom. The door was left ajar and the bed hadn't been made. Inside it felt chaotic - like a student's room. He opened the wardrobe where he could only find his own clothes. None of Jenny's jeans, dresses, coats were there. Being so perturbed at this point, he couldn't help breathing deeply as he tried the top draw of the chest, where she kept her underwear. Inside he found only his pants and t-shirts, all of them un-ironed and unfolded. There came only a shuddering blankness and indefinable loneliness. He tried to compose himself, as he dropped onto the bed, but all he could do was sit open-mouthed and tremble. Tears were streaming down his cheeks. What could he do? Things were completely different to how they were when he left the house this morning. Had the past been tinkered with like this just so that Jason could live again? Things were too much. He fell back into the pillow, physically and mentally exhausted, and despite his horror and anxiety, sleep came.

In the morning, he was woken up by a hand shaking his shoulder. He looked up with bleary eyed and tried to get a focus on the face that was looking down at him. It was Jenny! Her pale blonde hair was dripping wet. It was a little shorter than when he'd last seen her. But she looked great. When she smiled her little piggy eyes lit up, her cheeks swelled, and her tongue pushed up hard against her front teeth. Did she know exactly how sexy that was? Was this a dream, or was yesterday a nightmare?

"What time did you come to bed last night?" said Jenny. "You look terrible."

He sprung out of the bed, and lifted her off the floor with a massive bear hug. She had the big white towel wrapped around her body.

"Hey. Easy there, Tiger. You'll have a hernia. What have you been taking?"

He had to say something. "It's just that… you know what? I had a really bad dream last night that Jason was alive again. I can't tell you how distressing it was."

Jenny pouted and squinted at the same time.

"Why is that bad? I thought he was your friend."

"Sure, he was my friend. But... Shit. It's too hard to explain."

She shook her head, reproachfully. "Sounds boring. Now put me down. I need to make the coffee."

He lowered her gently.

"Where did you go last night?" she asked. "I mean, Christ, you were out from lunchtime, right through to God knows what time, I went to sleep about eleven."

He tried to remember what had happened the day before, but for some reason it was all quite hazy.

A few weeks later Alan was working on a campaign at McCann Erickson, and he was running late on his way back from lunch with an old friend in a Thai restaurant on the Tottenham Court Road. He almost ran through Bedford Square, and across Gower Street, then through Keppel Street, towards Senate House. Alan loved that building, with all its art-deco features and its tall white Portland stone edifice. It was like a stunted version of the Empire State Building. He often used it as a shortcut to and from Russell Square. On entering the grand marble hall, he saw a strange figure in a baggy grey suit coming down the opposite entrance towards him. He looked fortyish, skinny and gangly, with a frizzy head of hair that reminded him of Bamber Gascoigne. He was carrying a battered old brown leather suitcase as he came straight up to Alan and stopped, so Alan had to stop too.

"I remember you," he said to Alan.

Alan wondered if this was some kind of scam. "Sorry?"

"You're the fellow who briefly interrupted my lecture a few weeks ago to collect your friend."

He was smiling as he spoke, and seemed to genuinely want to chat, feeling confident that he had the licence to be on familiar terms, because of that occasion he was describing. Unfortunately, Alan realised, this was obviously a case of mistaken identity.

"I don't mean to be rude, but I have to get to a meeting."

"You said you hadn't seen this fellow – your friend – for years." Continued the guy. "Though you did apologise, which I fully appreciated. So… was it a spectacular reunion? Was it worth missing out on the rest of the lecture?"

"Lecture? What lecture?"

THE INFERNO

Gary Beecham was dead, and Alan was totally mystified. How could it possibly have happened? He was supposed to have had a heart attack, at least that's what the obituary said in the press. Yet he was only in his early forties, at most. And there was no history of any kind of heart condition. You hear about these kinds of things happening in spy versus spy situations in the news, where they have some advanced, hi-tech means of inducing heart attacks that are untraceable, even by the most experienced pathologist. But Gary had no political or intelligence affiliations or connections whatsoever. He was just an animator. He drew cartoons, for fuck's sake. But the disturbing idea Alan wanted to get out of his head was that Gary's death was the result of some kind of curse, hex or voodoo, that it was some kind of devious scheme that was meticulously executed by sinister supernatural means. The thing is, Alan is a natural sceptic, and he still genuinely believed that the occult was involved, even though he had no real evidence. Just a strong suspicion. How did that suspicion come about?

After spending a year in Paris, Alan and Jenny moved to New York. They had a wonderful time there. Alan was working for a production company, while Jenny found work for an events magazine. With the help of friends who had been living there for nearly five years, they found a spacious and beautifully furnished apartment on the first floor of a former Victorian sewing machine factory in Brooklyn Heights. The owners were antique dealers, currently on sabbatical in Florence, and they weren't due back for two years. When Alan's contract was up eighteen months later, Alan and Jenny were sad to leave, but they were starting to get a bit homesick. It was coming up to Christmas when they left, and the snow had been falling so heavily that the cars on the street below lined up like sacred mounds.

London, as they expected, was grey and wet, and the skies over Kentish Town Road seemed to be perpetually dark. However, it was good to be back, and thanks to their New York earnings they were now able to pay off all their debts (mostly accrued in Paris). They even had a good sum left over, which they set aside in case of an emergency. But, as it happened, that emergency came around sooner than they expected, because Alan couldn't get any work. It soon became clear that the main obstacle to employment for Alan was that London's animation studios had become incredibly cliquey, and he'd simply been away too long. Six months after they returned home he hadn't even had a single day's work, so it was no surprise when their savings were all used up. Even though Jenny did get the odd bit of illustration work, their overdraft facility was still nearly stretched to the limit, and they were getting behind on their mortgage. These were worrying times. Neither Alan nor Jenny's family could help them out.

Luckily, Jason, did his bit. He lent Alan some money, and insisted he was in no rush to get it back. He also put the word out to various studios that he knew a great layout and storyboard artist who was now available. And while that message was percolating, Jason also had an idea of how he would go about getting Jason to work alongside him. This was at Jago Productions, the hot shop in the London animation scene. Jago was set up by Gary Beecham, an animation director from New York who had been living and working in London for nearly ten years. They had built up a fabulous reputation for creating a whole string of stylish animated commercials and also for their beautiful and entertaining, animation shorts, which picked up awards all over the world. Their achievements had eventually attracted attention from Dino Guinizelli, the famous Hollywood director behind the Vietnam classic *Two Days to Saigon*, and the Mafia feature *Capo dei Capi*. Their work had made such an impression on him that he chose Jago as the production company for his first animated feature - *Dante's Inferno*.

Gary Beecham was a talented animator, and a fine draughtsman too, and as Arthur Conan Doyle once said, since "Mediocrity knows nothing higher than itself; but talent instantly recognizes genius", he hired Jason to help design the project.

Jason was producing some stunning work. Gary loved everything he did, so he hoped he had enough brownie points to have enough influence to get Alan in there. So, when Gary Beecham came back from New York, Jason waited for an optimum moment to ask. On the afternoon that Gary said he knew and respected Alan and his work, but he didn't feel it was right to make any changes to the personnel at Jago. Jason let Gary know the next day.

The following Tuesday Alan spent the morning hawking his work around the visualising studios in Soho, in the hope that he would be appreciated in that side of the creative industry. But as he found with the animation companies, even though the people loved his work and they were very impressed by his experience, they also declared that business was slow at the moment, and they had all the artists they needed for now. He was starting to think that he may pose a threat to some of the senior creatives in these London companies. Whatever the reason, week after week of disappointment was taking its toll.

The last studio he went to was Snapper Art. He left there feeling useless and miserable. Within seconds of him stepping out onto the pavement in Cleveland Street, it began to rain. He ran to Goodge Street Station like a demon. From an ever-present old stallholder there, whose face he knew, he bought a cheap, fold-up brolly. Then, instead of making use of it, he decided to go into the underground station. He got on a southbound train to Embankment, where he switched over to the District Line. The whole time he was thinking about whether they should go abroad again, but neither he, nor Jenny would want to do that.

At South Kensington, he walked along the long tunnel leading to the Science Museum. When he went up the steps to Exhibition Road it had already stopped raining, and in fact the sun was out, and there was a patch of blue sky over the trees ahead in Hyde Park. He walked the short distance to the Royal College of Art. The RCA library subscribed to all the trade journals, and possessed an amazing collection of books on art & design, film, illustration and much more. It was an excellent place for him to dry out too. He spent some time going through D&AD annuals, especially the advertising concepts. Then he started scouring the back pages of various media publications.

By half past three he was on his way home, again via the underground. When he finally came off the escalator at Camden Town Station he discovered it was raining again. He thought about getting the bus to Prince of Wales Road, but he had his fold-up brolly, which he took out of his rucksack to put to good use. When he reached that part of Kentish Town Road going over the Regents Canal, the rain suddenly became torrential and a horrendously powerful gust of wind turned his flimsy umbrella inside out. In a fit of rage, he threw the spineless appendage into the canal. It took a fair bit of self-restraint now for him not to do the same with his portfolio.

Rain was dripping from his nose, hair and his coat. Jenny looked up from her drawing board and rushed to the airing cupboard to grab him a fresh towel.

163

"Been for a swim, have we?" she said, as she threw it over to him. She was clearly in a good mood.

"Something like that," he said as he started drying his hair with the towel.

She sat back at her desk and went back to her painting of an Edwardian waitress serving a young couple in an oak panelled room.

"Just had another wasted morning," he said. "Carting that fucking folder around. Then I also went over to the RCA to check out the magazines."

"Oh, right," she said. There followed a moment of silence, before she felt emboldened to ask," Did you look in Creative Review? I've just found something interesting for you."

He finished scrubbing his head and hung the towel over the back of a chair, on which he then sat down.

"I looked in the latest edition," he replied. "There was bugger-all there… far as I could see."

She stopped painting and grabbed a magazine from the small table to her right, where she kept her brushes and paints and walked over to hand it to him.

"Oh yeah? Well take a look at that."

She opened it out to the back pages, and she had ringed one of the small square ads with a red magic marker. Alan put on his glasses to take a closer look. He shook his head in disappointment.

"Yeah. I saw this," he said. "It's for a manufacturing company in Yorkshire. What are they doing advertising in Creative review? It says they're looking for film technicians. Jen - I'm not a fucking film technician."

Jenny sighed. "Just stop and think for a minute, Al. How the fuck would they know what a film technician is? They're a manufacturing company in Yorkshire. They've probably never made a fucking film in their lives and they wouldn't know where to start. But they obviously need to for some reason. With your experience in storyboarding, animation, working with special effects, cameramen, actors, technicians, and sitting in on script meetings and edits you could do it."

"But I'm just me. I'm not a studio."

"Yes. But you know plenty of people. You could even set up a little company."

Alan shook his head. "Jen. Listen. Even if you're right, we don't fucking live anywhere near Yorkshire. How the fuck could I get to work every day?"

Jenny shook her head in disappointment, like his old head of maths used to.

"What's come over you, all of a sudden? Yeah, okay. Like… you've had a hard time looking for work and getting lots of rejections. But that shouldn't mess your brain up. Look."

She went over and grabbed the magazine from him, and pointed to the ad again. "There's hardly any description there. Who knows? Maybe they don't need you to go up there to do the job. Maybe you can work here, then send the work in the post. Do me a favour love. It's not even half past four yet. Give this number a call. What've you got to lose?" She gave the magazine back to him.

Confused, he looked at it again. Jenny came over, hugged him to give him a big, long kiss, so that he began to have other things on his mind.

"Uh-uh!" she said. "Phone first."

He dialled the number and heard a voice that sounded like it belonged to a middle-aged woman sitting at a 1950s-telephone switchboard..

"Baskin Industries, how can I help?"

"Uh… I've seen your ad in Creative Review about you looking for someone with expertise in film making and I wondered if the position was still vacant?"

"Oh that. To be quite honest with you, we haven't had any enquiries at all. Are *you* a film technician?"

Alan avoided answering the question directly, but he did explain his background in media and animation.

After a couple of minutes of listening to Alan, she said, "I think the best thing is for you is to talk to Mr Marshall. Let me see if I can get him for you."

He heard her shout through a muffled receiver: "Harry, my love. Can you nip down and see if you can tell Mr Marshall there's a call for him?"

Alan was feeling like a fool. He felt as if he was in the middle of an Ealing comedy. It took over a minute before her voice came up again.

"Sorry about that, love. You still there?"

"Uh, yes. I'm here."

"Lovely. We've located Mr Marshall for you. Putting you through now."

There were a few clicks, and the odd crackle before he heard a male voice, with a thick Yorkshire accent say, "Alan White?"

Alan had to think about that for a second. "Uh, yeah that's me."

"Andrew Marshall. Good of you to get in touch. Sorry about the delay. Just been on the factory floor sorting out an order. I might be the chairman, but I still have to get my hands dirty from time to time."

Alan pictured a small, man in a waistcoat, with a military moustache on the other end of the line: a kind of modern equivalent of the benevolent mill owners of the mid-nineteenth century.

The man went on, "So, Brenda tells me you've had a lot of experience in film, is that right?"

"Uh, yes. That's right."

"Very good, very good. Tell me more."

Alan was prepared for everything, except a direct and positive response. It was an effort to suppress his excitement and stay focused. He described his educational qualifications, his degree in visual communication and his experience in animation and film, all of which impressed Andrew Marshall.

To reciprocate, Andrew Marshall told Alan that in the early days of home computing, Baskin developed their own version of the Sinclair ZX80, which was a success. Since then they've moved more and more into computing – including computer software. Now they're looking to get involved in computer games, which they see is the logical next step forward in a burgeoning market.

The problem is that they have no experience in creating the moving visuals, and they don't know where to start. And that's where Alan may be able to help.

The company is based in Scarborough, which is 250 miles away from London, but the work can be developed off-site. He asked if Alan could come up next week meet with him and the rest of the board at Baskin Industries. Alan agreed, without hesitation.

Alan put the phone down, clenched his fists and shouted, "Yes!"

Jenny looked at him in semi-disgust, as he charged around the table to swoop her up. He asked her how she was so sure that the small ad in Creative Review was going to be so such a winner.

"It just stood out for me," she said.

He looked incredulous. "Come on! I mean, there's absolutely nothing about it that could stand out," he responded. "It's just... completely utterly ignorable."

Jenny shook her head from side-to-side, and raised her eyebrows, as if surrendering to the inevitable. "Well if you must know,' she said, "it was because of the dream I had."

"What dream?"

"About us being back at college."

"Oh yes. And me presenting a drawing of a dog, or something."

"Yeah. It was the end of a three-week project, where we all had to do a book cover for Wuthering Heights. Along with the whole illustration group, we've had to put our work up on the wall. Then Geoff and Andrew and some other tutors (I think) are doing the crit. I remember you put up this drawing of a Yorkshire terrier, and everyone loves it."

"Ha-ha-ha-ha. That's a bit mad."

"But think about it for a minute. Where is Wuthering Heights set?"

Alan thinks for a second, before saying, "the Yorkshire Moors."

"That's right. And the dog was, wait for it… a Yorkshire terrier."

"Ah. That explains Yorkshire. But still…"

"And what did we used to call those gatherings, you know, when the tutors would assess all our work in front of us on Fridays?"

"They were creative reviews…" suddenly the penny dropped, and he nodded.

"Oh, I see."

The receptionist told Alan that Jason had gone out for a coffee with 'Dino', but he wouldn't be long. It suddenly struck Alan that she could only be referring to Dino Guinizelli. It was incredible to think how his old buddy from art school was hobnobbing with one of the biggest names in Hollywood, who also happened to be one of his favourite directors, up there with Hitchcock and Orson Wells. Just at that point Alan heard a voice in a distinct New York accent from behind him.

"Alan White, isn't it?"

He turned around to see a relaxed, smart casual guy in his thirties, with loose dark wavy hair, white

169

shirt with open collar, unbuttoned navy jacket and brand new Levis – hands in pockets. It took a moment before he realised this was Gary Beecham, Jason's boss and the owner of Jago Productions. This is the guy who told Jason he didn't want Alan in there, so Alan wasn't feeling sociable. He worked with him before, but without too much contact. Alan felt then that he was hard to work out, but he was always charming and friendly.

"Oh, hi Gary. Good to see you again. It's been a while."

"*The Silver Salamander*, wasn't it?" said Gary. "Seems like a lifetime ago."

Alan nodded. "A lot of talented people did some great work on that picture. I just wish the studio let Richard finish it!"

"Yeah. Jesus. Then I think… yeah, that's right. You were at Crossbow Pictures on that short directed by Harvey. He was there at the same time as me?"

"Yeah. But I met you before that at Jason's life class."

"Yeah. I remember you did some really neat life drawings. So how are things with you right now?

"I got back from New York in January. I was working for a visualising studio out there. Hard work, but I learned a lot. Been quiet since then, but I may have found something that could turn everything around for me."

"Sounds good. Any place I'd know?"

"Doubt it. It's a software/tech manufacturing company up in Yorkshire. They need a lot of help setting up a games division. I'm going to go up and talk to them next week."

"Wow. Sounds great. How the hell did you get a connection like that up there?"

"Saw it in an ad."

"An ad?"

"Yeah. In Creative Review, of all places."

"Wow. I never would've thought there'd be anything like that in the back pages of "Creative Review. "Not sure what they'll need exactly, but they seem keen to talk to me about drawing, storyboards, character design, concepts – who knows what else?"

"Well done. Hope it works out for you. You deserve a bit of luck."

"Cheers."

At that moment Gary was summoned by a producer to come in on a phone call.

"Sorry Alan. I need to take this call. Uh… why don't you go over and wait at Jason's desk. You can check out what he's been up to. He won't be too long. Good to see you again. Take care."

"Cheers Gary."

Gary held out his hand to Alan, who shook it, and with that Gary was away into a conference room.

Alan walked over to the corner of the room that Gary had indicated. Despite Alan's familiarity with Jason's work, these paintings still acted as a shock to the system for Alan. There was such distinct focus to all the elements, and everything was so perfectly proportioned, yet vigorously executed;

every character totally brimming with energy and life, every expression executed with perfection. This wasn't just Jason's vision of hell, it was an eruption of seething suffering and malice, torture and torment, a cacophony of unrest and upheaval beheld by two observers, who may appear undaunted, but there is a suggestion of suppressed horror tightly coiled up that is ready to spring at the slightest pressure. This wasn't a product of fantasy or romanticism, it was an outpouring, an expression. And it wasn't an attempt to slavishly depict a fantasy. It was a depiction of a place – and that place happened to be hell. The blasphemous creatures that soared and leered at the tortured souls below were so believable you would think they were painted from life. Jason was uncompromising in his desire to convey the haunting and stunningly real images in his mind's eye. His deep understanding of human anatomy, and profound knowledge of divine principles, including scared geometry, allowed him to create a composite reality of evil, that was a truly gruesome physiology of the demonic. With these images Jason stirred up smouldering sensations of strangeness from the primordial regions and shadowy ancestral memories buried in the subconscious mind. Jason had shown us the rush of ecstasy that a lizard-skinned demon is experiencing from the pain of the naked individuals immersed in the burning hot, treacle-like liquid below. His leathery wings are outstretched, as his minions hover nearby in wait, and his lascivious, red tongue protrudes obscenely through his glistening fangs.

"What do you think?" said a voice from behind.

Alan turned to see Jason hands plunged into his black jean pockets. A slight paunch was beginning to show over his belt, but he looked smart in a brand new, smart, two-tone, viridian green jacket with a silky beige shirt. Since he and Jenny were abroad, Jason's hairline had receded dramatically, making his high forehead seem even more pronounced. The top of his head now featured a sharp triangle of thin, wispy strands protruding from the mass of dark brown hair at the back. Angular, well-groomed sideburns divided his face vertically.

"Oh, Jas. Yeah. Fuck me, all that work it's brilliant. Beautiful stuff. What is it?"

"That, Alan my boy, is the eighth circle of hell.

Seems a bit sadistic though, what those geezers in the black goo are being put through."

"They're being totally burned and blistered every second they're in it. And, get this. If they stick out of it too far, then those flying demons with the leathery wings a hovering around, ready to tear them to shreds. Nice eh?"

"What exactly did they ever do to deserve that?"

"They committed fraud when they were alive."

"Fraud? Is that it? Seems a bit excessive if you ask me, boiling people for all of eternity and ripping them to shreds, just for ripping few people off."

"Nah. Fuck 'em. Fancy a beer then?"

"Let's go."

Jason kept his black trilby hat on in the pub, while Alan explained about his call to the Yorkshire company, and how it could lead to big things. Jason wasn't really listening. Something was bothering him. The best thing was to let him come out with it in his own time. Sure enough, when they sat in the Greek restaurant eating their main meal the formerly hidden thoughts were flowing freely. The trigger was when Alan asked him about his job.

"So how you getting on. It must be amazing working on an animated version of Dante's Inferno?"

He puckered his lips dismissively and shrugged. "Ah, it's OK."

Alan couldn't believe the blasé nature of his reply.

"What are you saying? This is a dream project. You're working for one of the top directors in Hollywood. How is that just 'OK?'"

Jason frowned forming a long, deep vertical furrow.

"You don't know him," said Jason. "I'm telling you... he's really frustrating. Keeps changing his mind about *everything.* I give him exactly what he wants, he almost orgasms over it. Then the next day it's, 'Hey Jason. I was just thinking how we could do that a little different.'

"But that's not an unusual thing for a director to do."

Jason sighed. "I'm having to do loads of variations of the same fucking scene, over and over again. Even though I followed the fucking script – to the letter."

"Does he give you a reason for the changes?"

"Yesterday it was because his wife had a good idea."

"What?"

"Alan. You know me. I don't like to re-do anything."

Alan was speechless. He couldn't quite believe that Jason could throw away this opportunity of a lifetime, through arrogance and impatience. Alan could read the concern in Jason's eyes, and it pleased him, in a mildly sadistic sort of way.

He pulled that firm-set, calm, self-satisfied, and knowing smile, which was enhanced by the intense stare of his pale blue eyes, and broad jaw and decided to twist the screw a little more. "Do you know what he blurted out to me the other day?"

"Surprise me," said Alan.

He said: 'Jason. You're right. I don't know what I want. But I do know what I don't want.'

Jason leaned back pushing his hands against the edge of the table, as if a plate of bad eggs had been put in front of him.

"Pf. How can you expect me to work with someone like that?"

Images of a Kamikaze pilot performing his last heroic act came to Alan's mind.

"Uh… OK. So, what did you say to him?"

"I said 'Dean, how the fuck did you ever get to make *Capo dei Capi* with an attitude like that?"

"Shit. How did he react to that?"

He went quiet, and then he burst out laughing. Then he said he liked me for being so straight with him.

Alan could see that this gesture might have not been as conciliatory as Jason believed it was.

"Does Gary know you said that?"

"Sure, he does. He was right there when I said it."

"What did he say?"

"Nothing."

"Nothing?"

"No."

Alan was getting increasingly excited about the meeting with Andrew Marshall in Yorkshire. On the morning before he was intending to take a walk along the canal to Kings Cross and pick up his train ticket, but on stepping out he found it was too hot and humid for his liking, so he decided to wait until later. He could hear Jenny answering it downstairs, and then he heard her yelling from the bottom of the stairs.

"Alan. It's for you!"

He put his guitar down and went over to pick up the phone that was on his side of the bed. A woman with a strong Northern accent said, "Hello. Is that Alan White?"

"Yes."

In a very matter-of-fact way she uttered, "Felicity Sidebottom, Andrew Marshall's secretary." Then she said that the meeting scheduled between Alan and Andrew for the next day had been cancelled. Alan supposed that Andrew must have double booked, so he asked when it would be good to re-schedule it to.

"That won't be necessary," she said.

Alan had only spoken to her four or five times and she had always been warm, friendly. Now her tone was assertive, cool and matter-of-fact.

"Sorry?" he replied.

"We wouldn't want you to waste any time and money."

Alan was lost for words. He tried to understand what it was that could have led to this snub. Nothing sprang to mind. Baskin surely couldn't have found someone else from their ad in Creative Review, could they? He considered if they'd perhaps thrown out the whole idea of setting up a computer games section. But that was unlikely, especially after all the time and research Andrew said they'd put into it. But even if they had made such a reversal surely, he at least deserved a chance to have a conversation with Andrew Marshall.

The cold fish voice became even colder. "Mr Marshall is busy. Thank you for your time. Goodbye."

And with that she hung up.

He stayed sitting on the bed in disbelief, slowly coming to terms with the finality of it all, feeling it. That was the end of his dream of launching a new chapter in his career. He thought about all the hope his forthcoming trip to Yorkshire held for him. The prospect raised him up in the morning to plan ahead, to forge new ideas, to work out where he could rent some space when things evolved beyond the capacity of a virtual studio to handle. This was the vision that enchanted him as he lay down at night. It was the one idea that seduced him, the rose-tinted window between him and the world. And now it was gone.

Jenny was even more surprised than Alan when she heard. Had she read the dream wrong? Impossible. Still, the important thing was to console Alan, because this stupid phone call had left him feeling very low.

He went on long walks on his own most days, from the flat to Highgate and then Hampstead, and then back along Chalk Farm Road, stopping for the odd coffee or pint along the way. Sometimes he went to Muswell Hill and then trudged along the abandoned railway line to Finsbury Park. He wrote a lot in his diary a lot too. All of this helped him channel his initial despair.

After much soul-searching and reflection, he found himself reflecting on the time he was working in the visualising studio in New York. He was always curious about those various advertising people who used to breeze in and out of the studio to brief him and the other artists on how they wanted their scripts drawn up. They were generally smart and confident in themselves, much more so than the artists he was working. They were interesting, quick-thinking and confident, they also had a bit more style about them too. However, most of the scripts they brought in were often cheesy, and uninspiring. Even the ones that were meant to be funny were usually just corny. There were exceptions, but in nearly every case he knew himself well enough to believe he could do better.

Maybe he should have a stab at getting a job in advertising.

The day after that Alan signed up for that three-month course. It was hard work, and very intense. They were taught by some fascinating senior figures in the industry, who were incredibly knowledgeable, and their enthusiasm was infectious. Those twelve weeks released his creativity like never before. He became the star pupil from his group.

At the end of it all, he was hired by J Walter Thompson, a very prestigious agency. He would, however, be starting at the bottom as a junior art-director, so the salary was low, and he and Jenny would continue to struggle financially. But luckily, within a few months, he was headhunted by another big American agency, based in London, and his salary was almost trebled. Life was good. He and Jenny were now hoping to buy a large house they had found in Crouch End, although someone was trying to gazump them, which was proving to be stressful.

Jason now had his own visualising and storyboard company. It came together just about the time Alan started on his advertising course, when Jason found himself out of work when Dante's Inferno was pulled from Jago films. He was approached by a print entrepreneur, who said he had wanted to set up a visualising studio. He offered to set Jason up in business, and give him 49% of the company. Jason could recruit his own team of artists and reps. And that's how Hey Presto Studios came to be.

It was good for Jason that, as an art-director in a busy ad agency, Alan could pass a fair bit of work Jason's way. Usually, Jason would come to his office in Charlotte Street to get briefed by Alan and his copywriter. Occasionally, Alan would head over to Jason's studio in Great Marlborough Street to talk him through what was required. On one such occasion Alan took a stroll over to Hey Presto Studios. They were based on the first floor of a 1950s building, in a small white box-room at the back of a large design and print studio, which belonged to Jason's backer. Alan went through, knocked on the door of Hey Presto, and entered. It was the sort of space W H Smith would store all their unsold books if they had a shop on the ground floor. There were two large, metal-frame portrait windows that faced onto the back yards between Poland Street and Carnaby Street. A fire escape ran down along one of them. Two of the window panes were open, but the room still reeked of magic markers. Hundreds of them were clustered on desktops, alongside lightboxes and layout pads. Jason was sitting on a tall stall, playing guitar by his drawing board, a black polo neck, black drainpipe trousers, and ultra-pointed Churches winkle-picker shoes. Dave, Geoff and Mick had obviously all gone home. Jason saw Alan and gave a broad smile. He stopped strumming and leaned his guitar against the wall.

"Hey Al. You want to do this here, or in the pub?"

Alan took his rucksack off, and rested it on a chair.

"I dunno. I reckon it's better if I spread all the bits out on your workbench. We can get a drink in later."

"Sure."

Alan started getting bits of paper out of his bag as Jason picked up one of the scripts. "Oh, this'll interest you," he said. "I bumped into Gary last Friday."

Alan shrugged. "Which Gary?"

You know, Gary Beecham - my old boss at Jago. He's moving his studio over to San Francisco."

Alan didn't much care. "OK. Why's that?"

"He's had a bit of good luck; picked up a project for Warner Brothers. It's kind of an animated version of "The Day the Earth Stood Still", set in the fifties and everything, like the original."

"Uh-huh."

"I was having a fry-up in Juliet's and he came in and sat at my table. We chatted a bit and I ended up back with him to Jago. They've been working on this computer game

"Oh, right."

"They're working on this cereal ad too. But their main bread and butter, since they lost Inferno, is the computer game job. It's for some tech company. I asked him how the fuck he managed to get connected with a business in Yorkshire. He said he felt a bit bad, but he heard about it from a freelancer who thought he had the job in the bag.

Now Alan pricked his ears up and stopped rummaging as Jason continued.

But Gary rang the company up and got in there first. Business is business, I guess."

"Fuck!"

"What's the matter?"

"I don't believe it."

Jason looked blankly at Alan.

"That fucking freelancer was *me.*"

"Huh?"

"I found that work in Creative Review, in an ad – or rather Jenny did, and she told me about it. This was when you were working on Inferno. I made a call and sorted out a meeting with that company. The CEO was really keen to meet me after I told him about my experience in animation at Disney, Universal, BBC and all that. I was gearing up to go up to Scarborough to meet the client, and then they cancelled on me, for no reason. It totally depressed me."

Jason said nothing in reply.

Alan continued, regardless. "Now I know why. What a cunt. Gary-fucking-Beecham is a fraud. He made out he was concerned about me being out of work, and coaxed information out of me when I said I found something interesting. Sounding all sympathetic. He must've gone off to make a sly phone call to steal my client the minute he walked into his office."

Jason still said nothing. His face was blank. It was impossible to read what he was thinking. It didn't look like concern. Maybe it was disbelief, or even utter confusion. He was like a rabbit caught in the headlights. Probably, he found it hard to believe Alan was the 'freelancer' in question. But Alan had no doubts.

This information brought back all the tension and anxieties of the time. He found himself plunged back into that familiar morass of moodiness. How should he respond? Gary Beecham was directly responsible for pulling the rug on the best opportunity he ever had to create his own film studio. Growing up in the tough, West London streets, that he and his pals had a harsh code for dealing with injustice. College and adapting to the people in film, animation and media in general had bred those rough edges out of him. Part of him wanted to waltz right over to Jago, and unceremoniously smacked Gary Beecham him in the face. But Beecham was an internationally renowned animator, and Alan was still a nobody. The story would get about, and Alan's name would become mud. Although he no longer worked in animation, the advertising industry intersected with animation in many ways. It could damage his career. But he felt, as if he was copping out for not taking some kind of revenge. In time, those feelings simmered down. Alan rose to middleweight status in less than a year. Things were getting better for him all the time. He and his copywriter won an award for one of their alcohol campaigns. It was at that award ceremony, during the meal, that Alan bit into an excessively chewy steak, and cracked a molar in half.

Alan and Jenny had never stopped going to the same dentist they had when they were students, which made having their teeth seen to a bit of a chore, involving a hundred-and-twenty-mile round trip to the seaside. Having worked until midday he took the train from Victoria and made it to the dentist by 2.30. The treatment didn't take too long. The thin cloud cover muted the sunlight just enough, and as there was also a cool breeze coming in off the sea, he decided to walk to the station instead of getting the bus. There was plenty of time, as his train wasn't due for another forty-five minutes. He took the back streets, behind the law courts and his old college, and then crossed the main London road to meander through the old town roads. This was the time of year when the foreign language students prowled the street in packs, outnumbering the locals, and outdoing them in volume too. It made the streets seem remarkably busy for a Tuesday. He stopped in at a second-hand bookshop, where he rummaged around and picked up a battered old paperback of Camus' Myth of Sisyphus for a quid. Pleased with his purchase, he went further along for a short distance before deciding to walk back a bit and check out what was happening at the Bell and Candle. What he discovered was a long-overdue new window display, featuring an antique, white enamel Ouija board, surrounded by five small ceramic skulls, a large, illustrated astrology book, a nine-prong candelabra, and an ornately framed image of a pentagram. All these things were placed onto the ends of two long pieces of purple velvet curtain fabric. In the V-shaped gap, between the draperies he could see Cornelia and her daughter Bella sitting together at their table. Cornelia was taking a payment from a customer, while Bella was typing. He decided to go in to say a quick hello.

The customer was just preparing to go as Cornelia said, "Oh yes. It's so typical of a dead parent to keep hounding you. I wouldn't worry. I'm always being pestered by my dead father, you know, and I simply find myself having to give him a good telling off when it becomes a bit of a nuisance. There you go. Lovely to see you again as always. Take care."

As the customer was heading out past Alan, who had just entered, Cornelia spotted him. She put her hands on her hips in a matronly manner, that reminded him so much of Mrs Tiggywinkle.

"Well I never! Look who it is Bella."

Bella stopped typing immediately, looked up open mouthed. "Alan!"

Cornelia tilted her head to one side and beckoned him over, like a policeman conducting traffic. He gave her a hug and a kiss on each cheek. Bella, meanwhile, merely smiled and said, "How have you been?"

"Very good, thanks. Keeping busy. I've just been to the dentist. Broken tooth."

"Oh, you poor thing," said Cornelia. "Is your mouth numb?"

"No no. It was a dead tooth. I had a root canal done on it years ago. The dentist just put in a temporary filling, and I'm going to have to come back to have a crown fitted in a few weeks."

"Oh. So… Alan, what exciting things have been happening in your film career then?"

"You mean animation?"

"Yes."

"Well, since we got back from New York I've not worked in animation. I now have a successful career in advertising."

"Oh. What happened. Why did you change careers like that?"

"Well, it's a long story, but I was hawking my wares about for 6 months trying to get work from animation studios in London, but there were no takers. I was out of work for over six months, and it was getting a bit scary. We could've lost the flat."

Cornelia was listening with genuine concern. "Oh dear. I'm sorry to hear that."

"The straw that broke the camel's back was when I found what I thought was a great lead that would not only get me back into animation again, it was going to be a fantastic source of work. I would have had to set up my own animation studio to get it all done."

"That sounds wonderful. So, what happened?"

"Someone stole the work from me.

"What?" Cornelia shook her head in disbelief.

"Was it someone you trusted," asked Bella.

"Well, yeah, I guess it was," shrugged Alan. "But I was naïve. Maybe I should've been more careful. You know I… I just didn't believe anyone

186

would do such a thing, especially when they already had a successful business."

"Oh dear," said Cornelia. "Was it a big company that did that to you?"

"Not huge."

"Would I have heard of them?"

"Unlikely."

"Try me."

"Jago Productions."

"Quite right. No idea. And was it their CEO who did the foul deed?"

"Haha. You make it sound Shakespearean. I'm not exactly sure if he's their CEO. He's certainly their animation director."

"Oh. Famous, is he?

"Only in the business – within the London animation scene. Maybe in New York too. You won't know of him."

"Try me."

"Name is Gary Beecham."

"You're right. I've never heard of him. Will you have a cup of tea with us…please."

Alan frowned and looked at his watch. "Well, I was going to get the ten-past-four to Victoria…"

"Oh, come on." Said Cornelia. "We haven't seen you for, what… three years? You can't just rush off now."

He shrugged, in complete surrender. "OK. Make it a tea."

"Milk, no sugar?"

"Perfect."

"Good." Cornelia weaved her way around to the back room, and Bella leaned over to make sure her mother had gone in. When she was satisfied Cornelia was quite out of sight, she stood up and walked over to Alan purposefully. Her black hair was now shoulder length. She was wearing a black polo neck sweater and cream slacks. When she came closer, Alan was expecting a peck on the cheek, but she pushed her breasts into him, grabbed the back of his neck with one hand, and thrust her tongue into his mouth. When she pulled back a little a strand of saliva stretched away with her.

"It's good to see you again, Alan," she said.

She was back at her seat before Cornelia came out with the tea tray. At that point Alan was glad he was wearing a long coat, because he needed something to hide the bulge Bella had left him with.

The rest of the conversation was about his current job, which he explained was full-time, and that he was really enjoying creating ads for Martini, Coke and other big products. His pay has already matched what he had been earning in animation, and he and Jenny no longer have any worry about losing the flat. In fact, they were hoping to buy a house in north London - a wonderful place, near Crouch End, that needed a bit of work – but it had a big garden and lots of space. Cornelia said that that was great news. But they both see Alan's pained expression."

"You look worried. Is it up in the air about your house?" asked Bella.

Alan's eyes widened, and he raised his brows. "Well… they've put in an offer, and we're anxiously waiting to hear back. I'm pretty sure it's a very well-off couple in their thirties, so, we'll need some luck."

Cornelia put her hands on her hips again, as if she meant business. "Ok. Leave it to us."

"Pardon?"

Bella interrupted. "Mama and I will help you."

"Uh, great. Thank you. And how exactly will you do that?"

Cornelia gave him a stern look. "We'll perform an incantation."

Alan shook his head, in mild embarrassment. "I'm… you'll… how will you do that?"

"We'll make a fire with wood, and sprinkle incense, while we walk around it and chant."

Alan knew they meant well, and he didn't want to insult them both by advertising his incredulity. "That's very thoughtful of you both," he said.

"Not at all," smiled Cornelia, as she gave him a big hug. "It's our pleasure."

It was too late to go back to work by the time he got back into London.

A few weeks later, Jason came into the agency to get a re-brief on a job his studio had done for Martin, Alan's boss. Jason, Dave and Geoff drew up a storyboard for an alcohol campaign and it wasn't quite what Martin was looking for. Martin insisted that Jason come in to take the debrief himself, and not to send his rep. Jason was not happy about that. He hated being made to change his work, and he didn't like formal meetings.

Alan waited until Jason came out of Martin's office, and then took him for lunch down the road to the little restaurant, Italia Uno. They got in before the lunchtime rush, and Alan treated him to a tasty ciabatta sandwich with salami, sun dried tomatoes, mozzarella, with the usual dab of Felice's, secret basil, lemon and garlic sauce. After a few bites Jason's grim expression softened. Alan waited for that to happen to ask about how his drink with his staff had gone.

Jason perked up a bit more, "Oh, it was a good laugh. Geoff, Dave and Mick were all there. Richard turned up, and I took Rebecca along too. I did a few of my tricks. Picked up a few new ones from the magic shop under Charring Cross Station."

"Sounds good."

"Richard had a bit of shocking news though."

"Really?"

"Yeah. Get this… Gary Beecham is dead."

Alan stopped chewing, and coughed. He spluttered out, "What?"

"He's dead. Massive heart attack. He only just set up that studio in the states, you know – to work on that feature - and then that happens."

Alan's pulse quickened.

"Fuck. Did he like… did he have a history of heart trouble, or what?"

"That's what I asked. No, he didn't. Nothing like that. He was sitting at home watching TV and that was it."

"Shit." An alarm went off at the back of Alan's mind, and he couldn't quite work out why he was feeling so guilty.

The time came for Alan to head off to the south coast again for his next dental appointment for his new crown to be fitted, which took less then fifteen minutes. No anaesthetic was needed. And as he did before, he walked through the old town, this time more purposefully, and popped in to the Bell & Candle. Both Cornelia and Bella were there. When the formalities and greetings were over, he told them that he and Jenny had moved into the house they were after, and the couple that tried to gazump them had found somewhere else near Stoke Newington. Then, half-jokingly, he thanked them both for whatever they did to make that possible.

"Oh, it was our pleasure," said Cornelia, in all earnestness.

"Bella just smiled and said as of half distracted by some paperwork on the table.

"So, whatever happened to that fellow who defrauded you of all that work?"

The blood ran from Alan's face.

"Since you ask. He uh.. it just so happens that Gary Beecham, the animation director who stitched me up so I lost all that work, had a massive stroke, or heart attack, or whatever a few days ago."

Just at that moment Bella sniggered, and Cornelia nudged her.

"Uh, did he recover alright?"

"Uh, no. He's dead."

Bella snorted again and it turned into a coughing fit. Alan thought Cornelia was suppressing a smile. Alan strongly suspected they were toying with him.

"Bella! Spreading your germs around the shop. Go and get yourself a glass of water!" said Cornelia.

Bella excused herself and did just that.

"I'm sorry Alan," said Cornelia. "She's not been feeling herself today. A touch of flu I think."

By the time Alan left them both he took a few steps along the street, before getting the compulsion to sneak back and peak through the Bell and Candle shop window discreetly. What he saw through the velvet fabric was disquieting. Cornelia and Bella were laughing so much they had to hug each other. It was as if he could hear their cackling through the plate glass, causing the colour to drain from his face.

What had those witches been up to?

THE SUCCUBUS

Chapter 1

It was the second time he had worked in New York. The first occasion was a couple of years before the children came along. Back then he was working as an illustrator in a storyboard studio, which was dissatisfying, in itself, but it was an experience that whetted his appetite to make the switch, to become an advertising art-director. In the studio, he was working from mostly unexciting, poorly written scripts, most of which weren't particular good ideas, (most of them were terrible). He felt that (given half the chance) he could do much better. On his return to London, he signed up for a specialist course in advertising, became the star of the class, and was picked up by a big London agency. He built a solid reputation and moved on to a much more fashionable agency, within a few years he became a golden boy there too. The CCO needed him to transfer to the New York office to work on an account that needed some resuscitation. It happened so fast that he had to travel without Jenny and the kids, living in a hotel for three months, then moving to a fantastic apartment in Brooklyn. The family would be joining him before Christmas. What could go wrong?

When he met Juliette Doyle, she was working at Seraphim Sound, on West Broadway. What happened was that Gary, Alan's copywriter, accidentally slammed the door into her as she was carrying a tray of drinks in to their studio. The hot coffee and tea went flying. She was a bit shaken up. Alan held the door open for her and asked if she was OK. She said she would be fine, and ran off almost in tears to return with a plastic bowl full of hot, soapy water. She crouched down to clean up the mess, and Alan noticed her long, dark auburn hair, tied in a tight bun at the nape of her neck. He found himself making small talk. She said she was a drama student at Juilliard, and was only scheduled to be at Seraphim for two weeks. As she had just finished clearing up the spillage, Gary came back in.

Then two hours later, the were listening to the final edit, when Larry, the client announced that he wasn't happy. Gary, Alan and Sally looked at each other nervously.

Sally asked him what the problem was.

He said he hated the actress doing voice-over. (Luckily, she couldn't hear him, because, at that moment, the intercom was turned off in the recording booth). Sally reminded Larry the ad was due to be aired the next morning, so the audio recording had to be delivered to the various radio stations in the next two hours. There was no time to book another actress. Larry didn't care. Gary had his face in his hands.

Alan bit his lower lip. He had an idea.

"Listen," he said. "We can fix this. It's going to be OK. There's another actress here. We should give her a go. What's the worst that can happen?"

Sally thanked Aurelia Quinn, the actress whose voice Larry disliked, and told her she was done. Meanwhile, Alan went along the hallway to the main kitchen and saw Juliette preparing drinks. He tapped her on the shoulder and she turned around surprised when he told her to stop what she was doing and to come into Studio 4 straight away to do a sound test.

"I can't," she said. "I have to take these to Studio 2 straight away."

"They can wait."

He led Juliette back to Studio 4, and ushered her into the recording booth.

It couldn't have gone better. Larry, the (up to now) monstrously difficult and obstructive client, thought she was great. The ad was recorded in double-quick time and Juliette was so delighted about having earned a ton of money for less than an hour's work, that she wanted to thank Alan personally. She snuck out of the booth, and rushed straight over to him. When Sally had finished going through Gary and Alan's next schedule she pounced, in her own demur, but rather emphatic way.

He listened politely.

"Uh, Alan. I wanted to say thank you and, uh... just an idea... (cough) I know you must be very busy and everything... but some amazing musicians from Juilliard I know, well they're playing tonight at a place in East Village. I mean, they are *so* cool.

195

Be great if you could come along. Well, I at least owe you a drink. Will you?"

Juliette arrived just as the band was covering Round Midnight. She stopped near the door to make small talk with the staff, with whom she was obviously very familiar. She eventually caught Alan's eye with the sweetest of smiles, and made her excuses to her friends, before gracefully negotiating the closely packed tables on her way over to him. She took off her fake fur jacket to reveal a black Chanel-style sleeveless dress, and her hair was loose, silky and flowing. Her legs were bare, despite the chill in the air.

"Well!" she said, holding out her smooth white hand. "He half stood up to take her hand and kiss her on the cheek. A plane gold bracelet clung to her arm, and she wore a black leather watchstrap loosely against the base of her thumb. A silver cross, dangled over the table from her neck when she leaned forward to get comfortable in her seat.

"I see you're a celebrity in these parts," he said.

She laughed a little. "Oh, I used to work here," she said. "Bernardo is so lovely."

"You mean the guy at the door?" asked Alan.

She didn't answer, as she was twisting around to hang her bag from the back of her chair.

"What do you think of the band?" she asked. "Aren't they brilliant?"

"Impressive. They've been playing some sophisticated tunes in a remarkably mature way," he said.

Her mischievous smile made him melt. "You

said that like you were sixty or something."

He feigned disapproval. "How do you know I'm not?" he said.

She frowned, and her pixie-like features screwed up. "Are you cold?" she asked, not waiting for a reply. "I should've told Bernardo to turn up the heating."

Alan studied her long eyelashes, and transparent brown eyes as she casually glanced around the room. Something had obviously grabbed her attention.

"There's Janice and Simon, she said. "I won't chat to them now, though."

Alan had no idea who Janice and Simon were.

"I hope he doesn't bring up his boring journalism course again." She seemed to be talking for her own pleasure. Stream of consciousness. Nothing mattered. It was like being in flux.

The musicians were picking up their instruments again for the second set. Alan examined her profile against the spotlight falling on the small stage: her button nose and thin upper lip, the chin, faintly pointed. There were smiles and nods being aimed at her from all directions. She was in her element.

Alan summoned the waitress and ordered a bottle of Chateauneuf, while they looked at the menus. Juliette recommended the onion soup and that the steak frites was to die for.

The whole time, he didn't mention he was married with kids, and she didn't ask.

Later he would look back and ask himself how he had ever allowed things to get so far. But he was totally under her spell. Any thoughts that even threatened to intrude on any feelings of affection and tenderness evaporated at the very sight of her.

After the first set, two of the band strolled over to Juliette and Alan's table. Juliette's eyes lit up, as she sipped her wine.

"Hey!" She stood up to greet them both with a kiss on each cheek.

"So, what'd you think, Jules," asked Dan, a smart-casual, swarthy, square-jawed, slim boy, with a slicked-back mane of black hair.

"You know how much I love you guys. You were amazing."

"Jules, you're always exaggerating." said Mike, shaking his head and turning to Alan, as if for confirmation.

"It's true." said Alan, "and that's coming from a big Miles Davis fan."

"Hey," interjected Dan, as if in a moment of revelation. You the advertising guy who gave Jules the radio gig?"

"Guilty, as charged."

"Cool."

"We're gonna go get some beers," Said Mike. "But, listen, if you ever need any cool music for a TV ad, or radio thing... whatever, we're your boys."

He pulled a business card from his shirt pocket and handed it to Alan, who took it respectfully.

As Alan and Mike headed off to the bar, Juliette touched the back of Alan's hand, which was resting on the table. "It would do them so much good if you could do that."

Alan smiled and said nothing.

"How are you finding it here?" she asked Alan, taking her hand away now.

"You mean the restaurant - or New York?" he said.

She gave an ironic smirk. "What do you think?"

"This isn't my first visit, by any means. I've been coming over to New York since I was a student – (and do I need to say?) - that was a long time ago."

"How long?"

"I'm not saying. Are you originally from New York?"

"Not exactly, but not too far away. I moved over when I started at Juilliard's. I grew up in a small town in Connecticut called Groombridge, about an hour's drive from here."

"Was it like *Happy Days*?"

"Boring as hell. And it gets worse. I went to a Catholic School. So lots of guilt, punishment and repression."

"Ouch. Any brothers and sisters?"

"No. But I nearly had a sister."

"Nearly?"

"I was one of twins, but my sister didn't make it. Not that I remember anything about her. She died a few months after we were born."

"Oh. That's sad."

She shrugged. "I didn't know about that until I was about seven. I often think about what it would've been like to have a twin sister. You know, hanging out, and sharing clothes and make up and

199

stuff. Maybe even boyfriends! Only joking. Anyway. Mum said it was cot death. And we wouldn't have been identical."

She took a sip of wine, and caught him looking at her just a little too forensically over the glass. He reddened.

"I'm sorry," he said. "I couldn't help thinking how much you remind me of someone."

"Who?"

"Well, it's not anyone I actually know, or even knew. Just a person in a portrait by one of my favourite artists - John Singer Sargent. You are so much like her, or at least like the way he painted her. I think it was done in the mid-1880s, when he was in Boston. She was a society girl."

"Ooh. Now you've got me interested. Who's is this person?"

"Someone called Mrs Charles E. Inches."

She squinted. "Eeow! Inches? Sounds like she should have kept her maiden name."

"Ha-ha-ha. Yes. That had a much nicer ring to it - Louise Pommeroy."

She nodded in approval. "Oh, I like that."

"She was just twenty-two when she got married, and like a lot of marriages at the time, her husband was a lot older than her. But he was a highly respected general practitioner (doctor, in our language) rolling in money and, more importantly, he was stinking rich. He probably could have married any woman he wanted to. And I have to say he made a brilliant choice, she was absolutely beautiful."

He realised how much he had just revealed, but

it was too late. She looked at him pointedly. She seemed to be resisting a smile. "Oh."

"I uh… you know, Sargent was very taken with her looks. He painted her face with great sensitivity, care and detail. But for her arms and her red velvet dress he used thicker, bolder brushstrokes. Some critics say this girl, Louise Pommeroy, was typical of those fragile, beautiful and strong-willed heroines you often get in Henry James stories. And you know what? She may even have been a model for the heroine in *Turn of the Screw*."

"Ah! Now, I know that story very well. I didn't read it, but I saw an excellent play over at the rep in East Village. If I remember rightly, it's about a young governess, who's haunted by two dead, sinister, servants, and a couple of weird, precocious kids. Very creepy. Do you know that much about *everyone* Sargent painted?"

She swallowed a small mouthful of food and there was a mischievous glint in her eye.

Alan coughed, and some of his wine sprayed onto the white tablecloth. A few spots got onto the collar of his white shirt. He started dabbing at it with the corner of his napkin.

"Uh, no. I can't say I do."

Satisfied , she leaned back.

"So, when did you first discover all that about… what was her name again?"

"Louise. Louise Pommeroy. It was just the other day."

She smiled knowingly.

After desert, the waitress came back to clear the

dishes and ask if they would like to order coffee. Juliette beat Alan to the answer.

"Could you give us five minutes, Josie?"

"Sure," said the waitress. As the waitress departed with the dirty dishes Juliette leaned forwards and said in a conspiratorial whisper:

"The coffee here is a bit hit-and-miss."

"Oh?"

"Well. Depends on who's making it. Tonight, it's Maurice – and, excuse my English, he's crap. The good news is I have some lovely Columbian coffee at my place. It's just over on Park Slope. Oh... wait! It I left home in a bit of a hurry, so I didn't get a chance to clear up and it is a bit cramped. What's your place like?"

They didn't speak as the cab headed over Brooklyn Bridge, the dark clouds ahead twisted and stretched into different shapes. Alan made out a camel, a watering can and a map of Europe.

The driver pulled up on corner of Boerum and Court. Under the green awning Alan fumbled around in his pockets, and opened up the heavy door.

They went up the short flight of narrow stairs one flight and he opened the apartment door, taking her coat when he entered.

She looked around approvingly. "Nice place."

"Put on some music if you like," he said.

"What've you got?"

"Lots of stuff. Everything from Charlie Parker, through to the Thirteenth Floor Elevators, and The Cure – and some dub reggae too."

"Hmm." She didn't sound impressed.

By the time he came back into the lounge with the coffee tray, she had put on Joni Mitchell's *Blue.*, and she was looking more than a little distressed, turning her head from wall to wall as if she was lost and couldn't find the way out.

"What's the matter?" he said.

She shook her head and looked at him, like a child who had lost her toy.

"All these photographs…" were the only words she could muster.

"Photographs?"

"Of your children – and it must be your partner?

"My wife. Jenny."

Juliette picked up a small, framed photo from the mantlepiece and held it out at arm's length, then bought it up really close to her face. "She's very pretty."

Alan pretended he hadn't heard that as he put the tray down onto the small table.

She put the picture back and walked around the coffee table to sit next to him.

"So uh… what do your mum and dad do?" he said, handing her small the milk jug.

"No thanks," she said, touching his hand to stop him pouring. I take it black."

"Sugar?"

"No."

She took a sip, coughed nervously, raising her hand to her mouth.

"My dad owns a construction company. Mom

was a district judge, but she also does a lot of work for children's charities and the local community, that kind of thing... mostly through the local business association. Dad's involved in that a bit too."

"Right." He didn't let on, but that made him feel inferior. His mother worked in a shop, and his dad was a barber. Luckily, she didn't ask about that.

"What's your star sign?" she said suddenly.

That stumped him. "Are you into all that?"

"Does it offend you?

"No. Not at all."

"Then I'd like to know."

He shrugged. "My birthday is January 6th. What does that make me?"

She curled one corner of her lip up and shook her head in mock despair.

"Oh dear."

"What do you mean?"

"Capricorn. You're rigorous in the way you do things and... you move ahead in a very systematic manner, with rules and systems. You're determined, and always aim to turn plans into action and enjoy leading others with your matter-of-fact personality and pragmatism."

"That's completely wrong," laughed Alan. "I'm a mess when it comes to organisation."

She looked at him for a moment and then stared at her knees, rubbing them self-consciously.

"I saw you in action at the recording studio. The way you sorted out everything without any stress. The rest of your team... Sally, you know... your partner, what's his name?"

"Gary."

"Yes. Him too. They were all blind-sided by the client. Not you. You're a Capricorn all right."

Normally, he had nothing but disdain for the subject of astrology. However, he had no desire to shatter the atmosphere of sensitivity and revelation that was building up, so he went with the flow.

"When's your birthday?" he asked.

"June 21st."

"So you're a... "

"Gemini. Well, I'm on the cusp actually. That makes me flighty and disorganised, and I focus on too many things at the same time." She spoke hurriedly, and with enthusiasm, as she continued to rub her knees.

"Oh, how terrible," he said in mock-disapproval.

"Hey!" She nudged him playfully. Geminis are great - totally adaptable. You don't know how lucky you are, having a Gemini for company. We accept people for what they are, and we're probably the most sociable star sign of all." She looked a bit lost then – as if she'd run out of things to say.

They both smiled, and then turned away from each other, embarrassed by this unexpected gap in their conversation. She eventually thought of something to say.

"Gary doesn't like me, does he?"

"What?" Alan leaned back, wide-eyed with surprise. "Where'd you get that from?"

"C'mon, he was giving me the evils the whole time I was in the studio."

"Ah... You just caught him at a bad time.

205

When you get to know him, he's like a big Teddy Bear."

"Don't forget. He was the one who pushed the door into me while I was carrying the tray."

"That's not fair. He didn't even know you were there. I'll tell you something right now... he loves the job you did on the V/O."

"Really?" She turned to Alan, pouting and frowning at the same time.

"Sure."

She stopped to think about that for a minute, looked over at the sound system, and then she turned back to him.

"Did he know we were meeting tonight?"

"Why should he?"

"Do you always answer a question with another question?"

Alan shrugged, and she looked away. This time the silence was longer and deeper. They had run out of things to say, and the discomfort was growing by the second. He could have come up with random small talk, but something told him that was inappropriate. She gazed blankly at the opposite wall. Clusters of half-formed ideas whirled around in his head. He studied her elegant, gently tapering neck, her calm face and her thick eyebrows for clues. What if she was just waiting? What if it wasn't right to say anything at all? Without thinking he touched the side of her face with his thumb and forefinger, slowly turning it towards his. He saw a sleepy, sad and submissive look. He leaned forwards and his lips touched hers. Their tongues rolled around each other in a sweet, wet frenzy.

Their teeth clashed. A wave of electricity ran through him. They stood up and undressed wordlessly, as if it was the most serious task imaginable, and words would shatter everything. Her skin was pale and flawless, and her breasts small and firm, with dark, clearly defined nipples. She was supple and disarming. He had fallen under a spell, and the wonderful part was that, even at the time, he didn't want to resist. Something inside him was turning away from the deeper things he had always valued. She lay back diagonally across the sofa, her head resting on the corner of the hand rest, where it met the back of the sofa, and her legs stretched.

"Let's go into the bedroom," he said.

"I can't." she moaned.

"It would be much more comfortable."

She looked scared. "It's your wife's bed."

"She's never even been here."

"But…"

Soon she was crying softly. Then she shuddered, making a baby noise and her nails bit deep into his upper arm. When it was over, she stroked his face, and a tear travelled down her cheek. "Hold me," she said.

He lay down beside her, in what little room there was on that sofa, stroking her like a cat. They stayed there, saying nothing. He noticed her toenails were painted a rich, glossy black as she twisted around to face him, open mouthed and needy, like a hungry baby. They kissed hard, twisting into each other. She gazed up to the ceiling, breathing hard and moving her head from side to side. Tears flooded along her cheeks. She seemed startled and things went a bit weird. Another face seemed superimposed over hers, vibrating erratically, forming a faint double image; slightly harsher, yet still beautiful, but with a more intense stare. He thought perhaps this was a flashback. But you get that with acid, and he'd never had that, although he did try magic mushrooms as a student. Perhaps he's had more wine than he realised

He started to withdraw, partly through fear and confusion, but she whispered, "No."

Soon after they fell asleep. When he woke up, he lifted her into his arms and carried her over to the double bed, and got in, pulling the duvet cover over them both.

At dawn, he was woken by a squealing sound, which he associated with a child being hurt. Juliette was rolling around in her sleep, looking pained and in a sweat. He touched her forehead, and it seemed she had a temperature. She was repeating something, quietly at first. Eventually he made out what she was saying. It was the name Vanessa. Who was Vanessa?

But that wasn't the only question on his mind. They had already rented out the house in London, and in just three months Jenny and the boys would be moving in with him to the new apartment. They had a school and nursery sorted out for the boys too. What the fuck was he going to do?

Chapter 2

Alan had to make a decision. And he did. He decided not to decide. He took Juliette with him to Martha's Vineyard one weekend, fielding a few interrogative phone calls from Jenny while they were there. Another time he and Juliette went to dinner at Windows on the World, in the World Trade Centre. They would spend a couple of nights together at her place some weeks, and other times she would do the same at his. Most Fridays they would do lunch. One Saturday they saw La Traviata at the Met. They even did that cheesy thing and took a horse and carriage around Central Park. It was like an advent calendar leading to an explosive inevitability. What finally shattered the illusion was an impromptu visit from a friend.

Jason was on his way back to London from Los Angeles. Alan was really pleased to hear his voice. They had a long lunch at his favourite Irish bar, throughout which Jason wore his brown trilby hat, with its little partridge feather in the brim. Alan suspected it was to cover up his fast-balding cranium. Over a pie and mash, and a couple of pints of Guinness, Jason insisted on discussing the philosophical merits of Plato and Socrates over the "dark, nihilistic, free-for-all" of Sartre and Camus (who Jason had never read). Jason then showed Alan some of the images in an A4 portfolio he had in his bag, of the stunningly beautiful work he had created for the animated feature, *The Adventures of Randolph Carter.* Then he took out some pictures of the spacious, colonial style house in LA he and Rebecca had settled into, with its huge swimming pool and incredible views of the city below.

Alan was pleased Jason appeared to be thriving, not just because he worked so hard, but also because he was an unbelievable talent. The only trouble was he had a kamikaze-like propensity to throw it all away.

Alan then told him that Jenny and the boys would be coming over to live with him in New York soon, in the apartment he had recently moved into in Brooklyn Heights. After he'd bought another round of drinks, Alan couldn't help putting on his mischievous grin, and telling Jason about the little fling he was having with this gorgeous young girl, who was just twenty-four. Jason's reaction was not at all what Alan expected. He slammed his jug of Guinness on the table, his huge forehead furrowed, and his eyes stared straight at him in terrifying and unadulterated fury, Alan was more than a little startled.

"What the fuck are you playing at?"

"Well I…" Alan was too stunned to make a cohesive reply, just stammering an explanation of sorts, about how he could easily keep Juliette in the shadows when Jenny and the boys were here.

"I know how you operate, said Jason, raising one corner of his mouth into a sneer. "You're such a big kid. You just follow your nose every time you meet a new bird. What's the matter with you? You were like that at college. Remember what happened with that girl Erica, when you were seeing Jan?

210

How many years ago was that? Haven't you learned anything since then?"

Alan was clearly taken aback. He wasn't expecting anything like this from Jason.

"Yeah, but that was then, and this is now," he said. "Honestly, Jas, this is not like what happened with Erica. I've got all this under control."

Jason shook his head. "I can't believe you. You're putting the future of your children and Jenny on the line for a... for a.... what is she? A fucking actress, only just out of her teenage years."

"She's twenty-four."

"You're an idiot."

That night Alan found it impossible to sleep. He couldn't get over what Jason had said. Finally, he came to the conclusion that Jason was right. Things had slipped away from him. Talking to Jenny was becoming a chore. He was painfully aware how wrong that was, but he couldn't stop himself feeling that way. It took all of his composure just to hide his sense of detachment from her. When the phone rang, he felt a horrible sense of dread and discomfort. He became resentful about even having to talk to the boys. He simply couldn't help it. But afterwards that feeling of disdain would go away, to be replaced by a dark cloud of energy-sapping guilt. The result was that he was drifting away from his family, and sinking into a sweet, and sticky quicksand of his own making. Suddenly the dark flow of his thoughts was interrupted by a loud dull thud on the window pane. He pulled on his dressing gown and raised the blinds. A thick covering of snow was everywhere, burying every parked car in sight. A group of boys, obviously on their way to school, were wading through it all just below, in the middle of a massive snowball fight.

In the office he struggled with the dark mood that had been eating away at him, hoping he could somehow hide it from everyone. But he failed. Most people noticed. Some didn't care, but others (especially those who had to brief him, or work with closely him on existing projects) became visibly irritated by his gloominess. Gary was in handling a photoshoot in South Africa, so it remained to be seen how he would react, if Alan's grim state of mind persisted. He was still able to concentrate in briefings (up to a point), and to communicate what he needed to, so as to deliver an acceptable job. But that wasn't good enough. He was hired to blow people away with his ideas. Something had to change.

The ice-cold wind rubbed against his cheeks like steel wool. A twenty-something mother in expensive designer ski gear was pulling her toddler along the sidewalk as he entered Washington Square Park. The kid was wrapped up warm in a long, tweed coat, woolly hat and scarf. The black, antique lampposts, and snow-covered branches created the vibe of a Victorian Christmas card. Near the fountain a woman let her Alsatian loose, as she brushed away some snow from the wooden bench with her bright pink mittens, and then parked her track-suited bottom on the exposed wood. Further along a middle-aged dad in a military style grey coat picked up an armful of snow that he'd rolled into a large ball and carried it over to a similar sized lump his young son had built up on the ground. Did he have the courage to do this?

Usually, the green wooden frontage of Cafe Reggio felt like a warm invitation from a much-loved friend, but not today. Dots of snow drifted down as he entered the small, dark, baroque interior and rush of warm air greeted him. He looked around and saw that his usual table, next to the ancient chrome espresso machine was free. Dangling light fittings spread a feeble glow over the marble-topped tables, wooden benches and metal-backed chairs. Sitting at a table by the main window was a student with Jimi Hendrix-style hair busily. He was busily writing notes in a small, spiral-bound pad. Behind him was a small old lady in a thick headscarf, leaning her elbows on the table while chewing a sandwich with apparent difficulty. The stage was set.

Juliette came in hurriedly, encumbered by a large Gucci carrier bag, dusting flecks of snow from her heavy black jacket. As she sat down, she seemed slightly taken aback by the brevity of his kiss.

"Been here long?" she asked, removing her white Russian hat and gloves.

"Not really," he said.

Her hair was in a bun again, and as she shook

her head a thick strand came loose and hung against the side of her forehead.

"Don't get me wrong," she said. "I love Bergdorf Goodman, but some of those floors are literally ghost towns. It took me fifteen minutes to track down some assistance."

She reached for his glass of water and took a sip, and her long, dark eyelashes flickered, as she looked at him over the rim of the glass.

"Are you OK?" she asked, as she put the glass back down.

"He squinted, as if in pain, and scratched his forehead. Why wouldn't I be?"

"I don't know… you look a bit sallow."

"Sallow?"

The waitress came over to hand out some menus.

"We're not really eating," said Juliette. "I'll just have a dry cappuccino and a Portuguese tart."

Alan ordered another Americano. Then the waitress trotted off and Juliette pulled out a little box that was beautifully wrapped in black paper with silver polka dots.

"For you," she said.

He studied it with some concern, rotating it slowly in his right hand, as if it might be a bomb.

"Oh."

"Go ahead. Open it up."

She watched eagerly as he peeled back the wrapping paper to reveal a white cardboard box. He lifted the lid and slowly pulled out a snow-globe, incorporating a New York skyline, set on a black Bakelite stand.

"Nice."

"It's antique," she informed him. "Fifties, I think."

"Right."

He shook it and put it on the table, and they watched the tiny flakes swirl around it in a spiral. He wanted to break the spell, so he looked up, with an unmistakable look of sadness.

"As if we haven't had enough snow this the last few days," he said.

She frowned. "'Thank you' would be nice," she said.

"Of course," he said. "Thank you."

She was biting her lower lip. "Well, do you like it?"

"Why wouldn't I? It's really sweet."

"I spent ages choosing it, from this darling little place in Tribeca."

He rested the globe next to his cup, and she looked at him quizzically. She was beginning to sense his mood.

"Oh Jules. What are we going to do?" he said.

"Um... maybe we could go to the galleries in SoHo."

"That's not what I mean."

"I know what you mean. You're going to go on about the age difference between us again."

"No, not that. But, let's face it, we've been burying our head in the sand bit, haven't we? Jenny and the boys will be here soon and..."

The waitress arrived at that point with her coffee and cake. When she departed Juliette brushed something from her shoulder.

"You know what that means."

"Look," she said. "I'm not trying to take you away from your family. That was never my intention. We've been through this."

"I know. I know," he replied. "But I've been thinking about things and… it won't work."

"What won't?" All this time she left her coffee and tart untouched. "What are you talking about? Where's all this coming from?"

"We can't duck and dive now. It won't work. Jenny is no fool. She can sense when my mind is elsewhere, even over the phone. Imagine when she's here."

A hot tear grew in her eye and rolled down her cheek slowly, like a glass bead. Her lips quivered.

"I can't lose you."

He couldn't remember ever having been so cruel. He tried to summon the state of mind he turned on for client meetings.

He couldn't help reaching out and squeezing her hand.

"Please don't think like that. It makes it worth for both of us. We always knew this time would come. And you've got so much ahead of you. You're getting offers from everywhere… Broadway, TV…"

She wiped her eyes with a napkin. "Stop patronizing me."

"Jules!"

She closed her eyes, almost as if in prayer, and then opened them again – focusing through him now. Outside the snow was falling heavily. It was hard to see the terrace of houses across the road.

She cried passively and noiselessly.

He fought back the compulsion to hold her in his arms.

"Why are you doing this to me?"

"I... I'm doing it to both of us."

"Sure." She leaned over, picked up all her bags, and stood up awkwardly.

"I have to go."

She hurried out.

He watched her leave and looked back to see the guy with the Hendrix hairstyle and the old lady in the headscarf must have noticed everything. He picked up his wallet pulled out a few bills, threw them on the table and ran out to grab a cab that had stopped outside to let out some passengers.

"You free?"

"Where to?"

"Park Avenue and East 50th"

"Jump in."

He would immerse himself with work at the agency.

Chapter 3

"Are you well?" asked the little Jewish lady who lived a few doors further along his floor as she was leaving the building. "You look so pale."

She studied his face with almost motherly concern. She passed him on the stairs and stopped on the step below and looked back up at him.

"Not too bad, thank you Mrs Spielman," said Alan, turning back to face her for a moment. "Just finished work, that's all - tough day. I'll be raring to go again, after I have a cup of tea."

She watched him go up, shrugged, and then turned to continue on her way out.

At his apartment door he fumbled and dropped the keys on the floor. His fingers were like sticks of ice. He picked the keys up and eventually managed to get the door open. He took off his damp shoes and found he was almost sliding along the wooden floor in his socks. The apartment was like an outdoor theatre to the neighbours opposite at night. He went over to pull the blinds down on all five sash windows. In the kitchen area he managed to make himself a pastrami sandwich on rye, without losing a single finger, which was quite an achievement, considering the state he was in.

He wondered if he should ring Gary up to tell him the script that they'd put together for Hershey's had been blown out completely by the client. Then he realised there was no point in doing that. Gary would just start yelling down the phone, hang up –

and lose sleep thinking about it. He'll break it to him at work in the morning. It wouldn't achieve anything ruining his evening now.

Alan only found out the bad news from Serena when he got back from the café. She was waiting for him to get back. What the fuck was the matter with these brand managers? No imagination. That was such a powerful concept. Original. Funny too. And the storyboard was beautiful. Continuity had done an amazing job. It was absolutely crazy to give that idea up. That's what he told Serena. He got her to fix up a meeting with him and Steve for the end of the day. That's when he tried to be upbeat and convincing, to bring Steve around to the idea of saving it, by just making a few tweaks. It wouldn't be hard. They could present again… only this time to the senior client, not that idiot Martin Moreland – the fucking middleman.

Steve listened for a while and finally raised his palms up.

"Alan. We need a new idea. The manic chicken script is dead. Move on."

To calm down he poured himself a JD with ice, and sat in the large armchair in front of the TV. Even the Star Trek Original Series episode that came on failed to cheer him up, not least because it featured a female android with long dark hair (who had fallen in love with Captain Kirk). She reminded him too much of Juliette.

He switched it off. The bits of pastrami stuck between his teeth were becoming really annoying. In a huff, he went to the bathroom to brush his teeth, when he was startled by a warm breath brushing against his cheek and a woman's voice whispering in his ear, "Alan!"

He twisted around, swallowing toothpaste while coughing and spluttering. There was no one there.

A sense of warm, scented air lingered. Maybe it was a lingering odour from the many times Jules had stayed over, some kind of after-shower cosmetic. She used to have a bag full of lotions, potions and sprays. But this particular fragrance wasn't one he was familiar with. Not that he was an expert. It could be a perfume used by the previous tenant, after all, he hadn't been living there that long. Somebody told him that some smells like cigarette smoke or spicy cooking can be absorbed into wallpaper. But there was no wallpaper in the bathroom. It was completely tiled over. Hmm. Perhaps... the grout between the tiles soaks up smells, or maybe the blinds or shower curtain.

Baffled, he went back to armchair, and knocked a whole glass of JD back in one go, enjoying the sweet burning sensation at the back of his throat. He then poured another glass, and took a sip. It was probably just nonsense, the lingering smell, the smoke that never was. He couldn't deny he was kind of, tinged with fear. And now he understood why. It really felt like there was a woman in there with him, in the bathroom – even though he couldn't see her. Maybe he was going mad. That's what stress at work can do to you. Or was it what happened with Jules?

That night, he took The Age of Reason to bed with him, but he was reading the same paragraph again and again. Surrendering to the inevitable, he turned the lights out and fell asleep almost immediately.

He is outside the office – the huge glass agency skyscraper on Park Avenue. It's daytime, but for some reason it's dark. A storm is brewing. He is waiting for Jenny on Madison Avenue, but the buildings are not in their proper places. He can't work out why. The street is empty of people and cars. He has an idea verging on a premonition that this is all an empty stage waiting for something terrible to play out. There is a sense of inevitability and helplessness – a blind fatalism. He knows how it's going to play out, and there's nothing he can do to stop it. Why isn't Jenny here yet? He doesn't want to be there any longer than he has to. In the sky there are thick, time-lapse, dark clouds, twisting and flowing, obscuring the day, merging into a blanket of darkness. A bright scar, opens up between them, flooding the top stories of the buildings opposite with light. But at street level all is cold, dark shadow.

Behind him, over the entrance to his offices, are the words *Sam Hayne House, instead of* Goulding Graham and Puller son (GGP). When he looks back there are people there now, walking along – oblivious to him and each other. Where did they come from? They all have curious red spots on their faces. 'Is it measles?"

It is going to happen now. He is afraid. An old couple come towards him. As they lean toward him, close to his face they fill him with horror. The old man is a leering, and heavy-set. His wife thin wife is lascivious, with an evil grin. Their salivating lips and look of wide-eyed lust are disgusting

They start up a chant:

"The yellow truck is coming. The yellow truck is coming."

The passers join in, encircling him. The rhythm becomes fearful, hypnotic. He can feel his heart pump faster and faster. He can't stand it. He wants them to go away, closing his eyes tight. A low humming noise starts. It builds slowly, changing from the sound of an electricity generator to the sound of a truck... becoming louder.

It stops. He opens his eyes again. The street is empty again.

A noise like a slowed down car horn starts, followed by a low, rumbling sound. He wishes Jenny would hurry. The rumbling gets louder. The street is shaking from the vibration. He looks both ways for the source of the sound, but there's nothing. Terrified, he runs back into the office through the revolving door, but it won't turn. The noise of the engine is now a terrible roar. Behind a huge yellow truck is closing in. He can't move.

He woke up in a cold sweat, shaking. The digital clock said 2.35.

Chapter 4

Alan was having a hard time putting together any ideas.

Gary didn't stress about it at first, because as long as one of them can comes up with the goods, there's no issue. We all have our off days. Trouble is this was turning into an off-week, then an off fortnight, and it was now approaching an off-month.

Gary was definitely coming up with the lion's share of the ideas, and this is the stuff that team break-ups are made of. To add to the burden, Gary was also carrying the can when it came to fighting all the battles to get HIS ideas through the sifter – basically that means getting approval from the account team, the creative director(Steve), and the client.

At one presentation Alan found himself sinking into a soft, foggy, sweet oblivion. Everything around him seemed to be happening behind a wall of glass. Gary was presenting a Chrysler TV spot to the account team at the time. The script was based on a great idea (Gary's) which was clever, witty, and edgy. The difficulty was that the Chrysler account team were the most boring, risk-averse bastards in the agency. Their natural inclination to buy safe ideas to make it easier to present to the client.

That was what Gary and Alan – and most importantly Steve – did not want to give them. Steve needed them to sell this risky and powerful idea to the team. As Gary was trying his level best to do that, from the corner of his eye he could see the vacant expression on Alan's face. This was not good.

Alan was becoming fascinated with Gary's lips. He remembered a goldfish that he won in a funfair on Hampstead Heath as a small boy. It was in a clear plastic bag. He recalled holding it up against the bright blue summer sky and staring at it in fascination. Gulp, gulp, gulp it went – just like Gary.

By now, Gary was now in a fierce argument with Paul, Brendan, Christine and Elaine. He desperately needed some support from Alan, who was still staring straight ahead, glassy-eyed. Gary gave him a discreet kick. Alan's eyes flickered into life, and he began to bring the room back into focus. He saw the alarm in Gary's face, and voices raised in anger, but he couldn't attach any meaning to it all. Words were all going over his head. The idea was dead.

The minute they were back in the office, Gary exploded.

"What the fuck is the matter with you?"

Alan was incapable of explaining away his state of mind. He didn't know what was happening to him, and he said so. Gary glared at him and then, palms down, slammed the desk, before storming out of the office. Momentarily stunned, Alan tried to spark himself into action, so he could rush out and calm him down. But he was totally unable to do that, as he was struck by a sudden rush of vertigo and had to drop down into his chair again, feeling impotent and confounded. Anything could happen now. It wasn't impossible for Gary, raging as he was, to barge into Steve's office and demand a new art-director. Steve might even agree, especially after how things had panned out the last few weeks. Alan could find himself out of a job. That's because there's no guarantee Steve would take the trouble to find someone else for Alan to partner up with. That sort of this can be a real hassle. What then? The three month's severance pay he'd get wouldn't even cover the money he'd laid out to secure a nursery and school for the boys and the deposit for the new apartment. And he'd signed an eighteen-month contract for that. No. Sitting here was no use. Gary was probably in O'Reilly's Bar. That's where he goes to let off steam. He tried again to get up, but now he felt incredibly drowsy. What was wrong with him, for fuck's sake? Things had gone completely tits up from the time he finished with Jules. But he was sure that couldn't be why all this shit was happening to him. This wasn't the first time he'd had to put an end toa relationship. He'd been through it all before. It was much worse when he finished with Anna. They'd been together for nearly three years when Jenny came along, so the guilt and ennui that came from that split was pretty deep. This wasn't enough of an emotional cataclysm to precipitate a psychological and physical crisis like this. The timing, ending with Juliette, was just a coincidence. Something else has caused this. Is it a virus? A genetic disorder?

I'm not used to this profound apathy, lethargy and despair.

Antipathy, despair – having no faith in the possibility of successfully explain his feeling of helplessness away.

Negative changes in thinking and mood

This must be what post-traumatic stress disorder is like

But I haven't been through an experience that warrants these sorts of symptoms.

Alan is at the doctors which was recommended by Mrs Spielman. he asked the her if she could recommend a doctor, which she did. The doctor listened with an expression of deep earnestness while stroking his goatee beard, then he recommended it would be a good idea if Alan could get some time off work, and finished up by writing up a prescription for anti-depressants. Alan had never had anti-depressants before.

Over the next few days Gary's frostiness began to thaw, although it was probably due more to necessity and the passage of time than anything Alan was doing to redeem himself.

That Friday he was in the office early, trying to come up with ideas for a product that was a kind of lazy person's cheese on toast. His stream of thought was broken by Gary pushing the door open violently, but in good humour.

"You still awake?" he shouted.

Gary seemed to have recovered his high spirits, which was a relief. They sat down together and threw around some ideas. It was as if the preceding bad atmosphere between them had never existed. Again, Alan's contribution that morning was simply to prompt Gary rather than to come up with anything new himself. And there were certain moments when he could feel himself slipping, but he made an excuse about having a weak bladder, and rushed out to splash some cold water on his face. Those kinds of emergency measures worked for a while, but he was aware he was on shaky ground now, and that he couldn't hold on this way forever.

When he was back home, he sat down to dinner and gazed at the photo of Jenny and the boys in Regents Park, taken the previous summer on one of their Saturday morning strolls. Jenny was sitting on a bench with her arms around the boys. Simon had been crying just a few moments before, because Jack had bitten a huge chunk out of his choc-ice.

He finished eating and went over to pour himself a drink, and then grabbed the remote and sat back to watch some television. The screen showed nothing but grey static. Suddenly he was overcome with drowsiness, causing him to drop the remote to the floor. A wave of fatigue came over him. The room felt out of phase with reality, and he had a powerful sensation of sinking. A shudder ran through him, which left him, weirdly, with a new sense of clarity that somehow segued into thoughts of Juliette. Then the phone rang, dragging him out of these sweet and delicate reflections. He didn't answer, instead waiting to hear that it was jenny, and that she was leaving a message.

"Hi darling. I guess you're either working late, or you're having a drink with the team.

I just wanted to have a quick chat with you about schools for Jack. I'm happy with the nursery we've found for Simon though. Give me a call if you don't get back too late. Bye. Love you."

He was in no frame of mind to discuss mundane issues, so he sat still for a little longer, building up the energy to stand up and stumble into the bathroom.

After an ice-cold shower, he recovered some composure and a little more sense of clarity. He intended to read in bed, but he kept going over the same paragraph again and again. Giving up, he turned out the lights.

Soon he began to slowly drift off into a sleep, but was never too far from wakefulness. He thought he heard a breathy sigh coming from the corner of the room at one moment. Instinctively, he opened his eyes and out of the velvety darkness he noticed a faint greenish glow coming from outside the door, which was slightly ajar. That soft light began to spill more and more into the room, like a slow, tide on a sandy beach. Then he noticed that the ceiling was throbbing, almost like a membrane. Suddenly he found that he couldn't move. A sense of cloudy anticipation welled up inside of him. A hidden and undefined change was happening, in the room and in him. Peering deeper and deeper into the velvety darkness, near the large wardrobe, a smoke like form was taking shape, slowly solidifying. He saw the form of a young woman, lithe and slim. Her long dark hair fell onto her shoulders and breasts, while the white light from her eyes seemed to pierce him. He was tingling with terror, yet couldn't move. The young, naked woman, looked at him with affection, like a mother adoring her sleeping baby. She tilted her head to one side and wriggled exquisitely, shuddering in and out of phase with the room. His fear was battling with his sense of incandescent lust. The room became ice cold and his breath came in clouds of vapour. Stunningly beautiful, she moved forward. His pulse raced and he thought his heart would explode. He managed to close his eyes, and when he opened them again the darkness had returned, and he found he could move. He twisted around to switch on the bed light. The brightness hurt his eyes. When he adjusted, he could see that the room was empty. Turning the light off again, he fell back flat onto the mattress, and fell into a horrible, unsettling drowsiness that transitioned into an unconnected sequence of short, rapid nightmares, and then dreamless sleep.

And then... boom! Suddenly he snapped awake again, like a drowning man coming up for air. This time he was too terrified to fall asleep, but he remained stretched out on the bed, in a nerve-tingling semi-wakefulness. It couldn't last. A quagmire of disturbing dreams returned. He saw flights of stairs, down which he was falling endlessly, deeper and deeper into slimy depths where nameless things were hiding in the shadows.

Once again, he awoke in a panic, now with pins and needles in his left arm. The bed covers tormented him. He kicked them away in anger, and then he realised that much of his discomfort was because his pyjamas were soaked with sweat. He took them off and threw them to the floor. When he lay back his whole body began to smart and tingle, as though he'd been stung by a swarm of insects. His temples throbbed but after a while, things appeared to settle down. The pain went away – before, temperature suddenly plummeted and he watched his breath come out in thick plumes of steam. The room was resonating now – and the paralysis returned. This was not a dream. His mind was racing and he sensed her before she appeared, in a perfumed tremor of horror and desire she appeared in the darkest depths of the room. Her breasts caught the dull green glow from the slightly open door, and her eyes burned an intense white. She took a step forward and his heart thudded uncontrollably. Somehow, he could sense her lust and desire, but also her deep melancholy. In a liquid-like motion, she was pulsing towards him. Reaching the end of the bed, she stopped and smiled, lowering her knee onto the mattress. Then she began crawling towards him on all fours, like a lynx stalking its prey. He wanted to scream. Licking her upper lips, she leaned onto him and her breasts teasingly fell on his chest. A shock of electricity, passed from her skin into his body. His soul wavered and shook deep within him. Her eyes fixed upon his with a look of curious intent, as a soft and silky fire ignited every part of him. His breathing came faster and faster, and he waited for the inevitable. But it never came. In an explosion of horror and unfulfilled passion, she was gone.

230

The only thing he understood clearly at that precise moment was that something in him had swiftly and magically changed

Chapter 5

He felt weak and tired, and his eyes were sore. He also had a pounding headache. When his thoughts coalesced, he realised that the doctor he had seen was a quack. Depression was the last thing he was suffering from. Yes, he was in a depressing situation, losing his composure and clarity of thought at work, and now he was experiencing horrific visions, but that's not the same thing as depression. The medical condition they call depression applies to people who are miserable for no reason. They have an irrational sadness. Their emotional response does not correspond to reality. That's a problem.

But that's not what Alan was experiencing. He was responding to a true state of affairs that was depressing, by being depressed. It was an authentic response to events. So, the pills were of no use. He would stop taking them.

But there was something wrong. It was an external cause; he was certain of that. Normally strong willed, and confident in everything he did, he was nervous and confused. His thinking was getting cloudy, and as a result he was fucking up at work. Whatever it was had nothing to do with depression. He had been putting his psychological malfunctions down to fatigue, maybe due to some kind of viral infection, or something. But something else was at play here. He had enough belief in himself to know that. Resisting a feverish yearning to go back to sleep, he went into the kitchen and brewed up a huge jug of strong coffee. He had to think. He drew back the blinds to see there was no moon or stars. He sat on a stool in the kitchen and watched the sky slowly turn from black to pale grey, and the atmosphere in the apartment lifted. His numbing fatigue had gone.

But what had precipitated these weird visitations?

Was it a coincidence that this phenomenon was happening while he was experiencing something that seemed to be equivalent to a kind of nervous breakdown?

And what if his problem wasn't something that could be explained by orthodox means; doctors, psychiatrists, psychologists, neurologists?

Who could he talk to about this?

Jason wouldn't be interested. He wanted to find material explanations for everything, although he was a great believer in the merits of astrology, which is a whole other topic. Although Jenny was into all this occultism business, but he didn't want to raise the topic with her at all. He wasn't sure why, but he suspected that his guilt about his relationship with Juliette might be connected to all this. Jenny would pick up on that.

Then it struck him – what about Cornelia and Bella? Ever since he wondered into their occult bookshop to ask a quick question when he was a student, they had and had taken a big interest in him and his career. Over in England now it was coming up to midday, even though it was only seven in the morning in New York.

Cornelia answered. She was delighted to hear from him.

"Hello stranger. We were talking about you this morning, Bella and I. How's life in America?"

Alan was relieved to hear her voice. "Good. How are things with you and Bella?"

"We're fine. But there's a heavy, cold mist that's rolled in from the sea, and as we look through the window now, it looks like a steamy shower out there. Not good for trade."

"Oh dear. Sorry to hear that."

"So what's all this about you having these strange, disturbing visitations?"

Alan was startled, and totally confused. "But... I didn't say anything about all that. How did you know? You're doing this to me again."

Cornelia sounded as if she was disappointed with him.

"Alan, I'm not doing anything. You probably mentioned it at the start of this conversation."

"But I didn't..."

She became more assertive, and her frustration was evident in her voice. "Alan. Will you get on with it and stop beating about the bush?"

He knew it was pointless to argue any further. He would only end up going around in circles and build up more frustration. Defeated, he described how the weirdness began: the shadow of the woman moving behind him in the bathroom and the woman's voice whispering his name in his ear, even though there was no one there. He also told her

234

about the naked girl glowing out of the darkness in his room (who may or may not have been the same girl who whispered to him before). Her eyes were spots of light in the gloom, his paralysis, and the waves of panic rushed through him as she approached.

Alan realised that Cornelia had put the conversation on speaker, so that Bella could also hear this, because suddenly Bella said:

"Hmm, interesting. Does she remind you, even just a little bit, of anyone you know?"

"Oh... hi Bella," he said.

"Yes, hi. Now answer the question."

"Uh, sorry. He had to think about that. "Hm. No. Not really."

"Are you sure about that? Think about it."

"Well, maybe just a little..."

I had this thing going on with a girl... a young actress. But that's all over now. Jenny and the boys are coming soon, so I had to nip all that in the bud."

Cornelia didn't sound convinced.

"It sounds to me that you should be getting some serious help."

"What kind of help?" asked Alan, now more worried than he was before he rang. "What exactly do you think is wrong with me?"

"There's nothing wrong with you, *per se*. But you are in a dangerous predicament that cannot be allowed to continue unabated. You need proper assistance."

Alan was speechless. He wondered if they were being over-cautious.

Bella, Cornelia's daughter, broke the silence.

"We know exactly the right person for you to talk to. He is an old friend of ours, and he is a very sincere, intelligent and professional. What's more, he lives in New York. But you will need to arrange to see him as soon as you can."

"But who is he? What's his background? Is he some kind of shrink?"

"No, no, no. He is certainly not a psychiatrist, or psychoanalyst, or anything of the kind," said Cornelia. He is an expert in phenomena. We invited him to lecture here at the Conway Hall a few years ago. He was quite brilliant. It was a sell-out.

"When did you two reach this conclusion?"

"Listen," said Cornelia, dismissing any further questioning. "Robert is a very serious man. The CIA would never hire a crank now, would they? He is also a decorated war hero"

"What war?"

"Vietnam. He graduated from West Point. He's also a classics scholar and a prolific author. Highly respected. And his wife, Isobel, is lovely."

"Oh yes," said Bella, to add emphasis, "I thought she was delightful company. And a very talented artist too."

Alan wondered where all this was leading. "What's his name, again?" he asked.

"Robert Stringfield.

"OK."

He then heard Cornelia give Bella some instructions.

"I think we've still got that book on demonic possession by Robert, haven't we?"

"Demonic possession?"

Chapter 6

Alan found Gary working hard at his keyboard in the morning, in a newly pressed, white shirt, and sporting a brand-new haircut. Tracy, the art buyer, was right behind him carrying a portfolio. Alan turned around to keep the door open for her.

"Hey Tracy," he said.

"Hey guys. Guess what?" she said. "The illustration samples have arrived."

Gary looked up. "Hey. About friggin' time!"

"Wash your mouth out, Cummings. Let's see them," said Alan, taking off his coat.

Tracy opened up the folio on the desk, and Alan sat down to go through all the delicate pen and wash studies. Gary was too busy typing to look. His concentration was interrupted by three rapid knocks on the glass. They all looked up. It was Gordon, in his black and white check short sleeve shirt and clipboard. He came in uninvited and looked over Alan's shoulder at the illustrations.

Tracey turned to say, "Gordon. Whatever it is, can you leave it till later? I need these guys to approve an illustrator."

"Not until they explain why the Boston Mutual ad in the Times went out with the wrong phone number."

"What the fuck? That's not possible," said Gary, breaking off from his typing.

"I was the last one to sign it off. The phone number was spot on when it left my desk."

Alan coughed nervously and mumbled, "Well, uh... I think I had one more look at it after you did, Gary."

Gary stared at him accusingly. There was a deathly silence for a few seconds.

"Run that by me again."

Tracy gave them both a frown.

"I called the artwork back to uh... fix something. What might have happened, you know, because of the lack of time, I might have rushed things and inadvertently used an earlier version as a template for my changes. It's a... possibility. I guess."

"Inadvertently?" Gary looked up at the ceiling, his arms raised, as if he was summoning a deity. "Let me get this straight," he said, flopping his arms back onto the desk. "You called back artwork which had final sign-off, to make changes and then you sent it out again - without telling me, or anyone else?"

Alan shrugged meekly. "Like I said, there was no time..."

Gary dropped his head in his arms, which were now folded on the desk. "I don't fucking believe this."

"Yeah well..." Gordon interrupted. "I do. The agency is coughing up for all the print costs. Thirty-five-grand, at the last count."

Gary looked up now, and his face became flush. Then he stood up and walked purposefully around the desk to, opened the glass door, and steer Gordon out. Gordon didn't offer much resistance. He'd already made his point.

Tracy left the illustrator's portfolio on the desk. "I'll come back later when you've made your selection," she said as she left. "I'm meeting a photographer in five minutes."

When she was gone, Gary sat down, dangling his arms at his side, as if he'd lost the use of them. Alan said nothing. There was nothing he could say. He had screwed up badly, and cost the agency a great deal of money. Never before in his career had he done anything like it. His mind was not working properly, that was becoming clearer by the day. He wanted to get away, to be out on his own. His self-respect had plummeted.

Then Gary suddenly lightened the mood. "Gordon's a jerk," he said suddenly, as he leaned forward and rested his elbows on the table.

"Uh, well yes... I suppose he is," said Alan, relieved.

"But you have to admit, he has a point."

Alan found himself looking through the window, as a distant airplane moved slowly left to right, between two skyscrapers.

Alan looked down at the desk, shook his head and sighed. "I wanted to make a tweak on the face of the girl in the photo. Her complexion seemed a little bit...you know, bright. That's all."

Gary made a little chuckle, in despair.

Something inside Alan snapped. "Fuck it. I made a mistake, OK? I'm human. People fuck up sometimes."

Gary gave him a cold, hard stare. "The day I go into a zombie state in a briefing, and make a fuck-up those costs the agency top dollar, you can get on

240

your high horse. Right now, in case you didn't know it, you're the guy with pie on his face. If I was you, I'd shut the fuck up."

They were getting louder. People were looking in as they walked past.

"You know what?" Alan said. "Before I came here, I lost count of just how many people warned me off of working with you."

Gary's mouth froze open, before he said, "Oh yeah?"

Alan nodded, "Yeah."

"I'd like to know who the fuck they were."

"I'm not naming names, but the words 'liability', and 'unstable' were used more than once."

Gary stood up and his face was beetroot red as he punched a framed movie poster of Apocalypse Now, on the wall. The glass cracked, and the soft skin under his little finger ripped open like a pigskin purse. Blood splashed onto his new shirt and it was dripped freely onto our desk. He studied the wound as if it was a rare and beautiful bird.

Alan stood up immediately.

"Stay there," he said. And then he rushed over to find Jackie. She stopped tapping away on her keyboard and looked up. "What's up?"

"Someone said you were the official First Aider on this floor?"

"And?"

"It's Gary."

She shook her head, like a disappointed primary school teacher.

She took out a metal box from her draw and went over to their office. Alan followed in her wake. She picked up Gary's hand and said, it's going to need stitches. That was Alan's queue to go and get the coffees.

He came back with a cardboard tray of drinks. "OK for me to come in?" he asked.

Jackie looked round. "We're all done here," she said, giving Alan a stern look as she took out one of the paper cups and left. Alan put one of the cups in front of Gary.

Gary leaned back with a pensive expression and showed Alan his newly stitched hand.

"See what you made me do?"

Chapter 7

A few days later Gary and Alan were working on the finishing touches for a car poster campaign when Alan's desk phone rang. It was Jackie, the creative director's secretary, putting on her curt, serious voice.

"Alan?"

Alan suspected he was going to get a dressing down for the fuck-up over the print job. "Hi Jax. Everything OK?"

"Can you get over here straight away? Steve wants to talk to you."

"You mean me – or me and Gary?"

"No. Just you."

Jackie, who sits just in front it of Steve's office, acting as passport control, told Alan to wait as she got up to tap on the glass door to Steve's enormous office. She then turned around. "Go right on in, she said."

Steve, with his mop of dark hair and thick, long Rudyard Kipling Moustache, was bent down facing the desk, writing elegantly with his stubby Mont Blanc pen. He was far too engrossed, at that moment, to acknowledge that Alan even existed. Alan sat down on the seat opposite him, studying the various awards on the shelves behind, waiting for Steve to acknowledge his existence. Eventually, Steve looked up with a disarming hang dog expression, which was somehow exacerbated by his black, Rudyard Kipling-style, Victorian moustache.

That look could mean anything from, I'm going to give you a raise, to can you make a few changes to this script, to get out of here, you're fired. He uses it in meetings with account people, biding his time with supreme calm, leaving them in suspense. However, on this occasion there was a hint of warmth in his dark eyes.

"How's everything?" said Steve.

"Pretty good I think," replied Alan.

There was an extended silence as Steve put his pen down and his lower lip came forward. He then threaded his fingers together and leaned back into his seat to give Alan an intense stare. "Your name's been coming up a lot lately."

Alan cleared his throat nervously. "Really?"

"A few people were concerned about you - more or less - dozing off in a briefing."

Alan leaned forward. "Steve, let me explain…"

Steve didn't want to hear. "And then there's the question of a press ad that has ended up costing the agency $55,000 to put right."

Alan squeezed his temple between his thumb and third finger and continued to listen, hoping the axe would fall fast so he could just go.

"Now, I know you've been going through a stressful time. I make it my business to be aware of things like that."

Alan nodded reluctantly.

Steve then broke the flow of the conversation to walk over to window and pull up the blinds. It was still snowing, forming a net curtain between them and the towers on the other side of Madison Avenue.

"I won't probe. I don't have the time or the inclination," he said, coming back to take his seat. "All I want is for you to be at your best. That's not because I'm a nice guy. Put it down to practicality. We have some important pitches coming up. I'm thinking of putting you on quite a few of them in a few weeks."

He stopped to drink his glass of Perrier.

"I want you to take some time out when your family get here from England."

He put his hands in his pockets, pulled out a set of keys and threw them on the table.

Alan was confused.

"I have a house upstate. Place called Cold Spring. It's on the Hudson, maybe sixty miles north. I don't know if you've ever seen the Hudson Valley, around West Point, but it really is beautiful."

He pointed to the keys with his chin. "Go on, pick them up."

Alan reached forward and did as he was told, very meekly.

"You'll like it there," said Steve, enjoying his own benevolence, "So, will your family. It's very pretty in the snow."

Alan couldn't help sighing with relief.

"And when you come back, I want to see the Alan White I hired. Understood?"

On the way out, Alan passed Jackie, who looked at him knowingly and smiled.

Gary wasn't in the office, so he grabbed his coat and went to lunch. In reception, he saw Jay and

Pete coming into the building through the revolving doors. They seemed pleased with themselves. They said they had just recorded a couple of scripts at Seraphim, with the actress Alan had discovered.

"You mean, Juliette," said Alan.

"Yeah, that's her."

"She's really good Al," said Pete. "Went like a dream."

"We were going to ask her if she wanted some lunch, but her boyfriend showed up near the end of the edit, to whisk her away."

All that steely resolve he had built up to break off with her was starting to fracture. He showed as little interest as he could, but inside he was burning.

"Oh, that's a shame. What was he like?" he asked, trying to sound blasé.

"Blonde, tall guy," said Jay. "Uptown-type. About her age."

"Yeah. Maybe a little older," said Pete.

Alan had a good idea who it might be. He had a sinking feeling.

"Oh right. Never met him," he said.

Alan didn't feel like to taking the subway, so he hailed a cab. At the other end of the Brooklyn Bridge he told the driver to stop. He had a powerful urge to walk. When he got down the steps leading to the riverside, he found there was thick, slippery ice packed hard beneath the soft, snow. He trod carefully, knowing his expensive, industrial, big-brand boots were not reliable in these conditions.

Across the river the towers of Wall Street made a beguiling, blue-grey geometry. A pencil thin cloud drifted behind the World Trade Centre, and a seagull circled over a barge, climbing higher, in consecutive spirals.

He turned left to Montague Street, by the play area, where he used to walk with Juliette on Sundays. That would after she slipped an apron on over her bra and panties to cook breakfast. How could she have found someone else so soon?

Later he was pouring himself a drink in the apartment, when there was a knock at the door. He saw a frail, bird-like old lady with died black hair who lives alone, only a few doors along the hallway. She had a small FedEx package in her hands.

"Mr White. Sorry to disturb you, but this came for you this afternoon. I was coming in from the doctors at the time, and the man asked me if I knew you, so he let me sign for it. Is that OK?"

"That's perfect Mrs Spielman. You are an angel."

"No problem. Pleasure to help. She tried to look either side of him, "So when are your family coming?"

Alan had to think about that. "Uh… Next week. Thanks again, Mrs Spielman."

He closed the door and sat down by the coffee table, and took a sip of his beer, before opening the package. It was from England, from the Bell and Candle. Inside was the book Cornelia had spoken about, 'A Study in Demoniality'. He opened the first page and a plain business card fell out, with the author's name.

Robert Springfield
Apartment 9F
800 Fifth Av
New York 10065

There was also a phone number. They hadn't included a letter, but there was a note from Bella on the inside cover.

"To Alan, with love. Cornelia and Bella x"

Just then the phone rang. It was Jenny. He didn't feel up to speaking to her right then, so he waited for her voice to come up on the answerphone:

"Hi darling. You must be out – or still at work. Give me a call if you get home in time. The boys are so excited. We're all packed and ready now. Love you. Bye."

He went back to browsing the contents page of the book when the phone rang again. This time it was Bella's voice.

"Hi Alan. Bella here. Did you get the book alright? I'm…"

This time he quickly shot over to answer the phone.

"Bella! Hi! I got the book fine. Thank you so much. How are you?"

"We're fine thank you. I'm alone in the shop this afternoon. I wish you were here!

Mama has gone to have tea with a friend at The Grand."

"Oh."

"Listen, I have to be quick, because we have a few customers in the shop. You need to read the first twenty pages and then call Robert. He is expecting to hear from you. See him as soon as possible. You are in danger."

Unsurprisingly, this unsettled Alan. He knew she was referring to the glowing green woman who had been appearing to him.

"Shit. What... I mean... what can happen?"

"Read those pages. Make that call to Robert. You will get on very well with him, I promise you. And his lovely wife, or companion, I can't remember which, Isobel. She's delightful. When I was at school she came over with Robert and she looked very fragile. She was recovering from intensive radiotherapy, and she had a lovely red scarf around her head to cover her baldness. I gather she's fine now. She's an artist, like you."

"I'm not really an artist..."

"Anyway, Mama and I have made a charm that will protect you in your flat – but it will only last a few days. We can't repeat it. It's too dangerous for us, or rather me. Mama would never be able to do it."

"Do what?"

"To complete the charm, I had to consume large amounts of fly agaric, to reach the required state of consciousness. It worked, but it's also poisoned my innards for a few days. That's what it does. I was retching for hours afterwards. I'm still getting stomach cramps."

"Jesus." Alan wasn't sure if this was a load of nonsense, but either way, they believed they were helping, and he was really touched by this sacrifice. "You did that for *me*?"

"For me too. I want you to visit the shop again when you're back, so we can do that lovely thing we did, a few years ago. If you don't call Robert, you'll never be able to do it again – with anyone."

And with that staggering point delivered, she hung up.

Chapter 8

The Chinese take away arrived just as he was coming out of the shower so he quickly grabbed a towel and went to the door to collect it. Then he got dressed and sat down at the dining table, listening to Chet Baker. He didn't bother to empty the food onto plates, grabbing a knife and fork from the kitchen, and taking the bag of food over to the dining table, where he ripped open the thin, white plastic bag of prawn crackers, and lined up the foil containers of egg fried rice, vegetable spring rolls, crispy shredded beef with chilli, and stir-fried vegetables and tucked in.

The apartment felt less oppressive now. He couldn't put his finger on it, but Bella may well have been right. There would be no haunting from his demon tonight. Whether that was down to Cornelia and Bella doing their weird mumbo jumbo or not... well he couldn't say. They claimed to have cast spells for him in the past: to help him and Jenny get the house, when there was a rich couple trying to gazump them. And then there was a dodgy situation where they hadn't claimed any credit at all. But he preferred not to think about that.

Having finished, he put away the various trays and lids into the bag it all came in, wiped the table and poured himself a glass of wine, then sat down to go through his new book, "A Study in Demoniality' by Robert Stringfield.

The book opened with a general history:

A succubus is a female sexual demon: a paranormal entity, with a history going back thousands of years. In recorded history and myth, the succubus has had many ways to creep up and seduce her victims, usually during sleep. Some men have described these experiences as pleasurable. Others have experienced malignant overtones, and an undeniable sense of evil. Some victims may suffer enormously after experiencing full sex with a female demonic entity. The experience can lead to a decline in physical and mental health, impotence, - and sometimes death.

In his principal work Antiquarum Lectionum, a fifteenth century Venetian writer, Cœlius Rhodiginus, described how a young man called Menippus Lycius, was having a sexual relationship with a woman who begged him to marry her. At this wedding, there happened to be a philosopher, and this man guessed the woman was actually a sexual demon. When he told Menippus of his suspicion she began screaming hysterically and t vanished into thin air.

Alan shuddered, and skipped over to a section about, Ludovico Maria Sinistrari, a seventeenth century author. Sinistrari was an advisor to the Supreme Sacred Congregation of the Roman and the Universal Inquisition in Rome. He was an expert on exorcism and was also a respected authority on demonology, and advised on investigations of people who were accused of sexual relations with demons. Sinistrari said that when a female sexual

252

demon has sex with a man, there is always an ulterior motive –usually to give birth to a half-demon. Sinistrari also believed that satanic cults and covens are the means by which a demon is summoned, through collective prayers to an evil deity and sacrifice.

"They must promise the Devil sacrifices and offerings, or a homicidal act of sorcery. In exchange, the demon declares she will fulfil their material desires in this world, and make them happy after their death. But for a demon to be able to appear a dead host is needed"

Apparently, the cult has to subject themselves completely to the demon's will, to pray to her, to do her every whim, to follow only the will of the demon to enjoy material wealth and riches in abundance.

in the hands of the Devil they vow obedience and subjection; they pay him homage and vassalage… to observe none of the divine precepts, to do no good work, but to obey the Demon alone and, to attend diligently the nightly conventicles.

The coven/cabal are then expected to do all they can to bring others to partake in sexual liaisons with the demon.

they promise to strive with all their power, for the enlistment of other males and females in the service of the Demon.

The demon, or Succubus, can also have sex with a man who is in no way connected to an evil religious cult, sect or coven. She is then just a passionate lover, with only one desire: the carnal possession of one she loves (the victim). There are examples of this in history.

Alan threw the book down in horror and then realised this was disrespectful to Cornelia and Bella, who only had his best interests at heart in going to the trouble to send him that book. They knew the content would be worrying and distasteful to him, but they had their reasons. He picked the book up again and skipped a few pages, to come across another significant section:

"French nineteenth century novelist and art critic Joris-Karl Huysmans, also a significant part of the history of the succubus. Some of Huysman's work was considered at the time to verge on blasphemy, especially his novel 'La Bas'.

But late in life Huysmans turned away from the 'dark side', by converting to Catholicism. In the early stages of his conversion, he had "a powerful and singular experience". In 1892, he was staying at a monastery called La Trappe.

Robert Baldick, his biographer, describes one very significant night there:

Again and again, he awoke from some dreadful nightmare, trembling with fear and convinced that he had just been visited by just such a succubus as he had described in his study of Satanism. As he later explained in En Route, these were no ordinary nightmares.

Then Alan read the specific autobiographical passage that Huysmans described in his novel En Route:"

"It was not at all that involuntary and commonplace act, that vision which is blotted out just at the moment when the sleeper clasps an amorous form in a passionate embrace. It happened as in nature, differing only in degree; it was long and complete, accompanied by every prelude, every detail, every sensation, and the orgasm occurred with a singularly painful acuteness, an incredible spasm."

Stringfield then states quite clearly: "From that moment on, Huysmans was unable to have sex with anyone again. He became impotent."
Alan's face turned white.

Chapter 9

For Alan's last week, before taking time out to be with the family, Alan and Gary were given the 'pass the parcel' brief. It was called that because, when you win, you open up the package and what you find is a metaphorical pile of steaming dog shit. The task was to create a new campaign, across all media, for a huge disinfectant brand. The job was actually worth millions of dollars to the agency, but it was a creative black hole. The client had no idea what they were doing or what they wanted, although they were happy to pay for all the man-hours that were going into it. The agency didn't mind, one bit, because the job was a big, fat cash cow. But it was also depressing, especially for creative people who wanted to do exciting work that was worthwhile. On that Monday, when Alan told Gary he was taking the afternoon off to pick up a few things for the boys, Gary said he didn't blame him.

"Sure. No worries. I might take the morning off tomorrow," he gave Alan a wink, "to see the dentist, if you know what I mean."

Alan laughed.

But what Gary didn't know was that Alan was going off to meet Robert Stringfield at his apartment on 61st St. The snow was still falling hard as he walked along Fifth Avenue, alongside the park. Despite wearing a thick ski jumper, his black puffa jacket, beige, brush cotton pants with long johns underneath, black Timberland boots and a thick, black woolly hat, he was bitterly cold, with the strong headwind. It was a relief to arrive at the massive metal awning of the tall, 1970s apartment building, on the corner of 61st Street. The doorman was a stocky, short, middle-aged, suntanned fellow, in a long, thick black coat, with matching flat cap, and looked like he could have been a driver for a sheik. He held the glass door open for Alan. The lobby was enormous, and had the feel of a Mausoleum, with grey granite walls. A small, much younger guy, with jet-black hair and a black uniform, minus the coat and flat cap sat behind a long, slab of dark stone. He extracted his gaze from the sports pages of the Post, to look up at Alan. Alan asked for Robert Stringfield and gave his name.

The guy stood up. "No problem, sir," he said. "Please come this way."

He escorted Alan to the elevator, located behind the large ornate, cast-iron grill, the sort you get outside the grounds of stately homes.

On the tenth floor Alan took off his gloves and stepped into a spacious granite hallway. A tall, well-built figure in a well cut, single-breasted suit was waiting there for him. It was hard to tell if the fellow was blonde or if his hair was going white. He reminded Alan very much of Lee Marvin. Despite being so relaxed, and welcoming, there was something about those steel grey eyes that told Alan he was looking into the face of a killer.

"Robert Stringfield," he said, smiling and holding out his hand.

"Thanks for taking the time to see me," said Alan.

"My pleasure. Any friend of Cornelia's is a friend of mine. Come on in."

Robert asked Alan if he wouldn't mind leaving his slush-covered boots in the hallway and helped him off with his snow-flecked jacket. A small, white-haired woman drifted out from a small room that was clearly an art studio. She was probably in her seventies, yet she dressed young, in fitted blue jeans and a loose woollen ski sweater. She reminded Alan of Catherine Hepburn in her later years: high cheekbones, flashing eyes and a very dignified posture. "Alan, isn't it?"

"That's me."

She wiped blue paint from her fingers with a heavily stained rag as she spoke.

"Cornelia and Bella have said so many nice things about you."

Alan laughed. "Don't believe a word of it."

She jogged him playfully with her elbow, as if she'd known him for years.

Behind her shoulder he saw a small, framed photo of her with a red silk scarf wrapped around her head. Alan pointed to it.

"That's a great photo," he said. "Bella was telling me about that scarf."

"Oh yes, I wore that for nearly a year after my radio therapy.

When we went to England, I had just completed my last session of radiotherapy. Robert was doing his first lecturing for the Bell & Candle lectures, organized by Cornelia in London. We stayed in

258

Cornelia's house in the country. Bella was still a schoolgirl at the time. Such a lovely, sensitive and intelligent child. But I adore Cornelia too. They're a great team."

Alan wondered what kind of team she meant.

"What will you have - coffee, tea? Being an Englishman you'll want Assam or Earl Grey, surely?"

"Oh no. Coffee please. Black. No sugar. Dark as the night.

Robert led him into the main lounge, which was really an extension of the front hall. The apartment was spacious and modern with a series of large windows at the far end facing Central Park. Below the traffic had ground to a standstill. A big, black, cloud was expanding slowly from Harlem, and would inevitably smother the sky. Snow was still falling, but more slowly now.

"Incoming guys!"

They both turned around to see Isobel coming down the two steps with a tray of drinks.

"Here we go guys. Coffee blacker than a coal miner's T-shirt, a pot of breakfast tea for his lordship, and home-made ginger cookies."

"Oh, ginger biscuits – my favourite." said Alan.

"Good. But I'd hurry up and tuck into the cookies before Robert pigs out on them."

She set the tray down on the table, and hurried back to her painting. Robert and Alan then came over to sit down. There was a black leather sofa on the left, and a green armchair facing it on the right, with a coffee table in between. Robert directed Alan to the sofa and sat facing him.

"So, you've been reading my book on demonology," he said. "Are you enjoying it."

Alan almost spat out a mouthful of coffee.

"Kfff. Excuse me. I'm certainly impressed with the writing and the research. It's not the sort of subject matter I would normally read, you understand, but I... you know... I've have had to take an interest in the subject, for my own good."

Robert shrugged. "Of course."

Alan continued, still with a hint of nervousness. "Some of what you wrote really struck a chord. I mean, that Huysmans fellow. Did... I mean, did he really go through all of that, you know... when he was in that monastery?"

Robert leaned back into his seat, spread his fingers into a makeshift comb, and then pushed them through his mop of white hair.

"Well yes, he was seduced by a succubus. He had full sex with her, leading to orgasm for both him – and more significantly - the demon. It's all documented."

Alan hung onto every word with horror. But Robert spoke as if he was telling a funny anecdote from his holiday travels.

"Of course, Huysmans had been a bit of a rogue, dabbling in all sorts of dark stuff, perversions and so on. Ironically, he was edging away from all that, towards Christianity, just before that – incident."

"And after that?"

"He was impotent."

Alan sat back and sighed. Robert leaned forward and dipped a biscuit in his tea, taking a bite, then started to speak while he was eating.

"The succubus is a demon." He stopped to take a sip of coffee to moisten his mouth, and then swallow. There was a kind of breathlessness in his measured tone when he continued. "She's neither corporeal nor imaginary. She lies waiting and hiding. Though dead, she is amazingly alive. You feel her touching you. She takes from you. She enriches herself. And when she leaves, you are less than you were before."

Neither of them said anything for a while. Alan looked at the wall behind Robert, and he could swear the large, framed painting was a genuine Egon Schiele. To the side was a small sculpture on a plinth that looked like the work of the Futurist, Umberto Boccioni. It allowed him to slow the pace of his thinking, which had been rapid and anarchic.

"Is it true, he said, "that you worked for the CIA?"

Robert laughed. "My word, those little witches Cornelia and Bella are going to get me into deep trouble. I took a security oath you know."

"Sorry."

"Not your fault. But in a sense, yes, I was part of team carrying out specialist work. It was part of a very hush-hush project in collaboration with the Stanford Research Institute in parapsychology. Isobel was there too, that's where we met. But we weren't doing the same kind of work."

"So, am I allowed to ask you what you did?"

Robert knitted his fingers together, and then pushed them out causing the bones to crack."

We sat in a darkened room in a basement in Langley and made observations."

"That's it?"

"That's it."

"So you didn't do anything sinister or unethical."

He laughed. "No. Neither Isobel nor I did anything of the sort. But there were a bunch of guys in the StarChild set up that kept themselves very much to themselves. We had an idea that they were up to some dark stuff: very dark stuff."

"Really?"

"I actually got to know one of them, and by socialising in that way we were breaking strict protocol. I learned enough from him to know the work he was doing was sending him over the edge, bigtime. He couldn't come to terms with what they made him do, but I am not at liberty to say any more about that.

"Alan winced, cleared his throat and then asked, "So what kind of observations did you make from that basement? Am I allowed to ask that, at least?"

Robert thought for a moment, took out a cigarette, lit it and blew out a plume of smoke.

"In the late 70s," he said, "we identified a Soviet Typhoon-class submarine that was under construction, before any of our field agents or military knew it even existed."

"You did all that by sitting in a basement in Virginia?"

Robert nodded, and continued, "During the SADF pullout from Angola some nuclear weapons ended up in the hands of fanatical, right-wing Afrikaners in the South African Defense Force. We found their exact location in Zululand, and they were eventually recovered safely."

Alan looked baffled. "So, the CIA really invested in an ESP type thing that worked?"

"I think that's enough about me. Now tell us about your problem. That's why you're here, isn't it?"

Alan shook his head, in an attempt to assimilate what he had just heard, but without success. He settled for bracketing it to the back of his mind for later consideration. Eventually, he went on to describe, as best he could, the crisis he had been going through, starting with the shadow of a girl flitting by in the bathroom that he only saw it from the corner of his eye, after which he was left with the distinct feeling that he had been kissed fully on the lips, even though there was no one to be seen: only a waft of scented air. He couldn't understand how he could be affected by that moment so intensely, from this vague presence of a woman, just a shadow, and yet she had set him on fire. He went on to describe the night of restless, broken sleep, and the partial manifestation of a naked woman in the darkness, followed by more broken sleep, and the full appearance of the beautiful naked woman in the room, lit by a strange, penumbral, green glow. He was totally paralysed as she walked seductively towards the end of the bed, then reached it and climbed smoothly onto the mattress, crawling towards him on all fours, like a she-wolf. Eventually she was propping herself over him, poised, and then she stared into his eyes as she lowered her torso so that her breasts pressed onto his heaving chest.

Alan described his horror at that moment, and also his desire.

Robert listened passively, occasionally pouring himself some more tea. When Alan was done, Robert simply nodded.

"I see," he said. "Can you explain to me what you felt her source of her power was?"

Alan went wide-eyed with confusion. "Sorry? I don't know what you mean."

"No. Of course, that's a difficult question for you to answer."

The day was fading leaving a soft, vaguely inadequate, melancholy blue glow in the room. Robert went over to the window to get a closer look. The lights were coming up in the buildings on the other side of the park. He looked out for a few seconds as Alan watched him, this big powerful figure, who was so difficult to fathom. Robert took the drawstring, obviously thinking about lowering the blinds, and then he changed his mind to come back to his armchair.

"And why do you think all this is happening to you?"

Alan's eyes were moistening, despite his best efforts. He wiped them with his sleeve. "I have no idea," he said.

"Did you have any unusual, slightly disturbing experiences before all that? Think about that for a minute. It could be a sudden oppressive mood clouding your thoughts, or a sequence of dreams?"

Alan interrupted him. "Yes. There was a particular dream. Horrible.

"Ah! Now we're getting somewhere. Start from the beginning."

Alan described the nightmare, which began with him waiting outside the agency, and although it was day, everything was in deep shadow. There was a sense of sinister and malignant intent, oppressiveness and evil. The crowds of people on the streets, and then the coming of the yellow truck – the rumbling, getting louder and the strange, leering couple with red spotted faces, like measles, and all those people with red, spotted faces too.

"Describe this strange couple."

"They're in their late fifties to mid-sixties, I think. She's sort of skinny, with glasses and curly, light-coloured hair. He's medium height, but stocky and balding at the front, with a big leering smile. Horrible."

"Any idea who they might be?" said Robert.

"To be honest, I've wracked my mind to try and work that out for myself. I can't connect them with anyone."

"I need you to let me know if you come across any signs of who these people might be. It could be very important."

"Sure. I can do that."

Although Alan felt emotionally drained, he was also more relaxed now. The sky had darkened and a few rogue snowflakes were blowing around, while ore lights had come on in the buildings across the park.

At that moment Isobel came out of her studio to ask if the guys wanted to drink anything a bit stronger. Alan said a glass of bourbon with ice would go down nicely. Alan opted for a brandy.

She came back with the drinks and cleared away the empties. Alan asked her about the painting. "Oh yes, it's Egon Schiele. It was passed on to me from my grandmother in Austria."

"Wow. I love his work. Him and Klimt."

"Oh yes. Wonderful work."

"And the sculpture?"

"Boccioni."

Alan took a deep breath, in awe and respect. "Christ."

"I've got this show coming up in a gallery downtown. Would you like me to send you an invite?"

Alan perked up. "That would be great, Isobel. Thank you. Is it a one-man show?"

"No. It will be a one *woman* show."

Alan laughed. "Of course.

And with that she left.

Robert took a sip of his brandy and said, "The girls, I mean, Cornelia and her daughter, tell me that they've cast a rather clever little spell, that will help to protect you from your nemesis, but it won't last long. The succubus - which I think is what we are dealing with here - will break through. The same spell will never work again. That's why it's good you are going to be away from that place when your family comes. While you are away, I would like to be able to see what we can discover about her. Is that OK with you?"

"Uh... in the apartment, you mean?"

"Yes. Would you mind if Isobel and I look around?"

"Yes, of course." He fumbled around in his pockets and took out a set of keys and pulled two of them off from a ring. He put them on the coffee table. These are my spares. I was going to give them to Jenny, but I can get a couple more cut."

Robert left them where they were.

"Good. Now can you tell me something about the history of your building?"

"Not that much really. It was built in the mid-nineteenth century. Red brick. It used to be a sewing machine factory."

"Have any of the other tenants said anything about hauntings, or strange stuff going on?"

"No, nothing. I'm on speaking terms with a couple of people on my floor, an old lady and a middle-aged woman whose husband works during the day. No one has mentioned anything like that to me."

"And do you know anything about the owners of your apartment?"

"No. I don't even know their names. We got the flat through a realty company and the contract is through them. The realty guy told me in passing that one of them is an antique restorer. He's on a three-year sabbatical in Italy with his boyfriend, who I think works in the clothing industry. That's all I know."

"Fine. Well I think we have enough to be getting on with. I'm sure you're exhausted by my interrogation."

Alan stood up and laughed. "Not at all. Thank you for your time. They walked over to the door, where Robert helped Alan with his jacket.

Before stepping into the elevator Alan turned to Robert and said:

"So, uh, I guess you've had plenty of experience of dealing with sexual demons, etcetera?"

Robert puffed out his lips and shook his head.

"No. My interest in the subject has been purely academic."

Alan nodded. "Oh."

Chapter 10

Having had his hopes raised by Cornelia and Bella, Alan went back to feeling despondent after his meeting with Robert. The only thing Robert had achieved was to let him know exactly what danger he was facing. Part of him was annoyed with Cornelia and Bella for pointing him in Robert's direction. But maybe there wasn't anything that anyone could do. Cornelia and Bella had – apparently – given him a few days grace from another succubus attack. He didn't really know quite what to think about that. Anyway, he'd given the keys to Stringfield, and there was no point asking for them back. Not that he had any expectations of anything coming from that.

The next day, he was understandably in a sour mood when he went to work to finish off the poster concepts that Gary and he had come up with for that dreaded disinfectant client. The concept was really quite pleasing, but there was no doubt in either of their minds that it would be rejected. They were just going through the motions. It was his last day before going to Steve's, and then Gary would be left to work on the campaign himself. When he came into the office, he set down his coffee, and as he began to take out equipment from his bag, he inadvertently pulled out the book on Demoniality and left it on the desk. Gary grabbed it, as Alan looked on in surprise.

"Ha! I didn't know you were into this," said Gary. "How the fuck do you know anything about Robert Stringfield? The occult isn't your bag."

Alan snatched the book away from him. "No. But this is, and my book goes into it."

"Wooo. That was intense."

"Anyway, what's it to you?"

"A lot. I interviewed him a few years back, when I was working at the Village Voice. That's one of the books they gave me for research. Powerful stuff, and very scary... if it's true."

Alan tried to focus the conversation away from the supernatural. "Ha! You worked for the Voice? I didn't know you were that far left."

"Easy tiger. You know me better than that. I did it for the money. Kept my head down and avoided any discussion about politics."

"I guess you would."

"I wasn't out of university that long, and we were doing this filler piece about hauntings in SoHo. They pointed me in the direction of this Stringfield guy, because he's an authority on anything supernatural. I have to say he turned out to be a very decent and intelligent guy. We ended up having a few beers. His wife, Isobel, she's a lovely lady. Comes from one of the older banking families. They live in this amazing pad over on the Upper East Side."

"So, you don't think he's a crank?"

"No way. He's a very serious guy. But why the hell are you reading that book?"

Chapter 11

It was a sunny morning, and it wasn't snowing any more. Jenny and the boys would be at the airport in a couple of hours, and before making coffee, Alan decided to shave. He was half done when he leaned forward to get a closer look at his chin. But when he straightened up there was a woman's face right next to his. Her big brown eyes peered through strands of dark brown hair. He couldn't see her nose and mouth. The sight startled him so he pushed too hard on the blade, scooping out a slice of skin. A small river of blood flowed onto his white dressing gown. He turned around furiously. There was no one there: so much for Cornelia and Bella's protective enchantment.

At JFK Arrivals Alan had a Band Aid on his chin and a pain in his neck. He soon found out that the earlier heavy snowfall was delaying all incoming flights. He found himself staring piously at the main airport monitor. It was like taking High Mass. No new information was filtering through. He went to one of the restaurants and took the opportunity to sit down and have a full breakfast, with endless refills of coffee.

But he was in no mood for all this uncertainty and waiting, not after the sleepless night he'd had. Still, at least it was demon free, and all that was happening was that he was trying to make sense of stuff.

It made a big difference to Alan that Gary respected the work of Robert Springfield. Now he

271

was more reassured that maybe Stringfield was someone who could actually help him out with this demon problem - and maybe his sex life will be saved. But who for? He thought of Juliette again, cooking breakfast with an apron thrown over her bra and panties, and then he squinted hard and immediately tried to banish the thought. Jason was right. Jenny and the boys were his life. Messing around with a pretty undergraduate was not the way forward. Just then there was an announcement: BA flight 714 was due to land at 20.36. Thank fuck for that, he thought.

After an inordinate amount of time, people started to flow out of arrivals. He noticed a small man in a brown suit being followed by his wife and three kids, dragging their cases behind them. More people followed, in a steadily increasing stream. Alan decided to entertain himself by picking out all the bored passengers who were having to head straight to work. This only occupied him for a short time, and once again he found himself thinking of Juliette and how badly he'd treated her.

Just then there was a tug at his elbow and he realised that little Jack was standing there in his duffel coat, ski jumper and yellow wellington boots. He was holding up a piece of paper with wax crayon scrawls on it and his nose was running.

He crouched down, took the drawing, kissed his eldest son and lifted him up. Jenny and Simon walked towards him among the throng now emerging from immigration. Her short blonde,

272

pixie-cut hair was brushed to one side, which emphasised the soft curves and beauty of her face. She was pushing a luggage trolley and holding Simon in her left arm who was wearing his superman pyjamas under his blue coat and hugging his mummy koala bear-style while sucking his thumb.

As she came close, he kissed her and said, "Hello love. Gosh. You look tired."

She gave him a soft, warm smile that filled him to the ears with guilt.

"You've lost weight," she replied. "What happened to your love of the great American breakfast?"

"Ha! No, that hasn't gone away. It's just the stresses and strains of the advertising business that are chipping away at me.

"Talking of stresses and strains, you should try travelling with these two on a plane for eight hours. I think everyone in business class will be asking for a refund. Here, can you take this one too?"

"If you take this," he said. Handing her the drawing. She let go of the trolley and took it, then leaned forward so he could scoop Simon off her back with his free arm. Now he was carrying both the boys.

Her three-quarter length, grey herringbone coat was open, revealing a grey green fine-weave sweater, tan-coloured, slim-fit jeans and brown Chelsea boots.

Shall we pick up some coffee and drinks or something?" he said.

"I'm shattered," she sighed. "First thing I need to do is get some sleep. Can you handle the boys for a couple of hours when we get to the apartment?"

"I guess so, but don't they need some sleep too?"

"Oh, they're much too excited for that. Maybe later." She smiled. "I really have missed you… but not your snoring."

"Right, well… I'll try not to breath tonight."

She shook her head, and gave him a sideways look. "Hey, guess what? Dorothy and Ralph next door are selling up and moving to Highgate. He's just had the most ridiculous bonus and pay rise."

"Fuck, why didn't I ever get into banking?"

Because you're crap at maths, remember?

"How could I forget?"

Jenny pointed to the Band-Aid on his chin. "What've you done to your face?"

"I was in such a hurry to get ready for you that…"

"Oh. So, it's my fault, is it?" she joked."

"Isn't everything?"

"They were both laughing now.

"Hey Dad," said Jack, as they headed towards exit doors. "You should've seen this great big robot. He could fly into space, and he blew up like this," he held out his arms, "POOOOOM!"

Alan looked at Jenny for enlightenment.

He saw "The Iron Giant" on the plane," she said, "but he actual…"

"YEEEE-OWWW!" yelled Alan.

Simon was pushing his finger onto the sticking plaster on Alan's chin. "What the fuck?"

"Language," said Jenny, as Simon burst into tears, and started to take deep breaths between each cry, attracting the attention of nearly everyone in Arrivals.

"Jenny snatched Simon away from him. "What the hell's the matter with you?" she hissed.

"It hurts," he said, lowering Jack to the floor. Jack became quiet and confused as she ushered him to her side. A pear-shaped Mexican man and his tall wife looked at him accusingly.

"Look,' said Alan, in his defence, showing her a dab of blood on his finger, after having touched the offending plaster. "It's starting to bleed again…"

"Let's get away from here," she hissed. "I'm not enjoying being the centre of attention."

They walked briskly towards the exit now, Alan pushing the trolley and Jenny carrying Simon, with Jack walking alongside her.

Once they were through the sliding doors Jenny asked them all to stop, so she could take the pushchair off the trolley and set it up for Simon. It seemed like an eternity before they reached the car park. Jenny got into the back of the Chrysler, with Simon and Jack, who she strapped into the kiddie seats. They set off without anyone saying a word. Alan felt more like a taxi driver than a husband and father.

The insipid sun was losing its battle with the stern winter sky, and the widely spaced out and battered warehouses of Queens didn't exactly soften the mood. Jenny told Simon not to be upset. "Daddy was just a little bit tired. He really does love you."

Simon sniffed, in reply.

"Yes. Daddy's very sorry, baby," said Alan.

Simon didn't respond. Jenny diffused the tension a little by telling the boys they could watch a Disney video before going to bed. Alan could see Simon trying to hide a smile. Jack finally perked up and asked if he could plug his DS in when they got home.

Alan had been waiting at the airport for hours, because of the flight delays, and it was almost dark, when they pulled up outside the apartment block.

Simon started to perk up. Jack was brimming with energy too.

Jenny went to the bathroom, to freshen up, while Alan put on *One Hundred and One Dalmatians,* and sat with the boys. Eventually they started to drop off, and Jenny came in bleary eyed to take them to their brand-new bedroom.

Alan, started to prepare the lasagne. He was mixing up the salad when he heard a sigh from behind him, and some arms hugging him from behind at the waist. He tensed up in anticipation.

"Hey relax," said Jenny. He turned around to kiss her. "Oh, sorry Jen. You startled me."

"Mm. Smells good, she said," letting him free.

Her warmth had felt good.

"You mean my after shave or the cooking?"

The kitchen spotlights highlighted her doe eyes. She had such a sad face just then, but also a passionate mouth. She kissed him softly, and then again – longer and harder. When she pulled back, she looked at him longingly and said,

"It's the lasagne."

There was a brief pause, and then he pretended to be angry, but he became serious for a moment.

"Jen. I'm really sorry fort getting mad at Simon in the airport."

She closed her eyes, as if not wanting to even think about it.

"Let's forget supper," she said, "and go to bed."

"Aren't you hungry?"

Her voice was soft and deep. "We can eat later."

Jenny went into the bedroom first, while he took the food out of the oven and covered it up. When he arrived, she was already naked under the covers. The sideways glance she often did through half-closed eyes never ceased to work its wonders on him. He stripped off and got in with her.

They lay on top of the duvet afterwards and he stroked her goose pimpled, milk white body while they chatted. He missed her more than he realised.

"You've done well to find this place," she said. "It's clean and classic and… you know, it still has a sort of modern feel about it too. If your job works out, maybe we should stay here."

"Those guys who own the place are moving back in two years. Remember?"

She made a sour face. "Shame that. I think I could really get to like it here."

He let out a little laugh. "Let's just wait and see how things pan out at the agency. I mean, you never know what's around the corner."

Leaning on her elbows, she hauled herself up a little, and sucked in her lips before saying,

"Alan, is there something you're not telling me? Because if you've got any doubts about job security now, what the hell are me and the boys doing here?"

"No, no. I don't mean anything like that. It's just that, you know, bosses come, bosses go, jobs change, opportunities arise… Look at Nick."

Nick was his old copywriter in London. Alan continued. "He went off to Hong Kong as a head of Copy, ostensibly for a year, but ended up being headhunted by TBWA Paris. He's Creative Director there now. Living in a plush apartment in the 16th Arrondissement and earning a fortune."

"Why doesn't that happen to you?"

"Well it sort of is, isn't it? Look. We're in New York. And you don't get to be creative director overnight. Give me some slack."

She stayed in the same position and thought for a bit, while Alan considered how her nipples were like dark flying saucers landing on snow-covered hills. Suddenly she sat up and grabbed her kimono.

"I'm starving. Are you going to get that food ready?"

They ate in their dressing gowns in the lounge, and then watched a bit of TV before going back to bed. He told her that Fiona and Gary were looking forward to seeing her and the boys the next day.

That made her worry about what she would wear. Alan joined her soon after he cleared up the dishes. She was already in a deep sleep by the time he went to bed. But when he got in, his brain was running overtime. He couldn't stop himself worrying. If that crazy, sexually rabid woman were to emerge out of the shadows again and find Jenny there beside him in bed, who knows what she would do? But Robert did say that Cornelia and Bella's charm would hold her off for a bit. He also read in Robert's book that a succubus generally chooses to appear only to her chosen victim, and some experts have said that the victim needs to have some special sensitivities, or in latter day lingo, psychic abilities, to see her. But that didn't explain how he could see her, because there was nothing psychic about him. Anyway, there was no sign of her.

Jenny was up bright and early. The first thing she did was to check to see if the boys were still asleep, which they were. Then she went for a shower, and when she came out Alan sat up and admired her beautifully varnished, red toenails as she towelled herself.

"I'll get breakfast together," she said. "What do you fancy?"

"Maybe just some toast and a grapefruit. I can make the coffee, if you like."

"OK. I'll go and get the boys up. I don't want them over sleeping."

When Jenny had just put on her kimono, the door opened slowly and Simon walked in his oversize pyjamas, dragging his teddy bear and sucking his thumb, which he pulled out just to say, "I'm hungry."

"Hi honey!" said Jenny, whisking him up. "Mummy is just going to make you some breakfast."

He scratched his nose and pulled his thumb and said with a very earnest expression. "Soldiers." Then the thumb went back.

"Great." She turned to Alan. "Do we have any eggs?"

"Yup. Fresh bread too."

Jenny sat him down on the bed next to Alan. "You stay and have cuddles with daddy, and I'll bring you in when your egg and toast is ready."

"OK."

When she left the room, he gave Alan a furtive glance with his big blue eyes, pulled his thumb out and said, "Daddy? Who was that shiny green lady in my bedroom last night?"

Chapter 12

"You are such a clever boy, and when we get to Cold Spring, daddy's going to buy you a big ice cream, with a chocolate in it and lots of syrup. How does that sound."

"Wow," said Simon, all wide eyed.

"Now, can you tell daddy what this lady was wearing – the one you saw last night? Or... maybe she wasn't wearing anything at all?"

Simon leaned back and gave him a look of complete disapproval.

"Don't be silly daddy. Of course, she was wearing clothes."

"Oh yes. What was I thinking?" He tried to hide his relief.

Alan wiped Simon's eyes and asked him to blow his nose in a tissue he handed him. He did that and then handed it back to his dad absent-mindedly, and went back to sucking his thumb. But very quickly he withdrew it.

"Clever boy," said Alan. "What happened next?"

He shook his head. "Nothing."

"Right. What did Jack say?"

"Nothing. He was asleep."

"Oh yes." Alan ruffled his hair affectionately.

"Can daddy ask one more thing?"

"Can I have a really, really big ice cream?"

"Of course."

Simon nodded, with a pretend sadness.

"Could you move?"

"What do you mean daddy?"

"Like… could you move around?"

"Well… I sat up and watched her, didn't I?"

Alan picked him up and kissed him on the forehead.

"Listen sweetheart. I don't think we should tell mummy about all this. She might think we have burglars or something and then she'd start worrying. We don't want that, do we?"

He looked to one side for a moment then faced his dad again.

"Are there lady burgule-lars?" he asked with a look of profound concern.

"Uh, could be."

"Oh."

"Maybe the lady you saw lives along the hallway and she got a bit lost."

"Uh-huh."

"Anyway, let's just keep this to ourselves, shall we?"

Simon nodded thoughtfully.

Alan was now desperate to find out what this all meant, the demon's appearance to Simon. He had to call Robert Stringfield to let him know what happened, but not with Jenny around. When he took Simon into the lounge Jenny was laying out the plates and cutlery. He put the boy into his new highchair, next to Jack.

"I'm going to nip out to get a newspaper and some French bread," he said.

"OK. But be quick - the bacon's nearly done."

"Sure!"

The cold air sharpened his thoughts. He took a couple of deep breaths, and sighed, watching the vapour leave his mouth. There was a call phone in the Italian coffee bar, next to the bookshop on Court. He made his way there and dialled Robert's number at the phone in the Italian coffee bar. What he couldn't know was that Robert and Isobel were walking downtown for brunch. They were going to kill enough time for Alan and his family to quit the apartment for their break in Cold Spring then they would head over to the apartment in Brooklyn to carry out their investigation. Alan was frustrated when he heard the phone go to answerphone. He didn't feel right about leaving a message, so he had to think fast. It occurred to him that Cornelia and Bella might be able to help. He dialled them at the Bell and Candle, and Bella answered.

"Listen, things are bad," he said. "I have to be quick. Jenny doesn't know I'm calling. I'm using a café phone."

"Are you calling to tell me you love me?"

"Bella, please. This is serious."

"OK. Tell me."

"I don't know how to put this but – that demon, the succubus, appeared to Simon, my youngest son, last night, in the boys' bedroom. Simon is a smart kid. He described her pretty well. He said he was sitting up and looking at her for a while. But it was different from my experiences. For a start, she wasn't naked."

"Shit. Mum and I didn't think about that. We set up the charm to protect you, not your family. He must be gifted, like you, if he can see her."

"Gifted? What kind of a gift is that?"

"Never mind. She is harmless to him. There's nothing he can do for her. She's trying to break through the charm, that's all."

"Are you sure?"

"Honestly Alan, I can't emphasis this enough. Robert will get to the heart of your problem. By the time you get back to your apartment in Brooklyn, there will be no demon or succubus to terrorise you."

Alan desperately wanted to believe Bella, but part of him was deeply sceptical. Yet since he was a student, Cornelia and Bella had, for some reason, taken his spiritual and material well-being to heart from the moment he walked into their occult bookshop to ask a few questions about his friend Jason, possibly being a reincarnation of the great Augustus John. That issue was never resolved, but they did offer him a great deal of information and time. He considered them to be genuine friends ever since. On that basis, he would accept Bella's assurances, for now.

When he got back to the apartment, Jenny and the boys were already having breakfast. "What took you?" said Jenny.

"There was a queue in the bakery," he said.

"Yours is in the oven," said Jenny, as she fed Simon with a spoon. "I made the coffee too."

By eleven o'clock the kids were strapped in the back of the car, and Alan had put all their luggage in the boot. They left before midday, and it took a good half hour just to get across the water and out of Manhattan.

When they set off, he felt tired from lack of sleep and worry. But by the time they were driving through Westchester, he thought how good it felt to be in the countryside, and it perked him up considerably. The sky was pale blue-grey, except for a glowing patch of yellow to the right. On one narrow stretch of road the ploughs hadn't done their work, so Alan couldn't do more than twenty. At one point they had to stop because Simon was getting restless. So, Jenny got into the back next to him with his head resting on her arm, while she read him The Tiger Who Came to Tea. Jack, meanwhile, was engrossed with his Gameboy.

When they finally arrived, Alan had to park on the road, because Steve's driveway was knee deep with snow. Jenny thought the place looked really sweet, 'like the house in *The Waltons*, she said. It was, being a small, white clapperboard structure, surrounded by snow-covered pine trees and a good few other trees that had shed their leaves weeks ago. The other houses were a fair distance from each other, and set back, so you could only see the gables. Alan started to unload the car, while Jenny got the boys out.

Although they were only fifty miles from Manhattan, he felt safe here, from you know what. He actually dreaded having to go back to the Brooklyn apartment. If there was only to be some way, he could convince Jenny they should move to another place, his worries would be solved. He felt a playful kick behind the knee.

"What are you waiting for, Christmas?" said Jenny. She was standing beside him with the boys at the front door.

"Sorry love," he said, as he put the bags down and fumbled for the keys.

As soon as they entered the place his mood brightened. Jenny took to it immediately too. Considering Steve was an unreconstructed modernist, he was surprised by just how traditional the style of the layout and furnishings was. And it let in plenty of natural light, especially in the hallway and lounge. Jack ran into the lounge t and flung himself onto the Red Indian rug by the hearth. Within seconds Simon jumped onto him and they were rolling around like pigs in mud.

The ground floor had a sort of captain's cabin feel about it, with pale green, wood slat walls, a white wooden ceiling, brown cross beams and narrow and white painted floorboards. Jenny went to the still wrestling boys, shaking her head in mock despair. Alan raised his eyebrows and then pointed upstairs with his chin.

He carried the bags up to the pink, main bedroom room, where he discovered there was a complex antique quilt covering the bed. On the walls were framed collections of pressed wild flowers, along with a black and white print of a nineteenth century whaling vessel. The bedside cabinet was home to a dozen or so embossed hardcover books by Nathaniel Hawthorne and Emerson. There was obviously another side to Steve he never knew.

He opened up one of the cases and was startled by a tap on the window. He turned around to see a branch beating against the glass. The wind must've been stronger than he thought. He went to take a better look at the view across the Hudson Valley. The luminous sky shone through the ice-coated, bare branches, making them collectively glow, like a giant spider's web. Through a gap between the firs, he could see the long line of rocky, snow-covered hills on the other side of the frozen river, when something caught his attention. A tiny, dark figure was walking slowly on the ice. Because the window glass was ancient, and uneven in thickness, there was some rippling and distortion, so he wasn't sure if he was looking at a fleck of dirt on the glass. Then he realised that there was actually something, or someone, walking on the ice. That was a very dangerous thing to do. The ice was definitely not very thick, and was very liable to crack. Perhaps it was a fox, he thought. Whatever it was, it stopped, becoming a smudge on a wintery scene, before dissolving away. Almost immediately he had an overwhelming foreboding: a sudden fogginess clouded his every thought, and when he tried to focus, he was left with nothing but worry and confusion. A dark mood was about to set in, that was interrupted by Jenny's voice.

"Are you done here?" she said.

He turned to find her at the door holding a grumpy Simon, with Jack standing expectantly at her side.

"These two fellas need to expend some energy."

"Sorry, I was miles away," said Alan.

"Daddy," said Jack. "We don't want no ice cream now. It's too cold."

"That's very sensible, Jack. We'll go out into town and sit down somewhere to have a nice hot chocolate with marshmallows. How does that sound?"

They both yelled together, "Yaaaay!"

Walking along the riverside, they came to a Victorian gazebo. To the right of that, a part of the pathway branched off inland, slipping underneath the railway track, towards Main Street, which is where they headed. It was a quirky small stretch of road made up of two rows of charming small-town stores, with wooden verandas and brass door handles. They visited a swell stocked, no nonsense general goods store that sold Levis 501s at an excellent price. There was even a shop that had nothing but Scottish goods, including tartan scarves and ties, Highland Whiskies of various varieties and prices, and of course haggis. A little further on was an 'English' shop that sold Marmite, marmalade, pale ale, Toby jugs, union jack mugs, and Lipton's Tea.

"I don't know anyone in England that drinks Lipton's Tea," said Jenny.

To keep his promise, they went into a cosy tearoom for hot chocolate. It was run by a friendly, East European couple in their thirties. There were five tables, all of them covered with charming, gingham waxed tablecloths.

The rest of the day went by fairly uneventfully. They went back to the house, had a rest, and then Alan started rummaging around in Steve's shed where, among the tools and pots he found a toboggan. The boys were really excited when they saw it. He had his work cut out for him then, because he ended up dragging the boys around in it for the next hour in the back garden. It was twilight by the time they went back inside. Jenny fed the kids and then Alan washed them and put their pyjamas on. When they were tucked up in bed and fast asleep Alan put on his coat, and went out onto the veranda. There was virtually no street lighting, and the grouping of fir trees in front of the place was now just a mass of darkness. Jenny put on her woolly hat, jacket and scarf to join him.

There were far more stars out than they'd ever seen before, and lower down in the sky was a gibbous moon. He felt this was an excellent opportunity to broach the subject he'd been thinking about all day.

"Oh, it's beautiful," she said.

"It certainly beats Brooklyn."

She turned to look at him in surprise. "Give the place a chance," she said. "We've only just arrived."

"Em... what do you think of our apartment?" he said, tentatively.

The crescent moon cast enough light to turn her eyes into pools and highlight the dimples in her cheeks. "I love it," she said.

"But don't you feel it's, you know, a bit awkward in shape. You know, with the bedrooms and kitchen all attached directly into that great big lounge like limpets. It seems, well, kind of disconcerting to me."

"Limpets? Where are you going with this? We looked at a dozen places and that was easily the best, maybe not the most affordable, but not the most expensive either. And it's such a great location, with two subways close by, some great shops, you can go running along the river to the Brooklyn Bridge and... I think we're very lucky to have it."

"Well I'm not so sure," he said. Trying to sound assertive. "I think the place is kind of getting to me and, to be honest, I'd like to consider moving."

Her eyes widened, and she opened her mouth a fraction. "Are you crazy?"

"Seriously. Something about it is putting me into a weird frame of mind, and it's affecting my work."

"What? How can the apartment be affecting your work? Sometimes you are so surreal."

"Well... I don't know how to say this, but I think it might be haunted."

"Jesus. What are you on? Haunted by what? Have you actually seen or heard anything strange?"

"Mm, not really. It's just a sort of… feeling."

"Alan. I don't want to hear any more nonsense about this. There's no way we could think of leaving that beautiful apartment. It's perfect for us. And anyway, we can't afford the financial penalties for breaking the lease."

"I'm sure there are ways round that…" he said hesitantly.

"Alan. That's enough. Do you want to go in and eat, or what? I'm hungry."

That was the end of that, then. He was in the hands of Robert Stringfield now. Hopefully, he would deliver.

Chapter 13

McDuff's is an old-style drinking and eating joint on the ground floor of a five-story brick building downtown that has survived the advance of the designer brands that have been invading SoHo. The plain black exterior is straight out of a Hopper painting, and so is the inside, with its mustard embossed wallpaper, black painted columns, and the fleur-de-lis tiled floor. The place features the same type of red chequered tablecloths they used during prohibition. George McDuff ran the place from the time he retired from baseball in the early nineteen-twenties right up to the early eighties. His grandson Liam was in charge now. Liam was built like a tank, but was really just a big softy.

Robert and Isobel were sitting down at one of the tables by the wall, which like all the other walls, was surrounded by framed photographs of the greatest baseball hitters of the twentieth century. Isobel seemed to be staring into space before she finally piped up.

"What the hell am I doing here? Jacob Schulz is having puppies because I haven't delivered enough work, and the opening is only days away. I should be in my studio painting, for Christ's sake. If my show goes wrong, you're gonna get it in the neck, Springfield."

Robert softly banged both his palms on the table and leaned back, waiting for her full attention before he spoke.

"Listen, Izzy. It's really no big deal. I need you for just this one thing. We'll eat here, digest and then make our way across the river to Brooklyn, do our thing and get a cab home. Easy-peasy."

Isobel watched him with deep reservation, uttering only, "Hm".

They sat together quietly for a while, before Isobel said, "Strange that Bella should bother to tell Alan about my recovery from cancer, don't you think?"

Robert shrugged. "Not really. That's how you were when she first saw you, at their house out in the country. She was only a kid then, but she absolutely adored you."

Isobel nodded. "And I her, though she was a strange child. There was something sad about her, I couldn't help but be motherly."

The waitress came to ask if they were ready. They ordered brunch and went back to their discussion.

"What I'm wondering is, where does a succubus come from?" asked Isobel.

"Good question. A Succubus doesn't just come out of thin air. She has to summoned: usually by more than one person - a cabal or a coven, maybe. It involves blasphemous oaths and sacrifices.

"How does that work?"

"The existing texts say that on certain unholy Sabbaths, witches can summon a Succubus for their sexual gratification – and also for the power they offer to any individual that the Succubus will serve. That's when they make sacrifices and offerings to the devil."

"Ugh! What kind of sacrifices?"

"Blood sacrifices. A woman, a child maybe."

"Ugh. Disgusting."

"If we were to find out who was behind it all - we could undo what they've done."

"But why choose Alan as the victim?"

"Hard to say. Maybe he was in the wrong place at the right time."

There was a trio of Wall Street-types at the table next to them who had been laughing like hyenas. Now one of them was kicking-up a fuss with a waitress because they were dissatisfied with their sausages. Robert was going to say something, but Isobel kicked him.

"The Demon has to be summoned by a sacrifice, but after she is summoned, she can choose to uh… copulate with men or women without any need for sacrifices, just because it desires the carnal possession of a certain man or woman."

"You mean because it – or she - fancies them?"

He nodded.

"You know what?" she said. "I was kind of curious about that series of dreams you said he described to you. You know, that couple with the measles?"

"He didn't say they had measles. He said they had red spots on their faces."

"Yeah, yeah. The thing is, what does it all mean?"

"I think those dreams are connected to the demon's appearance. I want to find out who that old couple are, or at least who they represent."

They concentrated on their meals for a while, and then Isobel perked up.

"Look. I'm going to play devil's advocate here, if you'll pardon the irony. Could it be maybe that there is no demon haunting Alan at all, and he's just losing it?"

Alan waited until he had finished chewing a mouthful of steak pie before saying, "You know me, Izzy. I like to play safe. Like these fellas here, I'm like hedging my bets."

One of the bankers looked over when Robert said that. Robert ignored him.

Just then their food arrived. They waited for the waitress to set everything down, including the drinks, and then Robert continued, after supping a bit of his beer.

"Psychologists talk about something called the 'Old Hag phenomenon'. That's when people imagine that some weird creature is visiting them in bed. This thing usually ends up sitting on their chest, making it impossible to move or speak. Some people describe it as a terrifyingly ugly, old woman with demonic or supernatural powers."

"Oh. Is that common?" asked Isobel.

"Not especially," said Robert,

"It's a kind of sleep paralysis, caused by the mind not being fully awake. It can happen when you're hovering between a dream-state and waking. Some people who've been through that think they're being visited by aliens."

"So, Alan could be nuts?"

"I'm not dismissing that possibility. The important thing to remember is that the Succubus –

or whatever you want to call it - did not appear to Alan till he moved into his new apartment. I need to find out as much as I can about that place."

"And what about his apartment, I mean his current landlords? What if they have something to do with all this? Who knows, they could be the leaders of some satanic cult, or whatever."

"Let's not get ahead of ourselves."

"You could make a call to Mitch to do some checking? He could get you some answers, using the company database."

"No. I don't want to get anyone at Langley involved in this. Those days are gone. Whatever I need to find out, I'll do it myself?"

"You are one stubborn son of a bitch."

Chapter 14

As Alan and his family were arriving outside Steve's house in Cold Spring, Robert and Isobel were under the marquee to the main doors of Alan's apartment building. The Victorian apartment block, formerly a factory building, was close to the subway at Bergen. It was in a narrow, residential, tree-lined street, lying just beyond a characterful fire station, and the red brick walls of the side of the building took up half the block. They entered the lobby, and Isobel followed Robert up the narrow stairs to the first floor. An old lady was coming out of a door at the far end of the hallway. She didn't seem interested in their presence.

Robert unlocked the apartment door and felt a little shudder, when it opened straight into the lounge. The room was about the size of a school hall. An eerie glow squeezed through the bottom of the blinds that made the place look like a museum after hours. He groped for the light switch and hit it. White walls and minimalist modern furniture flooded into view, resting on a polished wooden floor, and covered by only one comparatively small rectangle of rug; and that was between the black leather designer sofa and the TV.

In one corner was a desk stacked with a row of marker pens standing on their ends, at the side of a layout pad. White shelves crammed with books filled a large expanse of the wall facing the windows. Robert glimpsed at some of the titles. They must've been Alan's because they were mostly relating to mass communication and art theory, along with some advertising annuals, classic novels by Poe, Lovecraft, Sartre, Camus and Dickens, and a few American crime writers like Hammett and Chandler. On the wall there was a framed poster for an Edward Hopper Exhibition Isobel had visited in London, in the 80s.

In the main bedroom everything was white, apart from the wooden floor, an antique wardrobe, glass vase of purple freesias and a photo of the family on the dressing table. On entering Robert sensed the feint residue of an intangible miasma. He wasn't geared to perceiving the presence of supernatural activity, but

Isobel was. Her internal Geiger counter for spiritual activity went off the scale. She looked stunned. Robert had seen her do this type of work a dozen times during the Cold War, preventing parapsychological assassinations. This was different. She had that pallid look which he hadn't seen in her since the cancer was eating her up. He thought she would faint, and he quickly took her arm. She shook herself free of his hold and took a couple more steps into the room.

"It's OK", she said in a low whisper, as if she was in slight pain.

Heading towards a corner she turned around to stare at the window directly above the double bed, where the blind was still lowered. Her face developed an expression of bitter anguish, and she sank slowly into a kind of trance. For about a minute she was motionless. Robert looked on as she started to sway gently where she stood. Her hands brushed down her side to her thighs, like an exotic dancer then she hugged herself and writhed around, again as if she was suffering. He'd seen her hoovering up supernatural essences many times, but nothing like this. Her hands moved around each breast, in slow orbits, and then eventually slid across them and back down again and she looked like she was going to burst into tears any moment, but instead her eyes widened, giving her a startled appearance and with the caution of a tightrope walker she walked towards the bed. Again, she seemed to be fighting some inner pain when she stopped at the foot of the bed and fell slowly face-forward into the mattress, crying hysterically and beating at the mattress with her fists. Robert stood there helpless, knowing that he should not interfere, for fear of losing the thread she was connecting to, which could be vital to their investigation. The longer she was able to remain in this state, the more she would learn. When she stopped quivering, and it was clear that the experience had passed he went over to sit with her on the bed. He hugged her and said, "What is it, Izzy?"

She rolled her head so she could face him, glaring at him with utter fury and almost spat her words out.

"What the fuck am I even doing here? You are such a bastard. Did you know that was going to happen?"

"What?"

"Don't give me that, or I'll give you such a thump, Stringfield."

She always looked so cute when she was angry.

He got up and left her sitting there, as he walked over to the corner, where she began taking everything in, and then turned to speak to her.

"Honey. I had no idea. I brought you here hoping you could maybe pick up some sort of sign, you know... of this demon. Obviously, we got a lot more than we bargained for."

"You mean I did," she said.

She sat at the edge of the bed looking at her knees. There was a silence that lasted for maybe twenty seconds, but it seemed like an age.

She lifted her head and glanced at him wearily.

"Get me a glass of water," she said.

He fiddled with some spotlights, which came up softly in the kitchen to reveal white tiles to shoulder height all around and a top of the range coffee machine on the grey work surface. He found a bottle of mineral water in the baby blue Smeg fridge, poured some into a glass, and went back into the bedroom. She reached for it dreamily, took a slow sip and sighed.

"You want to maybe take a lie-down before we look around some more?" he said.

She looked up at him while her chin rested on her chest to say, "And what is it that makes you think I can get much of a rest on this bed?"

Robert sighed. "Sorry. Stupid question."

He waited until she was ready. Slowly, it came out:

"This essence is very intense, emotional – not just passionate, but sad?"

"Sad?"

"Yes, definitely, sad too. A bunch of mixed-up emotions. And it's definitely a she."

"So, Alan was on the level."

"The feeling I get is of wallowing in a deep, black pit of endless misery, occasionally broken up by lust incarnate, from which there is no escape."

"Wow. And... is there a clue as to what this mix of emotions are directed towards?"

"I get the words 'This man that must be loved.' That's all."

"Hmm. OK. That's good, Izzy. Take it easy now and we'll head back when you're ready."

She drank up the rest of the water, handed him back the glass, and walked out of the room. He went to pay a much-needed visit to the bathroom, and then went into the small bedroom. A Spiderman duvet covered one of the beds and on the other was a giant image of the Incredible Hulk. Alphabet charts and a large Star Wars poster were blue-tacked to the wall. There was a plastic crate full of toy trucks and robots and another full of cuddly toys.

She turned to face him and said, "She was in here too."

"This time all I'm getting from the ethereal residue is curiosity and sadness."

"From the succubus or the kids?"

"Her, stupid."

"What the hell would a Succubus be doing appearing to the kids?"

301

Isobel shrugged. "Can we go now?"

Robert remembered Alan saying that his landlords stored a few of their things in a wall cupboard near the front door. Robert tried the handle, and it didn't give.

"What are you doing?" said Isobel.

"I just need to take a quick look in here," he said.

She closed the front door, turned around and looked at him, confused. "Didn't Alan give you the key to that room?"

"No. He doesn't have one."

"Listen Stringfield, don't overstep boundaries. You're not working for the agency now."

"I feel responsible, Izzy. Those kids... Who knows what could happen? I need to find out a few things."

He pulled a standard issue lock-pick out of his pocket.

"Oh, for Christ's sake..." She scowled as he crouched down to poke around inside the keyhole.

After a short while there, footsteps getting louder from further down the hallway getting louder. They stopped directly outside the front door to the apartment; neither Isobel nor Robert said a word. Robert was half way through releasing the fourth lever on the lock, when there was a click. Immediately there were a series of loud knocks on the door. Isobel shook her head and quietly opened the door, just enough for anyone outside to see her standing against the wall by the entrance, and no further. She put on her singing voice, "Hello?"

It was an older woman, and she seemed to be nervous.

"Oh, hi," she stammered. "Is Alan still here with his family? We thought they'd gone upstate."

"Yes. They have. But Alan asked us to pick up a couple of things he needs to finish off a project. His office asked him to work on a couple of things while he's on vacation." Isobel then did her pantomime look of despair. "Typical."

"Oh, that's so unfair."

"Isn't it?"

"So, will you be staying with them?"

"No. We have a place in Poughkeepsie, so we're just going to be passing through Cold Spring. Probably have a bite to eat with Alan, Jenny and the boys... and then we'll just move on."

That seemed to diffuse any tension.

"Well lovely to meet you," said Isobel.

After the woman left, Robert managed to pick the lock. He stood up and opened the door. Although the cupboard was much deeper that he'd expected.

It was mostly boxes of books. Robert lifted a couple of out them out and opened them up. There were a lot of heavy, well-produced art, architecture and design books and quite a few antique texts too. One of them, the *Lives of the Most Excellent Painters, Sculptors, and Architects* had a green cloth cover, and title and author in gold, embossed letters. Isobel said it was one of the most important books on the Renaissance, originally written in Latin by a contemporary and friend of Michelangelo. In the same box was another 19th

303

century English first edition of *The Civilisation of the Renaissance in Italy* by Jacob Burckhardt. Isobel informed him again that this was a one of the most highly respected texts on the Renaissance. The book underneath that was a yellow tome. Isobel knew next to nothing about that, but Robert did. It was Cornelius Agrippa's *De Occulta Philosophia Libra Tres*. He only had schoolboy Latin, but he was totally familiar with the English translation of this work. In the same box were other titles, such as Robert Fludd's *Utriusque Cosmi Historia*, *The Most Holy Trinosophia* – attributed to Count of Saint Germain, *The Autobiography of Benvenuto Cellini*, and *Steganographia* by Johannes Trithemius.

Robert stood up, sucked in his lips, and shook his head.

"You know what?" he said to Isobel. "There's a good chance that the people who summoned that demon are the guys who own these books."

"Aren't you just jumping to conclusions here, Robert? The other books are Renaissance texts. Maybe they're just interested in the philosophical and general intellectual writings of the time."

"From where I'm sitting, you'd have to be a really dedicated scholar of mysticism, alchemy and dark magic to own these texts. They're practically instruction manuals on occult philosophy and mysticism, going back hundreds of years. Some of them even refer to the summoning of demons. Izzy, I'm not kidding, we have to check these guys out.

Chapter 15

Alan woke up, and before making coffee he went into the bathroom. His eyes were encrusted with sleep and he badly needed a pee. Afterwards, he rested his palms on the edge of the sink and leaned close to the mirror to look at his still half-closed eyes. He ran the cold tap, leaned down, and splashed some water onto his face. He wiped his face and looked in the mirror and was so horrified by what he saw he let out a scream. His face was now covered in blood-red gore, which was dripping from his nose and his chin. Some of the bits of entrail were coagulating around the plughole, partially blocking the sink. He looked up and the bathroom went out of focus. He was losing his sense of balance, and found himself stumbling back, almost into the bath. Jenny pulled open the door in utter confusion. He tried to say something, but no words came. In the mirror, his face was clean and he could see that there was no sign of any gore in the sink. Thinking on the hoof, he mumbled something about the water being too hot. Jenny gave him a cold stare, shook her head and walked away without saying a word. He toweled his face and sat on the edge of the bed, trying to convince himself it was just a hallucination, brought on by a lack of proper sleep. He was tormented with doubts and fears about the demon, and had been tossing and turning all night, which actually woke Jenny up a couple of times.

It was a bright morning, and after breakfast they decided to go for another walk. There had been a fresh snowfall overnight and the hills across the frozen river were no longer in mist, so the dark rocks jutting out of the snow were in sharp outline. They walked along the riverside while the boys ran on ahead. Jenny was discussing their itinerary for the next few days, while Alan nodded blankly and found his thoughts drifting off onto other things. He believed that Robert was probably right in saying that his dreams were all somehow connected to the demon. Jenny caught him in his waking reverie and spoke, as the boys charged around in the snow ahead.

She put her arm through his and said, "I didn't want to say anything, but you've been acting really weird since we got here. I've never seen you like this before. I was hoping you'd relax, and settle back into the Alan I know. Not this retard. But you're getting worse. You've been acting strange since we arrived at the airport, and what was all that shouting in the bathroom this morning?"

Alan was about to touch on the truth about the hallucinatory experience he went through that morning when Jenny suddenly interrupted him.

"Oh, for Christ's sake," she said, as she ran forward to see what had happened to Simon, who was face down in the snow. Jack was standing and pointing nervously at his brother.

"Did you trip him up Jack?" said Jenny, angrily.

"I... I didn't do anything mum, honest."

"Come here, baby boy." Jenny lifted Simon up,

he was red faced and blubbering. She dusted the snow off his cheeks.

Alan arrived on the scene as Simon calmed down a little, resting his chin on his mum's shoulder.

"What happened, Si?" he said.

"Did you just fall over?" asked Jenny.

He interrupted his crying to nod shakily.

"Jack didn't push you, did he?"

He shook his head and closed his eyes, then opened then again. She put him down and wiped his eyes. "Right. Now will you try to be a bit more careful?"

"Uh-huh."

She turned to Jack. "And will you try not to go so fast, because you know he'll try to keep up with you, and his little legs can't do that."

Jack nodded.

"Right. Now go easy."

"Look. I'm sorry love," said Alan. "I've been a bit stressed out with work and everything..."

"Is that why Steve let us have the cottage for the week?"

"Well, if you have to know..."

"Is your job under threat?"

"No. Nothing like that."

She gave him a sideways look. "Tell me the truth."

"Honestly," he said. "Things will be fine. Steve wouldn't lend me the house if he thought I wasn't worth it. I wasn't myself and he just wanted to help out. That's all. I've won too much business for them

307

to even think of kicking me out."

She said nothing, but her blank expression suggested she wasn't entirely convinced and was suspending judgment.

This was the mother of my children. I should be able to open up to her about anything that worried me. There shouldn't be any need for self-censorship. Why couldn't I have married someone with a calmer, more patient sensibility, someone who respected me? Juliette was far too sensitive to question him in this way. Jenny's attitude, showed distrust and felt like a type of rejection. It made him question his own manhood. He couldn't help feeling a sense of shame.

They came to the part of the riverside near the town centre, by the pagoda where a few families were milling about. The boys wanted to build a snowman near the old black canon. Alan started to help them while Jenny went over to the giant Christmas tree, close to the gazebo, where she took out her video camera and started to film Alan and the boys and the beautiful winter scene in general. As she filmed, Alan helped Jack and Simon roll a huge ball of snow for the base of the snowman. The boys then helped their dad make another giant ball of snow, which Alan lifted onto the first one they made. Alan then rolled another ball for the snowman's head,

while the boys ran off to find stones for the eyes and something to use for the nose.

When he had placed the head on the body of the snowman and started to smooth it all down,

Alan felt a touch on his shoulder. He turned to see a milk-white hand resting there briefly and heard a soft, low woman's voice.

"Excuse me," she said, "You're not from around here, are you?"

He turned to see a girl in her early twenties."

"Sadly not," he replied.

Despite the oversize round sunglasses, there was something quite dignified about her. She wore a black Russian fur hat, black three-quarter length double breasted coat, with a brown fur collar, black narrow hose trousers and brown boots. He studied her smooth, ivory skin, high forehead and the delicate shape of her nose, and was mesmerized by her blood red lips as she spoke.

"It's just that I'm a bit lost, and I was hoping you might know your way around here."

He wasn't listening. "Pardon?"

"I'm sorry," she said. Perhaps I was speaking too fast. "I was just wondering if you might know where the cemetery is?"

He was vainly trying to work out what it was about her that made him feel so beguiled by her. It wasn't simply her looks. She was like a living poem, with her calm eloquence and ease of speaking.

"No, I don't. But that's the Hudson House Hotel over there," he said, pointing to the large, quaint gray clapperboard building behind her. "I'm sure someone in there will be able to help you."

Alan could see in the distance that the boys were now talking to some other children. They ended up rushing over with them, two boys and a

309

girl, with a fistful of stones of various sizes.

Alan turned to face the children. "Well done lads," he said, holding out his hands to be filled by a pile of stones. "But we only need two for the eyes, and one for the nose.

"But the rest can be buttons," said Jack.

"Good idea!" said Alan.

"And he can have my scarf too," said Simon.

"No. Mummy would definitely not approve of you giving him that," said Alan. "Come on, let's just finish him up."

He looked around again and the girl with the Russian hat was gone. He looked to see if she had gone towards the hotel, as he had suggested, but she was nowhere to be seen. He supposed that she must've already gone inside the hotel, though he was baffled how she could have got there so fast. Dressed the way she was, she would have stood out like a silhouette in the whiteness of the scene ahead.

The boys started to take a few stones back from Alan to apply to the snowman, when Jenny turned up, having finished filming them. She suggested that they go into town for a hot drink and then head back to the house again. Maybe the boys could do some tobogganing.

"Yay!" They both said in unison.

They boys were exhausted by the time they got back to the house. Alan had to carry Simon all the way home. The tobogganing would have to wait until tomorrow. Jenny made Simon have something to eat before putting him to bed. Jack stayed up a bit longer and Alan eventually put him to bed, reading him a chapter of his new book, *Harry Potter and the Philosopher's Stone.*

When Jack had finally dropped off to sleep, Alan came back down to the lounge, where Jenny was struggling to connect her video camera to the back of the TV, to check the footage she'd shot that day. Alan said if she made the tea, he would sort out the connections.

She stood up with a sigh, arms on hips. "OK," she said. But please don't break anything."

"How the hell am I going to break anything?" he replied.

"Just don't," she said as she walked off.

Just as Jenny was coming back in with the tea tray, Alan had it working, so they sat back on the sofa to watch. The first thing that came up was some shaky camera work of Simon and Jack playing shots in goal in their back garden in London. That was followed by a short sequence from the school nativity, where Jack was playing Joseph. But straight after that was a lovely, slow panorama of the Hudson valley. It finished up on Jack and Simon rolling a big ball of snow. Then there is a shaky section, which is a zoom when Alan comes into frame. In it he is picking up another huge ball of snow to place it onto the body of the snowman. Then the camera follows the boys as they ran off to the bushes further back to dig up some stones. As Alan watched, he could see himself in the distance, a small figure wrapped up warm in a dark coat and woolly hat. But something was wrong.

"Hold that!" he shouted, as he snatched the remote from Jenny.

Jenny was quite perturbed, "Hey!"

"Sorry love. Just need to see this again."

She nudged him on the shoulder, as he pushed rewind and then play, rewind and then play over and over again.

"I... I don't understand," he said.

"What is it?"

Alan stared at the screen in disbelief. He could see himself turning away from the snowman to point out the hotel. But the girl he had been talking to is not there. It looks like he is having a conversation with thin air.

Alan told Jenny that he desperately needed to get some beers in, and before she had any time to reply, he was out of the house. He ran to a call box, a few hundred yards along the path and dialed Robert's number.

Robert Answered. He was in quite an ebullient mood, and didn't leave Alan much time to speak at first.

"Ah, Alan. Good to hear from you. Well, we had your landlords checked out, to see if they could be behind all this business, maybe through dabbling with the occult, or being involved with a coven, or something, and the results came back that they're clean. No weird membership of sects or weird groups."

Alan had no idea what to say to that, and when he thought about it for a bit all he could say was, "But why suspect them in the first place?"

Robert response verged on anger. "Why? Because the demon appeared to you in that apartment and so that must be where she was summoned. Those guys also happen to own a few items that made me suspicious, and..."

Alan felt he had to interrupt, because what he had to say was of far greater relevance. "Well she's now appeared here."

There followed a pregnant silence, before Robert said, "What?"

"I saw her here, in Cold Spring."

"Wait a minute. What are you saying?"

Alan was relieved to be finally getting his point across. "I felt her touch me on the shoulder. I heard her voice. I spoke to her. I *saw* her. And yet she wasn't there - at least not on camera. How was that possible? Jenny took a video of us hanging around in that area, and when I saw myself at the moment, I was talking to her, she isn't there. It looks like I'm talking to thin air."

"How can you be sure it was her?"

"I realized after seeing the video. On reflection, she had exactly the right body shape and face. I also had this inner sense of her... I can't really describe it. I didn't say anything about it at all to Jenny."

"OK. Now listen. You hang tight, and keep me in touch of any developments. It's going to be OK; I promise you. Just hang tight kid. You hear me?"

Alan was more nervous than ever now. "Uh... well, sure. OK."

Robert put the phone down and immediately turned to Isobel,

"Get everything ready in the spare room. I need to do some RV."

"You what?"

Chapter 16

Normal, everyday thinking is disjointed and hyperactive, being it's made up of numerous disconnected conclusions, perceptions and ideas, strung together unifying imperatives. It has to be that way – to reflect reality – and that's how waking consciousness works - normally. On an electroencephalogram (EEG) it shows up as a harsh and scraggy line of condensed peaks and troughs: condensed because of the short amount of time allotted to each peak and trough. We call this saw-toothed consciousness, beta wave thinking. This is as far as you can be from the state of mind that is required to do what Robert was taught to do by his controllers at Project StarChild, in Virginia.

Alpha wave consciousness is a calmer way of thinking, showing up as a slightly stretched out version of the beta wave, which still has the look of a mountain range, as jagged lines go, but less compressed, and with slightly reduced peaks and troughs. The remote viewer needs to pass through this phase to reach a calmer state of consciousness, akin to pre-consciousness. This type of thinking heightens the imagination, and the capacity to visualise, recollect, learn and perceive. It's also a bridge to the lower frequencies of the subconscious mind. But it's still not right for RV. You need to go even deeper, to get a smoother, much more stretched out wave, one that looks like soft, rolling hills on an EEG. You would only experience this state of thinking for a short time, for example, in the moments when you drift off, or wake slowly from a deep sleep. This is theta consciousness – and it can only be sustained for limited periods. Your mind's most deep-seated programs are at theta. Here you experience vivid images, and get your true inspiration, creativity and exceptional insight. Theta brain waves are indicators of deep meditation and light sleep, including the REM (or dream) state. To perform RV, you absolutely need to be in the theta state - and stay there for some time. That takes some doing.

It was about ten at night. The blinds were pulled down and the lights were low. They were in the spare room, which is basically Robert's office. It had a few bookshelves, computer equipment, and an EEG monitor, which was connected up to Robert, who was seated at the table. Isobel came over to put the wired headband on him, slightly messing up his mane of white hair. He squinted and gave her a look of annoyance. As he had requested, Isobel put on a Pink Floyd CD and selected the track, *Careful With That Axe Eugene,* which had always helped him relax, to achieve the required state of consciousness. Then she left him alone for about a quarter of an hour and then came back to sit opposite him.

"How are we doing," she said. But she could already see Robert was nicely transitioning through the alpha state, according to the monitor.

"I'm… good," he said, in a mellow tenor voice.

Isobel then got up to dim the lights a little more. Then she sat down again, facing him, and passed him a sheet of paper and a pen. She read out some numbers and he copied them down one by one. "Forty-three... seven... eight... three... three. OK?"

"OK."

"Eleven... two... five... zero... zero."

Unusually for Robert, with his chiselled, square-jawed, warrior's face, the hard steel grey eyes became calm and dreamy. Isobel passed him a pencil, which he calmly took, and began to draw a rectangle. Inside the rectangle he drew three rows of squares. This was his subconscious response to the numbers – or coordinates. In Langley they used to call this an ideogram. It facilitated his link to the deep subconscious. After a short while, he put the pencil down and looked at what he'd drawn.

"OK," said Isobel. "Have you started counting?"

He nodded sleepily. She turned to look at the monitor showing a beautifully, smooth theta wave. He was ready. His head dropped forward and his closed eyelids started to flicker, almost as in REM sleep.

"Falling, falling, falling," he said softly.

"OK", said Isobel."

He nodded, and then there was a long silence.

"I see snow."

Chapter 17

Jenny went to bed particularly early, so Alan stayed in the lounge and opened up a bottle of JD. He polished off half of it by the time he got into bed. Jenny was then in a deep sleep. When he turned off the light, a swarm of random thoughts swirled around in his head, making it impossible to relax. Eventually he couldn't deny that the temperature was plummeting, even though the heating was still on. Abstract fear kicked in. His breathing came with some difficulty, and his head throbbed. A series of gloomy, shapeless thoughts were weighing down on him, and when he tried to reflect on them, to create some sense, they dissolved away, like smoke in the wind. It was impossible to string together his thoughts - there were too many of them buzzing around like ball bearings in a centrifuge. When his thoughts did begin to coalesce, he didn't like where they were going. He had to try to distract himself from the darkness and depravity in his mind, so he crept out of bed and walked over to the window. He drew back the curtain. It was snowing heavily. He stood there and watched it fall for a while, but it was too cold. When he went back to bed, he was shivering so hard his teeth were chattering.

The clock ticked loudly, and his thoughts were still running away with themselves, but he gave up resisting, allowing the dark thoughts to overwhelm him. Exhausted and bewildered he drifted off.

He was about five years old, in his old primary school in West London. The other children played around him; he was sensing them more than actually seeing them. This was pure childhood – the total lack of responsibility, the innocence, the reassurance that he was loved and cared for. But that mood faded away, along with all of the children, and he was left on his own, surrounded by four ridiculously tall, Victorian brick walls. Somewhere a teacher's whistle blew, and a deep shadow started to grow from the wall opposite, moving like a pool of dark blood from a deep wound. As it edged closer and closer, he found that he couldn't move. Soon he was in total darkness. "Where's mum," he thought.

But deep down, he knew she was far away.

Then he heard the echo of a woman's voice singing a lullaby. He listened carefully to the words.

There's a long line of mourners driving down our little street
Their fancy cars are such a sight to see
They're all of your rich friends who you knew in the city
And now they finally brought you back to me

They meant nothing to him.

She sang it over and over again. He wanted it to stop. It frightened him. It wasn't a proper lullaby, and those strange words sent shivers through him. He woke up from that dream, almost crying.

A faint light came into the bedroom from the hallway through the door, which he had left slightly

319

ajar. He tried to sit up, and found that he had pins and needles in his arm, and that he was still shivering. Jenny was still fast asleep, breathing deeply and facing away from him. He whispered her name. She didn't move. The duvet was pulled up high. He tried to wake her by touching her shoulder. "Jen?" he said.

But she didn't respond, so he levered her gently towards him.

A rush of blood pounded his temples, and he screamed. His heart was beating madly. Instead of Jenny he saw a half-living, festering corpse next to him in the bed. It had long strands of lank hair, crawling with lice, and the face was a hideous, grinning skull with protruding, bloodshot, glassy, bulging eyes. There were patches of putrefying flesh and muscle, clinging to yellow, slime-covered bone. He drew away from it in disgust, and then it started to move. In a fear-driven frenzy, he gripped the thing around the throat - tighter and tighter he squeezed with all his might, with both hands. His face and hands were sprayed with its spittle as the half-dead thing squeaked and hissed in its struggle to break free. Then a blinding light filled the room and his brain swam. Suddenly he lost all sense of reason and grew deadly sick. His vision failed and he involuntarily loosened his grip as his eyes adjusted to the light. What he saw at first was that the bedroom door was now fully open and Simon and Jack were both standing at the foot of the bed. Both of them were crying. He wondered what was wrong.

He looked to his side, where the living cadaver had been and saw Jenny, coughing, crying and spluttering. Her neck had a bright pink bruise around it and her face was puffed and pale. She rolled her head to the edge of the bed and started to vomit.

He stood up and the room started to spin and he had to hold tight onto the bedpost to avoid fainting. He didn't know how long he was in that state. The sound of Jenny coughing and puking up seemed somehow muffled and distant. He tried to slow his breathing and as he relaxed his senses slowly returned to normal.

Jack and Simon were around Jenny's side of the bed, comforting her. He got out of bed and walked over there to try and comfort her, but when he reached over to touch her head she hissed at him, and twisted away from his reach, causing her to fall awkwardly to the floor.

"I hate you!" she whispered, while trying to shout. "Don't touch me. Get out. Get out!"

Jack was crying profusely. "Leave mummy alone daddy! Go away."

Simon was just crying. He was too upset to say anything.

Alan pleaded with them all, "I didn't... I thought it wasn't mummy. I would never, ever..."

"She squeezed her eyes shut and tried to yell with all her might, although it was still more of a gravelly hiss. "Go!"

The boys looked at him as if he was an imposter. Simon hugged Jenny, and looked back at Alan with a look of absolute horror.

"Boys. It's daddy."

Now both boys shouted at him. "Go away, daddy!"

What else could he do? He grabbed his dressing gown from the back of the door and left the room. For a while he stood on the landing, until it seemed that the sounds from the bedroom had calmed down. Then he opened the door quietly to look in. But the instant they saw him they all started to scream. Jenny stumbled over to the door red-faced and pushed it closed with all her might.

"Get out, you bastard," she growled.

He felt useless and unclean as he went dreamily down to the kitchen. He pulled out a tea bag from the ceramic jar, and his hand shook like a leaf. After filling the kettle and switching it on, he waited patiently, in the hope that someone would call him back upstairs. But it didn't happen. The kettle boiled and he filled the mug. After that he sat down in one of the old-fashioned armchairs, leaving a small light on in the kitchen so he could see what he was doing. While there, he found himself staring abstractedly at the ceiling, which started to wobble, like an oil slick in a puddle, refracting the light into the semblance of a crude, liquid rainbow. His eyelids were getting heavier and the whole room was shifting in and out of focus now, pulsing like a beating heart.

He had sunk into a dreamless sleep without realising it, and when he woke, it was still the middle of the night. He had no idea how long he'd slept. Although the grandfather clock ticked loudly, it never gave the correct time. Steve had warned him about that. He resolved to go and see how things were. Quietly, he made his way up the squeaky stairs, and along the landing until he came to the boy's bedroom. The door was open. He went in - but they weren't in there. He reasoned they must be in bed with Jenny. He became dizzy again, and had to pause and hold onto the door to stop himself from fainting. The entire hallway throbbed and shook as his head pulsed with each rush of blood. He took a deep breath and went on to the main bedroom. The bed was empty. Where were they all? He looked around, and noticed that the only clothes on the chair were his. He stumbled over to the wardrobe to find only his clothes in there. Jenny's clothes were gone, and so were the boys. The same was true of the chest of drawers. Finally, he opened the front door. The hire car was gone, and there were tyre tracks in the snow. He dropped down onto his knees and sobbed like a baby.

After a while he stood up and went back into the kitchen to splash some cold water on his face, soaking his pyjamas and dressing gown in the process. With a massive effort, he managed walk back towards the lounge, unintentionally kicking a large antiques vase over, and breaking it. In his drugged-like consciousness, the scattered pieces of blue and white bone china seemed like alien artefacts that suddenly acquired a deep and impenetrable sense of the esoteric.

Feeling less and less in control, he nevertheless knew that there was something acting directly on his nerves, sapping his strength and weakening his will. He hoped it wasn't her. But within a minute of sitting back in the armchair he began to shake uncontrollably. It was like a fever. He was bordering on a state of insensibility, sinking into a deeper and deeper stupor, as the grandfather clock chimed for an hour that had nothing to do with the time. The noise actually snapped him out of his stupor. Then it struck him - he should call Robert. It may be the middle of the night, but he'd understand. He reached around for the Bakelite phone on the coffee table, grabbed it and sank back into the seat, exhausted.

The phone now rested in his lap. Finally, he lifted the receiver, as if it was a holy relic. He had learnt Robert's number off by heart, for fear of just such a necessity, and he dialled and waited.

There was no reply.

It occurred to him that he could call Gary. Gary had some knowledge of the nature of a succubus. He was familiar with Robert's book on the succubus, and had even read it. He might appreciate the seriousness of his situation. He dialled Gary's home number, letting it ring for a good while. Eventually a sleepy female voice answered.

"Who is it?"

It was the most wonderful relief to hear another human being.

"Fiona. Thank God. You're there!"

"Where else would I be? I live here. Is that Alan?"

Alan found it hard to speak properly. His words came out too fast.

He tried to speak again. "Look I'm really, really sorry. Things are bad. I can't explain right now. Please... can I talk to Gary?"

She sighed and there was another long wait.

Alan heard a deep groan through a muffled receiver. It sounded like Gary, "Huh? What?"

"Phone call. For you."

"Now?"

Fiona's was speaking. She sounded angry, but he couldn't make out what she was saying. Then Gary's voice then came up, slow and sleepy.

"Alan? What the hell time is it? What are you doing?"

"I'm really sorry, but I'm in serious shit. Really bad - you're the only person who can help me."

"Me? What the hell are you talking about?"

"You read that book, the succubus book, right?"

"Oh, that. Yeah. So?"

"I'm being attacked by one."

"You what?"

"I didn't tell you anything about it, basically because it's all so embarrassing. But I went to see Robert Stringfield about it, and he has been trying to help me exorcise it."

"That's... that's just mad."

"Seriously, she has come for me several times. And something horrible just happened. I think she will be back to finish off what she started? You know what that means?"

"But aren't you with Jenny and the kids?"

"I was. Jenny has gone and she's taken the kids with her."

"Fuck."

"I... I did something terrible, I think this demon - whatever she is - she's fucking with my head, making me do terrible things, I was sort of still half in a dream and... I hurt Jen. Now she's driven off with the kids. I'm on my own – and the weirdness is starting again. This time she'll – she'll finish what she started. You've got to come over here before it's too late."

"But you're in Cold Spring still, right?"

"Yes."

"Not Brooklyn?"

"No."

"Call a cab. Get here now – whatever it costs! Alan, can you hear me?"

Alan had dropped the receiver with a thud to the floor. The energy began draining out of his body, along with all of his will. The strange, entrancing force was overwhelming him once more. It came like a tidal wave. He leaned back into the chair, his eyes only opening a thin slit. The room began to pulse again and a green mist ghosted up in the middle of the room. At first, it flickered and then slowly resolved itself, from the bottom up, into her. She was back, shimmering in the faint light, dissolving a little at the edges, before becoming absolutely in phase with the room. Slowly and purposefully, she stepped forward, naked again, moving with sinuous grace, her breasts shaking to the rhythm of her walk, filling him with horror and

326

delight. Now, he was sure. This was the girl he spoke to by the snowman.

Then everything went black and there was a hissing close to his ears. A husky woman's voice was whispering his name. He opened his eyes and it was her, leaning over him, twisting her upper body so that she brushed his face with each breast. He didn't remember taking off his pyjamas, and dressing gown, but he was naked. Her arms clasped him around the neck. His nerves were tingling. A shudder went through him. He couldn't move.

She brushed loose strands of hair from her face, as her smooth skin basked in the warm half-light. He didn't know how he it was possible, but he sensed her anguish, and melancholy. His moment of calm vanished when she stretched out her arms and pushed him down by the shoulders, and her long delicate fingers felt their way towards his crotch. He knew this would mean lifelong impotence. Yet how could he stop himself from reaching an orgasm? She faced him, knees bent, her body hovered a little above his crotch, levering herself from her feet, reaching for his prick and lifting it into position, before pushing herself down onto it, arching her back in a spasm of ecstasy.

But then something extraordinary happened. She flipped off him, as if he had become an electric fence, landing with a thud on the floor, where she thrashed around and screamed. It was as if she was fighting off an invisible weight pinning her down. She lashed out at one point, clawing at the air. And then she was gone.

After a while, he found he could move. He

barely had the energy to lean forward. And then the front door opened and he heard footsteps approaching.

Chapter 18

The moon was high, and partially obscured by thick dark clouds. There was very little street lighting in the residential districts. Gary and Fiona had been up to Steve's house a few times, and even in the daytime they always had a hard time finding the place. When he eventually found the road, he decided to stop outside the only house with no car outside, and with lights on.

On getting out of the car he heard a high pitch scream coming from the house. It was terrifying and bewildering, because it didn't sound human – more like an animal being tortured. Worried, he ran up the pathway and found that the front door was open. He nudged it in and stood in the hallway and shouted:

"Anybody in? Hey Al. Where you at?"

A couple of seconds later there was a cough followed by a groan. It came from the lounge, to his left. He entered that room saw the back of Alan's head over the top of an armchair. He walked around to see that the guy didn't have a stitch on. He was gripping the armrests, as if in pain, and then he looked up at Gary with moist and tired eyes, like a helpless old man.

"Gary? Thank fuck you're here," he said that almost in a whisper.

Gary reached down to the floor, picked up a dressing gown and threw it at him.

"Here," said Gary. "What do you think this is, a men's sauna?"

It just fell in Alan's lap, where he just looked at it weirdly, and then looked up at Gary squinting hard, as if an excessively bright lamp was being shone into his face.

"What time is it?" he asked.

"Time, I should be in bed."

"No, really."

"Coming up to two-forty-five in the AM. That clock is wrong," said Gary, pointing to the antique grandfather clock, which said nine-thirty.

"Put something on, will you. Then we can get the fuck out of here. I'll go make some coffee."

Alan started to find the strength to move.

"So, what the fuck was that screaming noise was just before I got here?" shouted Gary from the kitchen, while he ran some water into the kettle. Alan didn't answer.

"Was it… you know, *her?*"

He nodded with a completely blank expression. But obviously Gary didn't see that.

"Never mind," he said. "You can tell me all about it on the way home. Now, why don't you go upstairs, take a shower and get dressed and packed so we can get the hell out of here? You're crashing at my joint tonight. No arguments."

Alan managed to coerce his aching body to go upstairs, and into the shower. When he got into a shirt and thick woolly jumper, jeans and Caterpillar boots and packed, he went back down to find Gary sipping what must have been his third cup of black coffee. Gary pointed to the coffee pot on the table with this chin. "There's still a bit left."

330

Alan sat at the table and poured out a cup.

"I cleared up the pieces of broken vase," said Gary. "I hoped for your sake it wasn't a rare and expensive piece, or Steve will go ape-shit."

Alan shrugged. "Yeah well… That's the least of my worries. Anyway, I really appreciate you doing all this, Gary."

Gary cut him dead. "Hey! Forget about it. Drink up. I want to get back in time to grab whatever shut-eye I can."

"Just give me a minute."

"What happened?" Gary said. "Why did Jenny take off with the kids?"

The coffee seemed to give Alan some life.

"I was having this nightmare… I don't know what else to call it. I thought I'd woken up out of it, but without realising, I must have still been living in the nightmare. It was kind of mingling with my waking consciousness. So when I turned to see I was lying next to this living, rotting corpse, I panicked, and reacted instinctively, by trying to throttle it. But… it was Jenny, not a living corpse at all."

"Fuck."

"She was choking and vomiting, and the boys came in the room to see…"

"You idiot."

"Don't say it like that. I couldn't help what happened…"

Gary stood up suddenly.

"Let's get out of here."

Chapter 19

"They're not expected back in the office till Monday." Gary said, as they crossed the Hudson to Bear Mountain State Park, to pick up the Palisades Interstate Highway. They were driving through a real of darkness - unadulterated countryside, with not a single building or residence either side of them.

Alan scratched his head and stared ahead vacantly.

"So, what are your plans for tomorrow?"

Alan turned to Gary, raised his eyebrows and said, "Well, I guess I'll be trying to save my marriage."

There was no way that Gary was going to let the journey go by without hearing from Alan exactly what happened, particularly with respect to the she demon, and what drove him to know more was that he was sure that Robert Stringfield would never have taken Alan seriously if he didn't believe the succubus threat was real. Robert would only have become involved if he was genuinely concerned.

Gary had read the succubus book by Robert years before and been fascinated by it. He had always wondered exactly what it would mean to be selected as a victim to such a strange and malevolent supernatural entity that could give you the best sex you've ever had, and effectively castrate you. He wanted Alan to describe everything that happened that night in detail. What he saw, from the moment she appeared, what preceded her appearance, what she looked like, what she felt liked, how he felt at every stage - everything.

He told Alan to talk, because he was tired, and he didn't want to fall asleep at the wheel. Reluctantly Alan described the events, and the story had the strange effect on Gary of making him cringe, while also causing him to feel envy. Gary decided to try to help Alan, not just out of his Succubus crisis, but with his marriage troubles too.

When they crossed back over into the Bronx, Alan felt a sense of relief. But too much had happened in the last couple of days, and he needed time to think. Gary parked across from the apartment on Greenwich Avenue and slapped Alan on the thigh.

"OK. Out you get."

They trudged across the icy road with the bags. Alan saw that, even at this unearthly hour, the deli downstairs had a few customers.

Alan's head was still throbbing as they went up the stairs, and his thinking was very cloudy and disjointed. When they were up on the landing Gary opened the apartment door, and put his finger to his lips to whisper, "Sh."

Gary pulled off his shoes, and told Alan to take a seat in the living room as he made a much-needed visit to the bathroom. When he came back, he was carrying a pile of sheets, a duvet and a couple of pillows. Alan was sitting cross-legged on the floor rummaging around in his bag. Gary put the bedding on the sofa and told Alan to help himself to the bathroom.

A few hours later, Alan had a feeling of rising to the surface of a floatation tank. He knew it must be morning, but he didn't know what time. There were little sounds all around him: footsteps, running water, cupboards opening and closing, kettle boiling, toaster clicking off. He sneaked open his eyes to see it was still dark outside, then closed them again quickly. Fiona was getting ready for work. There was no way he wanted her to have the opportunity of questioning him about what had happened. He knew there was a moment when she hovered around looking down at him as he lay spread out on the sofa, but he kept his eyes shut throughout. She coughed loudly a couple of times, but he still didn't move. Finally, she gave up, and went off to work.

Gary was fully dressed with his heavy-duty black coat on when Alan sat up.

"What's happening this morning?' he said.

"How do you mean?" said Gary.

"At work."

"Oh… nothing. I'm working with Jeff on some ideas for Nike. He's a good designer, but not much of a *thinker*."

Alan grinned. "So, does that mean you miss me."

"Fuck off."

He took off his glasses and rubbed the lenses clean using the bottom of his sweater. When he put

334

them back on, he came to sit at the end of the sofa, near Alan's feet.

"Listen. I'm arranging for you to see that guy, Robert Stringfield, tonight."

Alan shrugged.

He lifted his holdall. "There's bacon, beans, juice, bread, whatever. Just don't leave a mess."

And then he was gone. Alan went to the bathroom and then decided to call Jenny. He would willingly fall on his knees for her to forgive him. He picked up Gary's phone and dialled her number. It rang for a long while before switching to answer phone, which he couldn't help himself listening to in full, for want of hearing her voice again.

"Hi, this is Jenny. Sorry I can't get to the phone right now, but if you leave your name and number and a short message after the beep, I promise I'll get back to you as soon as I can. Thanks. *Bye!*"

Should he say something? He's already waited a few seconds. He took the plunge:

"Hi Jen. It's me. Uh, I just really, just… please will you give me a chance to explain everything. I am so, so sorry. I can't tell you. That wasn't me. I would never do anything to hurt you. When have I ever laid a finger on you before? Something was screwing with my mind. Please believe me. I want you back. I need for us all to be together again. I love you. Call me. Please?"

When he hung up, he sat there and thought about what he'd said, and wondered if he could've said anything more. He tried to work out the best strategy from this point, and nothing worthwhile came to mind. But one thing he had decided was that he didn't belong here, in Gary's apartment. He folded up all the bedding and booked a cab. Then he got dressed as quickly as he could. When the doorbell rang, he grabbed his bags and ran down the stairs and out of the apartment.

It was slow going through Chinatown, but Brooklyn Bridge heading east was clear. When the cab pulled up outside the entrance to the building, Alan said he didn't need any help with the bags. He didn't bother to pick up the mail in the hallway. He wanted to feel at least a little relief about being back, but there was just numbness. He headed on up the narrow stairs. There was no one about in their hallway. He fumbled for the keys and entered the apartment and immediately noticed that the blinds were up. What's more both bedroom doors were open and there was the unmistakable odour of Jean Paul Gaultier Classique. Jenny must have been there in the last couple of hours.

The chest of drawers had been ransacked in the main bedroom, and just as in Steve's place, only Alan's clothes were left. In the boy's bedroom, there were no clothes, toys or books left at all, but the mobile he'd bought them was still hanging from the ceiling. He pulled at the draw string hanging from a rocket, so that the planets started wobbling and spinning around it. Alan sat down on Jack's bed and watched them blankly, wracking his brains to try to understand why all this was happening to him, and what he should do now. After a while, he went back into the lounge and found an envelope on the table with his name on it. It was near the black vase, which was full of black tulips. He opened it up. It was written hurriedly in a thin marker pen, and all it said was:

'Listen to the answerphone messages. Jenny"

How much worse could things get. He reached over and switched on the black machine. Almost immediately her voice came up. She said his name. We've gone, Alan. That's it now. We've all left you. It's not just because of the horrible thing you did to me last night. Things were wrong from the minute we saw you in the airport. Even the boys could see it. Jack never said anything to you, but he was really worried. Simon felt something bad was happening that we didn't know about, though he couldn't explain to me why he believed that. But he's always been sensitive. But... even if that's true... you didn't give us any clues. Your mind has been on other things. It's like you weren't really there. I felt strange, like a substitute when we made love. A part of you wasn't really there. Has there been someone else? It would have been so easy for you to meet someone while we were back in London. You're in advertising for God's sake. You can lie about anything. Maybe you've done something like that and you thought it wasn't important, and now you realise that perhaps it was. But that's all academic now. We're going home. I can never forgive you for the way you throttled me. Maybe you didn't know what you were doing, and there's some serious psychological shit happening to you, but I'm not about to hang around to find out.

You could've *killed* me. I... Anyway, I just don't know what else to say. I've said it all. And I've made up my mind. Don't try to call me. You'll be hearing from a lawyer soon."

And that was it.

He didn't have the strength to listen to it again. He was just dumbstruck. Did she have a point? Was it possible that the thing with me and Juliette had some effect on the way I was with Jenny and the boys? It never even occurred to me for a moment. It was all down to the fucking Succubus. He thought of Juliette's soft, dark brown hair tied back at the nape of her slim neck, and her eyes squinting when she laughs. Then something came over him, and he rested his head in his arms on the table and cried. Even when the tears dried up, he lay back and fell asleep. He stayed that way, until he heard the buzzing of the intercom. When he looked up the streetlamp outside was the only thing lighting the apartment.

Reluctantly he got up and walked over to the intercom.

"Hello?"

Gary's voice came up. "Took your time. Buzz me up for Christ's sake."

He left the door off the latch and went back in to put some lights on, and pull down the blinds. He was half way through doing that when the door flung open against the wall and Gary came in, in his long trench coat, striding in like a civil war officer after a battle.

"Did you come straight from work?" said Alan.

"What do you think?"

"Shit. Where did the day go?"

"What've you eaten today?"

"Huh?"

"Let me put it another way, have you eaten today?"

"I haven't really thought about it."

He exhaled again, leaned heavily to the left, took out a brown bag from his coat pocket and threw it on the table.

"Eat up," he said. "Then we'll go."

Alan picked up the still warm foil wrap and took out a cheeseburger wrapped in white, waxed paper.

"Go where?"

"Robert's. What are you waiting for? "Eat."

Chapter 20

That elevator took its time. Isobel seemed distracted when she opened the door. Alan could hear the female vocals from *White Rabbit* by Jefferson Airplane coming from the apartment. Gary had dropped him off outside the building and decided to leave him there, in the capable hands of Robert and Isobel.

"Oh hi, Alan. Go right on in." She ushered him towards the main lounge.

The place had a kind of sick room feeling about it, with the lights very low. Isobel steered him over to the drinks cabinet near the kitchen and poured a generous measure of Napoleon Brandy, and dropped in a few lumps of ice, using silver tongs.

"You'll probably notice Robert's not quite himself," she said. "He's just a little fragile. But he's been looking forward to seeing you."

Alan nodded, not knowing for sure if he could believe her.

"Perfect. Well... you'll have to excuse me," she said. "I'm still two paintings short for the show. I do hope you'll be there for the opening."

"Of course. Thanks Isobel."

He found Robert sitting in an armchair to one side facing the large window. His face was in profile against the scene across the park. and in soft shadow. Alan thought he might be in a dressing gown and slippers, since he was unwell, but he was smartly attired in black trousers, a green tweed jacket, over a peach-coloured silk shirt and a geometric brown and grey green patterned tie. Alan couldn't help noticing how shiny his face seemed, almost as if he'd been running. His normally impressive head of white hair seemed lank, and moist. Some of it was stuck to his face. It was as if he was recovering from a fever.

He was staring dreamily at the thick blanket of snow covering Central Park, and the buildings opposite. To Alan it occurred to him that at that moment the park seemed like a cemetery without headstones.

His manner was not particularly warm. Without turning to face Alan, he lifted his right arm and waved him regally over to the sofa across from him. Alan found himself looking at Robert through the stems of pussy willow on the coffee table.

"I was sorry to hear about your marriage," said Robert.

His voice seemed as deep and commanding as usual, but much quieter. It would be too simple to say he looked exhausted. But there was an element of self-satisfaction about him, as if from the glow of some imperceptible glory. He was like a swimmer who had gone beyond his physical limits and achieved something nameless and extraordinary.

Alan nodded politely, took a sip of brandy and said, "Thank you, but I don't think it will turn out to be as bad as it sounds. Time heals all wounds, doesn't it?" he said.

"I hope so," said Robert, still looking straight ahead, leaving him in profile to Alan.

"I have to say," continued Robert, "you seem impressively stoic for a man who has been through so much and found his life in complete upheaval."

Alan wiped his lips and let out a little laugh. "Perhaps it's just shell shock," he said.

Alan didn't want to discuss the trials and tribulations of his marriage, and he couldn't help feeling a little patronised at that moment. But he took a deep breath and hid his irritation. He needed Robert's help.

"I suppose Gary told you what happened with the Succubus last night?" he said.

He coughed before he spoke. "He didn't need to tell me."

Alan thought he had misheard. "Sorry?"

Then Robert turned to face him. "I was there."

Alan couldn't help noticing four luminous pink marks on Robert's left cheek. The sight of it gave him the shivers. He suddenly remembered the demon who had lashed out and clawed at what he thought was nothing but thin air.

He couldn't help saying, "Your face!"

"Oh yes, that," he said, touching the strange blemish with the tips of his fingers. "It might not look like much, but it stings like hell." He half smiled, and took a sip of his brandy.

"What happened to you?" asked Alan.

"I think you know."

Alan's disbelief was like a giant dam that had developed a huge crack and the flood came in one big unstoppable rush. He recalled the Succubus thrashing around on the floor, as if she was pinned

342

down by an invisible force, and then he was struck by the sight of her suddenly thrusting out and clawing at something he couldn't see. "Was that you who…"

"Yes, it was," said Robert. "And lucky for you I arrived when I did."

Alan felt at that moment as if he was talking to a vampire. Robert was starting to give him the creeps, and that was despite knowing that he had saved him from a terrible fate.

"I just… Christ. I don't know what to believe any more."

"I'm glad we're beginning to understand one another. As you know, if the succubus had achieved her end, that would have been curtains for your manhood, my boy.

She was at the point of orgasm, and I had to drag her off you – which wasn't easy. She is strong and vicious." He pointed to the four claw marks on his face.

By this point Alan was speechless.

"But it's not quite over."

Robert tried to describe how he had projected his transcendental self to the house in Cold Spring, which went over Alan's head. But what it did do is prompt him to

recall how the demon thrashed about wildly on the floor in Steve's lounge, and the nauseous sensation he was going through at the time, as he shifted in and out of consciousness, unable to determine what was real and what was imaginary.

Robert could see the glazed look in Alan's eyes.

"You're not really following me, are you?"

Alan snapped out of his reverie, feeling instant embarrassment. "I'm really sorry Robert. The whole experience... since she first appeared, or before even, has left me unable to think clearly, and focus properly.

"Never mind," said Robert, getting up with a bit of a struggle, to change the CD, and then stumbling awkwardly. Alan quickly rushed over to help him, but he held out an arm to make it clear he needed absolutely no assistance.

"Just lost my balance there for a second, I'm good. But she really did take it out of me, your girlfriend."

Alan felt the blood rush to his face. "Oh God. Don't call her that," he said.

Robert found the disc he was looking for. The low light of the orange laver lamp, next to the pile of CDs, cast a twisting, organic, orange light over his face, making him look almost demented.

"I hope you like The Dead," he said, taking out another CD from its case."

"Huh?" I was feeling a bit dizzy by now.

"The Grateful Dead. Something called Dark Star. The studio recording was two minutes-forty, which is pathetic. It doesn't allow Jerry and the guys the freedom to evolve freely. This version runs for over twenty minutes."

Alan feigned the requisite enthusiasm.

"Great."

The spacey, eastern-sounding, slow lead guitar came in, building a melody that was so spaced out that Alan thought that he'd dropped a tab of acid.

Robert stood where he was, with his eyes closed in a kind of semi-sleep. Eventually his eyes blinked open and he walked back cautiously to his armchair. After a little cough he said,

""I went along with Isobel to check out your building, and we concluded that your apartment wasn't the source of the succubus. It must be you. You took her there with you."

"What?"

"You were already infected with her, before you moved in."

"You've lost me," said Alan.

It was like he hadn't heard.

"That's mad."

"Her essence – her ethereal signature – is new. Very recent. What's more, the dreams with the spotted people. I don't believe they are the fruits of your subconscious. They're hers. She hitched a ride in your soul. You are dreaming her dreams. I know it's not easy for a guy like you who's living so much in the material world to understand, but she was inside you. And appears in the room in front of you, when she has built up enough strength, by draining your mental and spiritual energy."

Alan sighed in despair.

Robert smacked the armrest with his right hand. "Look. I don't want you feeling this is all hopeless, and that there is no answer to your problem. We will find the source of your 'infection' – because that's what it is. She is a parasite on your soul. She has already been weakened, in the struggle she had with me."

"Oh." Alan perked up a bit, and although he

345

was confused, he was also clearly somewhat relieved.

I need you to tell me anything important that occurs to you in connection with those dreams – especially those people with red spots, like that sinister old couple. They are the key to all this – and let me tell you, I would say they are totally unsavoury characters, if they actually exist – which I believe they do."

Alan thought about that, and recalled the image of their leering, red-spotted faces, which made his skin crawl.

"So how would I find out what you need to know?"

"Let me put it like this, if that information should ever come to you, you will know."

Chapter 21

The events of recent weeks had totally undermined Alan. His understanding of reality no longer fitted with the things happening around him. He was disconnected. Too much mysterious and strangeness had invaded his life for him to ever be able to restore his faith in his ability to assess the imaginary from the real. It wasn't so much that he was in a void. He was that void. Even simple things, like the view out of the window, had changed. The buildings opposite, which were once impressive and grandiose, were now oppressive and intimidating. This luminous pale blue sky outside that was untainted by clouds, should have filled him with inspiration, but nothing stirred. And the entropy of the crowded street below that would have normally stirred him with a vibrancy and impetus, had no effect. Its ripples were not reaching him in the usual way. These things were not happening in his world. He had sunk into his own silent, personal world – which had been invaded by an incubating demon.

Alan had been back at work just over a week when Gary had to go off for a debriefing on some copy he wrote when Alan was away. Unusually, most of the other guys on the creative floor were out, for different reasons. Some were on photo shoots, others were on edits, some were doing client presentations. That's why the creative department was unusually calm.

He decided to go to the deli around the corner for a cheese and tomato sandwich, in the hope that it would fix everything. On the elevator going down he spotted Sally, his producer on Supermint Gum, chatting with Juliette in the atrium below. After the initial shock, he was filled with an overwhelming desire to talk to her. Seconds later she was heading off out on her own, and without thinking he ran down the last few steps and chased after her, touching her shoulder just as she was about to go through the revolving door. She turned to face him with a look of surprise.

He was distracted by her delicate, round gold earrings and smooth flowing hair. There were a dozen things he wanted to say, but the words just wouldn't come.

"H-h-how are you?" was the best he could do.

She smiled nervously, with an innocent, natural wide-eyed look about her. She held no malice at all, it was written all over her face. "Uh, fine. You?"

It was lunchtime, and people were awkwardly trying to get around them to get to the door.

"Yeah OK. I guess. Oh, this isn't such a good place to talk," he said. "Hey! You got time for coffee?"

Immediately she winced and took a step away from the doors, tilting her head down while giving him a sheepish look with her big, watery eyes, and raised her dark eyebrows to give him a sad look. For no reason, he had a nightmarish flashback of the demon with her terrifying, ravenous expression. It vanished as quickly as it came, but it left him worried.

"I can't, Alan," she said.

She could clearly see the disappointment in his face, because she quickly followed up by saying, "Oh, I don't mean I *won't*. "I just can't. I'm meeting my parents for tea this afternoon downtown. They're down from Groombridge for the day."

He sighed with relief, "Oh, right."

There was an uncomfortable silence, as she waited for him to say something more, though he was all-out of courage by then. She reached out and touched his elbow, and it felt right then as if she was draining away all his worries of the last few weeks.

"Listen... we should be done around six," she said helpfully. "Dad has to get back tonight. Maybe you can even come along and meet me after you finish work? We'll be at Balthazar, on Spring Street. You know that?"

The shadow that had been hanging over him was gone. "Yeah, no problem. I'll find it. See you at six."

But there was a problem with that, because he was sure he had something booked in at work for the end of the day, though he couldn't remember what it was.

"Great," she replied. "I have to get over to Sophie's for 8.30, but we'll still have an hour or two."

After that he went over to his usual deli to grab a sandwich, which he took back to the office and, as usual, peeled off two-thirds of the massive slab of

349

cheese slices that they always put into their sandwiches, then closed the bread back up and took a huge bite. He found himself looking at the photograph of Simon, Jack and Jenny on the desk. He stopped chewing, and didn't swallow until he had opened a drawer and put the picture away.

Gary came in an hour later moaning about his debrief, which in actual fact had evolved into a total re-write. Alan was unsympathetic. Instead, he threw a layout pad full of ideas he'd put together for a banking client and said, "Feast your eyes on this lot. The Chemical Bank brief is cracked."

Gary took a sip of coffee, and turned over a few pages of the pad slowly.

"Hey. Not bad for a Limey."

"You're very kind," was Alan's ironic response.

After a while Gary picked up a black magic marker and began to add a few tweaks to what Alan had done, here and there. He also drew up a few of his own concepts.

Alan said nothing about bumping into Juliette.

At Spring Street Alan got out of the subway station and walked as fast as he could in the deep snow. A little ahead he spotted a yellow cab pulling up outside the large, modern glass, restaurant frontage of Balthazar. Juliette emerged from and walked towards the red awning, then turned around to rush back and say something to the cab driver. Then she looked up and saw Alan approaching.

So, you finally made it," she said while shaking

her head.

"I would've been here twenty minutes ago," he said. "But I got dragged into a departmental meeting at five."

She gave him her little frown. "I forgive you," she said.

He glanced behind her. "So... where are your parents?" he asked.

"Dad wouldn't let me pay, even though I'm a working girl. He's picking up the tab. We almost had a scene over it."

Alan laughed. "Does he know how much you're making?"

She didn't have time to answer, because the restaurant doors swung open again and Alan guessed that it was Juliette's parents who were coming through. But he wasn't at all prepared for what he saw. The blood drained from his face. Where had he seen these people before? Then it hit him. The man with the leering smile and the woman with the horrible, cackling laugh. This was the sinister old couple from his dreams. He was sure of it. The only thing missing was the red spots covering their faces. If he ever needed confirmation that the real world was merging with dreams and fantasy, this was it.

"So, you must be Alan," said Mr Doyle holding out his hand. "Abe and Molly. We've heard all about you." He was wearing a long, heavy, expensive looking cashmere coat, and Mrs Doyle was in white fur.

"Hi," Alan said, nervously taking Mr Doyle's hand and shaking it as warmly as he could in the circumstances. However, his heart was beating fast, and his hand was shaking. Mrs Doyle noticed that.

"My, you're a very nervous young man. No need to be anxious in our presence, Alan. Juliette thinks the world of you, and if she's come to that conclusion, I'm sure we will too."

Alan didn't believe for one minute that Juliette would have mentioned anything about the fact that he was married, with two kids. Mrs Doyle came closer to give him a look of concern.

"Are you feeling OK,' she said. "Maybe you should go inside and get a glass of water."

"No need," said Alan. "I'll be fine."

Juliette tried to make light of the situation: "See the effect I have on men, mom?"

"Oh, Juliette!" said Mrs Doyle, as she nudged her daughter playfully

"I'm sorry," said Alan. "I've been recovering from a virus."

"Poor you, said Mrs Doyle. You shouldn't be out if you're not well. You should be at home getting some rest."

"I wish I could," said Alan. "But there's just too much to be getting on with at work."

"I can guess what those corporate slave drivers in the advertising industry must be like. Wanting every pound of flesh."

"But the pay's good," he replied.

They all laughed. Then Mr Doyle slapped the sides of his heavy coat, bringing the chat to an abrupt end.

"You'll have to excuse us Alan," he said. "It's been a pleasure meeting you, but we need to get to the station pronto. I have a Rotary Club meeting tonight, and I'm the chair. It wouldn't look too good if I didn't show up."

"No problem," said Alan.

When Mr and Mrs Doyle were comfortably seated in the back of the cab Mr Doyle lowered the window of the cab. "Do you play golf?" he said, looking over at Alan.

"Uh... no. I'm afraid not," said Alan, rather ashamedly.

"Never mind. You should come over sometime."

"Uh... sure. Sounds great."

"Juliette, fix it up, will you?"

Juliet nodded. "Sure dad. If Alan has the time."

"He'd better! Bye."

When the cab sped away Juliette turned to Alan and sighed, as if she was relieved they'd gone.

It wasn't easy shaking off the state of mind he was in. Dreams are supposed to be the distorted reflections of waking life, aren't they? That's how Alan saw it. So how did he manage to dream of people he never saw before in his life? And why should such a very ordinary looking, seventy-something, wholesome, all-American couple come across in such a hideous and terrifying way in his dreams? Nothing made sense to him anymore.

Just then, Juliette interrupted his reflections. "Are you feeling well enough for a glass of vino, Mr White?"

They touched glasses and said cheers. After they'd taken a sip, he felt compelled to spill it all out. He took a deep breath.

"Juliette. I want you to know this. My wife has left me and taken the kids."

She raised her eyebrows, and stayed open mouthed. "Oh."

With his hand, he gently turned her face towards him and tears welled up in her eyes. "You were a mean, selfish bastard," she said almost in a whisper.

"You're not the only one who thinks that," he said.

She opened her mouth to speak, and then thought better of it.

"Don't be afraid," he said. "Say what you need to say."

Now she became angry. "What do you want me to say?"

"I'm not expecting you to say anything." he shrugged. "I just don't want you to hold back. I deserve your anger. I admit it. I've fucked my life up, and everyone I love."

People in the wine bar were looking at them, almost as if they were watching TV. Juliette wiped her eyes.

After a moment she said, "That was real strange back then."

Alan fell back into his seat. "What was?"

"The way you fell to pieces in front of mom and dad? And don't give me all that bullshit about being ill. You have this schoolboy-type tendency to

354

look up quickly before telling a fib, like you're reading from an autocue above your head."

"Am I that much of an open book?"

"Yes."

She had him cornered. He considered telling her how since they had split up, he had lost control of his life, but he knew that didn't explain his shakiness earlier. What was the point of lying?

"I've seen them before," he said.

Juliette gave him a look that suggested she was worried about his sanity. "What?"

"It's true. I've seen your parents before - in my dreams."

She shook her head. "What are you talking about?"

He scratched his head in shame. "I know. It sounds crazy. You don't have to believe me. Look, you know normally how cynical and sceptical I am about anything remotely esoteric, or mind, body and spirit, or whatever you want to call it. Remember my views on astrology?"

"How could I forget?" She squinted, looked at her watch, stood up and said, "Shit, I have to get going. But you know what? Against my better judgement, I'll go this far... I believe that you believe you're telling the truth. Now... I'm running late. Sophie is cooking a meal for me and..."

"OK. But... will I see you again?"

She lowered her head, and took on the most enigmatic expression he'd ever seen in his life. "Bye Al."

Alan stayed behind to finish the wine, of which there was still had two-thirds of a bottle left. He also ordered a Salad Nicoise. His appetite had returned a little, since being with Juliette. But the discovery that her parents were the nightmarish couple from his dreams had left him feeling disorientated and afraid. What did it all mean? They couldn't have been any warmer in welcoming of him. And yet the power of his dream, and the memory of it, left him disgusted to be around them. It was like treading on dog shit in bare feet.

He left there after an hour, and had a horribly restless night. The images of Mr and Mrs Doyle plagued him. Jules had always said nothing but good things about them. They were, apparently, loving parents, and true pillars of their community, helping many charitable causes. How did that idea correspond to the evil, leering characters in his dream? There was only one person who might be able to make any sense of all this, and that was Robert Stringfield.

Alan's natural inclination was towards scepticism, and he wished it still was. That was despite a few little happenings in the past almost tempting him to reconsider. Now, however hard he tried, he couldn't discount the almost inexplicable perversity and coincidence of the dream alongside the unfolding of reality. His natural empiricism had been shaken to its foundations, first by the appearance of the demon. But now he was going through a mental revolution he couldn't ignore. He thought about phoning Cornelia and Bella, to ask their opinion about coming across these nightmare characters in real life. But they had emphasised that he should trust Robert Stringfield in anything connected to the demon problem. But Stringfield made him nervous, perhaps because of his military and intelligence background. Those kinds of people are never easy to work out, and their motives for whatever they do are beyond what they may appear to be.

However, the next day, when Gary left the office for a meeting with a photographer, Alan took the opportunity to dial Robert, who answered in his usual calm, business-like voice.

Alan proceeded to explain the events of last night. Suddenly Robert became assertive. "Wait. Stop right there. Let me get this straight. What you're telling me now is that you came across those two people that featured prominently in your dreams?"

"That's right."

"And who are they?"

"They're Juliette's parents – you know, that girl that I had a sort of relationship with."

"Oh. Of course, yes. I remember now. Juliette."

"What are their names?"

Alan went quiet for a second.

"Abe and Molly Doyle.

"What do you know about them?" Robert was totally business-like now, almost scary.

"They're in their sixties, and they live in a place called Groombridge, Connecticut."

"Groombridge. Yes. I know it. OK, I'll take it from here."

"Uh… so, what are you going to do."

"You don't need to know."

358

Chapter 22

"So, what's your plan?" said Isobel. "Will you do some RV, I mean, to find out if this freaky couple are connected to the succubus somehow?"

"I need a lot more information. Like where these people lived for the last twenty-five years, their backgrounds, if they have any criminal records, their connections – stuff like that, so I can build a detailed picture. The main thing is to locate a place – and of course a time."

Isobel brought over a glass of brandy with ice.

"That could take a while and a ton of digging around in public records offices and reference libraries."

"Yes. It would normally. But I'm calling Mitch."

She looked at Robert in disbelief. "What? You can't keep asking for favours from Langley. You do that enough times and they'll draw you back in."

He coughed. "Listen Izzy. This kind of request is small beer. And anyway, after what I went through for the flag, they owe me."

Chapter 23

At work, Alan was starting to feel marginalized, and things with Jenny were actually getting worse. But even if she really wanted to go the whole hog, with separation and divorce and everything, he wanted to resolve things amicably, just between themselves. It would have been great just to get some common sense from her. If for no other reason than so he could talk to the boys. But it was useless. She had made herself uncontactable. He got no reply from his calls or messages. Just letters from her lawyer, with a date for the hearing and a whole lot of miserable demands. It was looking like he would have to get himself a lawyer too, sooner rather than later. More than once he found himself sobbing in the apartment at night.

He called Barry Tonks, a copywriter friend of his working in the London office of GGP. Barry thought he wanted to discuss campaign ideas. But they didn't talk about advertising for long, because Alan needed some advice about other things. Barry had been through it all with his wife kicking him out of the house a few years back, and after a lot of shit, he had now come out the other end. Barry told him straight, if there was any way to fix his marriage he should give it his best shot – because he wouldn't wish this crap on his worst enemy. "She hurts you, you hurt her, and the kids get hurt for the rest of their lives."

Alan listened with trepidation, but said he

wasn't hopeful of any reconciliation. By the end of the call, Barry gave Alan the contact details for his solicitor.

Alan had the number in front of him when he picked up the phone again, but then he changed his mind and dialed another number. He honestly thought Juliette would tell him to get lost when he asked if she would like to join him to an opening night in a gallery downtown. After a long silence, she said it happened to be her night off from the play. She was only going to stay in and watch TV.

She'd been standing outside her front door in her grey three-quarter length coat freezing. As soon as she saw him look out of the taxi window, she trotted down the steps of her brownstone. Her hair was a slightly redder shade of auburn now and it was tied up in a loose bun. She got into the back with him and held up her cheek for him to kiss, which he did sheepishly, after which she smiled and buckled up. He couldn't help wanting to take her in his arms and carry her back up those stairs and into the bedroom.

Traffic was moving at a snail's pace, so they got out at Broadway and Lafayette and walked the rest of the way, even though it was snowing heavily. The conversation between them was not exactly flowing freely, so it was a relief when they arrived. The Sylvia Lake Gallery was sandwiched between two clothing boutiques on Greene. Its white marble entrance was made up of neo-classical columns, framing four windows. There was a large grey-green granite statue of the god Shiva at the front.

The crowd was already pretty healthy. Chamber music was coming through the speakers. Some people were even looking at the artwork. Alan and Juliette declined to hand in their bags and coats. However, they did accept a glass of wine each, and made their way through a crowd of people into a space where they could actually appreciate some of Isobel's paintings.

They were mostly early evening or nighttime scenes of New York. People didn't feature much, and when they did, they seemed very much alone, and unconnected to one another. Alan wondered if Isobel was an existentialist.

Alan steered Juliette towards one of the walls where some of the smaller paintings were hung, and from the corner of his eye, he noticed Isobel, in a tight fitting, sky-blue, silk brocade dress with short sleeves, and silver high heels. She was talking to some people at the back of the room: a big balding, Middle Eastern looking man, in a blue suit, and a thin woman, with her hair in a sharp bob. There was also a forty-something couple there, both of them dressed in black. All of them appeared to be hanging onto every word Isobel said. Nearby was the obviously disinterested and lonely figure of Robert Stringfield. He was in a single-breasted grey mohair suit. Robert eventually saw Alan, and his face came to life. He hurried over to him, his voice resonating as he approached.

"Alan! Well, aren't you going to introduce me to your lovely friend?"

Juliette seemed awed by this huge man who exuded such power and self-assurance. She looked at Alan and reddened.

"Sure. This is Juliette. We… uh work together occasionally. Jules, this is Robert."

'Oh," said Juliette.

Robert knew exactly who Juliette was. He shook her hand and showed her his pure white toothy grin.

"Charmed!" said Robert. "So, Juliette… tell me, are you enjoying the show? You can be completely open with me, because it's not my work, it's my wife's."

Juliette and Alan both laughed.

"Oh, well… I'm no expert," said Juliette, "but the paintings I've just seen are really beautiful."

Robert rubbed his hands together while leaning forward slightly, as if inviting Juliette into a confidence. "Well don't tell Isobel. Her ego's swollen enough as it is."

"Oh, I'm sure she…"

Juliette was interrupted by the voice of Isobel, who had just come over at that moment. "Excuse me, I heard that."

Robert pulled a fake look of terror.

"Ah. About time you broke away from those boring people."

"Shush Robert, or the reviews tomorrow will be less than flattering."

He put his arm around her and left it there. "Sorry sweetheart."

Alan then leaned forward to kiss her on the cheek. "Hello Alan."

"Hey Isobel," said Alan, pointing all around. "What can I say? Lovely work."

"Oh you, naughty flatterer. Stop right there. But speaking of lovely… who is this delightful creature at your side this evening?"

Alan hadn't expected Isobel and Robert to be so welcoming to Juliette, and was secretly pleased about it. "I'll let her introduce herself," he said.

She held out her hand. "Juliette Doyle. Pleasure to meet you."

Isobel then took it "Likewise…"

As Isobel held Juliette's hand Alan noticed that she threw the briefest look of astonishment to Robert, but she quickly composed herself. She let go of Juliette's hand and pointed to a large painting on the wall beside where we stood.

"So, what do you think of this one, Alan?"

Alan turned to his left and stepped a little more towards the painting.

"Ah. Now let me think," he replied, "It has a kind of Edward Hopper flavour, and maybe also a touch of Frank Brangwyn too, if you don't mind me saying."

"Clever boy. I love both those painters."

Robert shook his head in mock despair and took Julia by the elbow.

"Why don't we leave these two to go through their memorized list of Who's Who in Fine Art, and go meet some interesting people?"

And they went off, to enter into deep discussion for quite a while. Alan wondered what they were talking about.

Meanwhile he moved a fraction closer to the

painting Isobel pointed out. It was a strange picture, because it took for its subject matter the entrance to a tunnel. A shadowy modern block type building took up much of the picture, with a steel-ribbed structure that seemed to be stretched over the mouth of the tunnel. The sky was painted in a rich blue-violet, and the cars at the bottom of the picture moving towards the entrance were like phantoms.

"Is it the Holland Tunnel?" Alan asked.

She laughed. "Got it in one. You've obviously travelled to New Jersey a few times?"

"Actually no," he said. "I'm familiar with it only because it's just around the corner from the hotel I stayed at before I found the apartment."

"Ah."

"So, what inspired you to paint this scene?" he asked.

"Are you just being polite?"

"No. Really. Please."

"Well... I did it years ago. Just a few weeks before I was due to go for an operation to remove a tumour. I didn't know if I would come out the other end, if you know what I mean, and a dark ominous tunnel seemed about right..."

"Oh, I see the..."

Just then Alan felt a strong tap on his shoulder, and as he turned around, he felt an almighty slap in his face. He was shocked and bewildered. His right cheek throbbed as he realized, the culprit was Gary's wife, Fiona. She faced him with a look of intense, glare-eyed malice. From behind her people were staring at him open mouthed. Right then, he wanted to be anywhere but here. Fiona seemed to be struggling to find the words to express her venom. Eventually she found them:

"Is that how you get your kicks Alan White? Beating on your wife? Do your friends know about you? Huh? Do they?"

Thoughts were popping on and off in his brain like so many cheap firecrackers, and none of them fitted. He felt too dirty and unworthy, and couldn't bring himself to respond in any way, particularly with anger, even though Fiona was making a complete spectacle of him – and herself. Ironically, he had always been very fond of her, having imagined she was sociable and warm, as well as great fun to be around. But the depressing thing was, everything she was saying was right. Fortunately, Gary, stepped into the fray to drag her away.

"Come on Fi. This is no good, honey."

He looked at Alan and is face said, "Sorry."

But she wriggled free from him and yelled, "No!"

Two over-sized security people in black suits and electronic earpieces came over, but Isobel stepped in to assure them everything was under control. Reluctantly they moved away. Isobel then approached Fiona and spoke calmly.

"I know you mean well, Fiona… but Alan was not responsible for his actions the other night. He meant no harm to Jenny at all."

"Really? Well he sure went about it the wrong way. I spoke to Jenny this afternoon - and she can still barely talk. She sounds like she has a bad case of laryngitis. Aside from the bruising that goes all the way round her neck, she has bleeding and swelling *inside*. She's also suffering from blurred vision and ringing in her ears. She can't sleep and she's a nervous wreck. Happy with your night's work Mr. White?"

Alan was taken aback, because he had no way knowing any of that. Her lawyers hadn't mentioned those issues, but he supposed they were saving it for the courts. Before he could say anything, Robert stepped in:

"Fiona, please. I know you mean well, but Jenny is not aware of the terrible stress Alan was going through. Like Isobel said, he was not himself at the time and…"

Gary was now looking more embarrassed than Alan had ever seen him before. Fiona had her face in her hands and weeping. Gary put his arm around her again, trying to lead her away. "We'd better go, love."

Fiona turned to him and spat out, "Oh piss off!"

Then she shook herself free to walk briskly towards the exit of her own accord. Gary shrugged and followed.

Juliette, who had been watching all this from a distance, came over with Robert.

"What the hell was all that about?" she asked.

"Let's get out of here, and I'll tell you everything."

Isobel decided to leave them to it, and go off to be the hostess again. As Alan and Juliette started to leave Robert called out to them. "Hey, Alan, Juliette."

They stopped and turned around, and saw him

367

holding two wine glasses for them.

"Where are you guys going? I got you these."

"I'm sorry, Robert," said Alan. "But we really have to get going."

Robert seemed anxious about something.

"Are you sure?"

Juliette stood in and said, "I have a bit of a headache and…"

"Sure. And it couldn't have been easy for you Alan, with Fiona going off like that."

"That's OK, Robert. I'm a big boy now."

He bit his lower lip and then said, "I… I wanted to tell you..." He flicked a glance at Juliette and then back to Alan, as if to say that he really didn't want anyone else to hear what he was trying to tell him. "Uh, how can I put this? You know I said before that there was a chance you could have, you know… those problems again with that…"

He waited for Alan to show some sign to confirm that I knew what Robert was referring to.

"Yes?"

"Well, I want to assure you now, your troubles are over."

"Really?"

"Let's not go into details now. Call me later."

The snow was falling heavily when Juliette and Alan left the gallery. They walked towards Houston when Juliette stopped dead and the flakes started to settle on her hair.

"Alan. What the fuck is going on? Did you really beat on your wife? I mean… Gary's wife said you tried to strangle her and… is she crazy, or

368

what?"

"No, I...."

"No, what?"

"No, she's not crazy."

"So, it's true?"

"It's complicated, that's what it is."

"Fuck!"

"Please give me a chance to explain..."

"Well?"

He scratched his head, then hailed a cab which pulled over. But Juliette would not get in until he answered her.

"Right. It's not what you think, and I promise I will tell you everything - but not here."

"Then where?"

"Let's just get in and we'll talk."

"Where to?"

"I don't know... what about if we go to my place and order a Chinese?"

She licked her lip and seemed unable to decide, but by this time the cab driver was getting irritated, so they both got in.

When they were on their way Alan asked, "So how did you get on with Robert?"

"Oh him. Jesus. Is he for real?"

"What was he talking to you about?"

"He was like, you know... really interrogating me about my *parents*. He must've asked me maybe *dozen* questions about them. Why would he do that? Don't you think that's kind of weird? What is it with my parents?"

Alan didn't say a thing.

Chapter 24

The next morning Robert was a little hung over. He dragged himself out of bed at around ten, and outside the apartment door was the Times newspaper, as usual, but also a few letters. He picked everything up and went in to make a much-needed pot of coffee. As he filled the kettle he shouted out to Isobel, "You want some coffee!"

There was no reply, although he thought he heard a groan or two.

He poured the water into the cafetiere and took it to the table, along with his cup, and started opening the mail. The first letter was a bill from the phone company. The next was a statement on his military pension. The third came from Virginia. He opened it up enthusiastically. As he hoped, it was from Mitch. He had come good - as always.

Hey Rob!

I knew you would only get around to writing when you had some kind of ulterior motive. Still, it's good to hear from you. Pease congratulate Isobel on the success of her new show. Always knew that girl had talent (other than the one she used here, I mean).

You two did the right thing getting out when you did. I'm tearing my hair out here. You won't believe what's going down. To make sure we all toe the line they've got this other General (Clamforth) to muscle in on the project, and he wants to change things around a bit, and he's started by trying to break our links with Stanford Research Institute. The word is Washington doesn't want any more "time-wasting nonsense warnings and questionable intel from overpaid mumbo-jumbo psychics". They're threatening to wind us up, or run a paired down operation out of Fort Mead. If things ever kick off, the military will be as ready as they were at Pearl Harbour. Right now, I'm sitting here doing nothing but watching the reports pile up. Which is why I had plenty of time to do some rooting for you.

That couple from Connecticut you want checked out: you crazy? The Agency is strictly *verboten* to gather intelligence on US citizens. OK, from time to time, out of extreme necessity, we might bend the rules. But, lucky for you, over at the Bureau, when they investigate specific domestic crimes, they can provide other law enforcement agencies (like ourselves) with cooperative services. They also have a huge database on just about everyone in the US of A. So, I gave my friend there a call, and he did some digging around.

You might find some of this interesting: Abraham Leonard Doyle and Margaret Elisabeth Philomena Doyle (affectionately known as 'Molly") are pillars of their community in Groombridge, a small town out on the edge of Cockaponset State Forest, Connecticut. It's an unusually wealthy place: population of under four thousand, 96.5% of which are white. And virtually none of the families are below the poverty line. Abe is a successful, self-made businessman, who has gone on to very big things and she is a respected judge, doting wife and mother, ceaseless charity worker, and chair of the town's women's institute. In 1962, he formed his own construction company that became highly successful within four years, and well known for the quality of its public building projects throughout Middlesex County. In 1966 Abe served as a member of the Connecticut Constitutional Convention, becoming President and C.E.O. of GD Bank, and serving as a member of the Board of Directors of the Federal Home Loan Bank of Groombridge, and Chairman of the National Council of Savings Organisations. Apart from that he is also on the board of directors of the William Walters Technical College, and the local Groombridge Town Advisory Board, as well as an active supporter of the Middlesex Community Foundation, and founding member of the Blackheath Golfing Association. He is now Chair of the Groombridge Symposium, which takes up a lot of his time these days. His wife's too.

You referred to her as 'Molly' Doyle, but in her professional life she is better known as Margaret Doyle, or rather Justice Margaret Doyle. Apart from being a mom and a district judge, Margaret Doyle is active in an array of community, charitable and business activities, that includes running various businesses from her home and becoming the President of the Groombridge Chapter of the Women's Institute. She graduated from Fairfield University (which is where she met Abe) and the University of Connecticut School of Law with High Honours, before she joined the law firm of

Waterhouse & Barnett, where she specialised in bankruptcy and financial restructuring. Accusations have been expressed as to her integrity, in respect to the possible misuse of public funds. It's interesting to point out here that the Connecticut Judicial Review member committee has fielded hundreds of complaints filed by citizens against judges in Groombridge, and Judge Doyle's name came up in several recent State legislative hearings, in which hundreds of Connecticut families claimed to have been victimised by corrupt public officials working within the State's courts and the Department of Children and Families. So far, any charges against Judge Margaret Doyle and other public officials in Groombridge have not stuck, for lack of evidence – (or obstructions put in the way by certain people in high places). However, U.S. Attorney Elizabeth Goring is working to set up a Connecticut Public Corruption Task Force in a joint initiative with the FBI, Internal Revenue Service, and the Inspector General's Offices of the United States Department of Health and Human Services, to investigate further. But don't hold your breath.

Now, like I said, Goombridge is mostly a town of white-collar types with plenty of disposable income and too much leisure time. Maybe that explains all the wife- swapping that goes on there, of which Abe and Molly are keen practitioners, as are a lot of their friends and associates in the Goombridge Symposium – a local business association.

In 1978 Abe's firm, Premier Construction, lost out on a massive $9 million restoration project in

Hartford, in a bid. The winners were, Kean & Butler, a local rival. Lucky for him almost the same week the internal revenue did an audit on Kean & Butler's business operation, following a detailed tip off from an unknown source. They raided their offices and took away several folders that resulted in charges against Kean & Butler of unlawful accounting and tax evasion. It led to a bill for back taxes of $5,678,104, and ultimately the suicide of Simon Kean, the lead partner in the firm. The company then filed for bankruptcy, meaning they were unable to carry out the major public works project and as a consequence Abe's company, coming second in the bid like they did, was then awarded the project. Now you can read what you like into this, but soon after that Victor Martinelli, the former chief accountant of Kean & Butler, was recruited by Abe into a senior position in his firm. If you were a gambling man, would you bet against Mr. Martinelli being the Internal Revenue's 'unknown source'?

Another story that could be of interest is in 1979 Abe fell out with his business partner, Hank Partridge, over a dispute relating to profit shares. Precise details are not known, but just before the case was due to be heard in court Hank's car careered into a tree on Route 8. Within fifteen minutes he was taken by ambulance to a hospital in Hartford, but died soon after arrival from severe internal injuries. After that his family didn't pursue the dispute with Doyle, because Abe settled with them out of court - probably for a tiny fraction of the figure in question. So, it seems like Abe has a fairy godmother, or someone up there (or maybe down there), watching over him. Don't you think?

Moving on: you specifically asked for any details that were available about the death of Abe and Molly's daughter. As you know, she was one of twins – both girls - Vanessa Maria Agatha Doyle, and Juliette Eva Alexandra Doyle: born June 21st, 1967, at the Banbury Medical Centre in Connecticut. Records state that it was at the same hospital at 2.05am on July 23rd, just four weeks after she was born, that Vanessa died. Cause of death is sited as pulmonary embolus (which I gather is some kind of a clot to the lung). But the coroner's report is a little too succinct for my friend's liking. The medic assigned was a Dr. Richard Fenwick, friend of Abraham Doyle and long-term member of Groombridge Symposium. The coroner was Professor Stephanie du Cann, wife of Richard Fenwick and member of Groombridge Symposium. The judge at the Coroner's Court was Justice Peter Marson, a good friend of Margaret (or Mollie) Doyle, and a member of the Groombridge Symposium. It's also worth noting that the cremation was done in a real hurry too. Oh, and the funeral director at the burial was James Clarkson, also a member of the Groombridge Symposium. Can you see a pattern building here?

I asked Matt, my friend at the bureau, to give me whatever he could on the Groombridge Symposium. I thought it might be like some kind of Rotary Club, dishing out support to children's groups and third world charities and the like. And it does do some of that. But it seems to be hard to pin down what the real point of this organisation is. If anything, it's closer to Freemasonry than Rotary, though it has many women members. My friend at the Bureau said there is evidence of an esoteric side to this organization, but he didn't have much time to dig up any more on that, though he may be able to at a later date.

But I have to say, I'm kind of curious. In all the years I've known you, you never showed a propensity for detective work, building up character profiles, or hunting people down - other than with the old RV, of course. So, what's all this about?

Anyway, don't be a stranger. Call me up if you ever go to these parts.

Ciao.

Mitch

As soon as he read it, he rushed off to the bedroom and nudged Isobel awake.

She turned around, sat up and started rubbing her eyes. Then she glared at him and said, "What the fuck are you doing?"

"I'm going to need your help, Izzy. I need to do a session."

Chapter 25

Gary felt a complete idiot when he followed Fiona out of the gallery that night. It was snowing heavily as she stormed out hugging her elbows and tensing her shoulders, trampling along the sidewalk in shoes that were totally inappropriate for the conditions. What a waste of an evening. There was still over an hour and a half on the meter when he found her waiting for him by the car. She didn't look at him as he unlocked it. She just got in, opened her door, slammed it shut and leaned her head against the side window, wiping her eyes and sniffing theatrically. He got into the car and sat down by the wheel, trying hard to think of something to say. All he could come up with was, "You want to pick up a Chinese?"

She turned to face him with a look of disgust. So, he turned away and started the engine. They were home in less than ten minutes, having not said another word to each other. They walked across Greenwich Avenue, and he felt sorry for the long line of people they passed outside the jazz club. Some of them were stomping up and down on the spot to keep warm, and others were brushing the settling snow off their shoulders. Obviously, whoever was playing there tonight must be really good, concluded Gary.

When they got upstairs, Gary unlocked the door and Fiona blew past him like a gust of wind, heading straight for the bedroom, and slamming the door behind her. It needed a braver man than Gary to follow her. So, he just sat down to watch the Giants and the Dallas Cowboys over a couple of beers. Just when it was getting tense (in the last quarter) she decided to come out and sit on the armrest near him. He realised this was his cue to switch off the game.

"Do you think I'm going a bit crazy?" she said.

He cleared his throat and tried hard to think of an appropriate reply. The best he could do was: "Oh, I wouldn't say that, hon. You're upset, is all. Jenny is your friend, and, understandably… the way you see things, Alan was, you know..."

She opened her eyes wide and furrowed her brow.

"I know what?" she said.

"You, uh, responded in a way which you thought appropriate when you saw him just now."

"Hm. And I went a bit overboard?"

Gary took a sip of his drink, and there was a moment there when they were both waiting for each other to react. Finally, Gary found he couldn't stop himself spraying out a mouthful of beer and laughing like a hyena. It was the best thing he could've done, because she started to giggle too, before reaching over to hug him around the neck. She lifted his arm around her shoulder and rested her head there.

She had a sullen look when she asked, "Do you still think Alan is an OK guy?"

From her reversion to baby talk, Gary realised she was giving him an opportunity to make a case for Alan. He gave it his best shot.

"It's not as simple as that," he said. "What he did to Jenny was totally, totally wrong. I know that. But, the important thing to remember here is that he didn't know it was Jenny. It was like a waking nightmare. And when he realised what he'd just done, well he was, uh, you know... absolutely horrified."

She moved out of his arms and sat up straight to face him. Her already dark complexion erupted into an even darker shade whenever she was angry.

"Oh, I see. He thought it was some other woman?"

"No, no, no! That's not what I'm saying. Jesus. Look. He was having some kind of episode. He had this terrible dream, with some kind of horrific monster in it, and he thought he'd woken up... but he hadn't, and he believed he had this hideous, half-dead thing next to him on the bed so he lunged for it. But... it was Jenny."

Fiona shook her head.

"He told me a while back that he occasionally gets these kinds of a flashbacks from an acid trip he had, when he was an art student. That experience, the trip I mean, really freaked him out, and made him think about death, and his thoughts went all kind of sinister, depressing and weird. Now don't get me wrong, he was never a junky or anything. Just experimenting. Unfortunately for him, his constitution was not suited to... you know, drug taking: certainly not psychedelic drugs, anyway. And it is a medically accepted fact that lysergic acid, can cause flashbacks years after the event."

379

"Oh." She nodded a few times, "That's very reassuring. So basically, what you're saying is... he could do something like this again?"

"What? No. You're not listening to me…"

"Pf. All this crap about him not being responsible for his actions, I bet that's what every wife-beater comes out with when they're pushed into a corner. Well, I won't fall for it. I still can't believe Jenny doesn't want to press criminal charges. I want him completely out of our lives. Do you understand me, Gary Cummins?"

She stood up, hands on hips, giving him her intense, schoolmistress stare, and repeated herself very slowly: "I-said-do-you-understand-me?"

Fiona's intensity was not to be challenged. Yes, he had to work with Alan every day. He was his partner – and friend. Creative teams that don't have the kind of camaraderie going on are missing something. And Fiona was demanding that he put the kibosh on all that. Bang! He thought for a moment about telling her the truth about what Alan was really going through, making reference to Robert Stringfield's book. But he knew very well the she would never have the patience to listen to that kind of reasoning – one that required reference to evidence and reason – especially when the supernatural was involved. Like the novocaine that blocks patient's ability to feel pain, her scepticism bars any sensory data that doesn't fit with her well ensconced world-view. If she saw a ghost at the end of her bed, she'd find a way to deny it, because to do otherwise would be to blow away her world, leaving her drowning in darkness. Gary became

380

reflective in his despair. He considered that maybe someday the piecing together of disconnected facts will reveal such a terrifying picture of reality, and the insignificance of our place in the universe, that even extreme sceptics like Fiona will either go mad or flee from the terrifying light of disclosure into the false safety of unknowing in a new dark age. But her attitude to other-worldliness is neither here nor there. Nevertheless, he needed her. She was his little Fi. Unfortunately, what she was saying was: 'It's either him or me'.

The next morning at work was a bit awkward. Alan came in way after Gary did, as usual. This time he was looking particularly sheepish as he took off his coat. To break the ice Gary said he was just going off to get some coffee, did he want anything?

Alan nodded. "Sure. Strong black, one sugar."

Ten minutes later he was checking his email when Gary pushed the door open with his backside. He came in and put his paper cup on top of his copy of Advertising Age and put one in front of Alan. Then he sat down, chin in his hands, staring at the steaming coffee in front of Alan.

"Drink it," he said. "You look like you fucking need it."

Alan took the tiniest sip and said, "I've decided not to fight Jenny's demands."

"You what?" said Gary in surprise, causing coffee to dribble down his chin. He wiped it on his sweater. "What about the fucking exclusion order? If you don't do anything about that, you won't see your kids."

Alan took off his watch and started fiddling with the winder.

"Watch is off its rocker... "

"Never mind the fucking watch."

But Alan kept on winding it. His mind was somewhere else. Eventually he focused on Gary again.

"Last night... I don't blame Fiona for saying what she did."

Alan's downheartedness was worrying Gary.

"Look bud, you don't have to be so magnanimous, really. I should be apologising. She was.... You know, out of order. Emotional."

"She was right."

"That's bullshit. But to fill her in on why you did what you did... I would have had to get into a discussion of the supernatural, and that's where I'd run into a road block.

I love her to bits - but her mind is about as open as Fort Knox. Anyway, she's got this regular phone call thing going with Jenny right now and - well, you don't need me to tell you..."

"Gary, listen. Fiona is one of the loveliest, most genuine people I know. She wears her heart on her sleeve, that's all. I just hope that one day all of this, calms down, and things can get back to how they were."

Gary leaned back into his seat and breathed in deeply. Alan frowned.

"You don't seem too hopeful."

"No. I'm thinking of something else, well, it's kind of related."

"What?"

"Look, there's no easy way for me to say this, because you're not just my art-director, you're a buddy."

"And?"

He leaned forward, chin still in his palms, elbows on the table and rubbed his eyes with his fingertips. "I am going to ask Steve to team me up with Jack," he said. "Sarah is going on maternity leave, and the likelihood is she's not coming back anytime in the next three years. Her husband is a Wall Street trader, so there's no pressure to earn a buck or anything. So Jack needs a writer."

Alan said nothing. He didn't even show any kind of response. Gary expected him to at least put up some kind of argument. Maybe they would even get into a shouting match, or something. But there was none of that. Alan simply pouted, then furrowed his brow, as if he was answering a trick question in a pub quiz. Then he nodded and said, "OK."

It didn't seem right.

Next morning Gary got into work early, as usual, and after sitting down to go through his messages he found there was an email from Alan saying he wasn't feeling too good, and he had a sore throat. But he might come in later.

He didn't.

Gary was furious. There was a ton of stuff to get through. He tried to call him at home several times throughout the morning, but he didn't pick up. By lunchtime he gave up and started working on the initial pitch ideas for Cheerios on his own. In the

383

afternoon he decided to call Juliette. Surely, she would know where to find him. But she didn't pick up either. So he left a message for her at Juilliard. At one point Steve popped his head in the office and asked where Alan was. Gary just said he'd picked up some kind of virus.

Steve took a deep breath then said, "What the fuck? After two weeks of doing nothing in the country?"

This was not good for Alan, or Gary.

Working on his own, Gary somehow managed to come up with some semi-decent ideas for the pitch. The trouble was they all needed more thinking, and the only way that would happen is if he could bounce things around with someone else, whether that was with Alan - or whoever. Just as he was packing away to go home, he got a call back from Juliette. She sounded a bit out of breath and apologised for getting back to him so late in the day, but she'd been at rehearsals. He asked if Alan was staying with her. She said no. He wanted to stay at his place the night before. But she did say she would go around there to check out if he was OK. (She had a key).

Back at their apartment in West Village, Fiona and Gary were sitting down to their supper, while watching TV when the phone rang. They thought about ignoring it, but Gary had a feeling it was important. It was Juliette. She sounded concerned. She said Alan was not home, and his bed had not been slept in. Did he think Alan may have flipped and got a flight back to London maybe?

Gary felt a wave of pins and needles pass through him. He didn't know what to think. He wasn't hungry any more. Fiona asked what was going on. He told her Alan may have taken a flight home, and she just snarled and said if he went anywhere near Jenny he would be arrested and locked up. Gary needed some space to think, so he used the bedroom phone to ring round the airports: JFK, Newark – even La Guardia, just in case Alan was getting an internal flight somewhere (God knows where). They all eventually said there was no Alan White registered for any flights yesterday or today, or tomorrow. Gary knew he had a good friend in LA, so maybe he took a train there, or maybe he even hired a car.

Alan didn't show up to work the next day either, but Gary was ready for that. He had arranged to hook up with Brian, another art-director, and they got down to working up the pitch ideas Gary did the day before. By lunchtime they had four solid routes to explore.

In the afternoon Gary had a meeting about some work for an existing client, with

The account team - Brendan, Elaine and Christine, in one of the smaller meeting rooms, which was interrupted by Steve's PA, Jackie, knocking on the door.

"Phone call from your wife. She says it's urgent."

He took the call in his office. "Hi Fi. I'm in a meeting." He could tell she was snivelling. "What's up, honey?"

"Oh God."

"What the hell is it?"

"I got a call from Jenny just now."

"Is she OK?"

"She's fine, given… given the circumstances."

"What circumstances?"

"She just got a call from NYPD. Alan's body was fished out of the East River this morning."

Chapter 26

Robert sat in the leather armchair, dreamily checking out the lights of the West Side across the white blanket of the park. An antique copy of *Saducismus Triumphatus* opened up in his lap, but he had enough of reading and was weighing up the idea of rolling up a special cigarette. That was when Isobel breezed into the lounge in her messed-up dungarees, wiping paint off her fingers and making noises like she was in pain:

"Argh! I hate doing portraits of rich people who refuse to sit, and then don't even let you take a proper photograph for reference."

"Turn the job down."

"I can't. She's my biggest patron."

"Who?" he said twisting around to face her.

"Philomena Steinberg. Who else? Heiress to the du Pont billions, if she lives long enough to inherit."

Isobel came closer to him and bent over his shoulder to get a look an illustration in his book of a bat-like demon summoned by witches.

"Jesus, What the hell is that?" she said pointing.

"You wouldn't understand," he said.

She gave him a look of contempt and threw the rag onto the coffee table.

"So anyhow, I'm ready now. You still want to do this thing?"

He slammed the book shut. "Very good."

They had everything set up in his office, as before. The EEG monitor was fine-tuned, the low lighting was selected.

"Right," said Robert. "Thanks to Mitch we know where Abe and Molly Doyle were living at the time. We also know that their girls, the twins, Vanessa and Juliette Doyle, were born on June 21, 1976, and that one of them died four weeks later."

"So, what does that mean?"

Robert looked up at the ceiling in disappointment.

"The first full moon after they were born was Sunday July 11, 1967," he said. "So that's my target. I'm going to check in just before midnight that day."

She bit the bent knuckle of her forefinger. Then she spoke while wincing, as if she was pained or embarrassed by what she was about to express.

"Robert, I'm only going to say it once, but I have a really bad feeling about this."

"About what?"

"I don't know. That weird couple, the one's in Alan's dream - your obsessiveness, everything."

"Jesus, how many viewings have you sat with me on? And how many have I done in total? Two hundred? Three?"

She shook her head, with a look of sadness and confusion.

"My skills are not so finely honed as yours, but my radar is up. And that's the truth. Maybe it's nothing."

He went over to kiss her on the forehead.

"I'd say you're tired from the work you put into your show, and Christ - you haven't given yourself a break since it went up. You need to slow down Izzy. After this maybe we should spend a few days on the coast."

She looked up at him with watery eyes and said, "That would be nice."

While Isobel fine-tuned the electroencephalogram (EEG monitor), Robert dimmed the lights and sat down facing the empty chair. She left the room to get changed while he relaxed through the various mental states. By When she came back, now in her French fisherman's striped sweater and a smart black skirt, she found he was sinking into a calm, warm and velvety beta state. She came in and sat opposite him and picked up the target folder, pulled out a piece of paper and slid it towards him. After he gave it a quick glance and then noticed that Isobel's short hair appeared to glow, because of the soft light behind her, making her look like a religious icon. Slowly his head dropped, as he reached the theta stage. He was now in the zone.

She put a pencil in front of him and he picked it up dreamily, along with a pad of paper on a board. Then she started to read out the coordinates.

"Seven, three, two, seven, one, nine... four, one, one, seven, five, eight."

He was sinking deeper and deeper. She took the pad from him to get a good look at it. He'd drawn a circle made up of much smaller circles with a small rectangle inside it, near the top.

"Is it a sort of clock that's stopped," she asked.

"I don't know'" he replied, as if in a dream.

"Well, there are thirteen circles going around, so maybe it's not a clock."

"No."

"So, what is it?"

He looked back at the drawing and his left eye started to water, as he dropped the pencil and grew more and more limp. A part of him was loosening up and the room seemed to be dissolving. Somewhere there was an intense tingling going on. He was aware of a dual consciousness that was out of synch with everything around him. He knew there was a body there, but he was only loosely connected to it. The room was now made up of pulsing semi-transparent squares. Nothing seemed fixed because everything was fading at the edges. It stayed that way for a while before things started to settle down and he was able to focus on entering those squares, to go in there... deeper and deeper, until he eventually lost track of his original frames of reference. By then he was almost a completely disembodied consciousness. Complex, kaleidoscopic patterns were shifting around chaotically, which disorientated him. He closed his eyes, but it made no difference, because it wasn't his eyes that were seeing – it was his mind. Soon a number of green dots appeared from nowhere. They started aligning themselves into an endless series of squares over a violet background. His thinking had become more focused, and he relaxed even further, floating between the complex arrangements of squares. Eventually the saturated colour drained away leaving behind a nighttime scene of rooftops, roads, driveways and countryside. He was falling gently now, like a feather in a breeze. A tingling sensation ran through him as he floated in a swirling blue-grey mist. There was a woman's voice coming from somewhere.

"Relax Robert. Get a sense of where you are. Let yourself find it. Focus on the coordinates."

It was a relief to know she was there.

"What can you see?" she asked.

He had to concentrate. Communication was not easy in this state.

"A big moon low in the sky and some dim stars between ominous clouds. I've... I've got a visual of a rooftop... a grey one. Hold on..."

He was shifting involuntarily around the target, and had to summon all his will to make his position more stable.

"OK now?" said Izzy.

"Mm."

"Good. What are you seeing?"

I had to think hard. "I... I...I'm now at street level outside this large, white, colonial house... A gust of wind is bringing in the fresh, faint smell of the sea..."

"Good. What else?"

"There's a classical portico and a generous lawn with a white picket fence on the street and a row of healthy-looking red roses growing behind it. Huge elm trees all around... and I'm getting a strong whiff of the freshly mown grass.

"OK..."

He paused for a moment to re-connect to his

innate syntactical abilities so he could describe what he was seeing, while he adjusted his movements in this phantom state.

"Parked outside the front lawn at the end of the gravel path, behind me, there's a big blue car, a Pontiac, I think. I'm looking round now. Wait… a thin man in his forties wearing a fitted leather jacket and Wyatt Earp moustache is leaning against the driver's door of the car, picking his fingernails with the nails of his other hand. Someone is calling him. Let me look back. Yes. A slightly shorter, but overweight guy in a lightweight and heavily crumpled suit is walking towards him from the house… waving aggressively to him to get into the car. Then the big set guy is going back to the porch – looks like he's waiting there, like a nervous best man at a wedding. The house door is opening and… yes. It's them. Abe and Mollie Doyle are stepping out of the house. They look much younger than the photo of them Mitch sent us. She is blonde and fair skinned, about 38. Abe is a little older, with a slightly receding head of medium length brown hair. They're each carrying a white bundle in their arms. There's a baby inside each bundle. The big guy in the crumpled suit is closing the front door and follows, catching up hurriedly to open the car doors and let them each in at the back; first Mollie, on the near side and then Abe at the far side. Now Fatso's getting in at the front."

"Get in with them."

"Me?"

"Yes, you."

"OK. I'm in the back of the car behind Abe and

Molly Doyle. The baby Molly is holding is crying and it's woken up the other one who is just starting to do the same. Mollie's taken out two dummies from a small bag, and… she's put one in each baby's mouth. It does the trick. They're quiet now. Suck, suck, suck."

"That's enough with the sound effects."

"Looking at the road… the town is thinning away. We've passed two large industrial warehouses and the streetlights have thinned out. We're rapidly approaching the outskirts, moving along country lanes: dark, thick woodland either side of us. The babies are looking back my way – obviously not at me… they can't see me, but they're watching the furry dice hanging at the back. The atmosphere is quite solemn. The fat guy's asking, 'We nearly there yet?'

The driver is throwing him a quick glance and nodding, like he's too cool to speak."

For a moment Robert lifted off the chair, and then jerked back again.

"What was that?" asked Isobel.

"Sorry. A bump. The road just dipped a bit. OK now. In the head-lights I can see the tops of bushes and tall trees jutting out of a sort of mist in front of us. The higher branches to my left are showing up black against the starry sky - even more so in front of the low, swollen moon. Abe Doyle has just said something. He's asked the guys in the front to put on some music. The fat guy is clicking the radio on, a Country Music station. The DJ is announcing a song, by Hank Williams - Long Black Limousine.

Miserable sounding song about a funeral procession and a dead lover.

There's a long line of mourners driving down our little street
Their fancy cars are such a sight to see
They're all of your rich friends who you knew in the city
And now they finally brought you back home to me
And…"

Robert was suddenly startled. "FUCK!"

"What is it?" said Isobel.

"The view in front of me, including the back of Abe and Molly, as well as the two guys sitting in front, was swinging in and out of focus because a huge, monstrous yellow truck pulled up out of nowhere. Its headlights were blinding.

We steered away and were inches from smashing into a huge oak tree over to our left. Hold on… Abe is shouting something. The driver's saying it wasn't his fault. The argument has cooled down now. He straightened up and we're continuing on, turning left into a narrow road where the branches of the tall trees are leaning over us either side, and meeting up at the top, making an arboreal archway. There's another bump. The driver is swinging left onto a muddy verge.

"They're all getting out of the car now. The driver's grabbed a pile of stuff from the boot. Looks like sacks. No. No… It's clothing of some sort. Abe and Mollie have given the babies to the driver and the fat man while they put these, sort of, monk's habits on."

"Can you fast forward a little," asked Isobel.

"OK. Abe and Mollie are fully changed into their monastic robes, hood up. Now the other guys are handing the babies back and putting their outfits on. They're locking the car and setting off into the woods."

"Robert. Now slow down into real time again."

"Right... OK. They're walking very silently now, stepping as gently as they can along the soft, dewy grass. Both the babies are asleep. Occasionally, a small frog croaks. Weaving through the trees in single file. The guy who was driving the car is leading the way. I think his name is Russ. At least that's what it sounded like when the big guy called him. It's really dark, but I can see a faint glow among the trees in front of me.

We've stepped into a sort of clearing. In the distance, I can see a bobbing lantern. The person carrying it has approached from the direction we're heading. He is talking to Russ and the big guy but I can't hear what they're saying. OK. Now we're on the move, following the lantern carrier. The air is oppressive and warm. There's drizzling rain spitting all around this. Surprisingly both babies are quiet as our mini procession continues on its way. We're back among the trees again, which are reaching an imposing height and the ground either side of us seems to be rising into banks, as if we're walking along a dried-up riverbed. They've started to move a bit faster ahead and Abe and Molly are struggling to keep up. The trees are thinning out. I'm looking

395

up at the big fat, dark clouds – but the moon is still in a clear area of sky. We're over the ridge. There are more points of light glowing in a hollow ahead of us. Lanterns. A few closely packed trees now, and then… we're coming into a clearing now. Like a meadow. Shadows and silhouettes caused by all the lanterns. It's still hard to make out exactly what's happening; there's quite a few other people dressed up in this monk's gear – with hoods up… getting chromatic aberration now. Like there's some kind of weird interference going on. I'm having trouble keeping it together."

Isobel touched his knee. "That's just transitional noise. Pay no attention to it. Just focus on the target. Breathe slow. Relax."

He took a deep breath and continued.

"Some of the people's faces are catching the lamp light. They're like actors readying themselves for something. This must be what my ideogram – my drawing - was pointing to. It's this circle of people: thirteen of them, with one lantern in front of each - and the square 'font' (that's really just a flat-topped piece of granite) in front of a slightly raised plinth. This clearing is a natural amphitheatre. I feel a terrible coldness, not from the weather – it's a warm night. It's maybe my anticipation.

There was quiet conversation and mumbling going just now. Reverential. It's like a congregation preparing for mass. The whispering and chatter just stopped, as if someone flicked a switch.

Abe is passing over the baby he was carrying to one of the other people nearby. I think it's a woman. Now he's standing at the font, like a priest about to perform a baptism. He's raised up his arms to make a 'V', in a gesture of power and shouting 'In the name of the Holy Master!'

At this point it seemed as if Robert was trying to fight off being sick, as if he was swallowing some bile. He coughed a little.

Isobel looked worried. "You OK?"

"I feel queasy. Not sure why."

"OK. Take it easy. Breathe slow."

"So what's happening now?"

"Someone just rang a bell. Abe Doyle is speaking in a low tone, building up towards some sort of invocation. Saying something about the four corners and the elements and... now he's almost entering a euphoric state – kind of self-hypnotising. He's invoking Lucifer, I think, and mentioning the names of what sound like demons, Yog-Sothoth, Dagon and Azathoth; conducting the emotions of the congregation like one of those slick Bible-belt preachers. The whole circle of the congregation seems to be entering a kind of trance-like state now. They're like stems of barley in the wind."

"Can you tell me exactly what he's saying?"

"I'll try...

'Lord of Darkness... I Beseech You that... You shall receive and accept this which I offer to You, I, upon whom You have set Your mark, I ask for thy unfailing guidance, to be purged of all conditioned ignorance... that has been forced upon me!'"

He stopped talking again. Isobel prompted him. "Yes?"

"One of the babies…"

"Yes, go on." What is happening to the child?"

"Mollie has handed her baby to someone and she's now approached the font. The other baby… someone gave it to Abe. He's taken off its wrapping and laid it down gently on the font."

"Yes? Robert. Robert!"

"Horrible, horrible."

He seemed to have become numbed by what he was seeing. His voice became high, as if he was being strangled. Isobel could see that he was actually frightened.

"I can't go on," he said.

Isobel tutted. "Don't be so stupid. Of course you can go on. What would be the point of stopping now? Man-up, and tell me what you see!"

"I-I-I see them…"

"See who?"

"Mollie and someone else are holding the baby down…"

He didn't tell Isobel that he could hear a prayer to Lucifer, which he knew was a literal translation of one that had been used by various covens in the eighteenth century, in and around Lyons in France:

"Deliver us, Lucifer, Lord of Light, bringer of Enlightenment,

from all past error and delusion,

with the Fires of Hell purify the void of my mind.

For we walk upon the Left Hand Path and have vowed to ever serve you.

We travel through Boundless Darkness illuminated by the Black Flame,

the breath of divinity at the very core of my being,

the Light of Lucifer infused."

Then Abe chanted alone:

"O Dark Lord, I am Thy Faithful Child,
I do trust in your boundless power and might.

It is through You that gifts come to us; knowledge,

power, wealth are yours to bestow upon Thy Spawn.

I renounce the spiritual paradise of the decadent and weak,

for I place my trust in myself and in You,
God of the Flesh, God of the Living.

In his darkened office, Robert was gritting his teeth, and making such tight fists his knuckles were white. He was too shaken to describe what he was seeing now - how the initiates were now writhing around feverishly, while still forming the circle. Their movements becoming more vigorous and jerkier, and somewhere else in time and space Robert's pulse was beating faster. He heard a woman speaking softly... it seemed full of love. Was it his mother? Or a nurse?

"No," he remembered. It was Isobel," Her voice echoed, as if heard from inside a deep, cave.

"What are they doing now?" she asked. "Say something, Robert."

He took a second or two to unravel his thoughts.

"I can't look," he yelled. "This place reeks of horror, perversion and death. I saw some terrible things in Nam, but nothing as sick as what these fucks were doing…"

He was almost sobbing now.

"Robert. Relax, slowly. Breath slow. That's it. Good… good. Excellent. Now *look*. Tell me what is going on there."

He could feel her wiping the tears from his cheeks. He was actually trembling now.

"Someone has just handed a long knife to Abe."

Isobel now took a deep breath. "Shit. Go on…"

"He's taking it and… and twisting back round to face the font again… gripping the handle with both hands. Everyone is chanting and… Christ."

"What?"

"He's… he's lifted up the blade high above his head, and it's pointing over the baby and… No."

"What?"

He let out a terrible scream. A wave of misery and pain swept through him.

Now he was shouting hysterically.

"He's plunged the blade into the baby's stomach. The baby made a horrible, ear-piercing shriek and blood spurted out like a fountain into his face and Molly's. Their faces are covered with little red spots."

Isobel put her hands to her mouth. She was speechless.

"The baby is making horrible gargling noises… arms flailing. Then they drop. Now it's just making a sort of dry rasping sound. It's over. Now more activity…"

"W-what?"

"Molly is taking a metal goblet and she's holding it underneath the edge of the font…

She's collecting the blood. It's half full now."

Isobel was now standing up and moving away from Robert.

"The person holding the other twin has stepped forward. Ugh. Molly is making the living twin swallow her sister's blood."

"Sick fucks." Said Isobel.

The baby is coughing and spluttering, but Molly doesn't care. She has a smiling, leering face. Sadistic. She is enjoying the baby's horror and discomfort, forcing it to drink more."

He could hear Isobel crying in another place - far from here.

"Now Mollie Doyle is drinking some of the blood, the crazy bitch. Callously wiping her upper lip with her tongue while passing the goblet to Abe. He drinks, smiles and passes the cup on. When they are done passing the goblet around Abe becomes master of ceremonies again."

Robert was crying so much that he couldn't repeat what they were chanting then:

Hail Lucifer, and Hail all the Gods of Liberation, by whose assistance we are liberated in conscience and in heart! Hail Thyself!

And so, it is done!

401

"The woman wearing glasses is ringing the bell again," he said. "The ceremony has ended."

Robert's phantom body dropped to its knees, while his physical body slumps sideways and fell onto the floor with a thud. Isobel helped him up, back onto the chair again.

"Robert? Robert. Listen, I want you to come back. Let everything go now and come back."

Her voice was like a cool summer breeze, brushing softly past his ear. He felt a brief sense of release, and his eyes flickered open. Small beads of sweat had formed on his forehead. He looked up and saw Isobel in soft focus, sitting in front of him again, tears running down her cheeks. He rubbed his eyes. he was exhausted.

"They can't be allowed to get away with it," he said.

"What can we do? You read that report from Mitch. They have so many friends in high places, politicians, law enforcers, police and the media. No charges have ever stuck against these two. They're untouchable."

Robert took the glass of water Isobel offered him and drank, soiling some down his chin and shirt.

"Oh no they're not," he said.

Chapter 27

Robert tried hard, but he couldn't shut out the memory of the evil grimace on that woman's face as she drank the blood of her own daughter. He fell back against the chair, totally exhausted, bewildered and almost feverish. A wave of nausea was welling up inside him again. The odour of corruption, and his memory of the evil and sick perversion he had seen choked him. But slowly he began to regain some composure.

"What are you going to do?" asked Isobel.

"I'm going back."

Isobel's eyes became wide with worry. "What?"

She watched his expression harden. His eyes were cold now. They had the look of death. The steely resolve horrified her. She knew she had no control over him now. He had become a warrior again.

She stood up shaking her head and frowning in disbelief. "You're crazy. You don't know what you're saying. Here, drink this."

She handed him a glass of water. He took a sip and handed it back to her, saying nothing. The sentient part of her was terrified. She smacked her hand on the table and glared at him, with such anger and frustration that he had to lean back and squint.

"Who the devil do you think you are? There's nothing you can do. All that would happen is you'd end up watching passively as the whole thing unfolds all over again and stress yourself out for no good reason. You're tired. You need a break. Nothing can be achieved from going back – other than getting yourself even more distressed. It's pointless." She stood up then. "I'm hungry. Splash some water on your face and let's go get a pizza at Al Forno. We haven't seen Gino for ages."

He shook his head slowly. "Later maybe. Got to do this thing now."

She sat back down and sucked in her lips. He could see she was getting a handle on where he was going with all this.

"Wait a minute," she said. "Are you thinking you can pull off what those weird, black-ops guys used to get up to in StarChild? The ones we never spoke to. Is that what you're thinking?"

He shrugged. "I-I'm not sure. But I need to go back in."

"Uh-oh. You're way out of line. You have no idea where to start. We are not schooled in that type of thing. Forget about it."

"Fucking hell, Izzy. How do you expect me to forget about what I just saw? Someone needs to do something."

"It happened twenty-one years ago, Robert. Leave it alone."

"Time is not linear, Izzy. You know that better than anyone."

She thought about that and got up hurriedly to walk to the coat stand, and came back with a packet of Camels and lit one up with a silver Ronson.

Neither of them spoke as she smoked. Her hands were shaking throughout. When she finally put the stub out Robert said:

"Are you going to help me, or am I doing this thing on my own?"

She blew a thick plume of smoke in his face. "You are one stubborn son-of-a-bitch."

As she prepared the monitor again, he thought about how he would make this up to her. Maybe he could take her down to Mexico for a couple of weeks, to escape the winter. She'd like that.

She came back and stood over him to make sure he was properly wired-up, and then sat down again. "Let's get this over with," she muttered under her breath.

But Robert wanted to straighten out something first.

"What is it?" she said. "I thought you wanted to get on with this."

"Yeah but... Izzy. This is going to be a little bit different."

"What are you getting at?" she said.

He put the side of his fist to his mouth and coughed. "I want to do this without questions and answers."

She leaned her head back. "Huh?"

"Stick with me on this," he said. "It's not a big deal, really. I will do the viewing then come back. It'll be quick, I promise you."

"But..."

"Trust me."

She sunk back into her chair and sighed. "Whatever."

It didn't take long for him to reach the alpha wave state again, as he was already halfway in it. Theta was pretty rapid too. At first there was a restless kaleidoscopic blur. He was becoming dizzy, experiencing a kind of vertigo, and then there was a feeling of sliding through a winding chute, with flashing, coloured lights going off all around. He was being sucked down in a spiral for what seemed like an age, before jerking to a sudden stop. The scene ahead of him was completely blurred, but it eventually came into better focus, until it seemed like a stained-glass window version of where he was before, back in the car on the way to the woodland clearing with Abe and Molly, Russ (the guy with the Wyatt Earp moustache) and the Big Guy sitting in the car in front. Eventually the saturated colour drained away leaving the stark reality and the shadows. This was the moment where the car was leaving the outskirts of the town, on the way to the ceremony in the woods. One of the babies was making cooing noises and looking through Robert at the furry dice. He was sure the child could see his transcendental self. This was something new. In the past, he had always been an inert observer. He never became involved in the events unfolding in the viewing. Anyhow, they were told that interference was impossible. But that was a lie.

He was a floating consciousness, but he threw caution to the wind and merged into the driver's head. Wham. His thoughts were now floating around in the driver's skull, mingling with his and marginalising them, like wasps in a jam-jar killing off helpless bees. Alien, seedy thoughts were cluttering his consciousness, such as desiring a plate of fried chicken, winning at poker, visiting a brothel in Bridgeport. It was like listening to a radio that's too close to your ears. The feeling of disgust was overwhelming. But Robert hung on – and soon there were only his thoughts left.

Somewhere there was a quiet echo that sounded remarkably like Isobel, and he heard it saying, "No. You can't do a one-eight-seven, not in a viewing Robert. No! We don't do that!"

It kept repeating, and then it faded away completely, like a gust of wind in the fall.

The hands on the steering wheel were his now. The yellow truck suddenly appeared round the sharp bend ahead, and the driver's heart rate shot up. He was afraid as Robert drove head on into the yellow truck. Then blackness. There was an enormous pounding. Everything shook. Robert pulled away, out of the car, through the roof. The impact had sent the car spinning over, into the verge. It was now a twisted wreck. Robert was now floating out of the crashed vehicle.

The truck driver screeched to a halt and jumped out of the cabin. The moon was still low behind the dark woods to Roberts left. Only the front headlamps of the truck lit the scene. The upturned Pontiac rocked for a bit and then became still. Robert waited, hovering nearby, until he could hear crying: two babies crying.

Then everything was sucked into blackness. His breathing became heavy – and there was a glaring flash, painful in its intensity. It faded into glowing blobs that floated in front of him. When they dissolved away, he could see again. He was in a shadowy room that looked a lot like his office in the apartment.

His breathing slowed down to normal as he began to pull out of the theta, semi dream state. For a while he didn't have the strength to get up out of the chair, and he actually dropped back down when he first tried. At first, he couldn't recall what he had just viewed. But as the fogginess dissipated, things were starting to look wrong. Where was Isobel? She would never leave him during a viewing. He called out her name and waited. Nothing. Again, he tried to get up. This time he was able to stumble forward towards the door. He wondered along the hallway, almost as if he was sleepwalking and ended up at her studio, opposite the kitchen. After waiting for his sense of balance to come back, he needed light so he reached for the pull-string. But there was no pull-string. There was only a wall switch.

"When did that happen?" he said to himself.

He walked into the bedroom and it seemed less warm somehow, less welcoming. Emptier. In a panic, he went back out into the hallway and opened the door to Isobel's studio. What he found there left him in shock. Instead of her easel and canvases there were piles of dusty cardboard boxes and bags. This was now no more than a storeroom. This was all so wrong. Then an idea struck him, and he went over to the cabinet in the lounge to pull out his photo album and sat by the coffee table flicking through the pages with photographs of himself and Isobel at Langley with Mitch, Jerry, Stella and the guys, and there were some of their vacation in Sweden, as well as the log cabin in Concorde... but after that he didn't recognise any of the pictures at all. This was crazy. And then he came across a spread of pictures of himself and the guys at a funeral. Brett and Stephanie are there, and so is Mitch and also everyone else at Starchild, including himself. But not Isobel. When he turned the page, he came across a picture of a headstone:

Isabel Greene 1941-1989
She made the mundane beautiful

Being so weak, he could barely move. He ended up taking a few steps and standing still again, wondering, fearing and doubting. The silence in the apartment was endless, and the stillness was unbearable. he could only whisper her name, and then he collapsed.

ADDENDUM

Robert discovered that Isobel Greene died, following unsuccessful treatment for cancer in 1989. She had her operation at a different hospital, and by a different doctor to the one who succeeded in removing Isobel's aggressive tumour successfully in the previous reality. Robert visited her grave in Green-Wood Cemetery, Brooklyn several days in succession that winter.

His journal entries become considerably shorter and sporadic after this point. The bulk of them can best be described as incomplete and irregularly composed, loose jottings.

He succeeded in tracking down Gary Cummins to a public high school in the Bronx, where he had been teaching English for several years. Gary is married to fellow schoolteacher Mary-Anne Tracey, with whom he has three children. They live in a small brownstone within walking distance of the school.

The following week Stringfield tried to make contact with his former line chief at Langley, Michael Craig (affectionately known as 'Mitch'). He was hoping this would help him get some things in place with regard to the changes that were now existent. But he failed to make contact*.

Stringfield then traveled to England, making his base at the comfortable and discreet Brown's Hotel in central London. From here he set about tracking down Alan White. After searching public records for a couple of days his investigations led him to an address in Canonbury, North London. He found that Alan lived there and worked as a (not very successful) sculptor. Stringfield took a bus there from Piccadilly the following week. He had prepared a cover story about having an interest in moving into the area, and he wondered if this particular property was for sale. Alan White did not encourage conversation, but when Stringfield feigned interest in the sculptures on display in the hallway he was invited in. Eventually Stringfield commissioned a bust from Alan, which he agreed to sit for over two days. Alan's wife, Melanie Elisabeth Leech, is a wealthy city banker. She was away on business in Zurich at the time. They have no children.

Stringfield spent an additional three weeks in London in an attempt to track down Jenny White, but not knowing her maiden name, or even her date of birth the quest proved fruitless.

On returning to New York, Robert used the information he remembered from the hospital records of the birth of Vanessa and Juliette Doyle. He discovered that a local court handed custody of the children after the crash to a half-sister of Molly Doyle, who lived in Montreal, Canada. Christine Devereux was not on speaking terms with her sister, but she accepted the responsibility. Christine and her husband Trevor had no children of their own, and they were clearly devoted to the girls. Vanessa and Juliette took on the surname of their aunt and uncle and were educated in a convent on the outskirts of the city. Trevor was an insurance salesman at the time. Stringfield learned that Vanessa and Juliette Devereux had graduated from McGill University recently. Juliette majored in Film and Vanessa achieved a First in Art History. They now both live in a small apartment above a vintage magazine shop in 8th St. Juliette works as a junior assistant to the editor of a magazine. Vanessa was a waitress in a bar in Greenwich Village when Stringfield went there and sat down to order a coffee. Vanessa was the girl he had fought so desperately with on the floor of the house in Cold Spring in another reality, the girl who had been transformed to a demon by her evil parents, existing in limbo – unless she was made manifest by sexual contact with a victim. He was totally struck by her gentle nature and her beauty. She had a mole high up on her left cheek, which was very becoming.

At this point he becomes a little more informative in his journal:

"On a dull, warm afternoon, I wondered down town to the café in Greenwich Village. It was one of those oak panelled places, with a huge chandelier and wooden floor. I recognised her instantly. She wore a white blouse and newly pressed black skirt. Her long black hair was tied in a ponytail, and her eyes were violet. She had a definite shyness about her. I managed to start up a conversation after making my order, by asking if a facsimile painting on display was by Rubens. Her accent definitely had a Canadian flavour. She said 'aboot' instead of 'about'. I learned that this would actually be her last week as a waitress, as she recently had a successful interview to become a photographer's assistant. She stopped talking to give me a look of concern. 'Mister," she said. "Are you OK? Why are you crying?"

MATTHEW BLACKWOOD and *LAWRENCE DE FRIES*
Atlantean Research Group,
Vancouver, August 22, 2007

*Through the efforts of several members of our group we have discovered that 'Mitch' now works for the office of Naval Intelligence.

LAST ONE IN

It was a dull October Monday morning, with the sun struggling to break through a blanket of thick white cloud (and failing – as usual), as Dan made his way through the crowds emerging onto pavement level from the northeast exit of Tottenham Court Road Station. Reaching the grey, concrete monstrosity of the YMCA, he turned into the tree-lined street that led directly to his office in Bloomsbury, leaving the bulk of the crowd behind him. Opposite the modernist Trade Union Building, he stopped at a little Italian café for his usual cappuccino and two slices of buttered toast. Soon after he left there, he couldn't resist studying some sable brushes that had caught his eye just a few shops along, before looking at his watch and realising he was already a quarter of an hour late.

He was really chuffed to be working at Pepper. It was a prestigious little production company, so he didn't want to take too many liberties. The director, Paul Asher, and producer, George Locke, had built up a solid reputation internationally for producing quality animated films. Pepper Films was based in a large building, from the first floor up, at the end of an elegant Georgian terrace. He was just across from it when he charged over the zebra crossing outside the hotel and stopped in front of the entrance, which was a black wooden door at the far left-hand side of a shop that occupied the whole ground floor, specialising in Scottish highland clothing, including tartan scarves, coats, mohair jumpers, and even kilts. Most of its customers were European tourists. It wouldn't be open for business for another forty-five minutes. Its huge window displays extended around the corner into the road leading to the British Museum. Dan pressed the button and waited, eventually speaking his name into the intercom and getting buzzed in, probably by Marion.

He trudged up the three flights of hessian-carpeted stairs to the equally hessian-carpeted layout department studio, which was staffed by just himself and Dino. He reached the third-floor offices and, as usual, Dino was already at his desk, sipping a dry cappuccino from a pale blue cardboard cup, and biting into a ham and cheese croissant, while studying the drawing of a farmyard scene he was about to get stuck into.

Hearing Dan dump his heavy bag behind him, Dino turned around and blinked a kind of hello through his black-framed specs, which Dan immediately understood. Dino was a few years older than Dan and was instrumental in bringing him into the animation business, away from the advertising visualising wilderness, first by recommending him to the producer of an animated feature of Swan Lake the previous year (which led to seven months of work), and now as his partner on this current project, *Bertie Badger Goes South*. Everyone involved in the production was helpful and encouraging to him, from the director right down to the in-betweeners and colourists, so he had settled in very quickly and was doing some good stuff. Dan was grateful to Dino, and Dino was really pleased to have Dan working alongside him. This job offered them both great possibilities because the director, Paul, and producer, George had given them a huge amount of creative freedom in the way they design and style the production, so they were pulling out all the stops to do their best work.

"Hey, Dan. Good weekend?"

Dan started unbuttoning his coat and then he froze for a moment, before bending his torso and laughing at the floor.

Dino shook his head. "Was it something I said?"

"Look, I can't explain it yet. But something happened that I can't work out. I mean it. Let me just explain everything that happened, all the little bits… because, I think I'm going nuts, I need you to tell me what the fuck *you* think was going on, because… to tell you the truth, it's a little bit disturbing."

"Disturbing?"

"Yeah. I'm not kidding. Just hear me out, and you'll see what I mean."

"Is this a wind-up?"

"Will you just *listen*?"

"OK. OK. Go on then."

"Right. So, after you went to the dentist on Friday, I was hunched over my desk working on that fucking thing," he pointed to the five feet long, unfinished drawing of cartoon badgers running away from an angry farmer, in a luscious country scene, which was stretched out on his desk, which was surrounded by various pencils of all lengths and

416

colours, an electric sharpener, two scalpels, a putty rubber and a metal ruler.

"My nose was maybe three inches from the paper, so I was totally zoned out. I must have been like that for a while before I couldn't focus any more, and I had to lean right back into my chair and stretch my arms out. Then I was rubbing my eyes for a bit and I looked out the window. It was getting dark. The lights were on in the offices at the back opposite. I looked at my watch and it was only twenty past six. I got up and looked to see if anyone was in the room next door. Dead as a doornail in there. Then it hit me. There was no music coming from downstairs."

"Marion must've gone home."

"Or her ghetto blaster was broken."

"I wish. No more Phil Collins and Bruce Springsteen every day."

"No such luck.

At that moment George stepped out of his office hurrying through into Paul's office, uttering, "Morning chaps," and flashing them a less than gracious stare. They took it as a signal to begin work, but it didn't stop them from carrying on their conversation unabated.

"I've never been the last one in the building before," said Dan. "It made me feel, you know... uncomfortable. I had a lot more stuff I wanted to draw, but I just wanted to get out of there. I thought, fuck it and I grabbed my coat and bag and shot out of here. On the way down I saw the light was on in paint and trace. I got curious and checked to see if there was anyone in there. Their white gloves were chucked on the lightboxes and freshly painted cells of Bertie Badger were hanging up to dry. Oh, and Marian's ghetto blaster was left on, with a Bruce Springsteen CD left in its open pocket."

Dino laughed. "No one's going to nick that."

"In the back room some clown had plonked a potted plant on the glass screen of the Grant enlarger," said Dan. "But there was no one in there. Even Christine and Syd were gone."

"That's not like them. Missing out on overtime."

"On the next floor, I went into the background department. It was like a morgue in there."

Dino laughed. "Ha! It's like that even when they're in there."

Dan turned to face Dino with a sneer.

"That's a bit harsh."

Dan was about to respond when a girl with long dark hair, and a hippy-ish style of dressing breezed in from the hallway with a whiff of patchouli oil. She was carrying a pile of green cardboard folders in both arms, which the boys knew were dope sheets that the animators needed to time out their scenes.

Dan interrupted his narrative. "Hi, Nicola.

Both of them respected Nicola, even though they thought she was a bit eccentric, and because she was such a brilliant animator.

"Hi, guys! Nice weekend?"

Dino looked up at her, smiled and shrugged. "It was too short."

Nicola paused for a moment, pursed her lips and nodded in agreement.

Dan waited for her to go through to Paul's office before continuing.

"When I saw there was no one in backgrounds I really felt strange. I had this urge to get out of there as soon as possible, and I don't know why. It wasn't like I had anything to be afraid of."

Dino shook his head and turned back to his drawing.

"This is when it starts to get weird. I couldn't get out."

Dino stopped drawing again and twisted around. "Huh?"

"It's true. When I got down to the ground floor, I turned the handle on the Yale lock, only the door wouldn't open. Someone had gone and double locked."

"The Chubb lock?"

"Yeah."

"Shit. What did you do then?"

Well at first, I lost it. I kicked the fucking door and stood there staring at it and yelling, like I was daring it to hit me."

Dino was back drawing again and chuckling to himself.

"Ha. What were you yelling?"

"Can't remember." He wasn't entirely open about how he felt at the time. He didn't want to discuss how the silence of the empty building was starting to get to him.

At this stage, Dino stopped drawing and turned round to face Dan directly.

"I thought about calling Marian to get her to come over and to let me out, but I don't have her number. Anyway, I don't know how to get an outside line on the phones."

Dino concurred. "Mm. Come to think of it, I don't either. I always go through Eileen on switchboard."

Just at that instant, George stepped out of his office in his ankle-length grey coat, carrying his satchel over his shoulder, followed by his editor (and much younger) French girlfriend, Murielle in a mink jacket, with her long black hair tied in a ponytail. George reminded Dino of General Custer, with his shoulder length and wild ginger hair, goatee beard and a long moustache hanging down the side of the lips. George stopped to look at what the boys were working on, and Murielle went on out to the hallway, not realising.

"Is this the first part of the chase scene?" asked George.

"Yep," said Dino. "Long way to go."

"Did you chaps have a good weekend?"

"I did," says Dino, "but Dan nearly didn't. He was locked in here on Friday night."

"What?"

Dan. "Long story."

George put his hand on his hips and gazed at Dan in mock disappointment.

Murielle interrupted.

"George, we have to be at Portland House in ten minutes."

"Oh yes. See you soon, boys."

After George and Murielle had gone, Dan asked, "Where are the going?"

"BBC. They're trying to get the next lot of funding early. So what happened next? How did you finally get out?"

Dan sucked in his cheeks and looked up at the ceiling for a moment. He was considering what Dino had just said, which concerned him a bit, because it could mean the budget is being burned up too fast and they could be laid off. But he was also thinking that he wouldn't reveal how he had to struggle to pull himself together when he realised he was trapped, and how he had to pull himself together to shake off these weird negative vibes he was feeling, that he knew were unrelated to him being locked in.

"The only thing I could think of was maybe getting out through one of the windows onto the roofs and ledges upstairs, he said." So I turned to go back up and there was a slither of light coming from the back of the hallway."

"What was that?"

"It was coming from the right, under the stairs. I went around there, to the back of the hallway, and saw this white wooden door. It was open a crack, and that's where the light was coming from. I opened it a bit more and saw stone steps going down. There was a sort of slurping sound followed by a rattle coming from somewhere down there."

"Weird."

"I thought there could maybe be a door down there, leading into a courtyard or something, so I started walking down."

"Weren't you a bit worried?"

"I just wanted to get out."

Dan was lying. He felt a shudder up his spine at that moment, and he felt it get colder with every step.

"After a few steps I was looking down on this old man wearing a flat cap."

"Really. What was he doing there?"

"He was busy sucking the meat out of a stack of oyster shells from a dirty metal plate and then throwing the empty shells into a fireplace grate. I think he was meant to be decorating the basement, but he must've been on his break. Quite a big guy, with a white moustache and beard. He was sitting on a paint-splattered bench, wearing paint splattered overalls under a dark, paint splattered suit jacket. He didn't look bothered about me being there at all."

"That sounds weird."

"Who owns that room?"

"I guess it's the landlord of our building, or maybe the shop downstairs. Anyway, he

didn't speak, and the only thing I could think to say was, 'Working late?'"

Dino stopped drawing and looked baffled.

"Are you winding me up?"

"No way. I'm telling you, this is how it went down. He had a small stepladder beside him. There were brushes in glass pots and tools on the floor all around him. He looked up and saw me, and chucked another empty oyster shell into the grating. It clattered into a whole pile of other empty oyster shells."

"But how could a painter and decorator afford to eat oysters? I mean, they're not cheap are they?

I've forgotten what the price is for a plate of them in Wheelers. Not that I like them. The one time I tried one, I nearly vomited."

"Well, Wheelers is a restaurant. He wouldn't want to pay those kinds of prices. He must've got them from a fishmonger."

"What fishmonger? There isn't one within miles of Bloomsbury."

"How the fuck do I know. I'm not an expert on fishmongers."

"So what happened when you got down there?"

He just said, 'Evening lad', in a gravelly voice, then let out a huge burp, and put his fist to his mouth."

"Very pleasant."

"Then he stood up, wiped his nose with his jacket sleeve and pulled out a packet of cigarettes from his pocket. He put one it in his mouth and pointed the packet towards me, with a blank face, not unfriendly, just... kind of expressionless, or maybe it was serious. I felt he was saying, "These are really good, and we're both fellow sufferers in this world, so I'm sharing one with you.' He looked like an old seadog, the kind you see in some of those black-and-white films.

Is that what he said?

No. That's what I imagined he said.

So what did he actually say?

"Smoke?"

That was it?

"Yeah. The fag packet was green. Brand I've never seen before: Woodbines? You smoke now and again. You ever heard of them?"

Dino was intrigued. He stopped drawing, and had turned around in his swivel chair to face Dan.

"Yeah," said Dino. "I've heard of Woodbines. Do they still sell them?"

"Well, *he* had some. And I noticed there were quite a few empty packs in the fireplace too, mixed in with the pile of empty oyster shells he'd thrown over there."

"Weird. So did you take one?"

"Why would I? I don't smoke."

"Just to be polite."

"I suppose I should have... anyway, I didn't. I just asked him if he had a key to the front door. I told him that I worked upstairs for Pepper Films, and that everyone had gone and left me locked inside without a key. He had a think about that, and sat back down again, and took a box of Swan Vestas matches that was lying on the bench beside him, and lit his fag. Then he spoke with the cigarette still in his mouth.

"I ain't got one," he said. "Me gaffer's got one, but he's nipped out. He'll be back after he's knocked back a couple of bevvies."

Dino chuffed at that. "Sounds like a bit of a retard."

"No... I'd say the opposite. I thought he was deceptively clever and shifty."

Dino, who was still facing Dan, was now quite entranced by all this strangeness in the basement. He scratched his nose and said, "What made you come to that conclusion?"

"To be honest, I can't say. It's just a feeling I got while I was there... that he wasn't to be trusted.

There was something not right about him. I don't know if it was his eyes, his lack of expression, or that I might've felt he was lying about not having the keys.

So I asked him if I could wait until his mate came back. He took a long drag on his cigarette, and breathed out a couple of smoke rings. It all seemed a bit arrogant and nonchalant to me. I didn't like it.

"Couldn't tell you, son," he said. "Might not be back till the pubs close – know what I mean? He does like his drink."

Dino shook his head. "What a wanker."

Dan shook his head. "Yeah. That's what I thought. He seemed a bit devious, to be honest. But I was too stressed out to think about that too much because I saw there was a small window near the ceiling that I might be able to squeeze through.

"Does that open up," I said, pointing to it.

"No idea," he shrugged. "Never tried it."

Dino laughed. "Helpful sort of chap. A bit 'Right Said Fred."

"You could say that. Anyway, he didn't object to me moving the ladder over a bit to see if I could get it to open. Trouble is, I kicked a jar of dirty turps with a paintbrush in it onto the stone floor. That got him animated. He started to get up, but sat back down again after his arse hovered over the bench precariously a moment.

"Oi! Steady on, lad," he said, thumping himself back down again.

"I was going to pick up a rag to give the milky spillage a wipe, but he told me not to bother. So I stood up and dragged the steps over to get up to that window. I could only get up about five steps before my head hit the ceiling. I then managed to lean forward to look through the dirty glass of the rectangular, tea tray size window into a small, narrow paved courtyard, bordered on three sides by tall Georgian, dark-bricked buildings. I wiped away some of the dust, and to the right I could make out a black, wooden gate about seven feet high. I thought it wouldn't be that hard to clamber over, if I could get through this goddamn window. It had a little lever lock, which I lifted up, and then I took a step down, so I could stretch my arms right out to get more strength into it, and pushed with all my strength at the window, which was hinged at the top and designed to open outward. I pushed with everything I had, you know I can lift a couple of hundred pounds in the gym, but it was completely stuck. I couldn't shift it a single millimetre."

Dino was vaguely interested in all this, but he turned back to his desk, being conscious of the fact that his drawing needed to be done by the end of the day, as the animator, was starting work on this scene the next day.

"So what did you do, smash it?"

"Bollocks, did I. My idea was, if I could scrape away some of that thick paint that had sealed the joint, I could maybe prise it open. So I turned around to ask the old geezer, "Hey mate, you got a screwdriver so I…"

But he was gone. The bench was empty, and so was the room.

"What? He must've gone to the loo or something."

"No. He was gone. That was it. I climbed back down the ladder and ran up the back stairs to the hallway to find him. There was no one there. I tried the front door again, but if he had gone out, he definitely locked up behind him again. I guessed he must've been lying about his mate having the key. I thought he must have always had the key, and he just let himself out."

"Maybe he just went upstairs"

"No. I went back up. I never found him. Anyway, he didn't have any business being up here. George and Paul never mentioned anything about having decorators in."

Dan and Dino suddenly became alert, when they could hear stomping coming up the stairs, but it was just Marion. She came in carrying another pile of dope sheets in their green cardboard folders. She stopped abruptly, on her way through to Paul's office, to look at the boys' drawings, on her way to Paul.

"He-y-y-y. Nice work, guys."

They replied in unison, "Cheers Marion."

She turned to address Dan directly, with an expression of pain.

"Oh gosh, I'm so sorry. I hear I locked you in on Friday. Honestly, I know it's stupid, but I thought everyone had gone home. And I was in a terrible hurry to meet Amanda – we were going to see Aladdin. I didn't realise the time, and when I looked, I was running late. I didn't have time to do the usual check, and I just went halfway up the stairs and yelled out, 'Anyone there' and of course, I got no reply. So I thought it was empty up here."

Dan shrugged. "Oh well…"

Dino laughed and said, "I bet he had his headphones on listening to Prince at maximum volume, Marion."

"It wasn't Prince. It was the Commodores… probably Nightshift," said Dan. "I listened to it about ten times on Friday. Love that tune."

"And that's why you were locked in here, doing the Nightshift," snapped Dino.

Marion just looked mournful, and Dan wasn't impressed.

Just as she was about to ask Dan how he managed to get out, Paul's voice bellowed from the other room: "Marion!"

She looked at Dan and then Dino, her eyes wide with fear and with her left lower lip twisted low, revealing her teeth gritted. Then she hunched her shoulders and hurried sheepishly away.

Dan and Dino waited for her to go, before snickering quietly. They both turned back to their work. They carried on working that way without speaking for a while. Eventually Dino felt satisfied with himself, arched himself right back and yawned.

Dan looked over and laughed. "What's the matter? Didn't you get any sleep last night?"

"Not much. Sally and me were watching Godfather Part II till god knows what time. Then we entertained ourselves for a while, if you know what I mean… So anyway, what happened after you found out the old man wasn't there."

Dino swivelled around on his chair to face Dan to find a combination of fear and laughter written on Dan's face.

"Shit. By then I was mad, you know – steaming. I just wanted to get the fuck out of this place, and that whole fucking basement incident was like a horrible joke. I don't know what it was all about, but the old geezer was a time-waster, wherever he was now. I'd had enough. I didn't have a plan or anything. I just ran straight back up to the first floor again, because I couldn't think what else to do. I went into the background studio and groped around in there to switch on the lights. The two windows in there had locks on them; you know, the ones behind Alan and Fiona's desk. No chance of shifting them and I looked in all the drawers and I couldn't find any keys in to open them up. So I tried the next floor, in animation and then in production. Same thing there. Those fucking steel, oval window locks are a bitch. I tried every window on every floor. It was useless. By then I was going bonkers. The adrenaline was starting to pump now, I was shaking, and I think that's why I knocked over the statue of the Badger, you know, the main model the animators use for reference. A bit of the ear broke off. It was on Nicola's desk when I squeezed around to try the window in there."

"You idiot. They'll go mad if they find out. That cost George a fortune to commission from that sculptor from Madame Tussaud's."

"Who gives a shit?"

Dino laughed, but Dan's mind was wandering. They worked quietly for a minute, and then Dino decided to break the silence.

"You still haven't told me how you eventually got out."

"Oh yeah. Well, after backgrounds, I came up to this floor and went through to Paul's main studio. You know there's that door that leads to the flat roof at the back, where we sat and had drinks and snacks in the summer a couple of times when we celebrated finishing a sequence."

"Oh yeah. Is that how you got out?"

"No. It was locked."

"But I suddenly remembered that little cubby hole that Paul works in. No one else is supposed to go in there. It's in the very corner, up a little narrow set of stairs at the back. When he was in the pub with George, Jean, took me in there once to show me the new storyboard he was working on.."

"Yeah, I've been up there a couple of times. It's really tiny. It must have been the servant's quarters in the days when this building was a house."

"Probably was."

"I remember I hit my head on the low-sloping ceiling. All there is in there is a chair, a single wooden desk, an Anglepoise lamp, a telephone... and a poster from that film he made in the sixties."

"*The Pepper Pot Man.*"

"That's the one. Have you seen it?"

"No. Anyway, I went in there to have a look. There's a single tiny window in there. It's nothing like the other windows – kind of square. More like an original window. Not updated like all the other windows. It didn't feel like a window that you would bother securing. I dragged Paul's chair over and tried to stop it swivelling. Carefully poised, I tried the sash window to see if it lifted, and miracle of miracles, it did!"

430

"You lucky bastard."

"After that, I managed to lift myself up on the sill and squeeze through. It was quite a squeeze I can tell you. Not much bigger than a tea tray. I went through head first, sort of flapping through like a seal and cushioned my fall onto the flat roof with my hands. Meanwhile, the window I came out of dropped shut behind me. So I stood up and I went over to see if I could prise it open again, just in case I needed to get back in, because I didn't want to be stuck on the flat roof, four floors up all night. And I couldn't. So that was that. Still, the cool breeze felt good. I brushed myself down and looked around, to see if I could work out a way forward. I looked at all the buildings, all around, you know the upper floors are mostly offices, and I saw there was one window that was still lit. The rest had the lights off, so I guess in there everyone had locked up and gone home. This one window was my only chance. If there was someone in there I could ask for help. Trouble was it was about three flat rooftops further along, and I'd have to climb over a few low walls to get there – and, of course, I'd be trespassing. But what else could I do?"

"So you were doing a Spiderman."

"Not quite. Anyway, I got over there, it was about fifty yards from our building, The wall that this window was in butted right up to the flat roof I was on, so the flat roof I was standing on must have belonged to the same building. I manoeuvred myself into a position where I could look directly into those windows, set in the black brick wall of a tall Georgian building. I stood to one side of the

431

window because I wanted to be hidden at first. I
didn't want to frighten anyone. What I could see
was there were two girls in there, sitting at a long
desk: probably young graduates, that sort of age.
Casual, jeans and jumpers. They were putting these
little objects, that I couldn't make out, into little,
brown, square cardboard boxes, and writing
something on the lid. I could see there were shelves
full of these boxes filling two walls. I thought, fuck
it, it's now or never, and I went close and knocked
hard on the glass. They looked up at me straight,
and it was obvious I scared the shit out of them. I
pointed to our building, which was behind me then,
and shrugged – trying to express the fact that he was
not a burglar – or anything. I waved frantically and
shouted a bit, but they couldn't hear through the
double glazing. They watched me for a bit. One of
them was more confused than scared, and she went
off, out the room, leaving her friend a bit nervous,
still watching me, the strange black man standing
outside knocking on their window. Soon the other
girl came back with this guy in uniform. An old
fella, a bit bald, dark hair, glasses. He looked at me
for a bit, and then he opened the window and held it
up, inviting me to crawl through. The guy took one
look at me, shook his head, and told me to follow
him, as the girls just stared in disbelief. I wanted to
laugh, but I thought if I did, he might call the police,
or tell me to get back out there. So he told me to go
out and followed me down a few flights of stairs.
We came out on the left side of the courtyard of the
British Museum. There were these huge black
wooden double gates ahead of me, that I guess

would be opened up to let lorries through. He opened one up, and I came out onto Great Russell Street. "

"Fuck me, you were so lucky. He could've easily called the police and kept you in there."

At twelve-thirty, Dan and Dino decided to take their lunch break, and as they came down onto the ground floor hallway and were about to open the front door, a small girl in her early twenties, with beautifully long black hair, and wearing a green, tartan skirt, black polo neck, black tights and ballet shoes, while carrying a pile of jumpers, in their celluloid packaging, rushed past them both and through to the back of the hallway. Dino stopped Dan from stepping out into the street by grabbing his shoulder.

"Hold on Dan. That girl works for the clothes shop. She's taking those boxes to the basement. Let's see if your old geezer is still down there, working on decorating the basement.

Dan looked a bit baffled.

"You can't just ask to go down there…"

"Just watch me."

Dino rushed over to her, with Dan nervously following in his wake.

"Excuse me," said Dino. "Sorry to interrupt, my name's Dino and this is my colleague Dan. We work upstairs for Pepper Pot Films. The thing is, my friend here, he got locked in on Friday, and he says he ended up speaking to that guy you've got decorating down there."

The girl looked at them both, slightly perplexed. "What guy?"

Now Dan answered. "There was a guy decorating down there on Friday. Well, he said he had a mate who was out, for some reason. He was on his own when I found him, having a break from his painting and decorating."

The girl looked at Dan and leaned back as if she'd just eaten something odd-tasting."

"You must be imagining things. There's no one decorating for us down there. That's our stockroom, and it was locked up all weekend. I'm the only one who's been in there since Friday.

"What? No – that can't be."

Dino felt he should step in to resolve the confusion here.

"Look, sorry love. What's your name?

"Sarah."

"Sarah. Is there any chance that we can just take a quick look at the room, just to put my mate's mind at rest? I'm beginning to think he was dreaming the whole incident."

Dan protested. "I was not."

Dino ignored him. "Can we?"

The girl thought for a few seconds and seemed to come to the conclusion that they were harmless enough.

"Take these". She gave Dan the pile of sweaters to hold on to and then took out a set of keys from her skirt pocket and opened up using two different keys. She then pushed the door in, switched on a light inside, and took the pile of sweaters back from Dino.

434

"Right. Follow me."

Dino and Dan entered and Dan stood frozen, halfway down the carpeted stairs. He could not believe his eyes. There was no stone floor – just wall-to-wall carpet. The entire room was filled with boxes, neatly stacked. There were also a few clothes rails, with items of clothing on hangers squeezed in on each rail, including sweaters, coats, and jackets. There was hardly any room to move down there.

"B-but what happened... how is this possible? All this stuff... who moved it back in here?"

"What are you talking about?"

"All this room was empty apart from a step ladder a bench and some pots of paints on Friday. How..."

The girl was getting agitated now.

"Sorry guys, but I have to lock up and get back into the shop. It gets busy at lunchtime, and I've left my friend on her own in there."

A thick blanket of cloud loomed overhead as they walked towards their usual restaurant in Covent Garden. Dan was in a daze as they negotiated the obstacle course that was the crossing of New Oxford Street, on Shaftesbury Avenue. On the other side, Dan broke his silence.

"I don't get it. I mean, what happened to me on Friday in that fucking basement? Who was that old man?"

Dino just laughed. "Dan, I have no idea, but I tell you now – I believe you. I don't know what it was, but I know you well enough to know you're not lying. Sometimes, the laws of reality crumble.

They sort of just stop operating for a short time, nothing seems right. Reality is relegated. There's no explanation for it – it just happens, not for long. Before long, everything just goes back to normal. I've experienced it myself."

"You have?"

"Yeah."

"What happened?"

Dino pursed his lips and seemed anxious. Then he overrode his concerns and gave a sigh of relief.

"Christ, I haven't spoken about this for years, but when I was a kid I had a conversation with a tramp.' He looked down as he walked, then shook his head and continued. "I was about seven years old I think. This tramp, his trousers were knotted at the knee like sausages, because he had no lower legs. I was with a school friend my age, David White. We heard this voice calling us as we were walking to the school gate and we looked down to see this bearded, filthy tramp sitting on the pavement, leaning his back against a brick wall. He looked up and kept firing questions at us, and we felt compelled to answer them because it would have been rude for us to walk away. We had it rammed into our heads in those days by all our teachers, that we must never be rude to adults – ever. But this tramp was making us feel nervous with his questions. We just wanted to walk on... I felt I had to think of something to break the spell because that's what it felt like – a spell. And then I got this idea that I would ask *him* a question. So I did that, and it had an effect."

"How?"

"He suddenly stopped talking, just for a moment. I must have surprised him with what I said. I must confess, I felt really pleased with myself, thinking how clever and mature I was, to come up with something like that."

"Weird."

"Yeah, well it got even weirder, because suddenly he let loose this horrible cackling laugh, and vanished."

"What do you mean?"

"Poof! He was gone. He wasn't there anymore."

"What?"

"We were just left looking at the pavement he was sitting on and a bit of the wall he'd been leaning against. We were completely stunned. My friend wouldn't talk about it ever again. When I tried to bring it up a bit later he got so angry, we had a fight over it."

"That's mad. So, what question did you ask the tramp?"

"I just said, 'Where do you live?'"

"Is that it?"

"That's it."

"Shit."

"Yeah. That's what I thought."

The sun came out as they strolled past Freud's wine bar before turning into Neal Street. It changed the atmosphere completely. People all around had an extra spring to their step and at that moment Dan suddenly realised how hungry he was.